As Chief Product Officer
BRAHAM SINGH writes
Shifting gears, he now gi
He also wrote the screenp.,
Malaysia and based around their May 1969 race riots. *Emperor*, tne
novel, is near completion. He recently began research on his third
novel, *The Little Eunuch,* set in China.

He divides his time between Virginia and Hong Kong.

BOMBAY SWASTIKA

Braham Singh

Om Books International

First published in 2018 by

Om Books International

Corporate & Editorial Office
A-12, Sector 64, Noida 201 301
Uttar Pradesh, India
Phone: +91 120 477 4100
Email: editorial@ombooks.com
Website: www.ombooksinternational.com

Sales Office
107, Ansari Road, Darya Ganj,
New Delhi 110 002, India
Phone: +91 11 4000 9000
Fax: +91 11 2327 8091
Email: sales@ombooks.com
Website: www.ombooks.com

ISBN: 978-93-84625-57-3

Printed in India

10 9 8 7 6 5 4 3 2 1

Dedicated to Dr. Jyotsna Singh. Because which
Indian father wouldn't want the world
to know his daughter is an MD?

To those who think right is on their side, listen up, it means bugger-all. And those fighting injustice should remember, you will lose.

Contents

Acknowledgements

Fleshing out *Bombay Swastika* brings so much verifiable history to the fore that one is tempted to forgo disclaimers, deem it all true, and get on with it. Except that for starters, there are relatives from *Ernst's* dead, German wife's side—still alive but unreachable. No self-respecting member of the Virginia Bar would allow me to go write a purported true story without this other family's concurrence. It's not the only reason though, to run with fiction instead. It's also because *Bombay Swastika* has this Indian slant, and that gets tricky.

India has become a prickly nation. Denominational as well as a general sort of animus worn on shoulders like epaulettes. A narrative such as this may not escape lumpen rancor altogether (they may not read, their masters do). Some years ago, a Bollywood movie named *Billu Barber* was threatened into removing *Barber* from its title. The very real threats of violence came from a group—let's call them *hairstylists*—who find the term *barber* derogatory. This suggests even the fig leaf of fiction isn't much of a prophylactic, but one is entitled to minimise risk.

Besides *Ernst's* Indian family and friends who therefore may best be thanked anonymously, there are Indian curators, senior police officers, IAS officers, friends in government circles, friends in criminal circles and those thriving in both, who helped me research this novel. Also, Jesuits, schoolteachers, hotel managers, High Court advocates, doormen, and steadfast members of India's two major communities that remain in a permanent stand off against each other.

All of whom I also thank, while taking care not to name anyone. You know who you are.

Most of the events around which the story is built, are real. The people, barring some mentioned here, are not.

Ernst's parents Siegfried and Betty, were real. The staff at the Holocaust Museum in Washington DC located their histories for me. The Holocaust Museum, I can publicly thank. These days, rampaging hairstylists or Hindu fundamentalists are the least of their worries.

At the Museum, a kid in jeans and yamakeh heard me out and asked I come back after lunch. In that one hour he fleshed out Siegfried and his wife Betty from amongst the millions who died at Nazi hands. *Ernst's* father, Siegfried, never did enjoy that glorious death I accorded him in *Bombay Swastika*. And while I had *Ernst's* mother die of cancer to fit my story, in actual fact she and Siegfried, both Berliners, were picked up in Frankfurt, put in a cattle cart, taken to Riga via Berlin, and shot. We have a chilling type-written message from Nazi authorites to the local jurisdiction where the parents resided, informing them they can go ahead sequester Siegfried's property as the party in question is now deceased. The German fetish for documentation is one of the biggest hurdles Holocaust deniers face.

The Purandhar Fort Parole Interment Camp did exist and the German internees were amazing record keepers, especially the Lutheran priests. To them—Nazi sympathisers to a man—I convey my posthumous gratitude for helping build a Jewish hero. They kept diaries, wrote books and memorialised day-to-day events with Teutonic diligence. It was an extraordinary moment, every time a narration from their records matched one of the *Ernst's* tidbits.

Purandhar was unique in that German Jews and Nazis bunked next to each other in the same barracks, interned as equals. This delicious irony deserves a book unto itself about the actual people who entered and left Purandhar, and those who remain buried behind its frothy Deccan trap, stone walls.

Quaid-e-Azam Mohammed Ali Jinnah's last days make for fascinating drama and are extensively documented by various sources. I used Stanley Wolpert's biography as much as I could as well as his recommended bibliography to crosscheck Sindhi memories on 1948

Karachi. Taking a hint from his list of primary sources, I spent time in the India Office Library in London desperately trying to find an angle that may have eluded Wolpert.

The remarkable Jinnah was wasted on both India and Pakistan. It's a shame we meet him here so briefly and that too only after time's run out. Chabildas's escape from Karachi to Bombay was terrifyingly real. Its depiction in this book is fictionalised. His Sindhi Camp is still there in Chembur, changed and yet unchanged.

Ernst's refugee girl, the love of his life, is still alive and the Indian side of his family flourishing in Bombay, now Mumbai. They had two children, and now have grandchildren and great grandchildren, all blessed with rock star goodlooks—Sindhi and German DNA coursing through their veins. I thank the clan for all the love and affection showered on me even as I dissected them for this story.

As with Purandhar Fort, the war time goings-on at the *Krankenhaus der Jüdischen Gemeinde*, Berlin's Jewish Hospital at No.2 Iranische Strasse, is a tale in itself. Unlike the stories from Purandhar Fort, this one does get told—and brilliantly so—by Daniel B. Silver in his *Refuge in Hell: How Berlin's Jewish Hospital Outlasted the Nazis*, Boston, Houghton Mifflin, 2003, p. 352. It's from here I pilfered the collaborator, Doktor, Doktor Walter Lustig's inimitable character. Silver's *Refuge in Hell* was key to drawing up the plot around Schwester Ingrid. When it came to the detailed layout of the hospital compound during the war (the exact location of the Sammellager staging area to ship Jews, where the SS were stationed, the police wards, etc.) the book was extraordinarily helpful. This is the hospital complex Bombay Ingrid entered, and from where *Schwester Ingrid* never came out.

A suit with no literary background walks into a publishing house, wielding a manuscript. What could be the beginnings of a joke went on to become *Bombay Swastika*, thanks to Ajay Mago and his editor extraordinaire—Ipshita Mitra. If not for Ipshita, Dr. Homi Bhabha—India's nuclear mascot—would simply have snuck in and out of the story. Thanks to her persistence, he now lingers on while the game's afoot. The easiest thing one can do with fissionable material is to blow it up. Sixty years later, that's just about all the indomitable Dr. Bhabha's atomic energy program has got to show for itself. On the other hand, it does lend itself to a great story.

Still, how does a suit with no formal education in literature attempt a novel? By first learning to write movie scripts. Juliane Block, a die-hard Berliner, is an up and coming movie director who takes no prisoners. She taught me to manage a story arch across never more than 110 pages of a movie script. If *Bombay Swastika* stays on point, it's due to her. My other teachers though, were people I never met in person.

The Mahabharata tells us Ekalavya became the world's greatest archer by observing his teacher from afar. Ekalavya put up a mud statue of Dronacharya and would practise before it. Mine then, is a composite Dronacharya with Paul Theroux in the clay, along with V.S. Naipaul and Martin Cruz Smith and Khushwant Singh and Adam Johnson and Junot Diaz. One would also need to throw in Shobhaa De, Tarun Tejpal, Kiran Nagarkar and Chetan Bhagat. There are so many other influences, but these are my teachers. I would read everything they wrote and steal from them to write, write, re-write and write again, until one day I croaked in my own voice. There's no cutting off a thumb for my teachers the way Ekalavya did for Dronacharya; but I do thank each of them for being there for me.

The best part of any journey is when help pours in from unexpected quarters. Without Renaud Palliere, Om Books International wouldn't have known I exist. He championed *Bombay Swastika* like a boss. Then there's my dental clinic. Dr. Manisha Soni proved to be as much a stickler over grammar as she is about correct root canal procedure—finding punctuation errors where I could've sworn none existed. Then there were those who helped motivate, including a writers' group in Reston that got so offended by *Bombay Swastika*, I knew I was on to something. For positive reinforcement, nothing beats my daughter's work ethic as she ploughed away through her residency, doing eighteen hours a day to inspire and shame her father into staying up late. Then there's her mother, Harini—my rock. But for you, I'd probably be living it up, doing lines on some beach.

Preface
The Sardar's Run

The Sikh was big. Sikhs are big. This Sikh was bigger. A naphtha flare lit his face with a whoosh and he ran. For a moment, one would think it was Jesus running like crazy, his bearded face all lit up like that. A Jesus in a saffron turban. To celebrate this second coming Indian-style, the night broke into a dhrupad rhythm going, dhin tananana, dhin-dhin tananana.

The Sikh slowed for a bit, allowing security to catch up. Then he feinted, then dodged once more at the last moment to sprint off towards the naphtha towers. And because he knew his Chinee was rooting for him from the shadows over there, he started to show off.

'Oye, phuddus!' he called out without losing stride. 'Where did you learn to run?'

The security-wallahs abused him back—'phuddu yourself!'—although clearly in awe, hence somewhat demoralised; also straggling, out of shape and already tired. Even otherwise, they were dogs chasing a car. What if the car stopped? They say Sikhs can't multitask, but this one could sing and run while hefting a loaded gunny bag in one hand, holding his lungi up with the other. Dhin tananana, dhin-dhin tananana, he went, keeping up with the beat streaming across from the jhopadpatti slums.

There was never a time before jhopadpatti slums and they were everywhere. If you'd think of building something; anything, anywhere—the jhopadpatti would know what you were thinking and sneak up, just like that. Like what happened when they built the Fertiliser Complex, close to where Bombay steps out into the Arabian Sea. Using dwellings put together with tarp and Fertilisers gunny bags to encircle the factory perimeter, at first the jhopadpatti slum kept it low-key: we're just this one hovel here, one there, the starving poor, ignore us. See, we shit in the open, nothing to fear. Exactly how they laid siege on Sindhi Refugee Camp some years ago, then crawled their way into Trombay Proper to steal across Sion-Trombay Road into Sion and become the Dharavi sprawl—world-renowned for a stink that had aeroplanes brake in the air and turn around instead of landing properly at Santa Cruz Airport. Western reporters studied the phenomenon, inhaled, then wrote about it and filmed people squatting with brown bums on full display. The Sikh was a truck driver, but he knew this gora propaganda for what it was. He would discuss it with his Chinee lover and they would debate Lenin and Mao.

Coming in early morning with the Chinee on his mind, he drove through the jhopadpatti's cow dung smoke to where American consultants were still giving the finishing touches to Socialist India's A-1, first-class, second-hand Fertiliser Complex—transferred here lock, stock and barrel from Texas. During working hours, the Americans camped inside a solid piece of red, white and blue, bang in the middle of the complex—Indians not allowed.

'Fuck that', his Chinee had said. He wanted something from in there very badly and as far as the Sikh was concerned, that was that. He would get it for him. He would do anything for him. So, once it was dark, he scaled the chain-link fence to climb down into the American enclosure. The door to the air-conditioned, concrete block was left unlocked. It was like saying Indians didn't have the balls.

Once inside, it blew his mind, especially the Coca Cola machine, in spite of the stocked bar and pool table. It was night-time, no one present, and the air conditioner on. He couldn't believe one could shiver like this in Bombay. America had its shit together. On that, there could be no debate. He started looking for what his Chinee wanted and it was exactly where the Chinee said it would be. Phoren looking, with wires connecting to a stack of 12-volt car batteries, even though it was plugged into the wall through a transformer. Another wire crawled up the wall and went outside through a hole on one side. The Sikh took out a screwdriver from his salwaar and went to work.

A good half an hour later, he left clutching a Fertilisers gunny bag containing whatever this was he had unscrewed for his Chinee; wires sticking out from everywhere. When he looked through the chain-link fence, the security-wallahs were waiting for him on the other side.

'Sat Sri Akal, Sardarji,' they greeted. Big smiles. Caught red-handed, he had grinned right back through the chain-link fence—how a Sikh does in the face of adversity.

'Sat Sri Akal, bhenchodon,' he said, and proceeded to climb over to their side as if nothing to it. The security guards clearly hadn't thought this through because once he stood in their midst, they didn't know what to do with so much Sikh. He waited, they waited, and he waited. When they waited some more, he simply walked away; then yelled, 'Bole So Nihal!' before sprinting off, holding up his lungi with one hand, the heavy gunny bag swinging weightlessly from the other. Fertilisers' green swastika logo danced with the gunny bag whenever it caught the light. A naphtha flare went whoosh, painting a halo behind his bearded face to create that Jesus effect. All that was missing was a big, fat Sacred Heart to go with the picture.

'Oye!' the security yelled, and rushed en bloc after the lunatic. They were tired but fuck that; he had entered America without a visa.

~

Zigging while the security zagged, he turned a corner to ease into the shadows reaching out from the urea towers. Hidden from view now and with pipes scurrying around to provide additional cover, he searched for his Chinee. And there he was, a little porcelain doll looking lost. The Sikh put down the gunny bag and folded his lover gently into his arms. He could have that American thing he wanted so badly, the Sikh offered, in exchange for some mouth-to-mouth. They looked into each other's eyes and the Chinee used both his hands to readjust the Sikh's unravelling turban, pushing wayward, jet-black strands back in place.

'Actually when you're gone,' he whispered, 'I miss your chest hair the most.'

Oh yes, they were in love. The nonplussed security outside the urea complex sounded close, and the last thing the Sikh needed was for them to find out. So, they kissed Western-style and placing his porcelain doll back to the ground next to the heavy gunny bag, he stepped out from the shadows with the biggest hard-on known to man. Seeing his lungi tent like that, the guards couldn't believe their eyes.

'Oye, bhenchodon!' he said. 'What you looking at?'

And anyway, why the surprise? Sardar, after all. So they powered up again, to come after him in a half-heartedly dogged manner that is so Indian, it should be trademarked.

~

More Sikh laughter, lots of swearing and running like Milkha Singh, then boredom began setting in. The bhenchods weren't going to give up, or catch up. It dawned: this was bullshit. The urea plant released ammonia that tore into his eyes, his new leather Multanis were covered in dust, and his turban was all over the place. He on the other hand, was going nowhere. He decided to stop, turn around, raise his empty hands and say, guys, what the fuck, let's call it a day, and no harm done.

That's when a rifle went off. Indians know a .303 just from its sound and he jumped, not so much because it was fired at him, but because it was fired at all.

The Chinese were pleasantly surprised invading India in 1962, to learn that a .303 Lee Enfield is purely for show. Something every Indian by the way knows. Because no one can squeeze the trigger with that right amount of love, and even then it kicks like a bhenchod. Consequently, the bullet never strikes where aimed; meaning the Sikh wasn't worried about being hit, just being fired at in the first place.

Also, what was rented security doing with a .303? Turning around, he was startled at first to find dark blue police now running alongside the khaki security guards, then lost it because the police couldn't just fire at people. The British said so before leaving. Cane them, they argued, or beat them to a pulp. Even hanging a suspect was fine, as long as officially deemed suicide. But no shooting. The gunshot was therefore enough of an outrage for him to halt, swing around and accost his pursuers, who braked in turn to remain a safe distance from the giant maniac now yelling at them, asking, 'What the fuck?'

The police havaldar, the one who fired, looked ridiculous, still pointing a Lee Enfield like that, and the Sikh said so. 'Like the chootiya that you are, saale, Pandu Havaldar, bhenchod. Why don't you put it down so I can make you my bitch?'

No one spoke to the police like that. But because he did, no one was taking any chances. The havaldar lowered his rifle.

With both sides taking time-out, the Sikh looked around and saw they were near the sulphur burner all brightly lit and waiting to be fired up. Now that he noticed, must be shift change, because there was no one there except for more dark blue havaldars and a police jeep nearby. When did the police show up? No idea, but he acknowledged the balance of power had shifted. It was no longer a laughing matter. A shot had been fired—probably hit someone in the jhopadpatti slums because the music had stopped.

Only then he noticed the police sub-inspector with his polished, brown belt and buttoned-down, leather holster. Standing alongside was another officer, who looked too senior to get his shiny, black shoes dirty like this. The sub-inspector held a black umbrella, ready to open at a moment's notice for the Very Senior Officer.

'Sardarji,' the Very Senior Officer said. His voice was deep and low. He sounded English, looked Marathi. 'These fellows bothering you?'

'The bhenchod fired at me.'

'I heard it.' He looked at the dark blue culprit, who looked down. 'So did the rest of Bombay.'

'I could've been killed.'

'By a three-naught-three?'

The night air was cool and sickly-sweet from benzene. The smell of hydrogen sulphide was as if all of Bombay had farted as one. The Very Senior Officer studied his hand. His words were clipped like his nails.

'You took something that doesn't belong to you.'

'Sirji, I'm a Sardar. We don't steal.'

'You need to hand it back. Do the right thing.'

He would have, now that the police were involved. If not for the Chinee. The Chinee was a miracle that had happened, and the miracle was as follows. After pining for months and being ignored, he was ready to give up, write his last love letter and drive away in his Tata to never come back. Just about then, the little Chinee had for no reason giggled seeing him. The Sikh died and went to heaven. One thing led to another and before you knew it, he was spooning the little porcelain doll, kissing mouth-to-mouth while giving and receiving to his heart's content. He wasn't going to fuck with that.

'I'm told Sardars never lie,' the Very Senior Officer said.

Generally true, give or take. And while all Sardars aren't Sikhs, all Sikhs are Sardars, and therefore a people apart. So much so, during British rule, a Sikh's testimony in court required no corroborating evidence.

'I'm telling you Sirji, I simply climbed over for the fun of it. Wanted to see the Coca Cola machine.' He would charm the pants off this officer-type, if it were the last thing he did.

'Sardarji, you believe in God? In the Guru Granth Sahib?'

He nodded, even though these days he only believed in his Chinee. Where was the harm though? He liked people who were good at their jobs. The way the subject was being broached, this Very Senior Officer was clearly the best. The Sikh had to wonder what exactly was in the gunny bag, for someone like this to get here in no time.

'You've taken something, Sardarji, please return it,' the Very Senior Officer requested. The sub-inspector with the umbrella was more to the point. 'That gunny bag you were holding earlier. Where is it?' It wasn't a request.

The Sikh went, 'What gunny bag?'

The sub-inspector had a don't-fuck-with-me look. 'He doesn't have it now, but he did. Probably gave it to someone. Sir, we're wasting our time.'

A policeman and not stupid? This was a first.

'Maybe, maybe not.' The Very Senior Officer looked a reasonable man.

'I didn't take anything,' the Sikh repeated. 'Believe me, Sirji.'

The Very Senior Officer looked like maybe he would, maybe not.

'I was here last week, Sir,' the sub-inspector said. 'That naphtha pilfering case. I saw this Sardar hanging around with a Chinese-looking worker. Every time I looked, they were together.'

'You mean my Nepali cleaner-boy. He's asleep in the tanker. Go check.'

'We've checked,' the sub-inspector said. 'That's not him. I'm talking about a Chinee worker in blue overalls. Don't get all smart with me.'

'Come on, Sardarji,' said the Very Senior Officer, 'Let's get this over with.'

When the sub-inspector spoke again, it was as if he had taken his cue from the Very Senior Officer. He didn't use his standard police voice this time, the otherwise I'll-shove-a-fucking-baton-up-your-arse voice, or I'll-attach-a-12-volt-battery-to-your-testicles voice. He spoke like a human being, not police. You could say he was speaking to a friend, finally giving a Sardar the respect due.

'He's good-looking, the Chinee,' the sub-inspector conceded. The Sikh went, 'Yeah? What Chinee? You mean, Nepali.' The sub-inspector went, 'Really? Come on.' The Very Senior Officer went, 'He must be special. Tell me, where's he? I would love to meet your Chinese friend.'

Some other time and place and the Sikh may have crumbled. 'He's inside my head, Sirji,' he would have admitted, 'when I'm not inside him. Without him, I cannot eat, I cannot think, I cannot sleep. I just want to hear his voice. I'll follow him to China, if need be, like a cuckoo riding monsoon clouds.'

But he remained silent and saw the Very Senior Officer watching him intently. 'You were right,' the Officer said to his sub-inspector. 'This is a waste of time.'

The Very Senior Officer held his hand out with an expression to his face. The Sikh looked up at the skies, thinking he was asking for the sub-inspector's umbrella. The sub-inspector unbuttoned his holster and drew out his Indian Ordinance, .38/200 Webley. When he handed it to the Very Senior Officer, the Sikh realised time-out was over. No more niceties, and he hunkered down for a whole lot of threats and bluster. He was a truck driver and knew the drill. Fuck them.

The Very Senior Officer took the Webley from the sub-inspector's hand, then took a step back and shot the Sikh three times—right in the face, then the chest and neck. The Sikh didn't have time to flinch though his Chinee did, hiding out there in the shadows. His delicate hands shook and that gunny bag the police were after, it fell with a thud. Recalling how weightless it had looked swinging from his Sikh's massive hand earlier that night, the Chinee began to whimper.

1

Fertilisers

Public sector factories are the temples of modern India.
—*Pandit Jawaharlal Nehru*

Rumour had it they'd gone found some poor dead bastard at Fertilisers, and Ernst Steiger realised he too was out of luck. Times like this, he would rub the mole on his face. The fertiliser factory compound was emptying before his eyes and he thought, surely a skeleton shift stays back to man a continuous process plant?

It didn't appear that way, even though not everyone was headed for the gates. A crowd had gathered around the sulphur burner. A strong burst of ammonia caught Ernst in the eye and there was this pervasive smell of shit. The sound of children's laughter filled the air. A posse of havaldars in dark blue shorts moved towards the sulphur burner in absolutely no rush.

Like any Jew muddling through the diaspora, Ernst wore two hats. He had showed up at Fertilisers wearing the frayed Indian one to try mix freely, but there's no mistaking a white man. Seeing him, the police posse stopped to go, 'Sirji!'

Dead man over there, they said, all smiles, pointing towards the sulphur burner.

He smiled back, but felt the dead man could have chosen another day. Today was the annual tender opening and Ernst was here to play his part; plug his German-made stainless steel pipes, then wait in queue with other suppliers. Being German, his pipes were technically, German-made. Not Made in Germany, but this was India and that was enough. Every year, he walked away with something, sometimes large, usually not. Today though there was a dead man in queue, and so wouldn't matter whether Indian-made, German-made, or Made in Germany. He would go back home empty handed, he knew. Whereas, Salary Day was around the corner and his workers waiting to be paid.

Where exactly? The havaldars pointed towards the sulphur burner. Body burnt to a crisp, they said. How come? Because the place is wacked, they said, that's how come. Check those Lambadi women out, they suggested. Have you seen how they behave? The dead man was sniffing around them for sure, and probably why he's dead in the first place. Any which way, we will find out who did it, and Ernst agreed. Bombay Police, after all.

Some more back and forth, and the posse saluted before moving on. They strolled past a Lambadi kid on his haunches, a dog by his side. Then for the sheer joy of it, one of the havaldars goes kicks at the dog sniffing the child's naked bottom. Amidst the animal's howls and Lambadi children shitting in a public sector factory, Ernst recalled his wife saying, India could make a Jew pine for Nazi Germany. Some more policemen walked by with more smiles and Sirjis to remind Ernst that whatever Ingrid may have felt, in India, he was nothing less than a white man.

In Germany, he was a Jew.

I don't want to be one, he had told his parents on finding out what was in store. Besides, he said to them, I pass the Mischlinge Test—implying he was only half-Jew. His Aryan mother, Jew father, had looked at each other. It was like being half-pregnant. After that, Ernst's father took to patting his son's head for no reason at all. Siegfried Steiger was big and fat and loud and boisterous, but also a complex man, hard to understand. I'm sorry, Ernst felt his father was trying to say whenever he patted his head like that. Back then, Ernst didn't know what to make of it.

Truth be told, he still didn't know what to make of his father's life, or his mother's death. Everyone else did—said it was cancer. He, on the other hand, felt maybe not; that maybe she died from shouldering a shitload of guilt on behalf of her fellow Aryans. Sitting in his flat at Colaba, he would mull over how he left her behind with an illness, all that guilt, and a husband who would eventually go slit his wrists to escape being a Jew. Suicides are straightforward affairs, but not his father's—no suicide note, nothing; leaving room for conjecture, the size of a football field.

Siegfried made up for the missing suicide note by making regular visits instead. The visits began some years after he killed himself, slitting his wrists in a bathtub at the Jüdische Krankenhaus in Berlin. Ernst would have preferred his father didn't take the trouble. Not keeping in touch when alive was bad enough. Trying to compensate afterwards only made it worse.

~

A sub-inspector barked at his cohort, and pointed at a single mud-caked leather Multani lying by the sulphur burner. The havaldars gathered in a circle around the guilty footwear. An unnaturally tall, black man standing nearby ignored the proceedings.

The sub-inspector was loud and unequivocal. That Multani could only belong to a Sikh truck driver. A saffron Sikh turban lay coiled nearby, in case you felt like challenging the assertion. The open-toed Multani was caked brown, as if the sub-inspector's Sikh had walked all the way from the Punjab to come here to die.

Police havaldars began cordoning off the sulphur burner and the sub-inspector let go the forlorn Multani to focus on the Lambadi labour hired to carry sulphur to the melting pits. Watching the Bombay Police sub-inspector behave like one, Ernst could see where this was going and it wasn't going well. The police officer implying for all to hear, that the Lambadi had something to do with whatever happened. He had precedence on his side. This wasn't the first time some Sikh chatted up a tribal and disappeared, then reappeared dead.

'Probably why,' the sub-inspector deduced, 'the Multani's missing a Sikh.'

'Your menfolk,' he then asked the Lambadi women, 'why gone all of a sudden?'

Good point. Typically, kohl-eyed Lambadi men hovered close by while their women worked. Their hooked noses and curved daggers were a deterrent to anyone, except possibly some Sikh tired of spooning his cleaner-boy.

'Your men,' and the sub-inspector looked the women up and down. 'Where are they?'

The lack of response was deafening. Dealing with authority figures was an everyday affair for Lambadi women. The sub-inspector appeared torn between gypsy titties and gypsy truculence. The woman he kept running his eyes over wasn't exactly a spring chicken, but Indian men have a high tolerance when it comes to age. There was a pot-bellied child clinging to her leg and others playing nearby amongst mangy pye-dogs.

The very tall, black man standing nearby looked bored with all this. He also looked Tamilian, except for his height. Then out of nowhere, the havaldars dragged over a young worker half his size. His skin was like bone china.

'So, you fucking have it or not?' the big black man asked the Chinese-looking boy with the porcelain complexion. He spoke in Hindi, something Tamilians shouldn't do, and people around him cringed. 'It was in a gunny bag. Don't tell me you don't have it.'

The Chinese-looking boy simply shook his head. His eyes were red and looking past his inquisitioner towards the sulphur burner.

~

Neon stars twinkled along the upper reaches of the Government Fertilisers Complex amidst pipes and towering cylinders, cracker units and looming stainless steel vessels. The illumination was harsher though at ground level and Russian, high-pressure, sodium vapour lamps imported against rupee payment, created black shadows around brutal yellow pools. The lighting cast everyone in a sickly hue and because nothing had gone according to plan that day, Ernst felt this was more like it.

He had left Colaba around noon for the tender opening at Fertilisers, determined to make things go his way while doubting he could pull that off. It was an effort visualising anything going his way. But things had once, the first few years in India—no worries about money, or meeting payroll on Salary Day, or anything, except Ingrid.

He was all caught up toying with Ingrid's cold Bombay version, then the icy Berlin one, and back again to Bombay Ingrid, when Beatrice Taylor came by towing a young girl starting to bud. Going by the files the girl clutched for protection, Beatrice now had an assistant.

'Penny for your thoughts,' Beatrice said, smelling of Yardley lavender. She wanted to know what he was still doing here. There was no tender opening now by the way, what with this dead man thing. These people needed any excuse not to work. There was nothing to do. He might as well leave. The skinny assistant hovered by her side, straightening her sari, fingering her files, then looking away, then listening in. Ernst hadn't seen her around Beatrice before. Could have something to do with Beatrice Taylor's recent promotion. She was now Personal Assistant to Fertilisers' General Manager. It meant Beatrice Taylor was now entitled to a Personal Assistant.

Beatrice was Anglo-Indian, not to be confused with English people from the Raj, who also called themselves Anglo-Indians. According to them however, the correct, technical term for someone like Beatrice would be dingo, or kutcha butcha—half-baked. If you see a snake and a dingo, they advised before leaving India forever, kill the dingo.

Irish-white, you would never know she was half-baked. Her freckled face hovered over D-cups balanced by a solid backside at the far end. Her buttocks were watermelons, grown through competitive field hockey at St. Anthony's and had ripened over the years. Men would stare at that arse with a collective focus that burned a hole through her skirt.

'Look at them,' Beatrice said, nodding towards the sulphur burner. 'No wonder they don't prosper.'

As always, everyone was having a ball except her. These people, she said. Staring at you like that one moment, stabbing you the next. If you see a snake and an Indian, kill the Indian.

Ernst smiled, resisting giving in to a show of sympathy for her to then go misunderstand—half-baked dingos were dangerously attracted to Europeans in spite of everything. If a dingo saw a snake and a European, the snake was fucked.

There was a whoosh, and gas flared from a stack over at the urea plant. It lit up Beatrice's broad, freckled face from the back. The sun would do the same from behind Berlin Ingrid over long-drawn evenings on the Unter den Linden. That's where any similarity ended and wasn't just the looks. The Ingrids never harboured any of the urgency one saw flicker in Beatrice's eyes.

'Just look,' Beatrice said. 'God knows what they're up to over there.' Saying that, she walked right past the sub-inspector's dark blue cohort standing there, hypnotised by her thick backside. Her chit of an assistant scrambled to keep up, leaving behind a trail of jasmine sweat. There was this broad sweep to the girl's forehead and Ernst eyed those cheekbones, except that she was a very dark brown, bordering on black, and that wouldn't do. Indians were a flexible lot, though not when it came to colour. No amounts of Johnson Baby Powder on that face could change the fact that Fertilisers was as far as she would go. It also didn't help that her upper incisors stood out like piano keys. The two women were headed towards the crowded burner and Ernst thought it best to follow. He hurried, only to speed up further, avoided stepping on some shit lying in wait, and barely managed to edge past Beatrice's tits and arse cleaving through the crowd.

There was this buzzing sound. It rose to a crescendo as he clambered up the wicked, metal stairs to the viewing platform. Once there, he gagged, turned around and pushed Beatrice back down the stairs. Too late, because she was already biting down on her knuckles, staring past the buzzing flies at the charred carcass. The flies flew freely in and out through its open neck.

Beatrice Taylor stared at the headless torso, wide-eyed. The severed head lying next to it leered back. Cooked internal organs spilt out from linear fissures to dangle from the torso. They smelled of burnt liver. Topping it all was a metallic smell, making Ernst's head swim. It emanated from the burner's wide open viewing panel—all that iron-rich blood that had burnt inside. Then there was the odour from burnt hair and it clung to the nostrils.

There was no hair left though, on the head with that crazed rictus of a smile. So, anyone's guess whether Sikh or not. Just the khaki sub-inspector's word therefore, versus the bald, death mask grinning past flies fighting over brain matter coagulated on its left side. The neck had melted, leaving strings of blackened skin trailing down from the head and stuck in place with melted fat. Also, there was a hole bored clean through the forehead.

Anyone will tell you a Hindu skull bursts on cremation to allow the soul to ascend. But, this perfectly round aperture dead centre through the forehead, suggested Sikhs did things differently. Or, that the man was shot through the head, even though that would be ridiculous because this was India. True, servants, lovers, daughters-in-law, men of the wrong caste, women of any caste, and girls not boys, were routinely burnt alive across the land. And yes, Sikhs too, caught messing with Lambadi women. But shooting them first?

'That's a bullet hole.'

'What, Sirji?'

It was the same havaldar, the one all smiles earlier, then went kicked a dog. 'Where?' the havaldar asked, looking more like the dog-kicker now than a friendly policeman salaaming the European. Ernst pointed, wondering if there was an exit wound behind the skull, and should he ask the havaldar to check, or whether it was any of his business. People died all the time. He, on the other hand, still had to make payroll. The havaldar appeared adamant. 'I am not seeing anything, Sirji.' To demonstrate how he felt, the havaldar swung a leg at the same emaciated dog he'd kicked earlier, because now the tenacious little fucker was edging up the stairs towards the carcass. Its little mongrel head struck the rusted steps and howled as it took a tumble.

'Bhenchod!' the dog-kicker said, and there was laughter. Struggling upright, the dog stood there and howled away, distracting Ernst from the grinning skull with the bullet hole. At the same time, the sub-inspector declaimed loudly from below the steps, past the howling dog, and next to the unusually tall Tamilian bullying the little Chinese-looking worker with that porcelain complexion and red eyes. 'Do you have it?' he kept asking the beautiful, little man and Beatrice took it all in.

So there it was, the howling dog, the Tamilian asking the porcelain doll to return whatever it is he stole, Beatrice wide-eyed, and her assistant too, with jaw drooping to allow her buck teeth sway over the face. All this while the sub-inspector's pointing his finger at Lambadi titties and Ernst goes taps his shoulder. Caught up with so much cleavage the sub-inspector ignored him, but remained adamant about letting the world know what the Lambadis did to the Sikh.

'What about the bullet hole?' Ernst asked, tapping the sub-inspector once more on his epaulet. This time, the man turned. His eyes widened seeing a white man. Then they narrowed.

'Do any of you see a bullet hole?' the sub-inspector asked around. His havaldars shrugged.

'Make sure. The gora sahib wants to know about some bullet hole.'

The cohort looked towards the grinning head lying next to the torso. They peered. It was clear no one could see anything of that sort.

'Right there,' Ernst pointed.

'Where?' the sub-inspector asked. 'How can there be a bullet-hole? Lambadi don't carry guns.'

'Police do.'

In all fairness, the sub-inspector was unarmed. The only guns around were the .303 Enfields with a couple of havaldars, and the sub-inspector had this look that said, Seriously?

Ernst ventured with caution. 'Thought you sub-inspectors wore sidearms.'

'It's optional,' the sub-inspector said. 'I prefer not to. Not having one makes me think smarter, especially around people who feel they know everything.'

They were staring at him, the sub-inspector and his men. Ernst rubbed his mole, feeling somewhat less white under their scrutiny. He realised the little dog was still at it, the howls reminding him of his homo teacher's dachshund back in Berlin. He was surprised, not for the first time, at how so much sound could come from such a tiny body.

2

The Howling Dachshund

Swing Heil!
—*Swingkinder greeting*

Over the final year at his Berlin realschule, Ernst found many of his classmates looking bigger and blonder. Their evolution into a Master Race taught him early on how to be risk averse, not be his father, and to look down, look away, and look invisible.

Around this time, the Aryan kids began refusing to take turns wiping the blackboard or emptying wastepaper baskets. The chores fell to the Jewish students in class. The bigger and blonder boys also began answering back at the class teacher, even though he wasn't Jewish. 'Homo!' they would yell, whenever he turned to write something on the blackboard.

Now, no one in the class was blonder than Berlin Ingrid, who looked just like Hitler asked. So blonde, she was the alpha to an anglicised bunch of jazz-loving Swingkinder who loved poking fun at Nazi clowns in uniform—heckling them on the streets, then running away laughing. She could've been at the expensive girls' gymnasium her father lined up for her, but she chose Ernst's realschule instead because of her Swingkinder gang. Ernst, she ignored.

There was this stunned look to her face the day her Swingkinder friends explained how, blindingly blonde or not, and whatever they may think of Hitler, a Jew was a Jew, and how come she never told them? You could say it was a coming to Moses moment and in many ways, Berlin Ingrid would never be the same again. At least once a day, the school principal came borrowed her and the other Jews with a crook of his finger, and without even glancing at the class teacher. The Jewish children would then be assigned various tasks around the school compound.

Perhaps to show the law was law, and that there could be no favouritism towards a half-breed mischlinge, several janitorial duties befell Ernst even though the school had a custodian on payroll. Over an hour before the final school bell rang every afternoon, Ernst mastered the art of scrubbing yellow piss off the floor from around each urinal. Berlin Ingrid on the other hand was allowed leeway because of her platinum blonde hair, and also because she was learning how to look at men in that sideways manner. She would be tasked to help the principal and when she was there in his office with him, the door remained shut.

Amidst all this and with Berlin Ingrid behaving as if Ernst didn't exist, their class teacher was what made school tolerable. A tall, thin, monocle-bearing homosexual oblivious to his destitution, the man lived for Puccini and the pet dachshund he at times brought to class. He spoke extemporaneously on the opera and the Orient—dissecting *Madame Butterfly*, or coaxing the children to fly with him to Batavia or the Malabar Coast over geography lessons. All in all, a bit much for young, Aryan minds too busy with their shit to take a homo seriously.

Ernst however lapped it up and brightened one cold winter morning, when the teacher wanted to use the Flower Duet from Delibes' *Lakmé* to take them to India. Everything was grey that day—the road, the buildings, the people, the smoke, the ice, Ernst. Ignoring Wagner's *Ride of the Valkyries* compulsorily straining through school corridors, the teacher sang an aria from *Lakmé* to a class huddled in their coats like miserable penguins. 'Sous le dôme épais,' he sang in French, going on to trill the high notes better than any diva. 'Où le blanc jasmine, À la rose s'assemble, Sur la rive en fleurs…'

The sun began to shine and Ernst found himself standing on the banks of the Ganges. There, alongside two British soldiers sneaking a peek at the Brahmin priest's daughter Lakshmi bathing naked, he realised he wasn't cold anymore.

For the big, blonde Aryan boys however, this was the last fucking straw. To hell with waiting for him to turn his back, they yelled, 'Homo!' to their teacher's face, stopping him mid-aria. They kept shouting, 'Homo! Homo!' driving the dachshund nuts, until other grown-ups showed up amidst all that barking and noise to restore order. With the school principal leading, an all-Aryan staff dragged a surprised class teacher outside into the compound, his students cheering and kicking at the little brown dachshund scrambling behind his master.

During the Weimar Republic and even after Hitler was Führer, Ernst's father never failed to point out: what they taught or didn't teach in schools would determine whether Germany behaved itself in the future. Much later at the Jüdische Krankenhaus, he pissed off Nazis and Jews alike by saying they should've let that homosexual teacher run the entire verdammte school system, and saved themselves a Second World War. Instead, they strung him up before a cheering mob of his own school children. But not before first making him watch his dachshund dangle from a piano wire.

The grey morning became a carnival and a welcome diversion from the cold. The class found it hilarious, hearing their teacher scream in pain at what they were doing to his dog, and offering his own neck instead. The grown-ups took him up on that, and Ernst remembered the dog dangling like a counterweight to his master hanging alongside on the lamp post, each howling at what was happening to the other, until both stopped. He would never forget those few seconds of total silence, while Germany decided if this was how it would be. Then the crowd roared again, and Ernst saw the students and teachers, the young and old, Swingkinder and National Socialists, all come together into one nation. He could see there would be no stopping them now.

Berlin Ingrid saw it too, her eyes clamouring: I want to be part of this! Just look at me! No one will know!

The crowd was all caught up Sieg Heiling each other and they left her there ignoring Ernst.

Distracted, Ernst stepped into the shit he had avoided earlier chasing Beatrice to the sulphur burner. He didn't lose it, and just looked around to scrape it off his shoe. He found a rebar lying next to a shrunken, Lambadi kid squatting right there with ribs on display. The boy appeared caught up in a daydream, ignoring the recently kicked dog that was now happily attacking his turds as they emerged.

There was this other daydreamer in Nazi Germany, unilaterally deemed Jewish so they could fuck with him. He managed to escape to Bombay away from all that shit, only to learn one could escape anything over here in India, except that.

3

The Tamilian

Sikhs may be superior to Madrasis, but we are all Indians.
—*Partap Singh Kairon, Punjab Chief Minister*

Gas erupted again from the urea stack and the air became pungent with ammonia. The sodium lighting cast deep, dark shadows at ground level, and the distant oil refineries flared natural gas in loud belches from where the marshes ended and the Arabian Sea began. What with pye-dogs still trying to get at the charred torso, the police posse all caught up trying to pin it on Lambadi women trailing screaming children from between their legs, and the big black man in his parallel universe haranguing the little porcelain doll next to the sub-inspector studying gypsy titties; it was Dante's *Inferno* how an Indian would've written it.

The stricken doll wasn't Nepali, was too delicate to be Tibetan, and probably nothing more than an all-Indian, North-East Frontier tribal kid. Didn't matter; like the Lambadi gypsies, almond eyes are different and that was enough. After China invaded the country, people stopped looking askance at Muslims for a bit and began taking it out on anyone Chinese. On seeing a Chinese and a snake, an Indian would know what to do. Because there weren't enough Chinese to go around, one managed with anyone Chinese enough. Tribes from the east became the country's low-hanging fruit. There was even this one case of an Indian Army Sikh raping a seventy-year-old Naga tribal man he found shitting in the woods. People were shocked until told a Sikh did it, and then they just shrugged.

'Look at me when I'm talking,' the Tamilian said to the porcelain doll. 'Come on, good boy. Where's the gunny bag?'

'Don't pay attention,' Beatrice urged Ernst. She was now somewhat back to normal after how the headless Sikh had ambushed her at the sulphur burner.

The big Tamilian was carved in granite, holding a saucer cooling tea. There was something round and a discoloured ivory-white in his other hand. It could be a hockey ball and the Tamilian could be a senior plainclothesman, the way a uniformed constable in dark blue shorts held his teacup for him. The constable was being unctuous, whereas to the rest of India, Tamilians, or anyone from South India, is a Madrasi. Madrasi was the country's nigger-word, and dark skin totally a bad thing. Up North, they'll tell you point-blank: you see a Madrasi and a snake, kill the Madrasi. Regardless of what he might privately think, the constable refilled the saucer with tea for the Madrasi carved out of granite. He then remained awkwardly bent to continue kissing the big man's black arse.

Ernst watched the Tamilian sip from the saucer and bounce the leather ball off the dead ground. It sprang back into his cupped palm. The Tamilian held on to his bored expression. It accentuated his Tamil features and those full lips. He could be in some sort of street disguise because there was a red handkerchief around his neck. A laal rumaal—much thought of among street-gangs of the Muslim kind. It stood out. As did the porcelain doll in blue overalls—straight out of China he looked—at the receiving end of whatever was going on. Besides his cheap round-rimmed glasses, the porcelain doll had on this despondent look, as if facing detention after class.

'Don't be shaking that head of yours. Are you giving it back or not?'

The big Tamilian was being the schoolmaster, dressing down the young man with the porcelain complexion. He ignored the barbequed Sikh's body by the burner, the sub-inspector making a fool of himself over the Lambadi women, and Beatrice's stink-eyed look. As if none of that mattered. As if nothing existed outside his makeshift classroom.

'We know it was you,' said the man in granite, the English buckling under his Tamil accent. 'Bleddy bastard.'

A strained look grabbed Beatrice's lips, pursing them. The Tamilian was persistent.

'Come on, just return the gunny bag.'

The Chinese-looking kid shook his head.

No.

'You out of your bhenchod mind? Hand it over.'

No.

He shook his head once more, and then again, whenever the raspy voice asked he hand it over. The havaldar with the teacup began haranguing the kid in Marathi, vying at being brusque. It didn't help. Each time, the kid simply shook his head.

No.

Fuck that, the havaldar said and elbowed Porcelain Doll towards the Tamilian, who remained still in a bored sort of way except for a thumb and forefinger reaching out like a pincer for the young man's ear. When they came together in a pinch, it must have been painful, the way the kid winced. Neither spoke while the Tamilian continued wringing his ear, and the first one to say something, loses. How the Tamilian meted out punishment, the manner in which Porcelain Doll took it, the way the constable stood at attention, Ernst could see a point being made, a lesson being taught, and that there needed to be silence in the classroom. Beatrice's shocked assistant could see that too, and one would think, so could Beatrice.

There was a ripple and shouts of, 'Make way!' Two dark blue constables had somehow slung the Sikh's torso along with his severed head in his own saffron turban, and were coming through towards the jeep. Flies kept breaking away in tight formation and diving through the open neck to eat and lay eggs. Other flies were having a go at the Sikh's entrails spilling out from here and there. A sweet and musky smell took over. Ernst sniffed at the air.

'Cerebrospinal fluid,' the sub-inspector offered, giving Ernst a side glance, who in turn felt there was no harm looking impressed.

Seeing Beatrice cover her nose, he said to her, 'Come on, let's go.'

'Where to?' Beatrice asked. 'The whole country stinks.'

Ernst remained deadpan. He felt for her, but had no intention of coming across a phuddu. Maybe, the Anglo-Indian in Beatrice Taylor was still adjusting to a new world order, but he knew his place. It helped that he was comfortable by now in the skin of a white man who hadn't quite made it. India allowed him that, and though there was a price to pay, he could be someone here. Whatever Indians chose to do or not do in their own country, wasn't for him to judge and besides, he owed them. A Hindu would say he had eaten their salt.

Pointing to the headless Sikh, the big, black man said, 'Look. You want to become like that?'

The porcelain doll's delicate face came apart seeing the charred body. So much so that Ernst thought it strange, then realised it was probably the first time the kid had seen anything like this. Tears welled up in those almond eyes and the porcelain doll stretched out a trembling hand towards the headless Sikh. This was more than just shock. Clearly, the kid was grieving. Now, that was strange.

The big, black Tamilian came out from his slouch and slammed a heavy hand to the side of the boy's head, knocking him to the grass before it registered with those around. 'Bhenchod,' he said. Ernst thought he was seeing things. It was like a block of granite break into life and slip back again, spilling tea in the process. The porcelain doll laid there still as death, and Ernst realised the Tamilian had hit the boy with the hockey ball.

Beatrice gaped. The assistant too, her teeth more prominent with the lower jaw sagging like that. Something then started to happen behind those buck teeth; an engine was revving up. The Tamilian's constable recovered the empty saucer from his hand and poured some more tea on it, when the girl stepped forward. Her sari pallu was trailing behind though, allowing Beatrice to yank at it. The havaldars whooped in laughter.

'What are you laughing at?' Beatrice pointed at the damaged porcelain doll, while still holding the girl by her sari. 'This is what happens when the country's left to you people.'

The British couldn't have said it better. The Tamilian watched Beatrice from behind heavy eyelids. He could be falling asleep.

'Shut up, whore,' he said.

The silence following that was total. Ernst peered to see if Beatrice was okay. Her eyes had gone all funny, but she'd be fine—just an Anglo-Indian in an India that no longer gave a fuck. 'Rowdies,' she whispered. 'Is that how they talk to us now? These people, I tell you, they'll never prosper.'

The porcelain doll just lay there smashed to the ground, one side of the face cherry-red below the hairline. With the night shift coming in, the loudspeakers opened up with motivational music, now standard after the war with China. The song proceeded to remind one and all, India was the only place to be. Rulers come, rulers go, the singer waxed in colloquial Hindi, but India is still here; it continues to grow.

'Bhairavi!' Beatrice called out in a loud whisper to her tethered ward with the buck teeth and sagging jaw. 'Chalo, let's go.'

'Chalo!' she hissed again to the girl Bhairavi, taking on the white man's burden, who stood there rubbing at the mole on his face. Catching Ernst's eye, Beatrice Taylor gave him a look, jerking her head towards the gates as gas flared once more with a loud whoosh. All this, her look said, was unacceptable. These people, it declaimed, would never prosper. Please, it begged, take me away to a more European place.

He couldn't of course, but it reminded him he had an appointment tonight to take his friend Willie Lansdowne's wife, Daisy. Not something he enjoyed, just something he did. What he really wanted to take, was a shower.

4

The Cold Pilger

If phoren, then chalega.
—*Indian approach to imported goods*

Ernst's Goregaon workshop was on the Western Line, past early morning shitters scattered alongside the railway tracks. They congregated on the narrow strip between their shanties and the rails with locals whizzing past. Their numbers seemed to grow by the day and if someone crouching half-asleep by the tracks nodded off, it was over instantly and not a bad way to go. Looking out from the moving train, sunlight would glint momentarily off fresh turds coiled beneath brown arses like so many miniature, golden cobras. The railway carriages were open—no doors—and given that marigold sellers weren't allowed into first-class, the smell of shit would hit Ernst with blunt force.

At Goregaon, there was his elongated shed with its corrugated tin roof and prominently displayed SSI Certificate alongside framed labour laws and a lineup of Hindu gods and goddesses with Jesus thrown in along with pictures of Gandhi and fuck-knows-why John F. Kennedy. Here, Ernst's workers did pipes and tubing. He was on intimate terms with pipes and tubes, but not finance, and he didn't know how to deal with Salary Day. He would get short of breath as it approached. In its own way, the panic over raising money for salaries was similar to how he felt when it first dawned as a boy that he was nothing more than a Jew; even though, really, if one paused to think, where was the correlation?

Some months ago, facing Salary Day along with an unyielding bank overdraft, the panic grew seeing his workers all agitated outside the Goregaon workshop. The workshop manager Salim Ali—a dick any given day—was on leave, and the unsupervised labour being dicks for a change. They knew the bank had said a big, fat NO to Ernst and were curious—salaries being due in a week. Ernst's ears had turned red seeing them.

'No worries,' he said, and continued playing the European. The next day, he sold the workshop's flagship—its Pilger cold-rolling mill—to a bania trader for hard cash. Didn't matter he was still paying off another bania for the loan taken out to buy it. Some would challenge that assertion. They would say it did matter. Especially when this other bania, the one Ernst owed money for the Cold Pilger he sold without permission, was Seth Jamunadas Kejriwal. You fucked with him at your own peril. Still, Ernst had gone ahead, his simmering workers being the more immediate threat.

In Ernst's defence, it wasn't as if the Cold Pilger was working non-stop; more a symbol of what the workshop could have been, if everything had gone the way it didn't. The workers were nevertheless left stunned, and watched as the bania's hard-on grew under his dhoti each time he rubbed the Cold Pilger's imported metal skin. The bania looked ready to mount it right there and then in the workshop, but had shown restraint. He had the machine carted off, leaving behind a naked plinth and Ernst to take the blame. The workers took their salaries like a bitter pill. If machines were now being sold off to pay them, soon there would be no machines and no need to pay anyone.

The Cold Pilger sale kept the beast fed over several Salary Days, but good times were now over. Starting this month, the sinking feeling was back along with a constipation that would build up out of nowhere.

He had hoped for relief once Fertilisers gave him his purchase order. He could've borrowed against it. He was good at that, but then the Lambadi went broiled a Sikh in the sulphur burner. After putting a bullet through his head. Impoverished Indian gypsies owning guns, when even the police hardly ever carried them. .303 Lee Enfields didn't count.

~

Beatrice Taylor went all heavy-handed on behalf of Ernst and got the tender formalities rescheduled for the week following her encounter with the headless Sikh. 'Where would you be without me?' she asked Ernst, who felt it was best not to be anywhere too close and so he thanked her and took off. From Colaba he had dialled the Goregaon factory. Dialled and redialled and dialled again, when Salim Ali picked up.

'I know,' Salim Ali said, but was curious why Ernst wanted to be there for the tender opening. 'Leave it to me this time,' he suggested. 'No? Okay, you're the boss. You'll come pick me up? Are you sure? What an honour.'

Salim Ali was a Malayalee from Kerala on India's southern tip—home to this highly intelligent species that baffled the rest of India and Ernst could see why. Whenever Ernst pictured life without Salim Ali, it would be an idyllic, pastoral scene with blue skies and no cloud in sight. Salim Ali was useful though, in stormy weather.

'Why me?' he would ask, when navigating storms. 'Aren't you Germans supposed to be the technology kings?'

So, what Ernst did that Monday morning before leaving for Fertilisers, he climbed up two flights to the second floor of the Mian Building, opposite Sindhi Refugee Camp in Chembur. His stomach fought every step of the way leaving him drenched in sweat by the second floor. He felt old. Why Salim Ali would choose to live here, the only Marxist in a building full of devout Muslims was somewhat of a puzzle. Why the devout Muslims, let him, was the real question.

Ernst stood holding the banister for support, tired for no reason at all. The early morning smells made him dyspeptic. The deadweight in his intestines was like lead but his sphincter held steadfast; it could teach the army how to clench the next time China came tearing down the Himalayas. Coming up to Salim Ali's door, he rubbed the mole on the left side of his face. It felt bigger every time he touched it.

Maybe why he was tired like this, for no reason at all. Maybe also why there was this blockage up his arse. Maybe that's what the mole was: skin cancer like his mother's.

Dr. Waller had disagreed the last time he got it checked. Look at you, Waller had said. 'All tanned like a native. Do darkies get skin cancer? Get out of here, you bugger.'

There was a huge relief in being declared a hypochondriac. Dr. Waller diagnosed it a Jewish thing. Ernst had smiled before realising the good doctor wasn't joking.

Ernst was about to ring Salim Ali's doorbell when he heard the sound. Thaadup!

'Don't,' someone said.

His forefinger froze an inch from the bell. As with most buildings, bulbs were optional and the corridors cast long shadows. It was early morning, and the other man was in a singlet and a linen sarong worn South-Indian style. The red handkerchief was still around his neck. A permanent fixture like that bored expression, or the hockey ball he bounced again, going, Thaadup!

'Wait few minutes. His mother is undergoing morning namaaz.' He spoke a deliberate, Tamil-English, the voice deep and raspy, travelling up from the solar plexus and through gravel before hitting the air.

Ernst said, 'I saw you the other evening at Fertilisers.'

The Tamilian just stood there.

'That Chinese-looking fellow you were questioning. He had something to do with the dead body?'

'Who knows?'

'He stole something?'

The man bounced his ball. Thaadup! Ernst saw it smash into the porcelain doll's head; saw him crumple to the ground.

The Tamilian's singlet blazed from his black torso like a beacon, and all that whiteness brought back Beatrice's dark, skinny assistant with her shiny buck teeth. Last night, thrusting against Daisy Lansdowne with more enthusiasm than he felt, Ernst barely managed to swing it, and that too only after conjuring intertwined, chocolate bodies while thrusting against a pasty, white one. It had left him surprised. The trick apparently, was to imagine the girl's jasmine sweat play footsie with him while letting the man in granite pop in and out of the frame. He couldn't forget her engines revving up seeing the Tamilian smash the porcelain doll to the ground. Was it the girl who finally did it for him while he rode Willie's wife, or this man, or both of them working him in tandem to help out? Who could tell? Apparently, men his age needed all the help they could get. It was one more thing to worry about.

'What's the ball for?'

'Cricket.'

'It's a hockey ball.'

'A foreigner like you must find that strange.'

'You know, something else that's strange? The way that boy reacted, seeing the body being taken away. Almost as if he knew the dead man. Had to have known him, else why such grief?'

'You tell me.'

'The way he reached out to the body just before you hit him. Very strange. Or am I just imagining it?'

The door swung partially open though Ernst hadn't yet rung the bell. Salim Ali blinked past him and up at the Tamilian policeman. An oiled, jet-black, Kerala curl fell across Salim Ali's forehead. Making his way into the adjacent flat, the big black man rasped in his English to the little black man, 'I never see you at the mosque.' Strains from the Soviet National Anthem wafted past Salim Ali's oily head in response.

~

'Making new friends?' Salim Ali asked.

'What's his name?'

'Chhote Bhai.'

Chhote Bhai means little brother. 'That's not a name.'

'Doesn't matter. You shouldn't be speaking to him in the first place.'

'Who's he?'

'My landlord.'

'That's it?'

'That's not it. If you must know, he also provides protection.'

'You mean he is a slumlord.'

'Amongst other things.'

'And I thought he worked for the police.'

'They probably work for him, but that's neither here nor there. These past so many years I've greeted him, looked down and walked away. Next time, you do the same.'

'He appeared friendly enough.'

'Maybe, in a way,' Salim Ali said, praise for the Russian Motherland still coming through from the living room. 'He could've broken my legs at one time and didn't. That's a friendly act.'

'His hockey ball. He said it's for cricket.'

'I forget. How long have you been in India? You bounce a hockey ball to inspect the pitch before a cricket match. Every schoolkid knows that.'

'Or bounce it off people's heads. Why would he break your legs?'

Salim Ali looked at Ernst's legs, who then took off his shoes before entering the living room. That was a British era Victrola wobbling on three legs in one corner. An empty brown 45 rpm record sleeve with the hammer and sickle stenciled on it lay against one leg. Rich, Russian vocals energised the room.

Large charcoal portraits of Lenin and Castro sketched with Picasso-like panache nested amidst the holy-green calligraphy on the walls. Fidel Castro looked compelling hanging there, studying an elaborate verse from the Koran. A line-up of dark men in lungis stood behind Fidel, framed in another photograph, their eyes blazing directly at Ernst from the picture. There was a feel of imminent revolution in spite of the idyllic Kerala backdrop. Something was cooking in the kitchen and it smelt of spiced mutton and coconut. This was a Malayalee household from Kerala and there would be appam fritters to go with the mutton curry. The smell of fermented batter wafted through the air.

Ernst pointed to Fidel.

'Does your mother know you have your comrades hanging around the flat?'

There was a third comrade to Lenin's left, an Oriental in olive fatigues, flashing a red star on a ragged green cap. Four stars on each lapel, and a broad forehead like Mao's, but not him, not Chou En-lai, not Ho Chi Minh.

'General Ngyuen Von Giap of Vietnam.'

'Who?'

'Doesn't matter. You'll soon find out,' Salim Ali said. 'You'll all find out.'

The line up of lungis beneath those coconut trees now appeared to look approvingly at Salim Ali, their eyes blazing away. One of them though emerged with a benign smile instead, when Ernst peered at the framed photograph. He had a wizened, delicate face, and the Fu Manchu strands of hair straggling down from his chin was why Ernst was peering at him in the first place.

'Who are these guys? Your Politburo?'

'What did you think? The Kerala Cricket Club? They are the ones guiding us to a better tomorrow.'

'By the way, what's your slumlord-landlord got to do with cricket?'

'He arranges matches, takes bets, and then decides who wins. It's an excellent business plan, unlike ours.' Salim Ali paused. 'I still don't know why you're coming for the tender opening. I handled it last year.'

'Of course. How can I forget?'

Last year, Ernst had handed Salim Ali an envelope with four thousand rupees to give the Chief Engineer along with paperwork for the tender. To public sector chief engineers across the land, "paperwork" meant the bribe accompanying it—the actual documents and samples simply icing on the cake. Educated people like Salim Ali took it to be the other way around. So he went ahead, submitted the paperwork without the bribe. 'No need,' he said, and Ernst had gone to the Chief Engineer's home late evening with the envelope, stuffed with an extra five hundred to make up for the faux pas. The neighbours seeing a white man come to his home with money had saved the day, and the Chief Engineer let bygones be bygones. Salim Ali however became persona non grata. Everyone knew that, except Salim Ali.

'I'm going with you,' Ernst said.

~

They watched Salim Ali's mother as the blind diabetic rolled up her green prayer mat on the balcony outside; both men barefoot on a floor one could eat off. The spotless white cloth was already in place on the spotless floor where the dining table would be in non-Muslim households. Ernst's toes curled on the cool terrazzo tiles and they touched something. Tossed carelessly, the morning's *Times of India* lay at his feet. He was Indian enough by now to avoid placing his foot on reading material and pulled away. He picked up the newspaper and put it on top of a Fertilisers gunny bag lying in the corner. There were all sorts of wires sticking out from the Fertilisers gunny bag with its green swastika, but then, this was an engineer's flat.

PL 480 Food Aid Arrives, the *Times of India* headline said from atop the Fertilisers gunny bag. It went on to ask: If It's Food Aid, President Johnson, Why Do You Want Money?

Yesterday, it was: Why We Must Have The Bomb.

The day before: The Himalayan Blunder. Why We Lost To China.

Tomorrow the cycle would begin again—agonising over what China did, yearning for what The Bomb could do, then outrage over what America was doing.

They stepped aside as the tiny woman came in from the balcony muttering to herself or at Salim Ali; no idea. She wore a black crumpled sari, wrinkled as her face. Her eyes were covered—cupped in round black glasses with leather flaps—though the head wasn't. Her oiled hair knotted in a loose bun was luscious jet-black, in total contrast to all the wear-and-tear showing up everywhere else on the tired, little body. She was tiny enough for Salim Ali to look a clear evolutionary improvement. The air reeked of coconut oil as she hobbled past, minus three amputated toes. Besides the feet, diabetes had ravaged her heart, her kidneys, her immune system and Salim Ali's equanimity. Blind yes, but there was a cat-like, grimalkin quality to her, the way she looked around instead of straight ahead like any normal, blind person.

'How does she know which way's Mecca?' Ernst asked.

Fertilisers farted from the west, adding a tinge of ammonia to the methane and sweet-smelling benzene everyone around here considered normal.

'She smells it out.'

Salim Ali eyed Ernst with an animosity that had remained up a notch since the Cold Pilger incident. Kerala Malayalees prefer their angst fermented. Seeing him glower, Ernst wanted to be anywhere else.

Salim Ali was inconsolable learning what had happened to the Cold Pilger in his absence, and decided vocally there and then, on the shop floor, in front of the whole shift, to never forgive Ernst for as long as he lived. Ernst found it galling. As if Salim Ali alone was left mourning the loss—staring at the Cold Pilger's forlorn concrete plinth, its twisted cast iron brackets lying naked after the bania's men tore off the machine and hauled it away. Whereas and unbeknownst to others, the Cold Pilger sale also kicked in a new normal for Ernst. Until then, his nightmares had him stand and watch his father commit suicide; slashing both wrists using a straight razor, the bathtub going from pink to red, while Emmy Destinn sang Rusalka's "Song to the Moon". Ernst's ensuing screams as he made a grab for the straight razor would wake the dead along with the servants at his Colaba flat. A three-hundred-pound Parvatibai would bolt out of her bed in the servants' quarters to rush to his bedroom with a glass of milk and a wet cloth for his forehead.

In a whole new terror that opened after the sale, he would now grab at the Cold Pilger being carted away, the chill from its metal surface creeping up his arm and into his heart. Not so much because they were taking it away, but because he caught his future leave with it. With the dream refusing to put an end to itself, he too tries to leave, but they won't let him past Immigration and there's puzzlement over his passport at Santa Cruz Airport. The passport may be German, but he isn't.

'The passport's a mistake, Mr. Ernestji,' the babu at the Immigration counter says, chewing paan while fingering the good luck swastika around his neck. 'You're one of us. How can you leave like that? You've been deemed Hindu, you know.' And he cites a gazette reference number. Ernst tries explaining to the Immigration Man how fucked is that, because he's already deemed Jew; go check with the Germans if you don't believe. The Immigration Man keeps chewing paan with that babu-look of his. A German SS type, all in black and with the regulation swastika armband, steps up to save Ernst from the Indian Immigration Man. Now all of a sudden Ernst doesn't want to be saved, hell with Germany, and Bharat Mata ki Jai. The SS type is insistent however and reaches out for him, so Ernst starts to scream—Parvatibai's cue to do the baby elephant run down the corridor and come calm him with a cold compress.

Once done, she too would give him the look—like that Immigration guy from his dream—but only after he had quietened. Come next morning, Ernst would read a verse from Jayadev's *Gita Govinda* in English while sipping chai. Later, reciting the *Bija Mantra*, he would remind himself that here wasn't all that bad. He would then lift open the bedroom credenza and double-check the expiry date on his German passport.

5

The Second Floor Balcony

Sindhis had no where to go. So we went everywhere.
—Hari Harilela

You could say Salim Ali's second floor balcony overlooked the Sindhi Refugee Camp from across Vashigaon Road. Or you could say it overlooked the crumbling Krishna Temple under the banyan tree. Or, that it looked straight down into a garbage pile, the size of a Fiat car. Otherwise simply enjoy your chai, watch the children shit in neat rows alongside open nullahs, and wait for the Krishna Temple's blind woman to sing and kick-start your day. There was nothing else on offer this early.

Speaking of Fiat cars, there was one with a missing headlight parked opposite the temple, the driver slumped in his seat and staring ahead. Seeing his one-eyed Fiat parked on Vashigaon Road with Mohan Driver asleep inside with eyes wide open, Ernst felt it was time for a change. Both car and driver. Affording it was another matter.

A rising sun tackled what could be rain clouds, or not—the monsoons not sure whether to continue fucking with Bombay, or have some shame. Someone began to yell loudly and looking down at the Krishna Temple past the garbage heap, Ernst realised there would be no melody to be heard today, because the blind woman was in a rant instead. She was the other blind person in Salim Ali's life. In so many ways, Salim Ali's frame of mind depended on the blind people around him. Ernst once witnessed Salim Ali's blind, Muslim mother stare down the blind Hindu woman parked since forever outside the Krishna Temple. Salim Ali and Ernst had watched the two blind women eyeball each other.

'Is that even possible?' Ernst asked.

Salim Ali had looked bitter.

Anyway, around this time and once again in the evening, the blind woman would take to the air from the crumbling temple looking up into Salim Ali's balcony. A single roomed, whitewashed hovel for Lord Krishna built into the hollow of a majestic banyan, where even the priest refused to live full-time. Salim Ali claimed if by some miracle there really were a Lord Krishna, he wouldn't be seen dead in that rat-hole.

Permanently parked on the rat-hole's pockmarked patio, the blind woman would sing her heart out when not stoned on ganja, and also when she was. Breaking abruptly into song, she had a tendency to scare the shit out of passers-by before allowing them a glimpse of heaven. She sang to remind people like Salim Ali that it didn't matter the place was a rat-hole, because God resided in her throat. Over the years, every now and then, Ernst let her tie his stomach in knots. What's the greater sorrow she would sing, love unattained or love lost? Who could say, Ernst felt, remembering how his wife and he parted forever in an instant, whereas the teacher and his dachshund had remained hanging together side by side for as long as it mattered. Their howling aside, the two had at least looked into each other's eyes until the very end.

This morning, no song ascended to tie him up before tearing him apart. Instead, the blind woman was yelling at the skies. 'Do you see that light?' she shouted. 'It's coming from out there! Look, you bhenchods, look! It's so damn bright! How can't you see it?' Ernst heard the scold and saw the blind woman point in the air at some bright light only she could see. Next thing you know, every kid squatting over an open nullah had pulled up his shorts and was running over to her. They converged in a wolf pack.

'Maaji!' the little boys called out, and she let them. At other times, she would bite people's heads off. 'I'm not your bhenchod mother,' she would say.

'What's the matter, Maaji? Something bothering you?' the children asked, concerned looks on wee faces.

'Maybe it's her lice,' one little bastard offered. She couldn't care less and was on her own trip. 'Someone, do something!' she demanded. 'What's wrong with you people? Are you blind? Can't you see that light?' She went on and on, refusing to stop embarrassing herself, the ganja-induced harangue loud enough to wake the dead. Looking like row upon row of confused caterpillars, Sindhi Camp's Nissen huts appeared dazed as her unwashed finger continued pointing blindly past them towards Trombay Hill in the background. 'That place over there,' she said. 'It's giving out light. Do something!'

'What are you pointing at, Maaji?' another little genius asked, before pointing out, 'You're bhenchod blind, you know.' His friend went, 'It's top secret out there, Maaji. Don't point like that unless you want an atom bomb up your arse. Do you?'

The little buggers meant the nation's nuclear machinery ticking away behind Trombay Hill, where she was pointing. The location personally selected by India's Oppenheimer, Dr. Homi J. Bhabha—Mastermind & Sexiest Man Alive. Loved by one and all. So much so, they let him conduct nuclear experiments within pissing distance from the country's most densely populated city. A convenient, air-conditioned commute from his home at Malabar Hill. Anything you want, they assured him, because Indians yearned for The Bomb in a way others could never understand. Screw us, starve us, irradiate us, but build us one.

All this shouting going on, and there's this girl crouched outside one of Sindhi Camp's WWII vintage, army Nissen huts. Wearing a maroon sari and busy drawing a rangoli on her porch with chalk powder. When she looked up, Ernst recognised the teeth. Like piano keys. Her jaw sagged while squinting to see the hell was happening at the temple. It was Beatrice Taylor's skinny assistant from that evening with the headless Sardar. She looked more put together this morning without her boss around. I'm on my own turf, her glance said.

'Stop it,' Salim Ali said. 'She's known to me since school days. I have to live here, you know.'

Sugared up and chai in hand, Ernst stopped staring and leaned over the balcony, pressing his stomach against the ledge to trigger something inside. Anything. He eased back, and bore down again to try breaking the blockade up his colon.

'Careful,' Salim Ali cautioned, seeing him lean over. 'Parvatibai says you have a history of suicide in your family.'

'Not suicide. Escape. We have a history of escape.'

'Probably why you are at the Golf Club so much. How do you afford it?'

Credit chits, he wanted to tell Salim Ali, who was way ahead of him and said, 'Everyone should be white.'

~

To their left, was the police chowki where you turn from Vashigaon Road towards Trombay. A little further down the road, stood the Bombay Presidency Golf Club surrounded by Sindhi Refugee Camp—in turn corralled by the jhopadpatti.

The jhopadpatti was one big, open shithole where you could go wherever you please—meaning, anywhere. In Sindhi Refugee Camp however, decorum demanded you shat in nullahs running alongside the Nissen huts, whereas in the Golf Club, the toilets were unbelievably fine. The Golf Club's white picket fence kept Sindhi Refugee Camp from creeping in. Some months ago, typhoid stole into the club kitchen regardless; proving once again that do what you may, shit will happen.

It was still early morning and small stick figures teed off on the greens as the refugee camp slowly came alive. People carrying cans of water hurried past cows and goats to go defecate. Hidden from view a few feet away, No.1 wood connected with golf balls. The sharp cracks sounded like rifle shots this side of the border, making Salim Ali flinch.

'Join me there over a drink sometime,' Ernst said to him. 'I'll sign you in.'

'I don't think so,' Salim Ali replied. 'You know very well I don't drink. Besides, once we have a Soviet-type system, there'll be no need to sign anyone in.' Salim Ali pointed to a beggar sans legs careening across Vashigaon Road on a wooden pallet with wheels. Any given day, the legless man was all over Sindhi Refugee Camp, scooting at foolishly high speeds. Under Marxism, he could scoot into any club he wanted. 'They have holiday dachas for the proletariat in Russia.' Salim Ali cleared his throat. 'Let me educate you some more about a classless society.'

Ernst looked out to see if the girl in the maroon sari was still there. 'What's that?' he asked.

'What's what?'

'See that boy going up to the blind woman? What's he got in his hand?'

Ernst heard the fermented batter frying inside the kitchen as Salim Ali's mother ladled it on a pan over the gas flame. It was a toss-up who was in greater danger—that blind woman down by the temple, or this crazy, blind bat over at the stove asking for third-degree burns. When Ernst headed for the door, Salim Ali wanted to know where he was going, didn't get an answer, and said something about white people.

Ernst took the stairs two at a time with an alacrity absent when climbing up. The little wolf pack around the blind woman was still at it. She in turn was deep in her rant, pointing a finger toward Trombay Hill and there was this snake slithering down the patio towards her. Ernst had seen it wriggle in the boy's hand earlier. The empty basket near the mound of temple garbage would do and he picked it up to throw over the snake in one sweep. Then he grabbed the boy by his collar; who yelled in outrage, waking up Mohan Driver cocooned inside the one-eyed Fiat. The blind woman stopped mid-rant.

'Let him go,' she said, 'That's a rat snake. It's not poisonous.'

Ernst wanted to ask: I'm not blind so how would I know? He also felt like asking about the invisible light in the sky. And, why not just sing for your supper instead of freaking people out like this?

Down the mud path running parallel to Trombay Road with Nissen huts lined up on either side, Beatrice's girl was now standing erect outside her half of a hut. Looking his way, she flashed her buck teeth. He dropped the squirming boy and froze, unsure. Skin like polished teak and rubbing the pendant around her neck, she smiled again, the teeth lending her a bunny rabbit innocence. This time, he smiled back. It was only when she waved, he realised it was too good to be true.

Thinking it must be Salim Ali getting those smiles and waves, Ernst turned to look but the balcony was empty, although, the big, black Chhote Bhai was now on the balcony next door, sipping tea from a saucer. Then again, maybe her smiles and all that waving were for Chhote, made as he was out of granite. On the other hand, Ernst could be mistaken. He recalled her engine revving up when Chhote had assaulted the porcelain doll. She smiled past him again to confirm there was no mistake. She then returned to her rangoli and Ernst tried to return to normal. He couldn't keep from looking at her though, while she dabbed final touches to the design drawn on the porch. Elaborate in red, white, and saffron, this wasn't your traditional, good luck rangoli. It was a powder mandala. He recognised the Tantric symbols from where he stood, and found it strange someone this young would practise something so arcane.

Bhairavi. Beatrice had called the girl, Bhairavi.

There's this legend about Goddess Bhairavi. You will find her black as coal and ugly as sin on gaudy kitchen calendars across India. As long as she remains that way—black and ugly—all's well, you're fine; get on with life. Then one day you casually glance at the calendar on your fridge or are genuflecting at her temple, and find she's gone all radiant on you, and smiling instead of coal black with that tongue sticking out. That's when you should shit bricks. Because her smile means your time has come. It's ta-ta, bye-bye, so put your affairs in order. Smart thing to know when it comes to Goddess Bhairavi, ugly is good and beautiful is bad. Frown is good. Her smile, most definitely bad. Luckily, Sindhi Refugee Camp's Bhairavi preferred smiling at a slumlord carved in granite, and not at Ernst. All for the best because Ernst was anyway chained to the Ingrids any given time. He had tried breaking free last night with a little help from Daisy Lansdowne. It didn't work.

Meanwhile the blind woman resumed her rant, pointing away in the air towards Trombay Hill while the sun peeked out at her, unsure whether to show itself. Not bothered with either, Sindhi Refugee Camp went about its business. The girl was on her knees and bent over once again, reaching for the outer edge of her Tantric artwork. Doing so, her bottom blossomed into a perfect, tulip bulb. It filled his vision—frontal, peripheral, everything. I really don't know what I want, Ernst said to the Ingrids still riding him after all these years, while he remained caught up with the tulip out there, tightly bound in a maroon sari. But if you let me free, he appealed, I could try find out.

People were heading to work, lining up at the BEST bus stop opposite the police chowki for the 6 Limited to Colaba. Two-wheelers flew this way and that around the one-eyed Fiat. Lata Mangeshkar was on Sindhi Camp Radio, bemoaning the nation's Himalayan Tragedy through that one song that spoke on behalf of all India; the one every Indian knew by heart and played again and again and it still wasn't enough. An inspired moped rider went full-throat in unison, his voice rising patriotically above the metallic swell of his engine. When Ernst looked her way again, a woman was cleaning the porch where Beatrice's girl had chalked her Tantric powder mandala. The girl stood watch. Unlike her, the older woman was Sindhi-white with perfect teeth, so no idea why he took her to be the mother. A vacant smile to her face, and with bucket in both hands, she poured water on the powder mandala in a strong sweeping motion. Squatting with a wet cloth, the woman didn't stop until the porch was swept clean of all Tantric goings-on.

The girl stood there, looking satisfied at her hours of work being erased. She then did a quick namaste to acknowledge—as Tantrics do after intentionally destroying their work—that all material things are but maya, a temporary illusion. Then she hurried off to office.

6

Cowboy and Indians

Just because it isn't free, doesn't mean it isn't aid.
—*Dean Rusk, explaining America's PL 480 food assistance program*

Ernst stood under the full glare of a sullen Salim Ali. Humidity in Bombay builds like nowhere else. Even so, Ernst hadn't seen a wash-and-wear shirt go this bad, so fast. The man's body odour girded him for the day ahead. In the meantime, a Marxist protest at the factory gates ate away anything left of his brain. They were screaming something about American food aid and it didn't matter what, because Ernst didn't care.

'So this is why you didn't want me around today,' he said to Salim Ali, looking at the intentional chaos building up.

A comrade yelled, 'Europe's first, next America's dead, China leads, the East is Red!' Fighting back, India's world-famous Lata Mangeshkar trilled over factory loudspeakers reminding the nation, as always, to shed a tear for those martyred in China's wake during the War of '62.

The China lovers countered with, 'Long Live Mao, Chou En-lai; Johnson, Rusk, Hai, Hai!'

You had to hand it to Salim Ali's comrades hollering at the gates. No let up and no embarrassment at China's perfidy; as if the invasion never happened. Their yells tore through Ernst's head, ricocheting inside like so many red bullets. He thought of the Sindhi Refugee Camp girl's arse and calmed himself as Hindus do at times like these, acknowledging life is maya, an illusion to work past as we struggle towards the Place of the Hidden Moon. Salim Ali looked as if he could read Ernst's mind and curled his upper lip.

The agitators buffeted a green, jeep station wagon cutting through the wave of protesters and trying to get past the gates. The jeep threatened to plough through them and the proletariat went hysterical.

'PL 480 will not do!'

It dawned on Ernst what this was about. They were protesting the same PL 480 food aid from the morning's *Times of India* lying on Salim Ali's living room floor. The mob would go, 'Long Live Mao and Chou En-lai; Johnson, Rusk, Hai, Hai!' and then circle back to whatever it was about Lyndon Johnson's food aid causing so much pain and anguish to people facing impending famine. America's Public Law 480, Salim Ali would explain any chance he got, authorised wheat shipments to a rice-eating nation, against payment. Starving Indian villagers were spewing out the American staple from both ends, unable to hold down gluten. On the plus side, the Americans accepted payment in rupees.

The mob at the gates looked incensed, but why rage against American food outside a factory helping India grow its own? Ernst didn't get it.

Salim Ali did. 'This so-called food aid's to get America's foot in the door,' he explained. 'Then before you realise, it's up your arse. Got it?'

Someone yelled, 'American bhenchod!'

That, he got.

The jeep lurched through the protest, then lurching past the gates it stopped for breath. When a full-blown Texan stepped out wearing a twelve-gallon hat and real cowboy boots, Ernst knew this was God fucking with Salim Ali. The gargantuan American shimmered in the heat. The little Mallu engineer stared at the Texan mirage with such focus Ernst thought he would hurt himself. Salim Ali then swore some terrible oath in Malayalam. Ernst patted his shoulder, the sodden Terylene shirt wet to the touch. 'If you say anything to that man,' Ernst told him, 'I'll personally strangle you.'

'Why am I not surprised?' Salim Ali asked. 'When push comes to shove, Westerners will gang up.'

'You're stereotyping.'

'Am I? Do you know who ran like frightened pigs when the Japanese invaded French Vietnam?'

'No.'

'The French. It was their colony. The colonialist gone, the Vietnamese rallied under Ho Chi Minh to fight the Japanese imperialists. Know who helped them?'

'No.'

'The Americans. America and Vietnam fought side by side against Japan. Know who then helped ferry the French back to Vietnam after the Japanese left?'

'No.'

'The very same Americans. Like I said. When push comes to shove, Westerners come together.'

'Clearly, you know us better than we know ourselves.'

'I do. Why not make a difference, instead? Come join the fight.'

They made quite the pair. Ernst looking the white man he was, yet somewhat incomplete. In contrast, the pint-sized Salim Ali appeared larger-than-life. That could be because there were two of him. There was the IIT engineer here for the purchase order—to get a job done. Then there was the trade union leader, also here and lit up like the Charminars he smoked. The roasted tobacco ensured his body odour was off the charts.

Ernst had hired Salim Ali two years ago after not much of an interview. The little man answered every question in a withering barrage of Mallu English, resonating with idiom picked up on campus. He had curled his lip in contempt at the level of Ernst's technical inquiry. He appeared openly doubtful about Ernst's abilities as a businessman. It ended with him letting it being known, in the interest of full disclosure, that he was a card-holding member of The Communist Party of India (Marxist-Leninist). Salim Ali had looked surprised, almost disappointed, when Ernst employed him on the spot. Since then, he had done his best to get fired.

The Marxists at the gates yelled, 'Salim Ali, Zindabad!'

Head down, an astute Salim Ali raised his right fist to continue playing Lenin during working hours.

~

The workers milling around the gates were a motley crew. The ones yelling the loudest were of course Mallu, each a Salim Ali prototype. All Mallus are not Marxists—that's offensive—though most are. Therefore, and more so after China, if you saw a Mallu and a snake, the advisory said to kill the Mallu.

Also noteworthy: silent, smouldering non-Mallu-types could be seen loitering in one corner near the gates observing the proceedings. These were local Marathas, the original inhabitants of the islands that made up Bombay and the mountain ghats behind it. These days they were famously banded around Shiv Sena, a sectarian, Hindu supremacist party.

'Look at them,' Salim Ali said. 'Itching for trouble. Bleddy, communal rowdies. Fascist, American lackeys, all of them. If you see a Shiv Sena rowdy and a snake…'

'Yes, I know.'

There was another silent bystander—not Mallu, nor Maratha. A gaunt, bald man in civvies, his white bush shirt still crisp despite Bombay. He was about as out of place as, say, a Chinese professor in an Indian factory. Ernst thought the man didn't look ill, nor did he look well. He could be describing himself.

He appeared familiar, this Chinese-looking man, and resembled Porcelain Doll—the young man Salim Ali's landlord had smashed to the ground when they were taking away the headless Sikh last week. The two did look alike. Indians were convinced they all looked alike. After the Himalayan debacle, spooked Indian POWs swore the same Chinese infantryman guarding their barracks would go change uniforms, and come back to interrogate them as a colonel. Most of all, the bald gentleman looked tired. Very. He drooped, as if the starched shirt was all that kept him upright. Salim Ali walked over to him and put his arm around the man's shoulders.

Maybe because he stood out the way he did against Salim Ali, or could be those eyes giving out light instead of reflecting it, maybe the smile that refused to leave his tired face; whatever it was, the man's presence calmed Ernst. Seeing them approach with Salim Ali treating the bald man as if he was Mahatma Gandhi, Ernst felt an immediate affinity towards him—the bald man, not Salim Ali. They came up, the man all smiles and waiting to be introduced. Ernst had an urge to get closer, drown in all that compassion.

'Comrade, allow me to introduce Ernst Steiger,' Salim Ali said, surprising an Ernst unfamiliar with this flowery version. 'Our proprietor at Steiger Engineering, where I work.'

The professorial, Chinese-looking man reached out to shake hands with surprising vigour. It was then that Ernst noticed the red blotches on his face; the skin peeling off from too much open sun. The man's bald head was decorated with blisters looking wet to the touch.

'Comrade Tsering Tufan,' Salim Ali said. The name was a dead give-away. A North-East Frontier tribal. Salim Ali went on to say Tsering Tufan was his comrade and mentor. Also, Head Machinist at AEET, the popular acronym for Dr. Homi Bhabha's Atomic Energy Establishment at Trombay—his nuclear playground nesting behind Trombay Hill where every atom was peaceful.

'You should be resting. Why are you here?' Salim Ali asked, looking thrilled Comrade Tufan was there. It showed on his face and by the marked increase in body odour. You'll energise the protest though, Salim Ali ceded, looking fondly at his Comrade, who said not really, and he was here because of Arjun. What's with Arjun, Salim Ali wanted to know, all okay? And while Ernst didn't know who Arjun was, he didn't ask. Salim Ali and he were here for the tender opening and for the purchase order—to bribe people and to kiss arses—and he wanted to get on with it.

'Got nicely beaten up the other day, your friend Arjun,' Tsering Tufan said to Salim Ali. 'Head injury. I'm here to check on him. His mother and I don't need a repeat performance. He refuses to file a formal complaint. They say he stole something from the American compound. Probably why he won't file a complaint.'

'He won't file because he is Arjun. When was the last time he stole anything?' That settled, Salim Ali proceeded to channel Lenin. 'Besides, even if he did, he did for the working man. For the nation.'

'What exactly did he do?'

'How would I know?'

'He looks up to you. The more radical you are, the more radical he gets. In that frame of mind, people can behave stupidly. Maybe he did steal something from the Americans. Why not cool it down a notch? Temper things, yes?'

'Temper what, Comrade Tufan? Workers' welfare? Our fight against Imperialist aggression? Or maybe temper everything you taught us?'

Ernst made a note not to feel too singled-out in future. Tsering Tufan just smiled that smile of his. He didn't appear fazed by Salim Ali. He didn't appear fazed by anything. He'd go look for Arjun, he said, touching Salim Ali's forearm. 'Come, find me later.' He started to leave, shuffling slowly. The way he moved, it was seeing a dead man walk.

Ernst waited for a bit before edging up. 'Come on,' he said to Salim Ali. 'Let's go over the paperwork and close that PO. Hell with all this.'

'Hell with this?' Salim Ali went. 'No, hell with that. Besides, you don't have to worry about the bleddy PO. I have it covered.' Salim Ali looked ready to go to battle. 'Paperwork's done. Everything perfect, like my pipes. They will last forever, even though I have to do repeat draws on third-class, Ludhiana draw benches. You went sold the Cold Pilger, remember?'

True, there was never any sunburst cracking in his pipes even without the Cold Pilger and yes, they lasted forever. Thing was, who cared? What mattered was hard cash upfront for the Fertilisers management. That is, if Ernst wanted the order.

'Here. Take this.'

'The bleddy envelope again?' Salim Ali asked. 'All I want is to win without bribing babus and pimps. Is that asking too much?'

Yes. India without babus and pimps wouldn't be India at all.

'Fuck them,' Salim Ali said. 'We have a superior product. No need to bribe anyone. Let's show these buggers.'

Ernst didn't feel like showing anyone. He could understand why the Chief Engineer had said that he held Salim Ali in very high disregard. Ernst would cringe whenever Salim Ali wanted to "show" them. To, not compromise. His lack of confidence in Salim Ali was all the more evident today, probably because he didn't feel well. He was sure he didn't look well. His no-confidence vote fed Salim Ali's resentment. That in turn buggered Ernst's outlook further, making Salim Ali glower all the more.

'What is it with you? I thought you Germans had balls. Why not show some and refuse to propagate this sort of thing? We are a socialist country. Bribes are not necessary.'

'If they weren't necessary, I won't ask you to do it. Do I look like I have money to waste?'

'But you have money to waste at the Golf Club.' Salim Ali peered at him. 'You sell off the Cold Pilger because there's no money, then you invite me over to your club for an alcoholic drink?'

'How could you sell it,' he yelled at Ernst. 'How could you?'

~

Standing by the one-eyed Fiat, Mohan Driver watched Salim Ali as if nothing new, then went back to eyeing Lambadi titties as the gypsies hauled gravel. Pendulous breasts jiggled inside short black cholis resplendent in mirror-work. The women's dark pigmentation wasn't much help against the May sun. Blotches of skin peeled off their blistered faces. It reminded Ernst of the skin peeling off Tsering Tufan's bald head. Why would a Head Machinist at Atomic Energy go get blisters in the sun?

'Why can't we win on merit?' Salim Ali asked. 'Why? When we have a superior product?'

Ernst let it go. Not just because it was too hot to argue. The country was too nuanced for Salim Ali. The man had graduated from the prestigious Indian Institute of Technology and four years on campus leached all the Indian out of him. It left him with black and white logic to deal with a country that only recognised shades of grey. In contrast, Ernst found himself calmer during times like these—that much closer to the Place of the Hidden Moon.

'You've mastered Hindu fatalism, I see,' Salim Ali acknowledged. 'So much easier when you have a German passport.'

The cowboy who had stepped out from the jeep was walking by and he was so tall, he blotted the sun. If he reached up, he could touch it. Ernst remembered seeing him around at the Golf Club with his wife.

The couple didn't seem to need anyone else. The cowboy looked their way and it was clear he wanted to come up, say hello, but there was this force field around Salim Ali, and it wasn't just the body odour.

'Jack Hanson of Chemerica,' Salim Ali said. 'We know what he does.' He made it sound a war crime. 'And we know about Chemerica.'

Chemerica being the New York consultants providing plant and equipment to Fertilisers, as well as perks for its management. In return, they had run of the place; also a whole area cordoned off for them within the plant. Inside Chemerica's high chain-linked fence was an air-conditioned, concrete shed, and through its window one could see the top of a red Coca Cola machine. People said there was also a billiards table in there and pictures of naked, blonde women in unimaginable action poses. That the music you heard playing sometimes at nights, when all sorts of American things went on inside, was from a real, honest-to-God jukebox. It was the American dream, sectioned off with a warning in red, white & blue: ONLY CHEMERICA EMPLOYEES ALLOWED.

Salim Ali felt strongly about that sign. Why not just say what you mean? Like the British, who had no problems putting up warning signs like: DOGS AND INDIANS NOT ALLOWED. At least they had been upfront. Salim Ali liked upfront. Be upfront, he would preach in his nasal, Mallu English. 'Even when bad, upfront is good.'

Salim Ali was going at it, when the loudspeakers came alive. Not India's world-class Lata Mangeshkar this time, but instead, Beatrice Taylor's top-class boss. Fertilisers' General Manager, Venky Iyer. He was all over the air, taking on the Marxist protest at his gates in precise, clipped English. 'Is this what we want? Emulate China? Surely we are better than that. We socialists are not communists. We are Indians first.' People stopped to listen. In India, owning the microphone is a prerequisite to owning power. Salim Ali pointed towards a circle near the sulphur burner. General Manager Venky Iyer was there too, this time in flesh and blood—owning suppliers vying for his attention before tender formalities kicked in. Hearing his recorded message indict communism wholesale over the loudspeaker while seeing him standing there in person, Ernst felt he was in a news documentary.

With the clamour around Venky Iyer, it took a trained eye to capture the method to the madness. A bania-caste businessman or his convent-educated salesman would step up, give Venky Iyer a limp bania handshake or a firm convent one, depending, then step aside to slip a cash envelope to his Chief Engineer leaning against the sulphur burner—gone all cold since they shut it to scrape the Sikh out from inside.

'That's how it's done,' Ernst said to Salim Ali, who curled his upper lip. Over there, loud laughter arose from a polished group clinging to Iyer.

The starched A-Team of Punjabis surrounding Venky Iyer in an immediate circle was from Sassoon Industries. Beatrice Taylor hung from Venky Iyer in their midst like a big, fat ornament. Sales teams belonging to other bidders formed an outer circle. The military-erect Sassoon boys made the rest look like Indians. General Manager Venky Iyer leaned forward to say something and there was another bout of laughter from the Sassoon cohort. Venky Iyer was not one to bother with a show of impartiality when it came to the Sassoons. It wasn't just Iyer. The monsoons would fail and the city rendered bereft without them. Besides everything else it had done for Bombay, Sassoon Industries also paid for Venky Iyer's eldest son to go to CalTech.

Is probably why, year on year, Venky Iyer delivered Adam Sassoon a big, fat chunk of business commensurate to the great man's stature. Every year, as long as paperwork was in order and as long as accompanied by the cash envelope, Ernst got the crumbs commensurate to his. Ernst caught the General Manager glance his way as one would at someone living off crumbs. Venky Iyer nodded to allow for Ernst being a white man before calling out, 'German made! Not the same as Made in Germany, what?'

Ernst smiled, hoping people around didn't get that.

'Bleddy bastard,' Salim Ali said. 'Thinks we don't know what he means?'

'We have his attention, so go,' Ernst said to Salim Ali, nudging him towards Venky Iyer's Chief Engineer. 'Remember, firm handshake, then hand over the envelope and make sure Iyer sees you give it.'

'Why don't you do it?'

'You need the practice.'

Salim Ali went on to go die a thousand deaths—shake hands, hand over the bribe, curl his lip, then flee.

Ernst gave him an A-Okay sign. Stuffed envelopes after all, carried a piece of equipment across the winning post. Deliver to A, what should go to B. Make a millionaire out of Venky Iyer and fly his firstborn to be schooled overseas. Iyer knew it. His Chief Engineer knew it. The banias hovering in the distance knew it. Beatrice Taylor, leaning towards Venky Iyer and bursting out of a tight, grey, knee-length skirt, knew it. Ernst suspected she also knew that besides fretting over paperwork, the men were tearing off her top and skirt right now, to slobber all over those hefty breasts and thighs, leaving a trail of wet saliva. She looked towards Ernst standing in the burner's shadow and smiled that special smile she reserved for Europeans. Ernst felt the musky warmth from all the male eyes following Beatrice's gaze, and backed away behind the sulphur burner.

Triangular heaps of sulphur piled high, some two hundred feet away, couldn't turn the air any more toxic but did, biting into his skin and eyes. The sulphur left permanent sores on the Lambadi human-chain feeding the melting pits. Like the weaponry America recently shipped to the Indians to fight China and lose, Chemerica provided Fertilisers its best, pre-World War II technology. Ernst saw the Texan cowboy standing near Chemerica's second-hand urea plant that ate naphtha, shat urea and spat out sulphur. Where would socialism be without the United States?

There was something going on over there, with people gathered around the Texan cowboy. Then loud shouts, and Venky Iyer placing a protective arm around Beatrice. She leaned against him to complete the picture. Together, they surveyed the commotion. From where Ernst stood, it looked as if Lilliputians were clambering all over the Texan looming beneath the naphtha cracking towers. He swatted them off like flies. Ernst walked around the burner for a closer look at what appeared to be Salim Ali's long awaited attack on imperialist pigs of the American kind.

But it was nothing of that sort because Salim Ali went, 'What the fuck?'

7

The Porcelain Doll

They all looked alike.
—*Indian soldiers fleeing the Chinese*

Turns out, the Indians weren't attacking Chemerica's Jack Hanson. He was simply in the way as they reached for each other's throat. The Texan was surrounded, two semi-circles coming up to his midriff. The Maratha semi-circle was in blue overalls, while the opposing Mallus wore a red aura.

'Chinese bhenchod!' the Marathas went. Salim Ali's red clones roared right back in outraged Malayalam and no idea what the fuck they were saying. The air was palpable with an indigenous hostility, as Indians hollered abuse past each other in different languages.

Hanson waved at the only other white man around. 'Frisky Injuns!' he said out loud. 'Where's the Chief?'

The Chief was by the sulphur burner, arm around plump Anglo-Indian shoulders while a security guard held up an umbrella against the sun. Venky Iyer must have heard Hanson because he barked at the umbrella bearer, who scurried off towards the gate. What with white men yelling and the general managers finally taking heed, things kind of simmered down. Only then, Ernst noticed another group of blue overalls at work in the shadows. Near a pile of rusting, reinforced iron rods behind the sulphur burner, they appeared to be peering down at a white first-aid box. The lid was open and the Red Cross staring at Ernst. Like the Marathas crowding Jack Hanson below the naphtha towers, they wore standard moustaches.

Beyond the shadows over on the burner's bright and sunny side, Venky Iyer's Chief Engineer was also at work near the viewing platform, busy collecting bribes so India may rotate on its axis. It takes more than a minor riot for civil servants to stop working. The viewing platform looked swept clean and repainted, when just the other day it had a charred Sikh lying there next to his severed head. The cleaning had been surprisingly thorough and with a diligence one doesn't associate with the public sector. It was just that area though— spotless with fresh red-oxide paint. The little Lambadi shitter from that day stood at the bottom of the metal stairs with a paintbrush in one hand, can of red oxide in the other. Ernst recognised his fellow daydreamer, the one with the dog nuzzling his bottom.

The kid had this knowing look. 'They pay me too,' he made it clear, catching Ernst look at the Chief Engineer collecting cash in envelopes. 'Nothing's free. I can do another coat, if you want. Two rupees.'

'We don't want,' Salim Ali said. 'Go away.'

The lad pointed a finger with his thumb cocked, took a step back and shot at him three times. 'Dhishoom! Dhishoom! Dhishoom!' For the third shot, he aimed at Salim Ali's head.

'What was that?' Ernst asked the little shitter.

'That's how you shoot a Sardarji.'

'How do you know?'

'How do you think? I saw the police sahibs do it.' The kid took a step back and aimed at Salim Ali again. 'This one's Madrasi though.' He sounded disappointed.

'Bugger off,' Salim Ali said.

'No wonder people want to shoot at you,' Ernst noted. 'Why not try being nice?'

The Marathas working behind the burner watched the kid shoot Salim Ali. They looked inspired and one of them stood up, something in hand, the others still hunched over that first-aid box. The one standing up was a gorilla and so different from the rest that Ernst wondered why he hadn't noticed him earlier. If the Texan was tall, this man was broad, reducing those around him to matchstick figures. Tender, loving care had gone into his biceps and shoulders. That something he held, it resembled a short, curved poniard, except he kept opening and closing it like a pair of scissors or something; Ernst couldn't tell, other than it looked medical.

'Shiv Sena buggers,' Salim Ali said. They stared back at him like hungry carnivores. While any and all outsiders were natural prey, the Shiv Sena was partial to dark South Indians like Salim Ali.

The gorilla took a batsman's stance and holding the pointy scissors with both hands, he swung for a six, his red, little eyes riveted on the little engineer. Commenting on those close-set eyes, Ernst couldn't help but remark the gorilla would look a lot safer caged. Salim Ali curled his upper lip in contempt at such bourgeois, casteist, upper-class attitude towards the working classes. That man may be Shiv Sena and dangerous, still. Workers like him laboured for their money; didn't fritter it away at the Golf Club like some people. Salim Ali's words typically bounced off, but Ernst was particularly sensitive today. So when the gorilla pointed at them and his gang of three stood up, Ernst was torn between real concern, and the simple pleasure of seeing Salim Ali shit his pants.

Shuffling up to them now carrying an iron rod in hand, the gorilla was a sight to behold. Luckily for Ernst, Venky Iyer must have called for more security because guards were seen flooding the gates and a section tore off to come up from behind him. Unluckily for Ernst, the security proceeded to form a circle—more like a cage for people to battle it out. The gorilla had this pleasant expression approaching Salim Ali in the cage. He stopped, turned to the security guards.

'Are you sure these communist bhenchods have it?' he asked them. Then to Salim Ali, 'Do you?'

'Do I what? Here, we are fighting on behalf of the working class, and just look at you. Who's paying you to behave this way? The Americans? Why don't you come join us instead?'

'Why don't I just fuck you?' the gorilla suggested. He would break just the one leg, he promised, enough for Salim Ali to get his sense back and return what was stolen. Now if only the gora sahib would kindly step aside. The gorilla grinned, before grabbing out for the little engineer. Although those shoulders were massive and rounded, he himself was squat from too many dead lifts. Still, Ernst felt dwarfed. What made him then, slam the rigid edge of his right hand into the gorilla's throat, when surely there were other options, he didn't know. He regretted it the instant his arm jack-knifed like that towards the gorilla's Adam's apple.

Best to apologise now before something else ensued, so Ernst dropped his arm and stepped forward to try clear the air. The gorilla had dropped the iron rod and was clawing at the throat, gurgling, and couldn't be bothered. Tearing away at his neck as if choked by an invisible strangler, he coughed, gurgled some more, and struggled to breathe. Looking confused, then surprising Ernst more than anyone else, he fell like a log and the playbook went out the window. The gorilla's gang of three backed off, leaving their co-worker flailing in the dust. The security cordon fell into disarray, unravelling to demonstrate how the British could rule this country for two hundred and fifty years. The security guards had turned Buddhist, stepping aside the way they did. They threw friendly smiles at the European—no hard feelings.

Having escaped unscathed, Lenin was now back at the wheel.

'Any doubts the Americans are behind this?'

'Take me through your logic, step by step,' Ernst requested. 'I have time.'

Also, no show of gratitude or anything of that sort. Salim Ali simply asked, 'Where did you learn that karate thing?'

'In jail. What's this now?'

Police in dark blue shorts had appeared out of nowhere, scrambling to assist the gorilla. There was deference all around and considering the gorilla's heft, it wasn't surprising. Seeing his beady eyes search as he struggled to his feet—mouth opening and closing like a guppy fish—Ernst felt he could've easily shown the same respect and saved himself this tightening in the chest. He also felt short of breath and there was a cork lodged up his arse; not altogether a bad thing as the gorilla locked eyes.

'Mister!'

It was a police sub-inspector, materialising out of nowhere along with his men hoisting the gorilla. In fact, the same sub-inspector from that other day—the one interrogating Lambadi women about the headless Sardar. Only this time, he had his sidearm. Come to think of it, Ernst felt he looked a lot like Johnny Walker in uniform. Not the walking Johnny on the scotch bottle, but the famous Bombay film comedian who went by that name. The comedy however was missing.

'Clearly an unprovoked assault,' Johnny Walker said.

'Clearly,' Ernst agreed. 'Are you going to arrest that maniac?'

'I meant you,' Johnny Walker said. 'You assaulted a poor worker without provocation. Also, unlawful entry by undesirable character into prohibited area.'

'I'm here lawfully to meet Mr. Venkatesh Iyer. We're bidding in a public tender.'

'I meant him,' Johnny Walker said, pointing at Salim Ali. 'We have reasons to believe these communists sent someone into a restricted area to remove something.' He nodded towards the American enclave. 'You can't go in there just like that. These people need to respect the law. Return what they took. Also, what's with the communists anyway? Be patriotic! China may think it won, but we have to remain steadfast.'

'I have to get going, Officer,' Ernst said, doing the European thing. 'I'm sure we can clear up everything later.'

'Who did you say you have to meet for the tender?'

'The General Manager, Mr. Venkatesh Iyer. He's standing right over there. Look.'

'I know him. Good man.'

'The best. We'd better go now. He's waiting.'

'He is? Looks like he's ignoring you. But you go ahead, Sirji, and don't mind me,' Johnny Walker said. Then, looking at Salim Ali, 'I'll hold this fellow though, for questioning.'

'He comes with me,' Ernst said, but now the sub-inspector wasn't listening. Instead, he yelled out complicated Marathi at the gorilla. The sub-inspector along with the recovering gorilla, the respectful police supporting him up, a confused security, the busy Chief Engineer, smiling banias, their salesmen, and Venky Iyer with hands full of Beatrice Taylor—they were all craning towards the naphtha cracking towers where Jack Hanson was still holding out. It appeared he was also holding up someone, away from people snatching away at him.

Amidst all the tamasha, Ernst impressed himself by catching Johnny Walker and the gorilla exchange looks.

'That's him,' Johnny Walker said. 'The Chinee with the gunny bag.'

Salim Ali too was staring at the person Hanson had physically lifted up. 'Arjun?' he went, looking at what was happening and then, looking confused.

~

'What does he think he's doing?' Salim Ali asked. 'Lynching Negroes? What's with these Americans? If not one thing, then something else. Fuckers.'

To keep it even keeled, someone shouted, 'Bhenchod Chinee!'

Ernst nudged Salim Ali and pointed to Tsering Tufan standing behind the Marathas amidst all the sister-fucking abuse and name-calling. Couldn't be too much fun these days for anyone looking Chinese, let alone a Chinese-looking Marxist. Apparently aware of his situation, Tufan began pussy footing past the Marathas towards the opposing Red semi-circle and to safety. The Marathas saw him try to sneak past and licked their chops.

'Has he gone mad? We need to get him out from there.'

'Arjun too,' Salim Ali said, pointing. 'That's him the Yank's holding up like that.'

Arjun. Comrade Tufan's nephew. The boy looked familiar and Ernst felt guilty for thinking they all looked alike.

'They keep calling him Chinese. He's my friend and he's not Chinese. They are from our North-East Frontier Province. Nothing wrong being Chinese, mind you, just saying. That whole Indo-Chinese conflict, by the way, was India's fault. A Himalayan blunder.'

Ernst looked around. Indians were not enthused about the Chinese waltzing down the Himalayas and up their arse. To complete the humiliation, China then calmly turned around and went back home after showing India who was boss. The Indians never recovered.

Salim Ali pointed at the person Hanson was holding to his chest. 'Arjun works here, at Fertilisers. Never any problem before and now the ghatis go start this Chinese nonsense about a fellow Indian.'

'He may have stolen something, remember? Or did you forget already that gorilla almost killed you? He feels you know something about it. The sub-inspector thinks so too.'

'They're ghatis. They can't think.'

Ernst looked around again to see if anyone heard the racist slur. If the Marathas decided to have a go at Salim Ali, he wouldn't want to come in the way.

'The American,' Tsering Tufan said as Ernst hurried him away from the Marathas eyeing him for a meal. 'He saved Arjun.'

They could hear the one-man, Texan riot police and his loud, bellowing laugh as he put the man down. Taking the nephew's head in the crook of his arm, Hanson tousled the kid's hair. The nephew was an exquisite, younger version of his uncle, right down to the eyeglasses, but with hair. There was an ugly bluish-black discolouration around his left temple. It's Porcelain Doll, Ernst realised with a start. From that evening with the headless Sardar. This was the kid Chhote Bhai smashed to the ground with his hockey ball.

Jack Hanson reached into his pocket and took out a packet of glucose biscuits. The not-Chinese nephew and he chatted while munching, but Ernst couldn't hear a bloody thing. The more Hanson ignored the Marathas, the more abusive they became. The expressions on their faces; they reminded Ernst of those righteous burghers watching the school teacher dangling from the lamp post alongside his dachshund. Another detachment of security arrived from the gates to form a protective huddle around Venky Iyer and Beatrice. If the police were still around, you wouldn't know.

'Oye!' Salim Ali called out to security. 'You're needed here, not there!'

Iyer stared a bit, Beatrice looked duly offended, and the security guards ignored the fool. All this time the two opposing semi-circles remained resolutely apart and defined around their American nucleus. Looking disoriented—what with people baying for his blood—the nephew quivered in the magnetic field between the concave Blue and Red formations. Hanson's cheerful disposition remained at full wattage, but a hint of confusion crept on to his face.

Then, the Marathas surged forward.

A squat worker in blue at the rear of the pack caught Ernst's eye as he cut through towards the centre, his dumbbell-shaped shoulders gliding forward at high speed. A smile softened the hard focus on the gorilla's face and John noticed he was holding those curved, pointy scissors from that first-aid box.

Flowing around Hanson, the local Marathas in blue surged to mingle with the opposing Red Mallus on the other side. No one so much as touched the giant American. He stood stunned as the melee passed him by. The Marathas kept hollering abuse, moving past Hanson and past the Mallus to walk away and dispersed into the jungle of pipeline manifolds. The shouting stopped, and all you could hear were steel vessels hissing steam from the urea complex around the naphtha towers. The Marathas had gone off script, instead of at opposing Mallu throats. The Mallus looked sucker-punched by the silence.

Salim Ali pointed at Arjun. Tired of quivering, the not-Chinese nephew had collapsed—legs spread and head slumped forward like a porcelain doll in overalls. It was embarrassing, because it appeared he had urinated and was staring down at the dark puddle between his legs. Hanson had his hands under the armpits and was about to heave him up, when the boy raised his arms in abject surrender and fell back against Hanson to one side, his eyewear slipping off and on to his lap. The Texan put the boy down and Salim Ali rushed past the band of comrades tightening around Hanson.

The band loosened for Ernst, who squeezed in to see Hanson with Arjun's bruised head on his lap, his big Texan hand feeling around the wet crotch. It surprised Ernst that Hanson's hand was cherry red. Salim Ali was by Hanson's side, trying to understand why his friend's thigh was spurting blood like there was no tomorrow. Salim Ali then stood and yelled out at Venky Iyer in a way one should never address a Brahmin from the Civil Service. 'Why are you just standing there holding that woman? Call an ambulance! What the bleddy hell do they pay you for?'

It stunned the crowd into silence. Venky Iyer let go of Beatrice and held on to his stiff upper lip instead, staring into the distance where Ernst saw his purchase order floating away in triplicate. Beatrice patted Venky Iyer as if he was the victim. All this while

Hanson cradled his porcelain doll, using a beefy hand to try stem the blood erupting like lava from its left thigh. The Texan rocked Arjun as one would a child, tears welling from his furrowed, white face to fall on the kid's brow and then mingling with the blood everywhere, soaking his clothes, as the big man fell to pieces. Ernst thought Hanson was crooning a lullaby but when he bent down, what he heard through sobs racking the solid Texan frame was, 'He's only a boy…for fuck's sake, he's only a boy…look at him for fuck's sake, he's only a boy.'

'He's Indian, you know,' Tufan said, panic creeping up to dim those bright eyes even as the pupils dilated from fear. 'Not Chinese. He needs medical attention.'

There had to be more blood matting the ground and all over Hanson and Salim Ali than left in Arjun's delicate, not-Chinese body. So Ernst did what Beatrice was doing over there with Venky Iyer, and patted Tufan on the back. Meanwhile, Salim Ali screamed away, hurling abuses in Mallu Hindi at Iyer for allowing this, at Bombay for allowing the ghatis, at India for allowing someone like Iyer, at the universe for allowing India, and all the while waving his red palms.

Over the air, Iyer was long done with his pre-recorded exhortations against Marxist agitators and agent provocateurs. Lata Mangeshkar was now warbling across the speakers non-stop, asking fellow Indians to shed a tear for their dead, scattered across the Himalayas.

'Aye Mere Watan Ke Logon,' she sang, and India's favourite song it was, being warbled day in and day out across the land since the Himalayan debacle. Ernst looked down at the dying kid who would never, ever have to listen to it again.

8

Lenin

We wanted the maximum amount of chaos. So we sent them a virus.
—*Arthur Zimmermann, German Foreign Minister, on allowing Vladimir Lenin through to Russia*

It was afternoon, no clouds, the sun bearing down like a bhenchod, and the dust in the air with a life of its own. If dust got to you, then very likely India would too, but Ernst learnt way back when that one could get used to almost anything.

A gaggle of women passed by. They had looked Lambadi from afar, but turns out they were hijras—India's very own breed of eunuchs. Yes, Ernst agreed, nothing would surprise him anymore. Not even eunuchs wearing saris, cutting across a Government factory. Seeing the gora, they laughed, clapping their hands in that sideways manner but didn't approach for money, probably thinking he wouldn't understand. They did stare though, eyeing him until a curt command put an end to all that.

It was an older hijra in a sari; the creased, weathered face shorn of its female camouflage and with facial hair too sparse for a beard—white strands drooping from his chin. The face looked familiar. There was this picture of men staring out from inside an idyllic Kerala setting and then fleetingly, a close-up of an old man with strands of hair spouting from his chin.

An FCC station wagon had ferried Venky Iyer and Beatrice Taylor off to safety past somewhat green lawns and semi-trimmed hedges to the Administrative Building. Hanson's station wagon in turn, took Arjun's drained body to Sion Hospital, followed by a disinterested dark blue police jeep with a torn canvas top that showed up instead of an ambulance. Johnny Walker had jumped out and about to take charge of the body when Jack Hanson jumped in to cut his balls off.

'I'll bring the kid,' Hanson had said, and that, was that. Then to Salim Ali with Johnny Walker right there, 'Fuck knows how this asshole treats the body otherwise.'

'Not at all, Sirji,' Johnny Walker said.

Heaving his blood-soaked bulk into his station wagon, Jack Hanson had signalled to Salim Ali. 'I'm so sorry,' he called out. A disoriented Tufan sat in the rear, beside his dead nephew. Salim Ali must have felt foolish waving back at the American, but wave he did. Ernst noticed his eyes too were red like the hand.

He also noticed the white Mercedes parked just outside the gate. He knew that car and he knew the great man relaxed against the rear headrest. One-time boss, erstwhile friend, and overall Master of the Universe, Adam Sassoon. David and Solomon to Bombay's Baghdadi Jews, or whatever was left of them after Israel opened for business. Those had been his men back there at the sulphur burner, all suited and booted, clinging to Iyer in an inner circle.

Seeing the great man in real life was always unreal, and for a second time Ernst felt he was inside a news documentary. Why was the great man here? Ernst smiled and they locked eyes, but Adam Sassoon managed to look right through him. Sassoon's liveried driver leaned forward making the Mercedes purr. Ernst rubbed at the texture building up around the mole on his face. There was this feeling of being left behind and it wasn't just because the Mercedes had pulled away. Bhenchod. We were friends once. At least look at me.

'You were friends, I'm told,' Salim Ali observed. 'You and that man who fired you.'

'Yes. And I thought you said white people stuck together.'

'When push comes to shove,' Salim Ali said. 'When push comes to shove.'

~

The Marxist mob turned their eyes towards Salim Ali, and he swelled like Lenin must have on stepping out of his sealed train to greet the Bolsheviks at Petrograd's Finland Station. When he gesticulated, Lenin's hands were appropriately red.

'They killed Comrade Arjun!' he yelled, and not to be outdone, the mob yelled back, making Ernst jump like a kicked dachshund.

Definitely not the right time, but Ernst went ahead anyway, and leaned forward. 'Iyer's pissed off. The way you behaved. You were upset, of course. Who wouldn't be?' Ernst should have stopped right there and instead went on to suggest, 'I'd rather we calm things down though. What do you say?'

'Calm things down? Really? Okay, why not?'

Lata Mangeshkar was winding up to martial drumbeats over the loudspeakers and the union mob came to attention at some unspoken command. So did Salim Ali, staring straight back at the unionised guard of honour. The loudspeakers roared back to life, this time with the Soviet National Anthem.

The music was admittedly, awe-inspiring. Especially where it goes: "Long lives our Soviet Motherland, built by the people's mighty hand." Any other day and it would've been a welcome change; there being only so much of Lata Mangeshkar one can take. Mouthing the translated Soviet call-to-arms, the Red Mallu faction lined up, chests out, facing Salim Ali who thrust his pigeon chest back at them. If owning the microphone was a prerequisite for an Indian power grab, Salim Ali now ruled the skies. But how the fuck? That's what Ernst wanted to know. The public address system was on Beatrice Taylor's desk and for a Salim Ali to play his theme song from there, would be next to impossible.

'Not when we have comrades everywhere.' With that, Lenin dismissed Ernst, Venky Iyer, Beatrice Taylor, and any hopes of getting that purchase order today, tomorrow, or any time in the future. Mouthing the National Anthem of one foreign country in another foreign language, the Mallu Bolsheviks looked ready to go to war.

'Who killed Comrade Arjun?' Salim Ali demanded to know. The Soviet Anthem had them all fired up and the answer dancing on Mallu lips. The trade union-wallahs responded by roaring back larger than life. 'Americans! America killed our comrade!' Chants of 'America Hai, Hai!' and 'Down with American lackeys!' followed. And lest anyone forgot, 'Shiv Sena Ghatis Murdabad!' Then, some more ghati this, and ghati that.

Salim Ali rebuked them with a straight face. 'Comrades! No need for ethnic slurs! We're all workers!'

It was interesting though, how he didn't feel the need to chastise them for bad-mouthing America. Especially seeing how Hanson and he waved at each other a while ago. On the other hand, there was probably only so much one could ask of a Marxist.

~

Adam Sassoon's Mercedes out of the way, the security guardhouse materialised. The guard on duty was haranguing a hirsute, turbaned, Sikh truck driver. They appeared to be arguing over a young Nepali boy. Sikh drivers kept these boys—cleaners—to help around their truck, do repairs and maintenance, keep the vehicle clean, cook and make chai. But also because it was difficult driving a Tata truck day after day and sleeping alone night after night, without someone to spoon.

The argument with the security guard was getting personal. No idea how this could go down, so the Nepali boy had this neutral expression pasted on his face. Ernst felt he did look a bit like Arjun, although, not quite. There had been a quality to Arjun. Just as there was a quality to his uncle.

Salim Ali came over to watch Sassoon's Mercedes float towards the Administrative Building in the distance. The little fellow's face glistened and Ernst thought it was sweat but no, Lenin had taken leave and Salim Ali was crying. Ernst wanted to pull him close, regardless of the risk.

'It's my fault,' Salim Ali said. 'I instigated Arjun instead of turning a blind eye like bleddy Iyer does. And now he's dead.'

Of course, no one could turn a blind eye like Venky Iyer. His abilities were the stuff of legend.

'You instigated him to do what? They keep bringing up that gunny bag he stole. You think that's why this happened?'

'What the hell do you mean by that?'

'I'm just asking. You said you instigated him. And you keep blaming the Americans. Is it just you being Marxist, or is there something I don't know?'

'What's my being a Marxist got to do with American perfidy?'

'Nothing. Let's go find Beatrice. She'll help get our paperwork in.'

'Who gives a fuck?' came the revolutionary response. Lenin was back and riding roughshod. Ernst looked at the little Marxist—in tears over his dead friend. It dawned the man really didn't give a fuck.

'It's wrong,' Salim Ali said, finally putting the dead Arjun aside, to go embrace his other great sorrow. 'We shouldn't have to grovel to get our due. Why beg bleddy Iyer or Beatrice Taylor or anyone else for that matter? And why should she help you, anyway? Are you two having sexual intercourse?'

He pulled out a sample piece of brass tubing from his pocket and stared at it. One he had drawn himself on a wobbly, Ludhiana-made drawing bench, especially for today. Considering the quality of Ernst's Ludhiana-made equipment, the brass pipe was a work of art.

'Why won't Iyer buy my pipes?' Salim Ali asked. 'When they last forever?'

Yes, why wouldn't Iyer buy those pipes? After all, Salim Ali's pipes did last forever and so what if he had insulted Venky Iyer in public? Then gone fucked things further by, God-knows-how, sequestering Iyer's public address system to play Marxist music in honour of a dead comrade. And so what if Iyer went blacklisted Ernst, who would probably have to cut back, retrench workers, and kiss bania arse to try take out more loans? It didn't matter, and Ernst looked at the little shit with the respect he deserved.

A security guard had come up to them and after preparing himself to talk to a white man, he goes, 'They want you, Sirji, in Iyer Sahib's office.'

9

Brothers-in-arms

If twice born, O Brahmin, as you said,
Why weren't you born with your sacred thread?
—*Marxist ditty*

'Be a sport, Venky, and give the chap what he wants.'

No suit, tie, jacket, or anything of that sort and instead, a yellow T-shirt clinging to a fine body in gentle decline. Adam Sassoon's grey, patrician countenance and the British, upper-class gangle were in angular contrast to the rest of India. A stainless steel Rolex sealed the understatement around the King of the Jews. Next to him, his major domo, Major Punjabi—erect and miserable at what was happening. The Major threw a malignant look at Ernst to assign blame in a clear and straightforward manner.

'We're being taken for a ride.' General Manager Venky Iyer looked up from his executive-style chair first at Sassoon, who after all, was the Jew paying to educate Iyer's son in California. Next, he glanced at the other Jew, the one living off his crumbs. Venky Iyer was Brahmin, a twice-born Siva worshipper. It took a lot of money for Sassoon to bludgeon him into submission.

A large framed photograph stood on the Government-issue Godrej cabinet in green to his left, under the mandatory black & white Gandhi on the wall. Oxford, ICS class of 1941—the probationers grouped around a seated white-haired Englishman with hat in lap, and his wench of a memsahib wife. Ernst recognised Venky Iyer—standing on a bleacher along with others in the raised last row. Both hands rested on the skinny shoulders of the colleague in front. Not much change over the years, except for heavy greying at the temples. The chiselled features in the photograph, Brahmin brow, the deep eyes establishing an immediate divide, were all there across the table. Ernst wondered whether Venky Iyer secretly scrubbed up every time after shaking hands outside his caste.

'Mind you, this has nothing to do with his Muslim fellow abusing me in public, in my factory, in front of my workers,' Iyer clarified. Then, after a pregnant pause, 'These things don't matter to me. However, registration's all done, Adam. Tender's closed and they weren't even shortlisted. There'll be a next time.'

Spoken like a bureaucrat, but with such class. On occasion, Ernst had witnessed Venky Iyer cruise between Sanskrit, spoken Hindi, and Oxford English in the same sentence. This one was that much more impressive because of the accompanying subtext: These things do matter. In fact, nothing else matters. So, fuck you, this is my factory, and you're sitting in my office. You'll have to cut my dick off before I cede on this.

When it came to blame, the high caste Brahmin was in Major Punjabi's corner the way he looked at Ernst and the way he smiled. It was all very impressive. Equally impressive was how the morning events weren't allowed to intrude. A worker was dead and remained persona non grata in this room. No mention of what happened out there. The mandatory black & white Gandhi offered a toothless grin, just in case you missed the irony.

Above all, was the re-emergence of the old Adam Sassoon, holding forth in someone else's office. The great man winked past Venky Iyer at Ernst like a blood brother. Thirty minutes ago, he had looked right through him from his Mercedes, out there by the security guardhouse. Ernst didn't know what was going on, why this change of heart, but it was about time. Bad luck shouldn't be allowed a run of anything more than twenty-six years.

'We'd better reopen that tender then, old chap,' Sassoon said. 'Man needs a purchase order. Let's surprise ourselves and give him one.'

'Adam, you realise we're being played. You heard the bloody Soviet Anthem over the intercom. That damned fool Muslim of his is an anarchist and a troublemaker. Don't know how he did it, but he isn't getting away.'

Troublemaker? Salim Ali? Ernst pondered the impossible. 'He was just upset, that's all. The dead boy was his friend.'

'Just upset?' Iyer looked incredulous. 'They would have lynched Hanson.'

'I don't think so. It's fashionable to blame the Yanks for everything. Who takes it seriously?'

'We do. I know about that Muslim's Marxism.' Major Punjabi was emphatic. A Punjabi has to be seen to know all. 'Dangerous, bloody anti-national.'

With Sassoon nearby, Punjabi's Punjabi accent had dragged itself to attention. It was now more clipped, with no loose bits and pieces. The "bloody" no longer, "bluddy".

'Not at all,' Ernst insisted. 'You can trust Salim Ali.'

Major Punjabi nodded towards Ernst and lobbed a rhetorical.

'But, can we trust you?'

'He and I have history,' Sassoon said to the files on Iyer's desk. 'Still, Sirji.'

Having stretched uncomfortable silence all it could go, Adam Sassoon responded with what could only be a heavy heart.

'They locked him up during the war. A bloody spy they said our Ernst was. An enemy alien. Didn't take to it too well. Never forgave me. Thinks I left him to rot in Purandhar.'

Ernst smiled back at the great man.

A Jew jailed during the war for being German was nothing short of hilarious. Ernst was a big fan of the Law of Unintended Consequences. People would however make clucking sounds, then wonder why he laughed. It was more than over just how hysterical it was—being interned in British India because he was German, while his father took it in Germany for being a Jew. Truth be told, he only had fond memories from being interned at Purandhar Fort. He said to Beatrice once, 'Don't you ever dream of being cast on a desert island, where no one can reach you?'

Having said that, this desert island was more a school than retreat. The gardener's wife at Purandhar Fort was a Sahajiya sworn to secrecy, yet taught him their Tantric ways. The Japanese nationals locked up in there were arseholes, but taught him Jiu Jitsu. Ground fighting! They would yell at him. Ground fighting! And from the British he learnt on a daily basis that just because they were fighting Germany, didn't mean they liked Jews. Then there was this other thing. At some point, the Tommies went flipped a switch in his head and he began thinking in English.

Be that as it may, the real fun began only after his release. Turns out, the great man was waiting to wipe the floor with him when he was let out. Ernst never blamed Sassoon for not getting him out earlier. He couldn't have. Ernst knew that.

It's what you did after that, you fucker.

His old job ostensibly waiting, Ernst had slipped back into his routine. In the past, working for Adam Sassoon and regardless of the bonhomie bubbling over, one always worried he would screw you—he seemed that kind of a Jew. Then just when one relaxed and thought he wouldn't (after Purandhar, who would?), he did.

It's not working out, old chap, the great man had said the day he pulled the trigger. Not your fault. We to blame. It's not you, it's me.

He had kept his arm around Ernst's shoulders while walking him out, so the full import failed to sink in, and Ernst had left in a daze, but smiling. Eventually, with days becoming months becoming years and he starting to go invisible, Ernst couldn't think of the Sassoon building at Ballard Pier anymore, without his stomach cramping up. Stepping inside became out of the question.

The day after the sack however, he had marched back into Sassoon's office. Instead of a brilliant denouement, he asked—okay, begged—for something. Anything. Crumbs would do just fine, thank you. Also, let's do make sure I keep my Golf Club membership, old chap.

All this time had passed, and he still cringed.

Probably embarrassed at what he wrought, the great man made one of his grand gestures—granting Ernst minor supplier status, a good word here and a phone call there, Golf Club membership not cancelled, what not. Decades passed, times changed, and Adam Sassoon began to ignore him; as if more embarrassed by Ernst than by what he pulled. Major Punjabi became the interface with a Punjabi accent and there was no more direct access to the great man.

Until ten minutes ago, when they hauled him into Iyer's office.

~

There were wrinkles all over Venky Iyer's jacket as he struggled with why he just had his dick handed to him on a platter. Something Ernst too would have loved to know.

Venky Iyer put his pen away, straightened up, brushed around the shoulders, and kowtowed without too much heartfelt sincerity. He had to go, to deal with the aftermath from what he had just gone signed. Very irregular, what he did. Need to now go and iron out the wrinkles. No matter. What were managers for?

The air-conditioning hummed and gurgled and they relaxed in the face of Iyer's empty, executive chair staring them down—the Godrej to its left, a bank of phones to the right: black, green and red in an ascending order of importance. Sassoon reached to jiggle the black one. Beatrice Taylor floated through.

'Sir?' she enquired, her voice filling the room with the golden glow of smoky, single malt.

'A favour, Beatrice dear.'

'Absolutely, Mr. Sassoon,' she said, and waited. No rush, her silence assured.

'You see that Jehangir around, haul him in here.'

'Right away, Mr. Sassoon.'

'Special woman, our Beatrice,' Sassoon said, putting the handset down.

Ernst asked, 'Jehangir Merchant?'

Sassoon said, 'Yup.'

'Jehangir the bagman?'

'Is that what they call him? My bagman?'

'Okay. Then, Jehangir the ass?'

'The same. Am surrounded by them you may've noticed,' and he pointed at Venky Iyer's chair. 'But neither here nor there. You got your PO and that's what matters. Iyer's not happy though.' The great man kept looking at the empty chair. 'Your darkie's quite the provocateur. How do you tolerate him?'

'Not easy. By the way, did you hear? A worker died today.'

Quite something, Sassoon agreed and went on to commiserate. 'Two deaths, Iyer was telling me, in a little over a week. Truck driver gets burnt to death by gypsies, now this accident thing. The hell's happening?'

'About that truck driver. It wasn't gypsies, and today wasn't an accident.'

'What's that?'

'Couldn't be gypsies. Man was shot. Then burnt. Headless Sardar's what they're calling him. Has a bullet hole between the eyes the police refused to acknowledge. And then that kid today, he was stabbed in the femoral artery. No accident. There's a worker walking around with the weapon that was used. The police know this man. So whom do I point him out to?'

'Preposition,' Sassoon said, and it was Ernst's turn to ask, what's that? 'You ended your sentence with a preposition,' Sassoon went, and Ernst went, Oh. It brought back memories, now that the bullshit was starting again. A small price to pay, some would say, for such a big friendship.

'About this bullet hole in the head. You said the body was headless.'

'The head was found next to it.'

'Really? Sounds like one of your bad dreams.'

'Head was charred and skin gone, but you couldn't miss the small calibre hole. I saw it. Probably, a revolver. The police have it now. The head, along with the body. They'll confirm.'

Johnny Walker came to mind and one had to ask, why would they?

'Once again, old chap, going all German over something that doesn't matter. Brings back memories, what? We're in India. We burn people here, sure, but we don't shoot them first. Gypsies carrying revolvers? And this "weaponised" worker of yours. Most can't spell their names right, but this one goes locates the femoral artery? Why not leave guesswork to the police? They're good at it.'

The two deaths, Ernst suggested, could be related, is all. 'That man with the hole in the head, they say he stole something. May have handed it to the kid with the hole in his leg. Now both are dead.'

Sassoon wasn't listening and left Ernst feeling he was off-script again. One of your strengths, Sassoon had once assured him, and fired him the next day.

'The worker with the weapon, he thinks Salim Ali now has whatever the fuck was stolen. The police think so too. So maybe my man's next.'

'Who? Your darkie? May not be a bad thing. Anyway, moving on. Cathy was asking about you.'

To the best of Ernst's knowledge, Cathy Sassoon couldn't stand his guts.

'You're wondering,' Sassoon said.

'About what?'

'This, you and I.'

'Of course not.'

'Of course you are. Let's not forget, we were close once. I'm reaching out because we're getting old. You wake up one day, and there aren't too many friends left.'

There was this surreal feeling, listening to the great man. It would take some getting used to, but he was enjoying it already and didn't want it to stop. Salim Ali however, was on the loose. And so was the gorilla.

'Shall we go join Iyer?'

The great man was sanguine. 'Let him sort it out. He knows what to do.'

Be that as it may, Venky Iyer wouldn't know what to do if he bumped into Salim Ali. Left to his own devices, there was nothing to temper Salim Ali's singular reality regarding dialectical materialism. Made worse by today's events. Sassoon seemed to agree Salim Ali was an issue.

'That darkie of yours. Maybe the police are right. Maybe he has what his dead friend stole.'

'What did he steal?'

'Why not ask him? Man is clearly up to no good. You saw how Iyer reacted. I don't get it. Why keep him around? Do something.'

'I will,' Ernst said with such sincerity, his testicles shrank at the betrayal.

~

Outside, a Parsi-bawa scurried towards Venky Iyer's office, juggling long rolls of blueprint. It was Jehangir Merchant with that determined look of his. Suited and booted like that, he looked a shining success. Whereas, he lived in free housing provided by the Parsi Punchayet and lived off a stipend provided by Sassoon to be his bagman. Pay off Ministers, officers, clerks. The sort our great man wouldn't touch with a barge pole. The sort needed to get the barge started. Jehangir would get them aligned. Have them do the great man's bidding. It was a full-time job.

Asked why Jehangir of all people, Sassoon said because of the man's uncanny resemblance to his old friend, Pakistan's Quaid-e-Azam, Mohammed Ali Jinnah: the suave, erudite, hugely rich, enormously brave, scotch swigging, pork-loving, Parsi-marrying, Nehru-baiting, Gandhi-hating, now-dead founder of India's current Enemy #2: The Islamic Republic of Pakistan. Jinnah after all, talked and bribed his way into creating a whole new nation. Thereafter, Jehangir carefully adopted mannerisms to ensure he remained the Quaid's doppelganger. Ernst learnt never to underestimate the effect Sassoon's words had on people.

Seeing Jehangir try balance the rolls of paper while moving at high speed, things began making sense. About what the great man was doing here at Fertilisers today. As far as Sassoon was concerned, Fertilisers' pipes & tubing tender was a pimple on a gnat's arse. Those important-looking blueprints all over Jehangir, were probably why the great man was here. And being here, he had simply stepped up seeing old friend Ernst in a bind. After ignoring old friend Ernst for twenty-six years.

In a rush to meet Sassoon, Jehangir careened towards Venky Iyer's office in his buttoned-down jacket soaking in sweat. The babu-type bureaucrat hurrying alongside him came with a pince-nez from the Thirties that airlifted Ernst back to Berlin. Clocking their separate ways, both sides nodded at each other and Jehangir dropped a blueprint to the floor.

'Pipes?' Ernst asked, picking up the unravelled chart. 'What man, this is for a building full of pipes. We make them you know. Pipes and tubes. All German-made. Anything I can do for you?'

'Give it back! Hand it over, you fellow!'

Ernst rolled the unravelled drawings in slow motion, before giving them back to the wide-eyed Parsi-bawa gone nuts. He didn't think too much of it then. He knew Jehangir from the Golf Club. This was normal.

Jehangir snatched at the roll and the babu with the pince-nez was the one who said, 'Thank you, Sir.'

Ernst bowed with a heel-click, Prussian style.

'Come on, Paranjpe, come on!' Then, not caring whether Ernst heard or not, 'Phuddu this man is. Don't you know?'

One thing Jehangir never learnt, was how to behave like Jinnah.

~

Salim Ali was outside astride his abused Vespa; eyes still communist red, though the palms had gone rusty.

'Congratulations,' he said. 'So we got the order.'

'How did you know?'

'Know what? About white people coming together inside? The word spreads. What did I tell you? When push comes to shove, you guys will stick together. Goes to show.'

'Thought you'd be pleased.' Ernst remained curious. 'Still. How did you learn we are in play? It only just happened.'

'Why do you care?'

'Why should I care about anything you do? Which reminds me, they think you may have whatever it is your dead friend stole.'

'Who's they?'

'They. They're wrong of course. Yes?'

'You tell me. When were they ever right?'

'Any news from the hospital?'

'I sent Comrade Tufan home to rest. But the Yank insisted on remaining at the hospital. Did you see how he handled that bleddy sub-inspector?' Salim Ali would get this same surprised look when rifling through *Life* magazine.

'And yet, you think the Americans are responsible.'

'I don't think. I know.'

'Sure you do. What does the hospital say is the cause of death?'

'We're waiting on the coroner. You know, even if he certifies Arjun was intentionally stabbed, what are the police going to do? I'll tell you. They'll do fuck-all. They appeared more disinterested than usual, if that is possible.'

Ernst remembered Johnny Walker exchanging looks with the gorilla. The gorilla identifying Arjun as the Chinee. 'It's possible,' he said.

Beatrice Taylor walked by bearing two box files. A Fertilisers jeep had drawn up. Beatrice looked daggers at Salim Ali before turning to Ernst.

'Your PO,' she mouthed, pointing at the good box file holding the successful applicants, on top of the bad one holding those deceased. She made the A-Okay sign with a plump thumb and forefinger. Done making sure she wasn't seen blaming a European for anything, she threw something on the ground at Salim Ali's feet. It was a 45rpm record in a plain, brown paper sleeve with a stencilled, red hammer and sickle. Salim Ali picked it up and dusted it off.

'I'm going to find out who played that communist music for you rowdies,' Beatrice said to him. 'Then, we'll see.'

The Sindhi Refugee Camp girl—Bhairavi—came up from behind her, more files in hand and eyes red like Salim Ali's.

'Got everything?' Beatrice asked her.

'Yes, Madam.'

'Are you sure? You're not yourself today.'

'Yes, Madam.'

'Not too smart, our Bhairavi,' Beatrice said, the girl within comfortable hearing distance. 'Needs guidance. They all do. We should help the good ones like her, not that useless, communist, Muslim fellow of yours. Between you and me, both Iyer and Adam want him gone. He's a thief, you know. They all are.'

The girl Bhairavi adjusted her sari and the tulip blossomed into view again, threatening to burst through its wrapping any minute. She appeared distracted and straightening up, didn't make any effort to recognise him. Ernst found himself taking it personally. She wasn't smiling, not even looking. Forget how she had smiled at Chhote Bhai. At least smile the way you should at Europeans. He was shocked to feel this way, because he wasn't racist. Anyone would tell you that. He loved Indians. Same as Churchill, who then goes kills three million of them in one shot during the Bengal Famine by denying them their own rice. But only because Gandhi pissed him off.

Ernst waited for Beatrice to walk back from the jeep.

'Send her over,' he said. Beatrice looked confused, and he had to point at the girl. 'You said we should help her. I could use someone for filing and accounts. Part-time. So send her over. Anything to help.'

Beatrice mulled, her body parts stopped jiggling and the tableau around them took a pause from staring at her tits and arse. 'Good for you,' she said. 'If we don't help them, who will? Thursday then. She'll come over. I'll tell you how much to pay, but don't give her the money. They simply spend it. You know how they are. Best I keep it for her.' She sighed. 'Only hope she's grateful.'

If Bhairavi was grateful, it didn't show. Like Salim Ali earlier, she appeared to be in shock. Tell me why you've been crying, Ernst wanted to ask.

There was this smudged, gold pendant around her neck, a swastika—India's eternal good luck symbol. Staring back at him, it spoke up instead. No luck for you it said, but he had drifted already and was caught up with the rest of her. Her backside swayed on its own as she walked off behind Beatrice. A boy was just killed, and all he could think of was bending her over. 'Stop it,' Salim Ali had complained on the balcony catching Ernst stare at Bhairavi bending over her powder mandala. 'She's known to me since school days.'

'She's the one,' Ernst said to Salim Ali, just about to kick-start his Vespa. 'She told you. That girl, Bhairavi. She's your bloody childhood friend. That's how you knew we got the order. And she played that Soviet music for you over the bloody intercom.'

'If she played it,' Salim Ali replied, 'it wasn't for me.'

10

The Great Divide

Without gold, there is no dowry. Without dowry, there is no marriage.
—*Seth Jamunadas Kejriwal*

The invisible partition cutting through the Golf Club's dumbstruck piano was referred to as The Great Divide. The only ones comfortable crossing back and forth were the club staff. Also Ernst, who was neither here, nor there.

The Europeans at the Bombay Presidency Golf Club stuck to their side of The Great Divide like their lives depended on it. No moving those chess pieces unless over to the greens. Or to the permit room over on the Indian side where they served alcohol to anyone not Indian. An invisible Berlin Corridor connected the permit room to the Western side of The Great Divide.

Compared to single-minded Europeans, the Indians were more ambivalent and behaved like prisoners choosing sides at Arthur Road Jail. Jehangir Merchant and his suited-up wogs for one, could be seen curled up at Adam Sassoon's feet for protection.

'It means Westernised Oriental Gentleman,' Sassoon had explained to clear the air once and for all. 'Who says it's a slur? If anything, it's a compliment. Very respectful, I may add. Not racist at all.' Who could say whether they understood? Half the time the wogs had no idea what he was saying. But they listened carefully anyway, just in case the great man's thoughts came useful in the future.

On their part, desi Indians sought safety in numbers around Seth Jamunadas Kejriwal, perched on his divan in waistcoat and dhoti on the Indian side. You addressed him as Sethji. You referred to him as the Seth, and you did not take his name in vain. What Adam Sassoon was these days to a shrinking Westernised coterie, the Seth was to the rest of India that doubled in size every time he farted.

The Seth's divan dominated the Indian side, lodged in its own alcove next to the permit room. Sethji's one leg was tucked under an arse-cheek and the other swinging to hypnotise his audience. His spectacular non-compliance with the club's dress code refused to come up at any of the management committee meetings. The bearers were seen trying to keep up with demand as Westerners yelled, 'Chhokra!' from their side of The Great Divide. They served the Seth first regardless, before scurrying over to the hollering goras. Otherwise in full regalia, they wore rubber slippers that slapped against their heels as they then rushed across the border. The poor tend to be practical.

The Seth, not poor, was barefoot, his leather chappals tossed on the floor. His feet were sleek and fat like his baby face, and they dared anyone in the club to bring up the dress code.

He leaned his bulk against the gaddi-style divan put there just for him—the nation's most beloved of businessmen and patron to politicians, Krishna devotee and builder of temples, king of the banias and India's largest publisher of textbooks (the man spoke pidgin), besides being the only patriotic, Hindu gold smuggler in an otherwise Muslim-dominated business. Without him, there would be no gold for the average Hindu family. Without gold, their daughters would never get married to bear sons. The Seth was integral to the cycle of life.

The Seth was also bit of a loan shark. The goodwill from lending to a European was incalculable and he never missed an opportunity to show Ernst his appreciation. That was, of course, before the Cold Pilger incident. Ernst wondered, what happens now. Under their arrangement, Ernst could use the Cold Pilger the Seth had financed. Didn't mean it was his to sell until the loan was paid off. You didn't think of that before you sold it? Salim Ali had asked. Ernst had to admit it was a very good question.

Not a word about getting fucked over, and instead the Seth patted away to his right where his accountant would sit.

'Come, Mr. Ernestji,' he said.

Ernst came, placing his Bloody Mary on the table and being a foreigner, was allowed that trespass. Didn't mean he could sip. The Seth patted Ernst's thigh possessively. The powerful bania made him uneasy and today was no better, and a lot worse. Keep away from shiny objects, his father would say. The Seth was India's shiniest. Why heed a father who slashed his own wrists in a bathtub was a great question, but the advice took hold.

He looked around for the Seth's accountant. You couldn't have one without the other. He found Lala Prem tottering on the verandah edge. Lala Prem, with his lingering handshake. The sly wink every time his Seth complained about credit crunch. As always, he was in Frontier garb and looking more Muslim Pathan than Hindu Lala. His green, plumed turban fluttered in the breeze as he stood on the verandah edge, a heavy hand on some caddie-boy's shoulder. Turns out it's Kirti, the Sikh caddie-boy with creamy skin and a Hindu name. His unshorn hair was knotted on the top of the head in what they call a guth.

Caddies weren't allowed on the verandah and the boy remained on the lawn. Standing on the verandah's edge, the Lala reached out to massage the boy's shoulder. Ernst liked Kirti too, but the Lala's fondness was clearly special. Kirti the Poet, is what they called the boy. Always ready with gentle counsel on the greens—which iron, how to putt against the wind, do a quick cheat. When bullied enough, he would recite Urdu verse with a blush to the cheeks. Irresistible, those cheeks must have been because the Lala now reached out to pinch one.

'Chhokra!' a European called out to Kirti from the other side of The Great Divide. The voice boomed like a cannon.

'Who's that Englishman?' the Seth asked.

Ernst wanted to know where to begin.

'Someone I know, Sethji.' He didn't mention he also knew the man's wife, Daisy.

The Englishman was Willie Lansdowne, Ex-Club Secretary from when Indians were still not allowed in. You know, before enough was enough. After rounds of Government prodding and very little fanfare, an Indian replaced Willie as the club's secretary, as if Willie didn't dislike them enough already.

'Chhokra!' Willie yelled again, the pitch higher. Kirti jumped, the Lala stiffened, and a cloud of methane-tinged ammonia floated over unseen to smack the club in the face. Fertilisers wasn't visible from the greens but everyone knew who farted. The ammonia was sharp and tore into eyes.

'Useless buggers,' Willie said, using the back of a hairy hand like a towel. 'Bloody chimps at the controls.'

Meanwhile, the caddie-boy was finding it hard to disengage, the Lala refusing to let go his shoulder. This was death by embarrassment for Kirti the Poet—much in demand by the Indian golfers who jostled over him. He of course preferred caddying for Europeans, though one would think Willie would be the exception.

That's because Willie made it loud and clear he didn't suffer Indians easily. Frankly, he expected them to know their place. Adam Sassoon once declared he knew exactly how Willie would die. At a traffic signal, he predicted, with Willie in the middle of the road, a mottled red hand outstretched as he taught careening Indian truck drivers to obey traffic lights. Willie didn't take offense. Sassoon, after all. If Sassoon were to suggest a quick shag behind the bushes, Willie would consider it.

The Lala's hand on his shoulder over here, and Willie hollering for him from over there, young Kirti flushed from too much attention. Seeing Ernst sitting with the Seth, there was sudden hope in his eyes. Do something, they appealed.

'Chhokra!' Willie called out, pointing to his watch. Kirti struggled to escape and Ernst waited for the Lala to lose it. Kirti managed to free himself and panting delicately, he tore off. The Lala watched in dismay. Willie appeared satisfied, clueless what he had wrought in the Lala's bosom and pleased having his way; or from not allowing a darkie to have his.

The Seth sat next to Ernst like a Buddha and impervious through all this nonsense. That is, if you missed the shadow track across the buttery face. If the change to his disposition slipped by you. It didn't, and a chill blew down Ernst's spine. He so preferred open anger. Together they watched Willie strut off. Willie the little boy, somewhat a bully, and a little dense. Little Willie, playing with fire.

Ernst did his namastes and got up. The further from the Seth, the warmer he would feel.

~

Watching the action from across The Great Divide, Adam Sassoon sipped his scotch and smiled. He looked rested with Jehangir Merchant by his side. Then Sassoon's one eyebrow rose. Ernst saw the Lala making long strides his way, turban fluttering in the breeze. To those on Sassoon's side of The Great Divide, Lala Prem was from another planet.

'Mr. Ernestji,' the Lala said, looking towards Willie and Kirti disappearing on the greens. 'Your friend…'

'Let it go, Lala. The man's an ass.'

'If you say so, Mr. Ernestji. Only for you.' The Lala surveyed Ernst the way he'd looked at Kirti moments ago. You'll do instead, he seemed to say. Lala Prem was a friendly chap, always trying to get friendlier. They chatted. Ernst said this. The Lala spoke of that. It went on. Indians dislike straight talk. It insults a very complicated culture. After a while they appeared ready to converge.

'What happened?' the Lala asked. 'Sethji was surprised when he learnt you sold off his Cold Pilger. It was collateral, you know. Now Sethji has nothing. He is not happy.'

Over there though, the Seth looked happy enough. And over here if the Lala got any happier, it would involve sex. He squeezed Ernst's hand. 'Not to worry, Mr. Ernestji. You're one of us. What's collateral between friends?'

That settled, the Lala broached the lack of collateral. Painful, he would be first to admit, for Ernst to now pay principal and interest for a Cold Pilger not there anymore. He made googly eyes. Ernst looked vulnerable. The Lala squeezed Ernst's hands. Ernst let him. The Lala mulled. Ernst waited. The Lala brightened.

'Fuck the collateral. Just pay off the instalments as agreed. Monthly ten thousand. Happy? See? No more misunderstanding.' Ernst continued looking misunderstood. The Lala rose to the occasion. 'Tell you what. I will also help you pay back your own loan. This one time.' Ernst looked hopeful. The Lala looked encouraged. 'We will send our cheque to you. You then send your cheque to me.' It was time-honoured. The lender making out a new loan—usury deducted in advance—for the borrower to pay off the earlier loan. It kept things current and the Earth continued to rotate. Granted very Indian, and therefore sounding more complicated than it was. Ernst continued to look confused. The Lala capitulated. 'I know you have mouths to feed. How about if we include something extra for your payroll in the new loan?' Ernst smiled in gratitude. The Lala acknowledged it by squeezing Ernst's hand once more. Possession re-established, he continued to hold hands with Ernst; their fingers intertwined Indian style, while the Western half of the verandah watched.

With Sassoon and the Seth smiling back from their respective sides of The Great Divide, it was like discovering he could leave Germany before shit hit the fan and marry Berlin Ingrid at the same time. He remembered being euphoric then; nothing like what he felt now, smiling and going through the motions while carrying an ache God knows from what—all those memories Sassoon raked up, too much Seth, too much Lala, too much good news, or the cork up his arse.

Ernst wanted to ask the Lala what had changed since he sold the Cold Pilger without permission—meaning, why happy all of a sudden—when he saw Jack Hanson of Chemerica slumped alone on a rattan sofa behind Sassoon. With all heads up Sassoon's ass over here, and burrowing up the Seth's backside over there, no one noticed Hanson back from Sion Hospital. Hanson's shirt was soiled and there was a half-empty Coca Cola bottle in his hand. It looked like he had spilt the Coke on his chest. If you checked carefully though, it was the same shirt he wore that morning cradling Arjun, and that was blood caked on it, not Coca Cola.

Seeing Hanson's bloodied shirt, Ernst realised the unease he harboured, that ache within him, was from having to see the blood drain from a kid with almond eyes and porcelain skin. Arjun, the easily influenced Marxist who died a thief and no idea what he stole. Except maybe, Salim Ali knew. But he wasn't saying. Leaving Ernst aching to know why the kid would have to die such a miserable death. That ache inside him was just that, and had nothing to do with anything else.

11

The Gorilla

The English screwed us, so we screwed English.
—*Khushwant Singh*

Stepping into the club courtyard where members parked their vehicles, Ernst saw Murli Chowkidar freeze in salute.

Murli Chowkidar had been watchman since before the British. Ernst returned the greeting and only then it dawned that wasn't his arse being kissed. The terrified watchman was salaaming a trespassing Indian couple coming out of the greens and walking past a big, black Impala, renowned across Bombay streets as Sethji's ride. The man too was big and black like the Impala. He had a red handkerchief around his neck and it appeared to have left an indelible mark on the frozen chowkidar. Chhote Bhai on the other hand, looked bored as ever. He also looked through Ernst, who felt he might as well get used to this.

It was dark and no street lighting to help out after the abrupt sunset. Just Jhama Sweetmeats' blazing neon shining from across the road. It splashed the club courtyard to strike a parked Enfield Bullet on its handlebars.

A beauty of sorts crept into the night and a feeble moon looked down at India waiting outside the Golf Club's white picket fence. Chhote Bhai stopped, and stared at the parked Enfield. The gorilla from Fertilisers hovered next to the motorcycle. He peered at Chhote Bhai. He was in civvies instead of the blue overalls from Fertilisers and trying hard to read Chhote Bhai's face carved from granite.

The scene could be straight out of the Ramayana—Hanuman, the Monkey God cowering before Rama. Except for one thing. Rama cannot be black—a dark-skinned God impossible for this nation of dark-skinned people. Even Krishna, the original coal-black deity, was acceptable only when painted in blue.

When the gorilla spoke, the trademark rumble was a bleat. 'Nothing yet,' he replied, to whatever it was Chhote Bhai hadn't asked. In response, Chhote Bhai walked right past, causing some confusion. Then electricity sparked between his close-set eyes. He backed off to go sit on Murli Chowkidar's stool, leaving the Enfield bereft without his bulk. The motorcycle looked incomplete. Ignoring the gorilla to once again look past Ernst and through Murli Chowkidar, Chhote Bhai left the woman accompanying him to cover her face with one corner of the sari and turn away—how they do in the presence of strangers.

The Sindhi Refugee Camp girl had been in maroon earlier but this sari was emerald green, so maybe it wasn't her. On the other hand, though the face may be covered, there was no mistaking that backside. He almost felt its heft. Tufts of grass clinging to it, as she shimmied past to catch up with Chhote Bhai, leaving a trail of jasmine and sweat. Ernst felt his heart sink at how he could turn invisible just like that. If he couldn't evoke anything even in a refugee girl from Sindhi Refugee Camp, then who was left? The fat Beatrice Taylor? The sagging Daisy Lansdowne?

Jhama Sweetmeat's neon caught the fear on Murli Chowkidar's face as he rushed past the couple to go struggle with the big rusted hasp and open the gates. Not to be outdone, Mohan Driver held the one-eyed Fiat's rear door open for Ernst, who felt suicidal this beautiful evening, and so he strolled over instead to admire the gorilla's Enfield Bullet basking in neon light.

~

'Nineteen Fifty-Six make,' Ernst said, running his hand over the chrome finish.

The gorilla remained in the shadows, seated on Murli Chowkidar's stool by the Golf Club's brooding banyan.

'Cent per cent British import,' he said from over there.

'You've put a lot of work into this.'

The gorilla straightened and flexed, before strolling up to his bike. Seeing him coming up, Ernst remembered him offering to break Salim Ali's leg, then clawing at the throat and struggling for air after Ernst's tentative karate chop. He felt pretty confident he couldn't pull that off again.

The gorilla however was offering his hand. 'Hello,' he said. See? No hard feelings.

'My name is Henry Gomes.' Not just no hard feeling, but also personable.

'Goan?' Ernst asked.

'Yes, Sir. My grandfather was hundred per cent Portuguese blood.'

Ernst didn't know why Goans even bothered. Any Brit or German racially inimical towards Indians would feel no different towards the Portuguese.

'I'm Ernst Steiger. Sorry about this morning. But you were going after my friend.'

'That's okay. But Sethji's also your friend.' His expression suggested that meant something. He went on to ask, 'So why do you like Muslims?'

'Not all of them.' Not all Hindus and Goans either, or Christians and Jews, but this wasn't the time. 'By the way, very unfortunate, that boy Arjun's death. How do you think it happened?'

'What did you expect? Your friend's a communist. And a Muslim? Come on! You know wherever such people go, there's bound to be trouble. Take it from me. Guaranteed. Ask anyone. When China attacks us, they applaud. When America helps us, they protest. Besides, they stole something.'

'Who's they?'

'These communists. Who else?'

'What did they steal?'

'What does it matter? They stole. Just return it. Tell your Muslim. He probably has it.'

Ernst decided to probe further. He could always run hide behind Sethji.

'Is that why the boy was killed?'

'No need to tangent like that. He was pure accident.'

'He was stabbed. So can't be an accident, what?'

'Maybe. But if someone wanted to kill him, why stab his leg? You see what I mean?'

'I see what you mean,' Ernst said, walking towards the Fiat.

He waved getting in, and saw blood crusted underneath his fingernails. He didn't recall touching Arjun. Having said that, it was amazing how much blood a human body held and how easily it leaked and spread. Arjun's had spurted like a fountain from his thigh. Watching him die, Ernst thought he saw fear creeping into the kid's almond eyes from behind those soda glasses, but when he looked again, it was gone and there was nothing. 'Say something!' Salim Ali had screamed, snatching his friend from the Texan's lap and trying to shake him alive. There had been this look on Salim Ali's face of a person dealing with irrevocable change. He kept yelling, 'Say something! Can you hear me? Nod your head!'

Looking back, Arjun was already gone by then. Gomes, on the other hand, was vigorously polishing the handlebar with a yellow cloth when Mohan Driver crawled past towards the gates—held open with imperial panache by Murli Chowkidar. Ernst touched Mohan Driver's shoulder and rolled down his window. Gomes kept polishing the handlebars, focused on an invisible spot that refused to go. He spat on it and went back to work with loving care. It was interesting, how he could spit and polish and shake his head; do this and that and all the other things that Arjun couldn't anymore.

'Take same good care of yourself,' Ernst advised. 'Someone may have seen you with those curved scissors.'

Gomes stopped with the circular motion and looked up. He wasn't smiling anymore. Those beady, gorilla eyes went into a prolonged stare.

'By the way, that was Chhote Bhai,' Ernst said. 'Just now with the girl? How do you know him?'

Gomes was back to polishing the handlebar. 'You are Sethji's friend,' he said, and could be reminding himself. Possibly why Ernst was still in one piece.

'You had those pointy scissors when the accident happened,' Ernst said, going for broke Salim Ali style. 'Where are they now?'

Gomes got a dreamy look as if trying to remember. Then the invisible spot must have moved to Ernst's face the way he peered at him, scrunching his eyes and trying to find it.

'Good to have medical knowledge' Ernst said. 'You know where his femoral artery was. Very impressive.'

Gomes' lengthy stare continued to hold ground before he pulled his smile back out of nowhere. It was a nice smile with even teeth. Looking at them, Ernst regretted he didn't offer a dental plan. Salim Ali's mouth could use some work. His breath was murder. Then, Gomes lunged and thrust an arm through the window. Ernst flinched, expecting him to finally, at long last, go for his neck.

Instead, Gomes grinned and shook Ernst's hand once again. 'Tell your mian,' he said, squeezing Ernst's hand with gorilla strength. 'We want it back.'

12

Chai for Two

Women have half the brains of a man. It's a fact.
—*A.C. Bhaktivedanta Swami Prabhupada, founder of ISKON*

If Parvatibai took Bhairavi to be a working girl, she had cause.

'You are away all day,' she said. 'Any idea how many times people going up there, ring our bell by mistake?'

'The girls too? Or just customers?' Ernst asked.

'What do you mean? Really! If you must know, yes. What a question. Ever so often some new whore forgets her floor and shows up here. Why not move to a more respectable building?'

Ernst was on the fourth floor at the mildewed Karim Court, with a whorehouse one floor up at penthouse level—traditionally the landlord's residence. Given that most of his tenants were protected under rent control, only the whorehouse made Karim Court worth his while. The landlord was Khoja Muslim, a community with close ties to Gujaratis, Hindus, Parsis, and money. Aga Khan, the world's grandest bon viviant, was the Khoja's spiritual leader. Islam therefore took a back seat to commerce and a very liberal social intercourse. The Khoja Muslims couldn't decide what they were, and that was just as well.

'Who is she?' Parvatibai wanted to know.

'Oh her. No one. Works over at Fertilisers,' Ernst said. 'I had her come to help with the books and filing. Part-time. Our Munshiji is useless, I tell you. Doesn't know what's inside his own ledgers.'

Parvatibai looked him up and down, making it clear she knew him inside out.

'Also, she can help me with my Hindi.'

'Your Hindi's good enough for a gora.'

'She needs the extra income. We should help her. If we don't, who will?'

Parvatibai pointed upwards to suggest where the girl could go for extra income. 'At least she'll be paid hard cash.' She sounded envious.

It got tiring, standing at the door like that. Parvatibai however, would barricade the dark mahogany doorway as a matter of course. Even Ernst didn't warrant a free pass. A minor inquisition was mandatory before permitted inside. Today though, he felt decidedly unwelcome.

'I don't like all this.' Parvatibai was emphatic. When upset, she lapsed into Marathi from the pidgin the two had fallen into over the decades. Parvatibai knew her place when Ernst brought home Willie's wife those couple of times. Shameless sex between white people; there was nothing one could do about that. This though, this was unacceptable. Nevertheless, Ernst managed to squeeze past the hostile frame, trying his best to avoid those breasts. They were everywhere. He squirmed internally. It was like accidentally feeling up one's sister.

'She's waiting for you in the drawing room.'

The Maharaj was busy with a mutton curry in the kitchen over his battered, but imported, 1939 Magic Chef from Bombay Ingrid's halcyon days. His underage assistant squatted on the floor pulling on a beedi. In India, servants have servants. The employer being near broke, neither here nor there. The Maharaj leered on seeing Ernst. The mundu shoved the lit beedi into his khaki shorts.

'Phuddu,' Ernst said. 'Snuff it out first. Want to burn the building down with you?'

'She comes in, and straightaway wants to use the toilet,' Parvatibai said from behind. Ernst hurried down the corridor. 'Later I had to stop her touching the Menorah with her toilet hands. Why don't you display your shameless Tantric books instead? No one would touch those.'

'Don't bet on it. She makes powder mandalas on her porch.'

'What did you say?'

'Good with accounts. I said, she's good with accounts.'

The doorbell rang causing Parvatibai to brake and do a hard reverse. She left the household jangling in her wake.

'Have you seen her teeth?' she asked, reaching for the door. She may have said, 'Idiot,' too, but he wasn't sure.

In the living room and stretching up to the Menorah on the mantelpiece, the girl didn't notice him come in. Her foot nudged against one of Salim Ali's cold-rolled pipe samples on the floor. Now the damn things were everywhere. She pushed the pipe aside, her toe-ring grating against the red oxide floor tiles and she continued inspecting the Menorah with her toilet hands.

Today's sari was white, with a thick green border and tucked around the waist. The starched fabric fluffed out and her dark feet peeked from beneath the billowing cotton as she stood on crimson toes. For no reason at all, he swore to never fuck a Daisy Lansdowne again.

Seeing Ernst, she backed away from the mantelpiece, stepped on Salim Ali's pipe, stumbled as it rolled, then slipped, lost her balance, and fell against him. This was how Parvatibai found them when she walked in.

~

The girl had moved away, recklessly ignored Parvatibai and disengaging, deigned a curt namaste to Ernst. Falling into his arms, her body had felt hard. She had thrust apart on contact. He imagined her thrusting back instead. It left him irritated.

'What is it for anyway?' the girl asked, pointing to the Menorah. 'Candles?'

They sat across each other.

'Shouldn't we look at the ledgers? Your meter's running.'

She allowed the banter to fall flat and he got another whiff of her from where he sat. He found it impossible to put aside the visual of Chhote Bhai thrusting at her on the greens. There was this urge to confront. Was that really you? Did both of you go for it on the grass? There was grass sticking to the back of her sari as she had shimmied past that evening, so he must have been on top.

She had ignored him outside the Administrative Building, and she had ignored him emerging from the greens with Chhote Bhai. Seeing her sit on the sofa with legs pressed together underneath the sari, he found it got to him. What was it? Because with teeth like that and the receding chin, there was nothing there but youth. Is that all it took?

Knees together under the fluffed sari and with a purse at her feet, the girl studied her surroundings and wasn't impressed. He cleared his throat. Not looking at her helped clear his head.

'Parvatibai. Chai please. For two.'

'I need to ask you something.' Her starched cotton sari spread out on the sofa. She adjusted herself and a dark dot of a navel peeked through the folds of white fabric. Except for the dent it made, the veiled, brown stomach was a washboard.

When Parvatibai came in with the tea, she gave them both the look, then crouched to place the tray on the coffee table and didn't bother serving. Hefting her load with amazing grace she walked away, her mountainous arse cheeks grinding against each other through the Marathi-style, nine-yard sari. Usually times like this, conversation stopped and people would observe in silence.

~

I'm done with this, he thought, and said, 'The ledgers are in the dining room.'

'What are you going to do about Arjun?'

No doubt he had heard her correctly. He however refused to believe it.

'What am I doing about Arjun?'

'Yes. What are you doing about him dying like that?'

'What should I do about it?'

'Something.'

'Who says?'

'Salim Ali.'

As she got talking, Ernst learnt more about himself. Apparently, he could do anything. After all, he built the workshop from scratch and with phoren machines no one else had—probably the Cold Pilger is what she meant, in which case he didn't have it either. She went on to say that he did things other bosses wouldn't; she knew he sat with the workers over lunch.

'Salim Ali told you that?'

'He says you fought for the workers at Sassoons. He said that's why you lost your job.'

He says this, and he said that; it went on for a bit. Someone listening would mistakenly conclude Salim Ali held him in awe or something.

'Still, what makes you think I can do anything about Arjun's death?'

'I heard how you took panga with Henry Gomes at Fertilisers. Really, what were you thinking? Going for his throat like that. No wonder Salim Ali says you can do anything you want.'

'My father used to say anyone can do anything they want. Like Salim Ali, he was wrong.'

Her emphatic cheekbones made a triangle with the jaw and there was that grand sweep of her forehead; the extent of any resemblance with her mother—that Sindhi-white lady with the pail on the porch, holding on to a jhadoo and a vacant smile. The girl also resembled someone else he knew but her buck teeth came in the way. He couldn't put a finger to it. If she was self-conscious about her teeth, it didn't show.

'Are you going to do something, or what?'

The same day Arjun's killed, you go for a roll on the grass with a big, black man. And now you want something done about his death?

'Did Salim Ali talk you into this?'

'Of course not. He does mention you all the time though. Ernest this, Ernest that. When Beatrice Madam asked me to come here, I thought why not? Maybe you really are what Salim Ali claims. Maybe you can do something about Arjun. The police won't.' He saw her face harden. 'What? You think I came here for the money?'

'Of course not.'

Whatever the reason, at least she had come for him.

'I'm not going to see your money anyway,' she said. 'Beatrice Madam will keep it. I just came for Arjun. You need to do something.'

~

The evening was winding down by the time she pointed to the framed pictures in the photo corner.

'Who's that?'

The Kashmiri salver in silver on wooden legs was busy with Berlin memorabilia. It made his past deceptively presentable. Even so, he hadn't looked that way for a while. A long while. He preferred keeping a safe distance.

There was his mother with her chubby cheeks—Betty, the Aryan. His father, cheerfully chubby all around—Siegfried, the Jew. There was another worn-out photograph of the two of them together with him—their little, mixed-breed mischlinge.

He looked at his mother smile. You couldn't see the mole on her shoulder that had, just around then, taken on a life of its own. He remembered her shiny curls and how they dulled as the cancer took hold. The yellowish-brown picture, however, showed nothing of that sort and her chubby cheeks remained intact in the foxed photograph on the silver tray with its legs in walnut wood.

The girl however, wasn't pointing to his mother. As always, Berlin Ingrid stole the show. This time, from the picture with the silver frame; standing next to him on their wedding day: 10th April 1935. Nazi Brownshirts had thrown stones at the wedding party that day. He remembered protecting her from the shards as the synagogue's stained glass Tree of Life shattered about them.

Next to the wedding photograph was another one of Bombay Ingrid with the memsahibs on the Golf Club verandah. Bombay Ingrid looking into the camera and the memsahibs looking daggers. Then, the one of Bombay Ingrid with him and the Morris 8. Right next to that of Bombay Ingrid standing in front of the "Zaankert" at Sassoon Docks when it was time for bye-byes. He remembered she couldn't wait to turn around and walk up the gangplank.

Bhairavi rephrased.

'Who is she?'

He looked at his wife humouring him one last time as he had struggled with his Leica at Sassoon Docks for that one last picture.

'My wife,' he said.

'That one,' she said, pointing to what could be anywhere at the back of the clutter. 'With the children on her lap.'

Which one exactly? Oh yes, that, as if he didn't know. A svelte outline in platinum-white hair, marble skin, calves to die for, seated on a bench, two little children on her lap. And the barbed wire in the background, somewhat out of focus. It was difficult for anyone, and more so for the brilliantly blonde Ingrid, to believe she was a Jew.

'Same. It's my wife, Ingrid.'

'She's beautiful. Why is she wearing a uniform?'

Why indeed.

Parvatibai came by to interrupt the show & tell. She stretched across the doorway like the world's most successful goalie, an arse-cheek touching each side. Impregnable. 'Phone,' she said, fully articulating the 'ph' sound Marathi-style.

'Phor you,' she said to Ernst, looking directly at the Sindhi Refugee Camp girl, with those buck teeth.

13

Salim Ali versus the Rest of Us

Because we have a 90% literacy rate.
—*E.M.S. Namboodiripad, CPM leader, on why Kerala is communist*

He found Salim Ali squatting in the corridor, gaunt and with something eating him from within. He looked like a Mallu Sisyphus after the boulder had rolled downhill again. Parvatibai squatted opposite the troubled hero. The two just sat there, sipping chai and didn't bother standing. Parvatibai had her elbow resting on a gunny bag with wires spilling out. It looked like the one he'd seen at Salim Ali's place. He wished he hadn't seen it. She raised her arm to nudge Salim Ali.

'Unbelievable,' is how Salim Ali came at him. 'Less than half your bleddy age. To top it all, she's my friend.'

'I wouldn't need her help with accounts if you lot submitted your expenses properly.'

Salim Ali looked incredulous, then curled his lip to go full-sneer. Ernst wanted to sneer back. 'I see now why she would broadcast communist nonsense for you over the intercom. The question remains, why would you make her?'

'I told you, she didn't do it for me.'

'She did it for Arjun. So what? You could've stopped her risking her job.'

'It was to announce our intent. To let them know they will all pay.'

Ernst looked at the gunny bag with Fertilisers' green swastika logo and those wires sticking out. He pointed to it.

'More likely we will all pay.'

'And by that you mean?'

'Just because I'm too scared to add two plus two, doesn't mean you hide that in my home. Get it out of here.'

'It doesn't concern you.'

'Precisely. Get it out of here. Or tell me what's going on.'

Then there was this other matter. You've been saying nice things about me. He let that one go. Like the sulphur burner at Fertilisers, Salim Ali functioned best when fired up.

'Unbelievable,' Salim Ali repeated himself, as Ernst squeezed past to the telephone.

It was Sassoon's Major Punjabi. Ernst could hear him harangue a minor Punjabi from his sales team. He waited for the Major to revert.

'Mr. Ernest?'

'Hello Major. All well?'

'Of course, my dear. We go from strength to strength.'

'How is Sassoonji?'

'Sassoonji needs me,' the Major said, speaking as if not to Ernst, but a larger audience of minor Punjabis.

The last time Major Punjabi didn't speak to him was in Venky Iyer's office—the man as confused as Ernst at the turn of events. He seemed to have recovered his equanimity and the martial confidence was back; China beware. Without Sassoon around however, the Major's accent had regressed. He struggled past his Punjabi, to state, 'You draw stainless steel pipes.'

Ernst confirmed that was what he did.

'You have Cold Pilger, I'm told.'

'Yes, of course. Why?'

'Good question. Sassoonji wants a large order moved to you. God knows why, but boss is boss, what?'

Compared to banias like the Seth, reading a Punjabi was a breeze. Yet today Ernst didn't know what to make of this. Major Punjabi did.

'Be grateful.'

Ernst was. Truly. 'What grade stainless steel, Major, and what are the pipes for?'

'Why? So you can bypass us? We will supply you the design specs. No need to worry about what for.'

There was a pause and Ernst wanted to do a Sassoon and point out: Preposition! Instead he said how impressed he was with the Major's astuteness, also that really, there was nothing to worry about.

He worried, said the Major, because that was his job. 'It's large, the requirement. Almost three truckloads. So please note that's why the Cold Pilger. But you're German, so you know. Also, the inner diameter has to be thin. Not more than thirty-one millimetre.'

Rolling mill technology was almost exclusively German. Be that as it may, the fact remained Ernst did not have the Cold Pilger anymore. He did have two Ludhiana cold rolling benches, and they were perfectly fine for making lawn furniture. It was known far and wide that Salim Ali could get his unionised labour to work miracles on the crude, cold rolling benches. Given the size of this order though, even he couldn't make a Ludhiana machine do a Cold Pilger. The Major once again reminded Ernst he wanted thin, not thick.

Thin!

'Got it, Major. We'll need an advance of course.'

'If it's a must. But only because these are strict delivery dates. Best you deliver at your earliest convenience.'

'Of course. Anything else I can do for you?'

'Yes.' Major Punjabi kept silent until the tension threatened to snap the telephone line. Sassoon was a good teacher.

'Your Muslim communist. The Mian.'

Ernst took a deep breath and released it in a silent, meditative expunge.

'Sassoonji intervened to help you last week against my better judgement. Against my advice and caution. Now he also wants to give you this order. What's your problem?'

Hearing the Major being a Punjabi prick, Ernst travelled back in time to before he turned invisible. He was the one on Sassoon's flank in the original scheme of things, not this man. Having said that, would he too have stood to attention like Major Punjabi every time the great man farted? Probably not. But he did want all of everything else that came with standing erect at the sound of a Sassooni fart. In which case, Salim Ali had suggested on learning what happened back then, maybe he should've remained a corporate turd instead of wandering over to the worker's side.

'Maybe that's why you're so anti-workers these days,' was Salim Ali's prognosis. 'Because of what happened to you. You blame us.'

Sure. That's why I sold the Cold Pilger to pay for salaries.

Those were pitched battles at Sassoons, Ernst had to admit, admiring his own fervour from back in the day—the General Manager and a German to boot, taking up on behalf of the workers. It confused the hell out of everyone on both sides and there was palpable relief on Sassoon's face the day two Tommies showed up at the office—23rd October 1939—with the official gazetted announcement on enemy aliens.

I turned invisible that morning, Ernst would say about the day the Tommies took him away. He came out from confinement after the war, only to get fired. It still hurt and his heart still sank. Just like that heartbeat to the mole on his face, the hurt made no sense after all these years. Yet, there it was.

'I must ask again. What is your problem?'

'No problem, Major. Why do you ask?'

'Because I'm ex-army. I know operations. How do you plan to deliver on time when your mian spends all day being communist?'

'Not to worry. Trade union activity is only permitted outside of working hours.'

'Why allowed at all? Don't you have a business to run? And what about your good name?'

Actually, a good question. Did he have a business to run? Between his playing with that girl in the living room, and Salim Ali playing Lenin, one would never know.

'Did you know, Mr. Ernest, the 9th Punjab was my regiment?'

One didn't know that either.

'I was by then retired of course. Regardless, they fought the Chinese to the last man and the last bullet.'

There was a moment of silence.

'Now you understand? I don't like these communist kind of rascals. They should be thrown to the wolves. Besides, the man's a thief. Do something.'

As if something could be done. Ernst eyed Salim Ali spewing Marxist crap all over Parvatibai in fluent Marathi. Arm thrown over the Fertilisers gunny bag, a radicalised Parvatibai gave Ernst the look, as if all his fault. Caught up in a quick fantasy about throwing Salim Ali to the wolves, he didn't pay proper attention to Major Punjabi's exhortations. The Major began sounding mellower for reasons Ernst must have missed.

'I know you won't bugger with the status quo, Mr. Ernestji. I'll send over the advance. People like you and me hold this nation together. We don't encourage thievery. Just ask the mian to return what he stole. To not be such a Muslim.'

The bit about buggering the status quo; and earlier, don't you have a business to run? It was like talking to a Sassoon gone Punjabi. Ernst's sphincter clamped tight around a non-existent cork.

'By the way, what did he steal?'

'American valuables. Right from their enclosure. What is the meaning of this, I ask? They are our guests.'

'Salim Ali went into their enclosure and stole valuables? Why don't they arrest him?'

'Haven't you heard of the worldwide communist conspiracy? It's worldwide. He doesn't have to do anything himself, per se. He got it done. They are everywhere.'

'I'll bear that in mind, Major.'

'I have to go,' the Major said. 'Busy, as you know. What to do? Remember, thirty-one millimetre, otherwise we will reject the lot.'

In that case, best to be nice to the mian.

'Get rid of him,' the Major advised Ernst before hanging up.

Edging through the corridor, he resisted letting Salim Ali know he was pissing off powerful people left and right. It would only make his day. There was however the other matter the Major raised— rampant trade union activity and very likely accessory to theft. Such goings-on were out of line.

Salim Ali agreed. 'You should fire me,' he suggested.

They stared at each other, Parvatibai joining forces with Salim Ali to ensure a rout. Ernst felt a camaraderie with the 9th Punjab. It was difficult to manage a Salim Ali behaving like this. He squirmed. He was never constipated like this before the mole on his face developed a heartbeat.

'We need Punjabi on our side, if we want more orders.' It was the best he could offer.

'Why for?' Salim Ali asked. 'You have Sassoon.'

~

'How long have you known Salim Ali?'

'Since school.'

She paused to reach back. 'The boys played cricket after class. We girls would come to watch even though Salim Ali ignored us. The other boys all copied him. All, except Arjun. He would happily play with us girls when not playing cricket. This one day, we were standing outfield and a boy pointed straight at me and said loudly, "Cover that face and fuck the base".'

She had his complete attention.

'Salim Ali was about to bowl to Arjun. He was famous for his leg spin.' She smiled as she narrated. Total pride in someone who had ignored her, their whole childhood.

That day, Salim Ali delivered a full-toss that was so amateur, it was beneath his dignity. She was behind the wicketkeeper with the other girls. The ball rose high, coming in to Arjun and giving him all the time needed to hook and smash it straight into that boy's head—the one who had pointed at her and shouted, 'Cover the face and fuck the base!' The boy needed twenty-one stitches after that and the next day his father beat up Arjun very badly.

'Salim Ali went back to ignoring me, and I went back to following them like a puppy dog,' she said, grinning like a bunny rabbit.

She was sublime in her innocence, and with an openness found in children, sometimes in women, never in men. Her eyes were on fire, as she recalled Salim Ali's deliberate full toss to Arjun for him to smash the boy's skull. Or maybe she was getting off on that boy needing stitches, or maybe Arjun taking the beating for her. Ernst didn't enquire. He did remember Arjun calmly shaking his head— NO—and being clobbered by a hockey ball for that. It took a fatal stab to the femoral artery for him to show any panic.

'He was tough,' Ernst said, 'your Arjun.'

'He was the gentlest soul on earth. Out of place here, like his Uncle. Stray dogs in a mad city.'

'You loved him.'

'What's there not to love? He had a huge feminine side. That's why I still can't get over his hitting that boy like that.'

'He did it for you,' Ernst said, just to see her eyes light up again.

'Arjun loved cricket, but I know he would rather sit with my brother and me all day drawing rangolis.'

'That wasn't a rangoli, what you drew,' Ernst said. 'It was a powder mandala.'

'No one should know,' she said. 'No one should know.'

'Your mother does.'

'A mother's duty is to protect. Other people don't like our Tantra. They call it evil. But Arjun was from there,' she said, pointing to the east. 'There, they are more real. He taught my brother and me. Became our Tantaji and showed us the path. How did you know it was a powder mandala?'

He thought of his teacher, the gardener's Sahajiya wife at Purandhar. 'I found my Tantaji on a desert island.'

'He was Sahajiya at heart,' she said. 'Arjun. The perfect mix of male and female.' Looking somewhere into the distance while wiping her eyes, she recited from the Mahabharata. 'Prince Arjun was the third brother to enter the king's palace. His hair was long and braided, and he walked with the gait of a broad-hipped woman. His feminine attire attenuated his masculine glory, and at the same time, it did not.'

Her Prince Arjun, her champion. Smashing the skull of a bully who insulted her. Calmly taking a beating from the bully's father. Shaking his head in the face of a Chhote Bhai.

No.

Every time Chhote Bhai asked for the gunny bag, there was that shake of the head.

No.

Refusing to return whatever it was he stole, then dying for it. So much for the feminine side. Or maybe because of the feminine side.

Anyway, Arjun was how a Sindhi girl from Western India learnt about the Eastern Sahajiyas and their Tantric ways. Now he understood why she did that powder mandala on her porch every morning. Why her eyes were red the day Arjun died. She had been crying, like Salim Ali.

On the other hand, if Arjun was her Tantaji and best friend, what was she doing rolling on the grass with Chhote Bhai that very day they killed him?

~

'Your books are a mess,' she said. 'Just like you, Beatrice Madam says. She thinks you need to settle down, get married. To her.'

They sat across box files containing invoices and pink-voucher slips, next to ledgers with good-luck swastikas dancing across their red-cloth binding. Anxiety would build up facing financial paraphernalia, putting his insides into turmoil. Funny thing, he knew his books of account were beyond help and so was his business. The only reason he had her come, was because she ignored him that day at Fertilisers. The only reason she came, was Arjun.

Ernst reached to touch the mole on his face. It throbbed in response. Sitting with her at the dining table, the mole didn't bother as much as his financial past—towering in a pile the size of a migraine. Their legs touched, and he was surprised she didn't retract. Moving through the ledgers with professional ease, she allowed pressure build against his calf. He throbbed like his mole and a fearful thrill took over, throwing him into such a swivet that he remained an idiot for a full minute before taking his leg back; all the time trying to concentrate on her jottings.

Moving away, there was a flash of anger. Was that intentional? Teasing an older man? A bloody game, was it? A few deep breaths and he let it go, squinting at her ink squiggles spelling doom in double entry. She appeared more surprised at the mess he was in, than anything to do with him removing his leg.

'Should I have Munshiji explain the entries?'

'No need,' she said. 'Just tell him to do as I say.'

Salim Ali came in just about then or Ernst would have asked her about Chhote Bhai. Also, by the way, what did she think of older men?

Walking into the living room, Salim Ali worked at keeping it casual and when she smiled at him, it was the same one she had thrown past Ernst at Chhote Bhai.

'I didn't see you after that day,' she complained. 'The Mian Building swallowed you, or what?'

Salim Ali wasn't being himself and didn't say a thing. He appeared tamed. When Parvatibai came by to look daggers, for once he ignored her. Parvatibai then banished herself to the photo corner and kept dusting Bombay Ingrid's framed photograph—the one with Bombay Ingrid in front of Ernst's Morris 8 the day she went bye-bye.

~

Parvatibai had stood aside when Ernst took that photograph with his Leica some twenty-six years ago. She had remained to one side, crying into the corner of her sari while a younger, robust Mohan Driver loaded Bombay Ingrid's luggage into the Morris 8. Later when he drove them to Sassoon Docks, Ernst had sat next to Bombay Ingrid and tried holding on to her hand. Surrounded this evening with tenacious folk refusing to let their dead friend depart gracefully, Ernst felt inadequate at how easily he had let go when she pulled away.

Parvatibai didn't ever bring it up, but she couldn't understand why Bombay Ingrid would leave, then go disappear on them like that. As if Germany went swallowed her. Technically, you could say it was the Jüdische Krankenhaus that gulped her down. Berlin's Jewish Hospital swallowing its Jews, refusing to give them up. Except for his father who was an exception to every rule.

'What are we doing about Arjun?' Salim Ali asked. "We", not "you". He had a future as a diplomat.

'What do you want me to do?'

The girl stepped up. 'Salim Ali says it was no accident. Help us find who did it.'

But I know who did it, he wanted to say, and probably why. Although God knows how killing the kid helps recover what he stole. I can't tell you anything anyway, because your Salim Ali will go nuts, and then before you know it, there goes what's left of my life.

His mole shot out a distress flare searing his insides, and he asked himself whether it was time to put an end to this. At least ask what's in that damned gunny bag. One's entitled to know.

'Where were you that evening, the day Arjun died?'

She eyed him. 'I was a mess. Beatrice Madam excused me and I went home. Why?'

Now was the time to tell her why. Set her straight with: Maybe because I saw you walk out from the greens that evening with Chhote Bhai. Maybe because there was grass sticking to your arse. And then to Salim Ali: Are you aware Chhote Bhai knows the gorilla who stabbed Arjun in the thigh? Also, by the way, your landlord's fucking your Bhairavi.

'Do something,' Bhairavi demanded, looking at Ernst, both legs crossed on the sofa beneath the sari and the toes peeking out to taunt him.

He pointed at his watch. The 6-Limited bus service to Chembur stopped twenty minutes ago. 'Tell you what I can do. I can drop you both home.'

'You can do anything you want,' she said. 'You're European. Besides, you have a lucky mole.' It throbbed again when she said that, and he reached up to rub it.

They filed down the corridor past a Parvatibai using both hands to protect the Fertilisers gunny bag with all those wires sticking out. Try me, she seemed to say, thereby proving Bhairavi wrong. Clearly, there were some things he couldn't do.

14

Radioactive Showers

Total body exposure of 400 roentgens/rad (or 4 Gy) causes radiation
sickness and death in half of the individuals who are exposed.
Without medical treatment, nearly everyone who receives
more than this amount of radiation will die
within 30 days.
—*American Accreditation Healthcare Commission*

Colaba to Chembur takes you from Bombay to Mumbai—one world
to another—with Sion, a purgatory of sorts, where you wait while
traffic decides.

The rear seat was a war zone where Salim Ali's body odour
slugged it out with her jasmine sweat and Ernst's sensibilities. She
was pressed against her end, and Salim Ali lodged in-between. Mohan
Driver broke wind from the front seat suffocating Ernst further. He
stuck his head out of the open window. She did the same from her
side and seeing her looking out, he wanted to reach across Salim
Ali, take her hand and not let go—make up for abandoning Berlin
Ingrid at Sassoon Docks twenty-six years ago.

Sion Hospital was ahead, to their left. Also all over the news,
with its evolution into a teaching hospital; offering sixty MBBS
seats to six thousand applicants, twenty per cent reserved for
lower castes and minorities. He pictured Salim Ali in a white
coat and stethoscope, walking the corridors and knocking patients
unconscious with his body odour.

Ernst knew Dr. Waller, the Dean at Sion Medical. Technically, de-facto Dean. A placeholder, until they sorted out who got the job; yet Dean enough to be dangerous. Bombay's Europeans went to Breach Candy Hospital on Napean Sea Road. Ernst came to Sion Medical College. Waller had been a good doctor once. He was now a Pethidine addict. He was also free.

It was bright outside with the moon hovering close to the horizon. It lit up the city and rendered the feeble street lighting moot. The Fiat didn't need its one eye tonight. The girl looked up out of the window at the big apple-pie of a moon. Her expression probably stopped Salim Ali from curling his upper lip to ask what was the big deal.

Awash in moonlight, one could see Sion Hospital's spanking new outpatient building already crumbling. It stood in front of the functional remains of an older, ex-Army hospital—a rectangle of barracks facing Sion-Trombay Road. The outpatient building's brittle, whitewashed concrete glowed a bluish-white, and a single queue snaked into the entrance. The ginormous moon etched out each crease on every face in line. Ghatis came together here with Madrasis, and Muslim mingled with Hindu, all of them queued since afternoon. In their own localities, they would peer across at each other with hostility or alarm, whereas here they waited patiently together to take it up the arse.

'Uncle!' she exclaimed, leaning further out the window. 'Uncle!'

It was Tufan, standing out from the queue. The way she called him, all that affection in her voice, it was special. Maybe because of way back when Tufan's dead nephew had batted for her, cracked that other boy's skull, giving him a twenty-one stitch salute and taken a beating for it. Or could be because Prince Arjun with his huge feminine side had been her Tantric teacher, her Tantaji.

Salim Ali went, 'What the bleedy hell? He should be in bed.'

Why, Ernst wondered, because Tsering Tufan was lit up as if on stage. He reminded Ernst of Macheath—in the school's version of *The Threepenny Opera* his homosexual English teacher had them perform. A year later, the Nazis banned Brecht for being a communist agitator and killed the homosexual teacher for being himself. Young Ernst had sung 'Mack The Knife' from the wings.

Denn die einen sind im Dunkeln,
Und die andern sind im Licht,
Und man siehet die im Lichte,
Die im Dunkeln sieht man nicht.

There are some, who are in darkness,
And the others are in light,
And you see the ones in brightness,
Those in darkness, drop from sight.

A smile broke across Tufan's blistered face, sweeping away the darkness more than any moon could. The smile lit up Sion. The queue of sorrow snaking into Sion Hospital returned the smile as if it couldn't help itself. Mohan Driver braked without requiring a tap to the shoulder. Ernst studied the bald tribal with his blistered skull and those weeping sores, standing there all lit up and looking an alien in his own country. There was a quality to him: a Mercedes Benz among one-eyed Fiats.

'Arjun's body is in there,' Salim Ali said.

Ernst reached through the body odour and placed an arm around his engineer. Tufan came up to put his head in the open car window and when up close and smiling like that, he didn't look tired at all.

~

Jumping out from the backseat, the Sindhi Camp girl clung to Tufan holding his arm. 'Uncle,' she said. He tried wriggling free of that hard body being thrust at him, then gave up.

'The police calls Arjun's death an accident,' Tsering Tufan started explaining from above her head. 'I say no, it's not, let's have an autopsy. But who listens?'

Salim Ali announced, 'They're all in cahoots, I tell you. Bhenchods.'

Confirming this was exactly how you piss them off, two havaldars at the OPD entrance stared back at Salim Ali, then Tufan, then Salim Ali again. Tufan smiled at them as the Buddha would. The havaldars parted, saluting to allow a khaki uniform through. That would probably be the sub-inspector in charge. There was one permanently stationed at Sion Hospital because of all the police cases coming here to die. The khaki uniform spotted Tufan and walked up. It was a Deputy Commissioner of Police.

The black, acrylic badge on the chest said, Vijay Jahagirdar. Solid, flat-out, Poona-Brahmin. Deputy Commissioner Vijay Jahagirdar was a lean man with standard moustache. He looked tired and clearly had dinner on his mind. He did not look the type though, who took shortcuts. He switched on his own beam in response to Tufan's blinding smile.

'Tufanji,' he said, smile to smile. 'Let's come to terms. What do you say? Sooner or later you have to accept your dear nephew's body, no?'

His name was at odds with the accent, for he spoke like a St. Stephen's boy from Delhi, conquering the Vs and Ws insurmountable to most Indians. And Germans. The acid test would come should he get worked up; something Ernst knew all about first-hand. But the Deputy Commissioner didn't appear an excitable man.

Taking Tufan aside and flanked by the two havaldars, the Deputy Commissioner went into a huddle. The way he cajoled, film star Madhubala would have agreed to anal sex. Going by the dead nephew's performance at Fertilisers that other day, Ernst put his money on the wilting Tufan. Moonlight glinted off the three-headed lion on the police officer's epaulet, or maybe it was Tufan's smile being reflected from the DCP's polished silver insignias. A Deputy Commissioner, where a sub-inspector would suffice. It stunk to high heaven like the bullet hole in the Sardar's head. Or those scissors, surgically applied to Arjun's thigh by a gorilla. Deputy Commissioner of Police, Vijay Jahagirdar, was just one more instance of overkill, and it gave one pause. There were certain things one could reasonably demand be explained. Then there was this. Walking up to them, Ernst knew he should be walking away.

'The dead boy really stole something from the Americans, Commissioner?' Ernst asked, in spite of himself. 'I mean, are we sure?'

The DCP looked at the white man, mulled a bit and conceded, 'Great question. Maybe you should ask your little friend over there. By the way, is he Muslim or a communist? How can one be both? Maybe we should take him in to find out.'

'Or find out why the Texan was crying over the dead boy if the boy stole from him. Something very valuable, I'm told. But what?'

'That big Texan fellow! Have you seen his cowboy hat? It's the real deal. Incredible.'

'True. Nothing like it. But what do you think about him trying to save the boy's life? I mean, strange, isn't it? That's if the boy really stole from him.'

'I know. Very strange. And here I always thought Texans like to shoot first! Love their movies. Wish we could carry six-shooters the way they do. But as you can see, a DCP doesn't normally wear a sidearm. Not fair. Why are only Americans allowed to be cowboys?' And DCP Jahagirdar pretended to quick-draw from a side holster and aimed his finger at Ernst, smiling and shooting three times, first at the head, then twice at the torso. Everyone laughed when he went bang, bang, bang, with Ernst clutching half-heartedly at his chest.

Ernst out of the way, the DCP transferred his smile to Tufan. He put his arm around Tufan's shoulders and whispered something in his ear. Tufan buckled, as if under the weight of that arm, but then took a deep breath and was all smiles again.

Ernst, however, remained distracted. This was India, and that was a senior police officer over there, wrapping his Brahmin arm around a low caste tribal's shoulders; a tribal with oozing blisters all over his face and head.

~

'You know,' Salim Ali said, observing his comrade withstand the Deputy Commissioner's attempt at accord, 'Until recently, Comrade Tufan had long, flowing hair. Like a silver mane. He wore it in a ponytail.'

It would suit Tufan, Ernst thought, the ponytail.

'What happened?'

'He started losing it in tufts since about a week.'

Ernst waited for more, but the storyline faltered because there was flint in the Deputy Commissioner's voice now, audible past the flanking havaldars. No more whispers. Looked like he wasn't getting his point across. One had to wonder if the senior police officer would succumb to doing a Chhote Bhai and slap Tufan around. Withered state notwithstanding, nothing about Tufan suggested it would work. Deputy Commissioner Vijay Jahagirdar however must have felt he could wait this one out. Like he could wait for dinner. His type would wait patiently on the riverbank for dead enemies to float by. The timbre in his voice may have gone up for the acid test, but his St. Stephen's accent remained steadfast. As did his manners.

'No worries, Tufanji. We have time. You do not. The body will decompose. Sion Hospital, after all. It doesn't have an inexhaustible supply of ice.'

Even the queued patients appeared impressed at his demeanour. The two havaldars stood to attention for their boss, Salim Ali wavered, Tufan smiled, and this time Ernst kept his mouth shut. The Deputy Commissioner had everyone's undivided attention, allowing Bhairavi to break free.

'You have time?' she asked.

Her eyes were burning coals and the Deputy Commissioner reacted with a start—trying to grapple with the toothy maelstrom staring up at him from out of nowhere. 'Time for what, Uncle? Why not use that time to do your job?'

The Deputy Commissioner peered at her. 'You're Chabildas' daughter from Sindhi Camp.' He looked confused. More so when she asked, voice rising unwisely, 'Who killed our Arjun, Uncle? You knew him. You watched him play cricket. Why would you let it happen?'

The Deputy Commissioner's response was to go quiet. Tufan tried pulling her away and Ernst had this sudden urge to call out, The gunny bag, that's why! And guess who has it now!

Then Salim Ali, the voice of reason, stayed her with a gesture. She quietened, but stood there begging for the Deputy Commissioner to visit something upon her. She was outclassed and Jahagirdar smiled instead, declining to pick a fight with someone who had nothing to lose. He wasn't a Deputy Commissioner for nothing.

'You want an autopsy?' he asked, turning to Tufan with a look that said, Enough. 'We'll give you an autopsy. Please be here tomorrow morning for the post mortem procedure. I'll call the Assistant Coroner myself.' He smiled to establish his western style,

St. Stephen's College credentials. 'At least then, Tufanji, will you agree to kindly accept the body?'

~

They waited for the Deputy Commissioner's jeep to leave. After all, he blinked first.

Later, Mohan Driver held open the Fiat's front passenger door for Tufan, but he declined. He planned to stay on a bit, maybe shine more light around with his smile. He thanked Bhairavi, calling her 'Our Joan of Arc!' She clasped him and would have remained that way forever with her head buried in his chest; wouldn't let go until he gently disengaged. Ernst felt he was in the presence of a Chinese-looking Mahatma.

'Do you still practise?' Tufan asked her.

'With a kitchen knife.' She pouted. 'Promise to lend me your sword when I perform again.'

'My sister taught these two rascals our tribal dance for their school annual day,' Tufan said. 'Salim Ali was a reluctant performer. Claimed his Kerala martial arts to be superior. But he would practise the sword dance anyway. Maybe because of her.'

His dark skin saved Salim Ali from turning pink. Turning his gaze towards Bhairavi, Tufan said, 'It's a good exercise, the sword dance. But don't do it on stage anymore. You'll scare the men away and we want you married.'

Hearing her peals, Ernst thought, the Ingrids never laughed like this. As for Tufan, he just smiled and smiled.

When Ernst looked back after Mohan Driver sped off towards Sion Circle, Tufan's smile had switched off. The gentle tribal's forlorn gaze tore into Sion Hospital, through the crumbling concrete and past the corridors of misery to seek out and caress his nephew lying in there, decomposing. Ernst didn't want to picture the location. Wherever it was, he hoped there was some ice.

'The gunny bag at my place?' Ernst asked. 'The DCP may sound friendly and all, but I know his type. He won't give up. Why not just return whatever's in it? Leave the damn gunny bag somewhere they can find it?'

'No.'

'Want to tell me what's in it?'

'No.'

Up ahead and holding a meaningless grace from another era, Sion Circle lay past Sion Hospital and a few more Sion-Trombay potholes. It stood stupefied with the turn of events since Independence, paint flaking off its colonnades in surrender, and looking on as more and more cars, trucks, and buses twirled around in it. Even this late at night, it appeared confused. Not ill but not well. It reminded Ernst of Tufan. 'That you're involved in something shady doesn't surprise me,' he said, 'But where does Tufan fit in?'

'You saw him. What do you think?'

'I think he looks ready to drop dead.'

'Oh,' Salim Ali said. 'How did you know? I was telling you about his hair.'

~

Some two weeks ago, Tsering Tufan was passing by the CIRUS nuclear reactor at Bhabha's AEET where he works, when a fountain gushed up from the lawns. That whole area is a labyrinth of underground pipes, some carrying seawater for cooling the nuclear core inside CIRUS and others discharging from the reactor. A pipe had burst. It was a hot day, so the Lambadi women working on the lawns ran to douse themselves under the high-pressure leak.

'Seeing them do that, Comrade Tufan started yelling, stopped the bus, and got out to shoo the women away. They thought he was crazy. No one had protective gear and no dosimeter badges. There was nothing to see or smell, and therefore nothing to worry about. He got them out of the fountain with some difficulty, but he stayed on taking soil samples and getting soaked to the bone in the process.'

Ernst didn't want Salim Ali to continue.

'When the test results returned,' Salim Ali said, 'the water he had stood in showed up to forty Becquerel per millilitre. The soil tests were equally conclusive. Anyone under that radioactive shower received the equivalent of fifty chest X-rays in under thirty minutes.

Within the week, Comrade Tufan started showing symptoms from exposure to radiation.'

Anyway, when Tufan returned to the radioactive lawns the following day, there was no Lambadi labour and no signs of any pipe bursting, or anything like that. As if nothing had happened. That's what AEET maintained—nothing had happened. The Lambadi gypsies being casual labour, there were no employment or union records, no addresses, nothing. They didn't exist. But Comrade Tufan did, so the AEET Brahmins hit the panic button.

'I mean, total panic. Tufan said all they wanted to know was, how many roentgens. How many did he absorb? More than 400? Meant they were all fucked because he'd have to be quarantined. Meant, something happened. Meant the radioactive water leakage was official; heads would roll.

'You can imagine their relief learning he only absorbed around 200 roentgens. Sure, he'd probably still die, but slowly. No need to quarantine. Their jobs were safe.

'Comrade Tufan didn't care either way. His only worry were the tribals who had the radioactive shower. If the management took immediate action, those women could be traced, provided medical attention and saved. The AEET Brahmins gave him blank looks. With no one listening, he approached God.'

According to Salim Ali, Dr. Homi Bhabha, Mastermind, Father of the Indian Atom, and a deity to so many Indians, heard Tufan out. He assured him they would locate the Lambadi, knowing full well he couldn't. The gypsy women had vanished into thin air. Dr. Bhabha however, did set up a formal reactor safety committee. Their recommendations were published worldwide.

'And adopted by the AEET?'

'Of course not. But the achievement was recognised in all the newspapers. Bhabha's committee also undertook a complete audit of the incident as a learning lesson—to be read and put into practice. However, the audit report was deemed secret under the Official Secrets Act and sealed to ensure no one reads it.' Ernst hadn't seen Salim Ali look this miserable in a while. Like one of his Terylene shirts; just when you were confident it couldn't look any worse, it surprised you.

'Unlike the Lambadi, Comrade Tufan is a permanent employee and entitled to full medical treatment. It's become quite the quandary. If he is treated, it means something did go wrong that day. So he has to sign over his integrity in return. Put in writing that nothing had happened. They are still waiting for him to sign. He maintains if nothing had happened, how can he be sick? Sick or not, his hair keeps falling out in tufts. No one knows what the fuck to say and what the fuck to do, so no one does anything.'

Salim Ali then said Tufan's sister—the dead Arjun's mother—was taking care of Tufan. Or at least she tried. 'Have you met her? You should. She can take any amount of crap, and it would never show. The strong and silent type.'

There was silence in the car, then Mohan Driver farted. Bhairavi covered her nose with the hem of her sari.

'You said he looks ready to drop dead,' Salim Ali said. 'He is.'

The girl Bhairavi shifted her slim frame, and Ernst's heart lurched like the one-eyed Fiat when she reached across him to hold Salim Ali's hand.

15

Sindhi Refugee Camp

I won't deny Iqbal,
He gave me the Tarana-e-Hind.
He did love his mullahs though,
And took away my Sind.
—*Translated from the Urdu, by Kirti the Poet*

White people can't simply walk into Sindhi Camp. It creates wrinkles in the fabric and gets Mumbai into Bombay's face. So why even venture in there this time of the night? Mohan Driver posited, chooth ki pukaar was why; still thinking, after all these years, that Ernst didn't understand the crap he muttered in Hindi.

It was late and Jhama Sweetmeat's neon lighting was done for the day. The darkness enveloped Salim Ali, but Ernst shone like a white beacon. He had a fidgety Mohan Driver park the Fiat in the Golf Club compound and wait. Mohan Driver looked miserable seeing his employer make a fool of himself over a chawl girl. If Ernst wanted desi phudi this bad, just order home delivery from the whorehouse upstairs and be done with it. Even Foras Road whores were better than subjecting everyone to this.

Seeing the bile on Mohan Driver's face, a man in white dhoti walking by barefoot quickened his pace. The dhoti was knotted Marathi-style and he carried a lota in one hand. He looked like an E.M. Forster Brahmin carrying Ganga jal to sprinkle after ablutions.

The man held up an open umbrella to complete the picture. Ernst caught himself checking the skies.

Golf Club's Murli Chowkidar stood to attention and still not fully at grips with the situation. Until five minutes ago, he was crouched asleep on his stool, belt unbuckled and one hand comfortably cupping his crotch. The car's single headlight sent him stumbling for the gates holding up his trousers with one hand. His martial mask fell on seeing her dark face in the rear seat with Ernst. It was back in place now and so were the trousers, fly still open. He stared straight ahead, ears on the alert.

'Thank you,' she said to Ernst, 'but I can walk home from here. It's my neighbourhood.'

'I'll come along. It's not too far.'

'Okay,' she said and smiled with those teeth. It was irritating how the whole place lit up. 'You can meet my father. You both must be the same age.'

Ernst stepped out from the gates and on to Trombay Road, his mind lingering on that unnecessary comment. Salim Ali followed, accompanied by a dirty look. A white man walking into a refugee camp with an unmarried Indian girl as if nothing to it. She was already across the road, eyeing the gully next to Jhama Sweetmeats.

Salim Ali came up to remind him that the twenty-eighth was Salary Day, as if Ernst needed the reminder. 'My salary can wait,' Salim Ali said. 'It's the workers. There's a famine brewing the other side of the Ghats. They have to send money back home.'

Salary Days were touch and go, but the Seth's cheque would be there to support him this time; the Seth's Lala had squeezed Ernst's hand and promised it would be fine.

So Ernst said, 'Should be fine.'

Way past Sindhi Camp's dinner time, its refugee population was fast asleep and jhopadpatti slum dwellers feeling safe to encroach. They were India's toe fungus—the lowest in any pecking order, be it class or caste. The reason why Sindhi Camp refugees, however destitute themselves, understandably didn't want slum dwellers around. On the prowl for their evening meal, the jhopadpatti crowd spread through Sindhi Camp with singular purpose. From where the jhopadpatti garlanded Sindhi Camp, cow dung smoke rose into the air waiting for the ones foraging for food. Some of them chased a kid goat across the road and the legless beggar-on-wheels kept berating or encouraging them, one couldn't be sure. A slum boy rummaged through the garbage heap outside the Krishna Temple and the distaste on Bhairavi's face grew on behalf of Sindhi Camp. The look fortified her and made her the superior person. The road was unlit and no vehicles around, except for a Tata Mercedes truck turning the corner from Vashigaon Road.

Taking the turn like Jagannath, the truck came hurtling towards them. It rattled loud enough to wake the dead but Ernst was preoccupied. What with her comment on his age, and then Salim Ali with his Salary Day bulletin, conjuring scenes around the famine brewing behind the Western Ghats, and of people dying next to bags of indigestible American wheat. Then there was the dead Arjun, the dying Tufan—all at the same time as if the Furies from his school textbooks had decided to go real on him. He almost didn't notice the truck going for Salim Ali. When he did, it was clear what was about to happen, and also there was this loud bleating sound.

Seeing the Tata come at him, Salim Ali had pirouetted but didn't fall, not until Ernst tackled him from the side, going for his legs in a manner unseemly for someone his age. The tackle had them both drop into fresh cow dung, desperately grabbing each other as if going at it. The truck braked to a halt, mulled a bit, and a handlebar moustache appeared from the driver's side to see a white man and an Indian lying in cow dung holding each other. The man also saw Sindhi Camp Bhairavi, Murli Chowkidar and Mohan Driver rush over while slum dwellers gathered in what looked like the makings of a lynch mob. Bystanders routinely turned into one in Bombay, even over minor accidents. So rule of thumb when you hit, run. TATA OK BYE BYE said the truck's fleeing bumper, as does the rear bumper of every Tata-Mercedes truck across India.

The goat being chased earlier now lay on the road behind the disappearing truck, with Bhairavi on her knees next to it. For a moment there, Ernst thought she too was hit, but then saw her lift the kid goat's head to her lap. There was blood on the animal's white coat and Bhairavi looked stricken. Being Sindhi, she probably had mutton that week, but this was different. She stroked its head even though the kid goat was too far gone. Its eyes went opaque with a placid acceptance and there was none of that fleeting panic Ernst had witnessed in Arjun's eyes. Lying there in cow dung holding Salim Ali, it dawned on him, Hinduism was all about what a goat already knew.

Bhairavi put the kid goat's head down with a finality of sorts and was getting up, when something on wheels broke from the slum dwellers. Coming up at the speed of sound, the beggar-on-wheels snatched the kid goat and careened down the road towards the jhopadpatti slums. They heard him whoop, as he sped away with the dripping animal bobbing on his broad shoulders and leaving a trail of blood.

~

The girl, Mohan Driver, and Salim Ali, watched Ernst get to his feet, all self-conscious from the cow dung on his shoes, shirt and everywhere.

'Sorry about that,' he said to Salim Ali who just kept staring at him while he tried dusting off the man's Terylene shirt caked with everything India could throw at it. They watched him pause and rub his own shoulders. No one uttered a word; they just looked at each other.

'The way you tackled me. Learnt that in prison too?' Salim Ali finally asked.

Bhairavi went with, 'Are you all right?' He eyed the perfection of her silhouette in the dark while she lingered over his state of affairs. 'Have the driver walk you back to your car,' she said.

Mohan Driver was in no state. Ernst preferred the simmering fart he'd known for almost thirty years to this befuddled version. It got his goat. So did Salim Ali, now all of a sudden tacked to his sleeve and going on and on in a thick Mallu accent that made his instruction incomprehensible. Ernst tried to shake him off and cross the damn road, but the little Mallu was a pit bull that wouldn't let go. At the same time, he was a Chihuahua shying away from a Hindu refugee camp. Marxist to the core, Salim Ali's survival instincts were all Muslim.

'Go home,' Ernst said. 'I'll be fine.' Releasing Ernst's sleeve, a reluctant Salim Ali looked relieved.

On his part, Ernst felt light-headed crossing Trombay Road with the Furies playing a bongo on his shoulder. When he got woozy and stumbled on the other side, she surprised him by reaching out to grip his elbow with raw, male strength. Her hands were wet and bloody but he was used to blood by now, and she appeared to have no problem with him dripping cow dung that anyway, is more fuel than shit—ask any Indian. They squeezed through the gully, working past a day's worth of very slippery, Jhama garbage. She held him in a vice-like grip, insisting he take deep breaths. He found traction on garbage strewn around like organic confetti and they moved forward one step in filth at a time. She let go his elbow when they surfaced for air on the other side. A stroll through Sindhi Camp can change a white man forever.

Two lanes deep inside Sindhi Camp, an open umbrella aimed at them from the nullah that ran along her family's half of a Nissen hut. The umbrella jiggled a bit and then stood up to collapse with dignity, revealing the dhoti-clad E.M. Forster character scurrying past Mohan Driver's glare earlier that evening. The man's left hand was wet from scrubbing his arse with water from the lota. Caught shitting wet-handed in the enemy camp, the slum dweller sought to stare it out, his excrement lying coiled in the nullah. Ernst saw Bhairavi's eyes blaze back in the dark. She barked some complicated abuse in Marathi that he felt needed checking out with Parvatibai. Having just taken on a Deputy Commissioner of Police, she was back to busting balls and this time she kept at it with no one to stop her—a machine-gun peppering the shitter with invective.

The machine-gun then swivelled to aim at Ernst.

'You know how people die in refugee camps?'

Staring down the barrel, Ernst concluded there could be no correct answer.

'Do you?' she challenged again.

A big man—whiter than he—saved him just in time by emerging from the front door. He showed signs of a rude awakening and held on to a red notebook for support.

'Shame,' the girl's father said. 'They die of shame.'

16

Mauripur Road

Aayaa Mir, Bhaga Pir.

A wrapped body lay asleep inside just by the door. The dishevelled space next to it—where the father was before his daughter's spectacular vernacular brought him rushing out. There was torn notepaper around the empty space creating waves on the bed sheet. Ernst saw numbers crawl up and down the strewn notepapers' lined surface in neat rows going nowhere.

'My son,' her father said, and Ernst wondered if the swaddled son too was her colour, or Sindhi-white like his parents. The sleeping form appeared afloat on the sea of crumpled notepaper. The numbers looked familiar. Mohan Driver spent his spare time on them too, when not visiting whores on Foras Road. Clearly, Matka—Bombay's very own number game—had her old man by the balls.

She explained Ernst to her father, then the cow dung, and the blood. He took off on Sikh truck drivers. Ernst corrected him. The driver was Maratha with a handlebar moustache, straight out of Kolhapur. Her father appeared leery. Ghati at the wheel? Strange he said, because Marathas didn't drive trucks—Sikhs did—whereas, apparently, nothing strange about a white man covered in shit walking around in a refugee camp with his daughter.

A bucket inside the doorway collected water dripping in from a wet patch on the ceiling. 'No monsoon as yet, still…' the man looked at the bucket with an un-Sindhi resignation. It was embarrassing because one expected more of a challenge from so much bulk. If this big, defeated, Sindhi-white man was her father, any genes they shared were lying low and it wasn't just about the colour.

Ernst laughed.

'You should've seen the leak in my roof.'

'Your roof leaks?' He looked at the European.

'At Purandhar Fort. They interned Germans there during the war. Water would pour on my bunk from the roof when it rained. I asked if they could do something to stop the leak. I was told, "When the monsoon stops, the leak will stop."'

'Of course,' her father said. 'Very Indian.'

'They were British.'

All this while, the front door's left open, and the body on the floor sleeping through the chatter. Homes in Sindhi Camp and across chawls across Bombay came standard with the same furniture he saw inside: folding chairs, the charpoy laden with bedding, two pummelled sofas with frayed doilies, a green Godrej cupboard in the other room. Then the kitchen area, where the Bushane cylinder and gas stove held pride of place. Spotless utensils lined the flaking walls that didn't give a damn. An equally spotless floor called it quits, not too far from the open, shit-ridden nullah outside bubbling with raw sewage. An inch of cement across the threshold would usually keep the two domains apart. In this case, a raised porch delivered that extra separation and status.

While dismal when looking down from Salim Ali's balcony, at this angle the front room came into its own. There was a walnut-veneered HMV radiogram on display and a Guru Nanak portrait on the wall. Sindhi Hindus revered just this first of the ten Sikh Gurus. Enough for many Sindhis to have one son keep unshorn hair like a Sikh. The radiogram indicated a past frame of mind upbeat enough to make such a reckless purchase. 'We'll beat this,' it seemed to say. Guru Nanak, his open palm blessing the room, seemed to agree.

The two men sat on a listing string cot with the moonlight casting long shadows. The father appeared to relax.

He was Chabildas, he said. Chabildas Lalwani. 'Would you like to wash up?' he asked.

Ernst declined. It was fine. He had to leave soon anyway. Go home; take a proper shower. He looked at her father and smiled. He can't be my age.

~

Indians believe in churails, who are witches, only worse. Hot nights like these, a breeze would whistle in from the west and people who knew it was the sea granting pre-monsoon favours, would anyway blame this one, specific churail for fucking with them from the haunted house. That Bhoot Bangla, somewhere deep in the jhopadpatti slums cupping Sindhi Camp at its far end.

'It's that churail again,' the father said as a matter of fact, the breeze stirring his white mane. Bhairavi went indoors to wash the goat blood off and make chai. They heard her pump up the pressure in the primus stove, Bushane gas being strictly reserved for special occasions. Her mother was nowhere around, and the body on the floor slept on undisturbed. It would probably take an atom bomb to wake him. Or, the stove exploding as it did every other day on the third or fourth page of the *Times of India*.

'How did you get to Bombay, Dada?' Ernst asked, maybe the first time a European had addressed the man with the correct honorific for a Sindhi patriarch. He looked at Ernst, as if for the first time.

'It took one evening. Aayaa Mir, Bhaga Pir.'

Ernst leaned in.

'When Muslims come, wise men run. We ran, so now we are refugees.

'Me too.'

'It's not the same. I know your history. Your Government killed Yehudis and the Germans remained silent. Over here, Muslims killed Hindus while the Government remained silent.'

Ernst nodded his head Indian-style, ceding superiority to the one-sided version of the Partition and never mind the Muslims massacred. Someone should warn the man though. We Jews don't like sharing victim status.

'You lost everything?' he asked Ernst.

'Yes. You?'

'Everything. Even my charpoy. But now I have this one.' He bounced a bit on the knotted jute and Ernst bounced every time the larger frame descended. Bhairavi emerged with two steaming glasses for the bouncing men.

'You have her.'

'Her? I have a son.'

If she heard, it didn't show. He stopped bouncing.

'Ours was the only haveli, in fact, the only pukka structure in Mauripur Village. Fifteen miles out from Karachi. All the surrounding land was mine. When the British built their air force base in Mauripur, they had to buy the land from me.'

She was behind Ernst now, changed into a salwaar kameez to look like a schoolgirl handing him his chai. Her fingers were dark against his and wet from making tea. Touching them, he thought of Chhote Bhai's black on her brown and paused again to take in all that glistening, dark flesh sweating all over each other on the Golf Club greens. Chabildas stepped in. Her father, after all, even though moments ago he owned up to only a son. 'Millions fled, leaving their homes behind,' Chabildas said. 'We were just one of many. Be that as it may, the world will never forget the day I left Pakistan.'

Ernst leaned in once more.

'Eleventh September, Nineteen Forty-Eight. The Father of Pakistan, their Quaid-e-Azam, Mohammed Ali Jinnah, died the same day.'

Chabildas basked in happy thoughts.

'So much stuff... I hired a truck to carry our household goods to the Kiamari Docks in Karachi. We were booked on the P&O boat to Hong Kong where my business partners were waiting. We couldn't wait to get there. Start anew.

'My Alsatians were upset that day. It killed me to leave them behind. They snarled at the Pathan truck driver and his cleaner-boy, forcing them back into the truck. The truck driver was dark for a Pathan.' Bhairavi came to collect their empty glasses. 'Her colour,' he said. 'I should have heeded the dogs. Now I see his face every time I look at her. My wife was climbing the walls inside. She asked me how I could trust two Muslims. But they looked harmless enough, that truck driver and his little cleaner-boy.'

Chabildas produced a pencil out of thin air to flick against the red notebook in his hand.

'Bit late in the day, being Nineteen Forty Eight and already a year since Partition, but by August we were finally ready to leave Pakistan. I had everything, most of my money, the dowry my wife brought, everything I'd adorned her with, everything reduced to so many diamonds in four little pouches lying on my bed.

'There was rioting and the Karachi Pogrom in full swing since February that year. Hindus were being robbed and killed and all the while we're thinking it can't happen to us. Then Hindus start paying mobs to shoot them, instead of slitting their throats in accordance with the Koran. Time to go. We left home dressed like Muslims. My wife wore a burkha and held a Koran wrapped in green cloth. Other than the Pathan driver and his cleaner-boy, no Muslim could have known we were Hindus. The Pathan's truck went in front and we followed in the family car. A Packard Clipper. Ten thousand dollars. Those days.'

Chabildas coughed. He turned to ask her for some water, leaving Ernst with a one-eyed Fiat stuck in his craw.

The drive down Mauripur Road was relatively uneventful, even though dead bodies lay strewn around. Handcarts would come to carry away the corpses. Regardless, the Packard was making good time and the docks still forty minutes away. 'Then the bhenchod railway signal goes down on Lyari Bridge,' Chabildas said, stunning Ernst with the choice abuse out of nowhere.

Once on Karachi's Lyari Bridge, it appeared Chabildas had enough—with the story, with being the gracious patriarch, with Ernst, Pakistan, the whole damned world. His earlier bonhomie began losing air by the second. The family story stalled and sputtered to a halt behind the family's Packard, waiting at the railway crossing while a Mujahir mob gathered. They didn't look happy—Muslims who fled India to become refugees in their very own Islamic Republic. There was no sign of the truck carrying the family's stuff as the mob closed in. But the dark-skinned Pathan truck driver was there, leading the mob, pointing to the Packard, his cherubic little cleaner tugging at the Pathan's salwaar and jumping up and down in excitement.

~

'I'll take your leave now,' Chabildas said, struggling to get up. The girl took his elbow.

'What happened to the diamonds?'

'I put them in a hole carved with my knife in that Koran. Put the damn book to some use. At least the diamonds made it here.'

'Who didn't make it?'

Chabildas looked at him as if digesting something distasteful. Could be Teutonic persistence. The man didn't bother to reply and shrugging Bhairavi's hand away, he creaked up the porch. Once on top, he rallied. Straightening his back, Chabildas cast off a decade the way he dismissed his daughter's assistance. His tone changed as he spoke down to Ernst—the language gone coarse. That first bhenchod had set him free. He waved the red book like a Sindhi Mao.

'You want to know who didn't make it? Look around this refugee camp. See anyone who did?'

Chabildas lowered his little red book.

'Did you know Jinnah's airplane landed at the old RAF airbase behind my house when he flew into Karachi to die? The army ambulance went past our haveli with sirens blaring while we were getting ready to leave for Hong Kong.

'Then, we find the fucker's ambulance stalled at the Lyari Bridge railway crossing. That's why our car couldn't move even after the train had passed. We saw the ambulance back doors wide open for air. The Father of their bhenchod nation was inside on a stretcher, lying still. Two women beside him worked to keep the flies off their Quaid's face, mouth, eyes, lips, everywhere. One was an English nurse, using a piece of cardboard to fan the flies away.'

Chabildas peered at Ernst, as if to see if there were any flies around him. Bending forward, he grinned.

'Want to know the best part?' Adrenalin flared in those eyes and Ernst was now able to see Mauripur's zamindar clearly. The Mauripur landlord: owning so much of the surrounding acreage that the British had to come to him for their airbase. Chabildas finally looked the part.

'We saw the ambulance driver staring at a dry dipstick he had just pulled out from the petrol tank. The circumcised fucks put the Father of their nation in an ambulance without petrol! Mohammed Ali

Jinnah died in front of us and the rest of the bhenchod, sisterfucking refugees he and that fuck Gandhi went created.'

Chabildas was quiet, lost in staring Pakistan down.

'Mauripur Road,' he said. 'It ate Jinnah, then it ate me.'

And just like that, he went inside and to his bedding on the floor without bothering to shut the door. Knees creaked, knuckles cracked, and lying down next to his boy, Chabildas let out a healthy fart. Without so much as a fuck-off, he turned his back and vanished inside the thin bed sheet, leaving his unmarried daughter in the safe hands of a gora his own age.

~

'What just happened?' Ernst asked.

'His sugar gets the better of him late evenings. Besides, there's a certain protocol to the Partition. What happened, who got killed, who got raped, where's the need to ask? What happened, happened. There's nothing you can do about it.'

'Who got raped?'

'Salim Ali is right. You're the type who doesn't let go. That day in Karachi, things happened to my parents between Lyari Bridge and Chinna Creek. Dada was taking his wife to Hong Kong. Instead, they ended up here.' She looked at her sleeping father. 'He wanted his firstborn to be a son. After Mauripur Road, he had me instead. Not just the wrong sex, but wrong colour. Maybe he should've listened to my mother when she was climbing the walls that day, asking him not to trust the Pathan truck driver and his cleaner-boy. Now whenever he looks at me, he sees the dark-skinned Pathan truck driver. You know, I'd love to see my mother do that again—climb walls. She doesn't do wall-climbing anymore. She doesn't do much of anything anymore. Just smiles. All day, she just smiles.'

'What do you mean?'

'The Partition did strange things to its survivors. It did something to her on Mauripur Road, or maybe it was the Pathan truck driver and the Mujahir mob. Don't ask. Never ask what happened with her, or how I was born. Ask about my younger brother instead. The one conceived here. Born here, and pure. He, we can discuss.'

Maya—she who feeds our illusions—must have felt some pity for Ernst, because she went nudged Bhairavi's brother, who shifted in his sleep. He tossed around a bit, and the bed sheet fell off his face to reveal flowing hair and creamy-white skin. It partially covered his head like a sari, and the beauty of the boy was quite breathtaking.

'He is a poet,' Ernst said, nodding towards Kirti, the caddie-boy sleeping like a baby, and she didn't ask how he knew.

'What happened to the diamonds?' Ernst asked.

'Matka.'

Ernst saw the numbers around the sleeping boy, clambering over each other, trying to win back these four diamond pouches. She pointed towards the Mian Building, where a shadowy figure in granite stood watching from the second floor balcony next to Salim Ali's flat. Made sense. A slumlord would run all the gambling on his turf, not just cricket matches. Matka was the big one. Bombay's number game; played mainly by those who couldn't afford it.

'The diamonds. They paid for that building,' she said. 'And now I've to go run, do some chores.' With that, she walked off, leaving him standing on the mud path outside her home, just like her father did minutes ago. As she weaved in and out of the shadows, he wanted to shout and ask whether she was headed for the Mian Building. Really? You're going to him after what he did to your own father? And to Arjun?

He of course said fuck-all, but he did will her to stop. So she did, and turning her head sideways, brushed something off her shoulder before slipping into the shadow cast by the Mian Building.

17

ICE

To be rewarded, do some wrong.
—*The Business Mantra*

For cultural reasons the morgue was the furthest, most distant corner of the Sion Hospital complex. Brahmin doctors want nothing to do with dead bodies, and require the morgue to occupy the furthest, most distant corner in all hospitals. In this particular case it meant the desolate, semi-bunker type couple of rooms adjacent to where the general staff gathered for meals. Perfect. Brahmin doctors don't eat in hospital canteens. Their food came from home, untouched by human hands.

Two distinct queues crawled into the morgue-cum-canteen building. One was mainly family and relatives here to identify or collect a body, while the other made up of chattering hospital staff over an extended lunch break. There was no osmosis between the two. Lunchtime bonhomie and lifetime sorrow remained separated into two columns.

At a closer look though, things became more nuanced. The Friends & Family queue had pockets of gossiping Kohli fisherwomen with breasts bursting out of blouses, and nine-yard saris hitched high around thighs that could crack coconuts. The rest of Friends & Family remained lost in their grief, but with eyes fixated on those breasts, while maintaining the distance caste requires from Hindus. They shrank from the laughing fisherwomen, keeping a wide berth until arriving at the narrow entrance leading into Hades. There, they converged to mesh with all that smelly, lower caste, tits and arse.

Ernst stood with Salim Ali in Friends & Family. Tufan was a few vacant stares ahead of them. Over by the bosky compound wall, a man in white coat and stethoscope hunched over shrubbery running alongside the brickwork. There was a tremor to his surface from some heavy machinery rumbling inside, or could be something else. The stick he held quivered as if alive and he used it to poke at the shrubs and dead, brown leaves littered at his feet, rustling and scattering them with each thrust. Oblivious to the queue of sorrow and the fisherfolk titties on display, the man in white coat carried on with whatever he was doing; peering down at the leaves, then up into the compound's jamun and mango trees. Noticing a nervous Ernst all of a sudden also look around his feet, Salim Ali asked what the fuck was up.

'He's catching snakes.'

Seeing Ernst, the man in white coat yelped, rotated left on the balls of his feet as if in the army, and poked at the air while approaching. Ernst reached up to rub his mole.

'What you doing here, you bugger?'

Hearing him talk, people would automatically assume that de facto Dean, Dr. Dicky Waller was a half-baked dingo, an Anglo-Indian like Beatrice Taylor. They would be right.

~

'How come you didn't say you were friends with the Dean?' is what Salim Ali wanted to know. 'He could've stepped in, done something about Arjun's body. Why are we even in queue? Heights, I tell you.'

'De facto Dean. Not Dean. Besides, he's at the Medical College, not the hospital. Different setup. No one listens to him over here. Or there, for that matter.'

'How would you know? Did you try find out?'

Times like these, smile.

Salim Ali smiled back.

'Have you noticed how you always have a good reason to do nothing?'

However calm on the surface, a sanctimonious Mallu radiates heat. Ernst used his white man prerogative to push through the queue to Tsering Tufan's gentler aura up ahead. Also cooling in there were glowering comrades—out of place in this queue of sorrow. An oriental butterfly next to the gentle Tufan, even more so. The trade union shirts and kurtas were white like Ernst's, in deference to the impending Hindu cremation. Ernst thought maybe they all should've worn black instead; most North-East Frontier tribals were Christian converts.

It didn't matter, because the waning Tufan was in a defiant, communist-red kurta. Comrade Tufan, where it mattered. The oriental butterfly was also showing the finger to ritual standing there in her electric, copper-green silk blouse. Her sarong had broad horizontal stripes that defined tribal dress from Tibet and Bhutan, to Chiang Mai and beyond. The hair, cut and bobbed like Jacqueline Kennedy, was jet-black and seared white in broad streaks. As if something very hot had burnt paths across the top of her head. Yes, her hollow eye-sockets attested, those are third degree burns from one thing after another.

'We haven't been introduced,' the butterfly said, turning around to extend a hand. No namaste. 'I am Tobi Basar, Arjun's mother.' She could be in her twenties, if not for a dead son. A stubborn chin held that broad, ravaged face together. The strong and silent type. How had Salim Ali described her—something about being able to take any amount of crap and not show it.

'Tobi teaches at the Tata Institute of Social Sciences in Trombay,' Tufan said.

Tufan had mentioned earlier how she also taught Bhairavi and Salim Ali to sword dance. In happier times. He tried visualising the two women with swords and it wasn't difficult at all. Visualising Salim Ali dance was a different matter. Behind them, the little man looked at his HMT watch, then at the serpentine queue in front and shook his head. Ernst heard Dr. Waller rattle inside.

Comrade Tufan tried to put a positive spin to things. 'This shouldn't take too long. The Deputy Commissioner has given his go-ahead, remember?'

Not too reliable a weather forecast, because if you looked behind, Salim Ali was sniffing the air—a mouse sensing danger. The look on his face made you turn around, just in time to see a gorilla emerging from Hades.

No mistaking Henry Gomes: Once in Fertilisers blue and now in Sion Hospital khaki. The gorilla saw Salim Ali and squinted, then saw Ernst and brightened. A smiling Gomes brushed past Friends & Family, his gorilla gait pronounced as ever. The last time Ernst saw that smile was when he thought Gomes was going for his throat.

He considered making a dash for it.

~

'Mr. Ernest! Is everything in order?'

The concern was touching. A complete makeover from the murderous shift-worker, to a caring hospital employee. Ernst nodded, and found himself enveloped by the Goan's Christian compassion that went beyond him, to embrace Tsering Tufan, before dragging itself all over Tufan's sister while pausing over her breasts.

'Why for are you standing in line?' Gomes asked. 'Please do come with me. I understand Deputy Commissioner Sahib has given go-ahead to autopsy. That's good. Very good.'

'We must have the body released today without delay, for the last rites,' Salim Ali said, with the perfunctory authority vested in him by an engineering degree. Gomes glanced at the IIT man. He looked bemused such a species was allowed to roam free. 'You,' he said.

Then, 'I will be taking your good self straight to Assistant Coroner Sahib,' he offered Ernst.

'You work here too?' Ernst asked, while being ushered past the line-up of lost souls and fisherwomen titties. Gomes smiled back.

'Well, at least we now know where you get your medical knowledge,' Ernst said, then wondered why in the world poke a gorilla like that again.

Salim Ali also appeared puzzled. Gomes however, refused to stoop to that level. Smiling as if Ernst had enquired about his health, he pushed on ahead to clear a path through Friends & Family.

'What did you mean by that?' Salim Ali asked. 'What medical knowledge? Why? Why do I need to decipher everything you say?'

'Stick close to me,' Ernst advised, as Gomes looked back to smile at them. 'Very close.'

~

It was ancient inside, dilapidated, like the rest of the newly built hospital. The asbestos roof however confirmed the canteen-cum-morgue building was part of the older military hospital structure. Now eclipsed by tired-looking concrete blocks, put together recently for the new hospital and newer medical-schooling facility.

The subterranean bunker-type room was large, more than thirty feet square and very busy, as if all of Bombay decided to collect their dead that afternoon. Gomes brought the Tufan party in, past an uneasy queue coming down the concrete stairs with rusted iron rods sticking out at the edges waiting for a banister; some day, no rush. Once in the room, the queue rent apart with an urgency beyond mere racial prejudice, and it wasn't just the Kohli women's somewhat fishy smell.

And like the Lambadi gypsies, the Kohli fisherwomen couldn't care less. They weren't here to be admired, and surged in an explosion of female body parts towards a desk, where an elderly ward boy in khaki sat focused on the jiggling breasts. The neglected Friends & Family queue barely moved, registering none of the impatience shown by the fisher folk. From somewhere in his late sixties, the ward boy tried his best to manage the obstreperous fisherwomen. Not here to confront mortality as we all have to some day, the fisherwomen's bustle suggested they just wanted to get on with it. Two large wicker baskets sat by the wall—perfectly round, one on top of the other, blue jute ropes attached to allow for pulling. They were large—a person could sit in one. Silver fish scales glinted from here and there on the baskets, wet from holding ice long melted.

Gomes pointed at the wicker baskets. 'True public service. We allow them to keep their fish in the morgue's ice-room.'

From over at the school desk, Ernst heard the venerable ward boy instruct a fisherwoman on how to avail this public service. 'Five annas a kilo. Cash.'

Rising from behind the ward boy's school desk were four concrete slabs, six to seven feet long, each with a dead body, each body covered with a white bed sheet, except for one poor, naked bastard laid out on the second concrete block. On the floor around the slabs, shrouded bodies lay stacked—dragged out from cold storage to make space for fish. Someone had attempted at symmetry before going, bugger that, and piled the bodies on top of each other in woebegone heaps.

Behind the slabs, towards where Gomes pointed, was a bolted door with a thick dark-green sheen of lacquer as insulation. White streamers crept up from underneath to vapourise in the baking heat. The morgue's ice-room to store its dead; holding baskets of pomfret instead, while bodies piled up in the heat outside. Ernst gagged. The formaldehyde was there, yes, phenol too, providing a thin veneer to the stench only India can produce. Is why the Hindus discovered before science did: the sense of smell is the brain's only direct access to the outside world. Tobi Basar started to throw up. Salim Ali handed Ernst a lit Charminar, after having sucked on the roasted tobacco as if inhaling from an oxygen mask while the aeroplane goes down. Tufan supported his sister's forehead with his palm and she retched right there on to the floor until only dry heaves were left.

'I hate this country,' she said.

A semi-distinguished looking rake of a man in white coat and stethoscope leaned against the cool, green door, taking deep puffs. A police sub-inspector who wasn't Johnny Walker for a change, but who was fast asleep, had his chair tipped against the ice-room's wall—at minimum ten degrees cooler than the rest of the room. There were no microphones, recording, or photographic equipment around. On the other hand, no electricity either, or anywhere to wash and scrub up. A layer of dirt covered the floor, otherwise strewn with rags and burnt incense-sticks. Cobwebs swung from the ceiling.

Ernst remembered the one other time he visited a morgue: at the Jüdische Krankenhaus in Berlin over a school study trip. They had spotless stainless steel sinks, tape recorders for preserving commentary, and Leica cameras. In all fairness though, that's comparing Bombay in Nineteen Sixty-Four to Nineteen Thirty-Two Berlin. Ernst staggered over to the outer wall that reached just under six feet, and tried for air through an opening laced with chicken

wire. Looking out, you had a worm-eye view of the compound—
the two snaking queues, and the adjacent canteen from where the
wooden signage beckoned: RICE PLATE IS READY. If you leaned
further on tiptoes to try for more air, your feet touched something
decomposing against the wall.

Ernst leapt back with a yell and not just because he had stepped
on a limbless torso burst out of a length of saffron cloth binding it. A
blackened hipbone stuck out through a blanket of flies, while a small
but diligent rat worked on the body. Unevenly cooked, the torso had
bloat, recklessly bursting through its binding wherever it could in
swathes of fleshy dark blue. Its smell went with the colour scheme.
Ernst recognised the headless Sikh last seen at the sulphur burner.
The head with the bullet hole however, was no longer there to keep
it company. The rat having fled, he nudged the torso to straighten it
back to how it had been, and then a bit harder until somewhat aligned
with the wall below the chicken wire. A brass button lay where the
torso had slumped and Ernst picked it up. Ernst knew a Webley
.38 slug from his time with the Tommies at Purandhar Fort; even
one flattened somewhat after ricocheting inside a Sardar's rib cage,
and misshapen further from excessive heat. Sure, Exhibit A with
the bullet hole through its forehead was missing, but the .38 slug
suggested DCP Jahagirdar liked to go dhishoom more than once, as
the little shitter of an eyewitness had shown aiming at Salim Ali by
the sulphur burner. Jahagirdar himself had fired three times at Ernst
when playing cowboy with a cocked finger that evening outside Sion
Hospital—twice at Ernst's torso and one to the head. DCP Jahagirdar
wasn't just a thorough man. He was a creature of habit.

Ernst's yelp had succeeded in waking up the police sub-inspector.
The policeman nudged the man in white coat. All this while the
fisherwomen kept it moving, oiled with singular purpose; an army
of amazons collecting fish stored overnight and rushing it to the
Dadar and Crawford wholesale markets. Working alongside, khaki
ward boys carried shrouded bodies back inside the emptying ice-
room before they rotted any further.

A fisherwoman in a nine-yard sari came up to the septuagenarian
ward boy manning the desk. He presented a clipboard to her as if
it was the Constitution of India. They went into a huddle while the

ward boy pointed out this and that, pretending to guide her through the paperwork. She produced a wad of money out of nowhere and forked it over, saying something coarse in Marathi. The ward boy pocketed the bribe with finesse.

Ernst elbowed Salim Ali.

'See? That's how it's done. Learn something.'

Salim Ali saw the Government servant pocket money to illegally store fish in the Government morgue. He saw the dead bodies rotting in the heat. He saw Gomes keeping tally. There was so much anguish on his face that Tufan came up to hold him. Salim Ali burst into tears.

'It's okay,' Tsering Tufan said to his distraught comrade. 'It's okay. Arjun's at peace now.'

Ernst didn't have the heart to tell him that Salim Ali wasn't sobbing over Arjun. That he was crying over India.

18

Friends & Family

They bathe, then pray,
Put the chandan mark along with the cap,
And then they seat a whore on their lap.
—*Vijay Tendulkar's Ghashiram Kotwal*

The semi-distinguished white coat approached the naked body on the second concrete slab and stood there, looking bored and very Brahmin. Venky Iyer came to mind. A woman in a white sari materialised to join the white coat, along with a sweeper carrying a flat wooden box and a bucket of water. He laid the wooden box on the floor and opened it to reveal a clutter of surgical instruments. A ball of catgut rolled out to the floor.

'Assistant Coroner Sahib,' Gomes said. 'He's getting ready for post-mortem duties. Real, medical Sherlock Holmes, I tell you, no question.'

There was a hiccup in the room as it paused to pay respects, and then back to business. Gomes snapped off something in Marathi to the ward boy selling illegal cold storage space. The Assistant Coroner's team continued readying for the autopsy, unmindful of the commerce underway. The fisherwomen paid up one by one. They then proceeded to remove their fish baskets from the morgue's ice-room while the ward boys dragged back the rightful occupants, swaddled in white sheets.

~

The Assistant Coroner produced an empty Brylcreem jar, a packet of salt, a pair of rubber gloves and an elongated package of incense-sticks. He handed all that over to the woman in the white sari. She handed it all to the sweeper. He lit the incense-sticks and stuck them around the floor, mindful not to get in the way of the fish being removed from storage. A blast of chilled air came in their wake through the open, green door. Meanwhile, khaki ward boys lined the shrouded bodies on the floor, one by one. The burnt and bound Sardar by the wall—headless, limbless, and helpless—looked even more forlorn in the same room amidst these so much more dignified corpses, properly shrouded and with limbs and heads intact; their final sacrifice being to save baskets of fish from rotting. Ernst fingered the .38 slug in his pocket.

Friends & Family stood by, watching their dead line-up. Who belonged to whom? With no one bothered about them, there was ample time to read the writing on the wall—in English, Hindi and Marathi: OUR AIM IS TO EASE YOUR SUFFERING.

Handing over the gloves to the sweeper, Assistant Coroner Sahib was ready to commence with post-mortem duties. He ordered all lay personnel to leave. 'Only family and relatives of deceased allowed.' There was another hiccup around the room and a respectful pause, before everyone ignored him and went back to what they were doing. The sweeper had the rubber gloves on and made a wide sweep with his scalpel to where the Brahmin Assistant Coroner pointed. The Assistant Coroner then pointed out other body parts, careful not to touch anything low caste. The sweeper then took tissue samples so professionally, one had to stop and stare. The autopsy was being performed without the doctor even touching the body.

While everyone watched the proceedings, Henry Gomes watched Tobi Basar.

Made of stone, she stared at this unknown boy on the slab, maybe thinking of her Arjun coming up next to be sliced by a lower caste sweeper, directed by an upper caste doctor. Ernst wondered where Arjun was; under which shroud. Eenie, Meenie, Minee...

The sweeper coughed and spat on the floor. He was done, leaving behind a long cut from the base of the cadaver's neck to the pubic area, and another on the scalp from ear-to-ear within the hairline. A strip of cloth had been threaded through the wounds like a shoelace. Ernst wanted to protest the shoddy workmanship, but how was everything else in India, including him, any different?

'No autopsy,' Tobi Basar said, surrendering in her Assamese, Convent-English. 'They're not doing that to my boy. We'll take the body. Call it accident, whatever you want.'

'Not to worry,' Gomes assured her. He was looking towards the third concrete slab. 'No need to cut open your dear boy. Sahib had kindly agreed after much persuasion. He will declare the death an accident and all this isn't necessary. By the way, there's no need to pay for this courtesy. I am here for you.'

Now that they were all friends, Assistant Coroner Sahib came over to introduce himself as the Civil Surgeon at Sion Hospital.

'As well as Assistant Coroner. Dual role, double work, single salary.' He looked at Ernst to see if the heart bled. Chit-chatting after a hard day's work, the Assistant Coroner explained he had already done as required under Section 9 of said Act.

No one asked what Act, or this or that.

'Ruled accidental.' He was magnanimous. They were free to take the body.

Gomes smiled at Ernst. 'See? I told you!'

Gomes transferred a wad of notes, very thick, without commentary into the Assistant Coroner's white coat. With an expression that unequivocally conveyed his authority in spite of what you might think, the Additional Coroner left. Accompanying him was the woman in white sari, leaving behind the sweeper for any final sutures before handing over the slum dweller's body.

Next, official-looking forms materialised again out of nowhere. 'Sign here, please,' Gomes said. 'I have to ensure your dear boy is carried outside on a trolley.'

Tobi Basar was staring at the shrouded body on the third slab and ready to renege. 'How can this be right, when we know it wasn't an accident?'

Gomes repeated, 'Sign here, please.'

Tufan took the sheave from Gomes' hand and sidled his sister away from her son's murderer, who had just offered to wheel his victim up from the morgue. But first, *Sign here, please.* Ernst had to wonder what Tufan and Salim Ali would say if they knew, he knew. That he didn't tell them about the scissors. That, the scissors belonged to Gomes. That Gomes belonged to Chhote Bhai. That everyone, including Chhote Bhai and Gomes and Ernst, belonged to the Seth. He started feeling backed-up again.

'This accidental death business,' he said to Gomes. 'You can see how the family may have a problem with that.'

'What about you, Mr. Ernest? You have a problem too?'

Ernst felt for Gomes. Clearly, half of him wanted to continue being the caring, hospital orderly. The other half wanted to kill someone.

There was a tug to his sleeve. Salim Ali. Not the reinforcements one hoped. The field only evened up when Dr. Waller joined them and Gomes reverted to ward boy status under the Anglo-Indian's withering look.

'Gomes! You bhenchod,' Waller said. 'Still up to your no good, I see.' He then snapped his very shaky fingers and a sea of white, medical college uniforms clambered down the stairs, pushing past people to converge around Arjun's shrouded body on the third slab. In spite of the bravado, they appeared somewhat wary of Gomes.

Waller wasn't. 'Bugger this fellow, and move the body to the college section for a proper autopsy. I'll sign for it. The family has donated it to science. Get it out of this porki place.'

As Gomes stood down and the Medical College squad went to work, Salim Ali took the opportunity to spell out the moral of the story.

'I just went asked Dr. Waller for help. It's simple, really. All one has to do is something, instead of nothing.'

Gomes in the meantime had stiffened into a single block of muscle. He looked ready to do something too, and Waller be damned. There was only so much a gorilla could take. Salim Ali, however, appeared unaware of the Henry Gomes factor. Ernst was willing to do anything to keep it that way. The best way, of course, was to do nothing.

~

'Maybe, you should do something,' Dr. Waller said, pointing at the mole on Ernst's face as they climbed out from Hades. The mole throbbed in agreement. Moments ago, he wanted to thank Waller for saving him from the gorilla. Now, not so much.

'Thought you said it was nothing.'

'Could be something. What's the harm in playing safe?'

It was past seven and dark outside. In the courtyard, the jhopadpatti family was paying the sweeper-surgeon for a tarp to carry the body.

'It never ends,' Waller said, watching the family deal with their kismet. At least, he had Pethidine to help deal with his.

'We're going to the medical college,' Tufan called out. 'Arjun's already there.'

Looking back at Ernst, Dr. Waller said, 'Come along,' and touched his left cheek. 'Won't take a minute.'

They watched him walk away—a superannuated army surgeon. He appeared to have left a mark on Tsering Tufan.

'Saw the way he intervened for Arjun? An extraordinary Dean.'

'De facto Dean,' Ernst corrected.

Salim Ali though, was more impressed at how Gomes was staring their way from the morgue entrance with his tiny gorilla eyes. 'Why is he looking like that?'

Ernst played innocent. 'Who?'

'Who else? Your medical ape. Look at the useless fellow stare. As if he wants to kill us.'

'What do you mean, us? I'm not the one holding on to stolen property.'

~

Sion Hospital started life as a fifty-bed Military hospital installed across Sion's ramshackle army barracks in a snake-infested locality. It grew to its current size but the snake colonies remained, along with ex-army surgeons like Dicky Waller, many of whom became enthusiastic Pethidine addicts after the war.

In time, the post-Independence hospital administration realised they weren't the only ones robbing the place blind, and large stocks of missing pharmaceuticals were traced to Waller. There were demands for his head but they couldn't fire him just like that, not just because he knew how to deal with snakes. More importantly, being Anglo-Indian, he was considered neutral in a hospital administration drawn strictly along caste lines. He had absolutely no political ambitions and absolutely no desire to mingle. Most importantly, he disliked all Indians equally, irrespective of caste or creed. So they made him the de facto Dean of the new medical college and continued fighting over who would eventually become the actual Dean, and from which caste.

This worked superbly for all concerned. Waller spent most of his time searching for frightened snakes hiding in the shrubbery and in-between roof tiles. The rest of the time was spent searching for collapsed veins hiding in his arms. He kept live snakes in his surgery to mess with people and he encouraged the rumour he had a couple of Russell's Vipers on the loose in there. Ernst was convinced that was a lie. An unnecessary one, because just seeing snakes lined up in glass vitrines was enough to drive urban Indians insane with fear. Freed from patients on becoming the de facto Dean, Waller nevertheless kept himself available for Ernst, who found him either drowsy or dangerously revved, and should have known better. But then, Waller didn't charge, and there was never any need for an appointment.

Seated up high on an operating table in Waller's surgery, live snakes staring at him through glass jars, Ernst kept an eye open for any loose ones around. He refrained from commenting on Waller's change of mind regarding the mole.

'What's the harm?' Waller repeated, before lopping off an anesthetised slice with a medically steadied hand. He signalled a Mallu nurse to apply a big, square of sticky plaster he held out, but she refused to enter his surgery. Ernst stepped outside with the sticky plaster for her while holding an alcohol swab to where Waller had applied the scalpel to his cheek.

~

Supine, the dead Arjun appeared at peace amidst medical students his age. His glasses were gone, but the rest of him held on to the kind of equanimity his uncle displayed, looking down from the observer's gallery. The mother may have declined to watch her porcelain doll being cut up, but there was a complete calm on Tufan's visage.

'There is no reason for you to be present either,' Ernst had said to Tufan, seeing Waller's unnecessary relish wielding the scalpel in the theatre, down below.

'But I must,' Tufan replied, because there was no further trust left in him, it looked like, for any third-party information and best he confirmed with his own eyes what he knew happened. Trust issues aside, he could pass off as a Buddhist monk. Then there was Salim Ali.

Tufan held him tight to control his sobbing. Down below, the medical world carried on as detached as Tufan, but with none of his Buddhist empathy. The room smelled of formaldehyde and professional competence. Even Dr. Waller having a go at a medical student, appeared as de facto as the dean.

'You're working the wrong orifice, you bugger,' Waller said to his student victim, the humour delightfully Anglo-Indian. 'For a change, no need to finger the arsehole. Try checking the puncture on the left thigh instead. If you locate it, try advising us on cause of death.'

After humiliating the student some more for fun, Dr. Waller slashed downwards with a flick of the wrist, holding a pair of pointed surgical scissors to demonstrate how it went down. When it came to theory, the man was supreme. And when it was over with, there was all around agreement amongst the student body that a great amount of strength would be needed to thrust a pair of scissors with such precision into the thigh, and then tear open the femoral artery. That too, while in motion. Also, some amount of medical knowledge would be absolutely necessary.

'Medical knowledge?' Salim Ali asked of Ernst with a face all crunched up. 'That goon of yours, that Gomes. You said he had medical knowledge. What's the meaning of this?'

Now right through Waller's re-enactment and the subsequent autopsy, Ernst had failed to pay attention at how Salim Ali's eyes widened to take over his small, black face. He also didn't think too much of it when Salim Ali went into a huddle with Tufan. But now Salim Ali was looking his way once again in a manner that did not portend well. Then Tufan goes declines a lift home in the one-eyed Fiat, preferring to go pillion instead on Salim Ali's totally-blind Vespa. The two of them tore off into the night without as much as a bye-bye.

'I know everything now!' Ernst heard Salim Ali yell into the wind. 'Bhenchods! All of you!'

19

Darkies

After winter, must come spring,
After forty, no such thing.
—Jehangir Merchant

The nuance around what killed his mother hit Ernst again a few days later, after news spread Prime Minister Jawaharlal Nehru had died of a stroke. As with his mother, turns out the real reason the PM keeled over, was guilt. In the PM's case, because of how his Chinese friends shamed a fellow-socialist by coming over uninvited. They didn't knock, just barged in and slapped the army around, showed India who was what, and left.

Whereas, while Ernst's mother sank under all that guilt over all those Jews and silently vanished, Prime Minister Nehru's death became a JFK moment. Those going about their business would remember forever where they were when the news broke. To help them never forget, AIR looped the Lata Mangeshkar song over radio; yes, the same one she had sung to shore up a befuddled army after China's Himalayan waltz. The death of their very first prime minister was bad enough, and now the song was being played and re-played. All of India cried and took the rest of the week off. No fans of the socialist Nehru, Europeans refused to follow suit and were seen spending even more time at the Golf Club during working hours.

The wood-panelled walls and columns in the Golf Club's permit-room were a fair imitation of an English pub. A good try. It was May, but the green tinsel along the walls was from last Christmas. Someone would have to get a ladder one day and take it down, unless Christmas came first.

The vibrating Voltas had the room in its grip, shaking it as sweat dried off Ernst's back sending a chill up the spine. He squinted to adjust to the complete absence of natural light. It wasn't large, the permit-room, and could barely hold its quota of European gentry. One wondered what would happen should desi members venture in some day to sit alongside and drink openly. Willie Lansdowne foresaw permit-rooms wilting into dingy, sad haunts for alcoholics once the Indians took over. It was depressing enough already, with Willie's wife sitting there alone at the teak bar in breach of club decorum. The Goan bartender looked guilty seeing Ernst walk in, as if the drunken memsahib was his fault.

'Hello, D'Souza,' Ernst greeted, 'a Bloody Mary please, and how are you?'

'So-so, Sir. Chacha Nehru is dead. Broken heart for sure. The Chinese betrayed him, you see.'

'For goodness sake.'

Daisy Lansdowne was awake.

'They're behaving as if Churchill died.' She peered into her gin and tonic and swirled it around with a paper straw. A shaded bulb swung above Daisy with the sole purpose of basking her filigreed blonde hair with a radiant halo. Ernst thought: so that's how hammered goddesses look. She was taller than him, and stacked on the bar stool her torso cut a dark silhouette in contrast to the flushed, radiant face hogging the light. It would be horsy English if not for the pointed nose, making it more bird-like than equine. The eyes were all mare though, big and limpid, but it was the golden hair that drew the crowds. Becoming and all, though Ernst knew without the corset holding her together under the floral summer dress, she'd splay like her feet, minus those open-toed pumps.

Unlike his wife. With Bombay Ingrid, it had always been too much perfection. Perfect feet, perfect sex, perfect disdain. Perfect departure.

'I'm positive D'Souza can't blow you any better than I did,' Daisy said. 'So why no hello-hello for me?'

~

Daisy Lansdowne happened without Ernst thinking it through. Before he knew, she was on all fours on his bed, her bum staring him in the face. She happened, because she didn't dwell on his shortcomings, did not comment on any fashion faux pas, didn't nitpick or touch on his money situation, and all in all, was nothing like Bombay Ingrid. Truth be told, after his wife was done with him, Ernst Steiger could only feel confident around someone like Daisy. Except that these days, not even that. He felt lost in his flapping clothes, being slapped around by a pair of bloodshot eyes. Ernst patted the precious strands still vying for air from his bald spot. Also, there was a plaster pasted on the left side of his face where Waller had dug in. He realised he was in a limbo awaiting results from Sion Medical College. The thought made him ill.

'It's been more than two weeks, Ernst. One would think you'd have the decency to call.'

'Hello, Daisy,' Ernst said, as he trod through the minefield to a bar stool near her.

Daisy stood up with the extreme caution of the very drunk. Standing upright, she looked like a crane—an attractive crane—with a blonde wig on. She stumbled and Ernst reached out.

'No need,' Daisy said, veering away with admirable control. 'I'm sure you didn't come here looking for me.'

'It's nice to see you anyway.'

'Is it?' she asked, with a smile that invited him to step on a landmine. She looked him up and down, peering with interest at the handiwork on his left cheek. She then went back to balancing the tottering structure. 'You look bloody awful,' she said. The iron grip slipped and she slurred. 'You think Willie knows about us?'

Ernst glanced towards D'Souza. The Goan had his back to them, busy capturing rainbows in a whiskey glass he held up to the light.

'I doubt it,' Ernst said, 'though now D'Souza does.'

A look of genuine surprise flashed across her face, as if that mattered. Daisy Lansdowne then turned to go, putting her arse on display. Ernst recalled his surprise at its strength in spite of a jelly-like consistency. The sway to her hip, even in this state, suggested that women like her and Bombay Ingrid, and those others with that special something, had all attended the same course in mocking men with undulating backsides while remaining aloof. Even when compromised.

Especially when compromised. That other night, while emerging from the greens with Chhote Bhai, the girl had registered alarm, covering her face with the hem of her sari. Then something happened and straightening up, she had taken back control to sway past him just like Daisy Lansdowne; or how Bombay Ingrid had walked up the ship's plank when she left India forever. Daisy struggled with the heavy teak door and edged out before Ernst realised he should have gotten up to help.

'Another Bloody Mary, D'Souza, and my chit please,' Ernst said. 'I'll take the drink outside, if you don't mind.'

D'Souza placed little squares of carbon between the first three white, light blue, and yellow pages of the chit book and handed it to Ernst along with a pencil stub. Club chits were Britain's greatest gift to mankind. Ernst signed off without looking. He then removed the celery stick from the Bloody Mary, toyed around with it, and took a sip after placing the celery on a napkin.

'D'Souza…'

'Sir?'

'Fuck that bhenchod, Churchill. Don't mind what she said. He should've died instead of Nehru.'

~

Ernst's eyes readjusted to settle on the American couple on the verandah. The glistening Texan looked sweaty, having just returned from his morning sortie into India.

Worlds would collide when Jack Hanson stepped out from the Golf Club mornings to exercise charity, something he did more and more these days. Why, what the hell for, who knew? American guilt, Christian love, some Texan thing, whatever it was, he would come out swinging with pockets full of anna coins and Parle Glucose biscuits. Murli Chowkidar would stagger behind with his bamboo lathi under an armpit, arms piled high with textbooks.

Aroused at the sight of a white man, the huddled masses would turn into a mob. Unfazed, Hanson showered them with anna coins, handed out Parle Glucose biscuits, and ruffled their heads the way he did that day with Arjun. He would soon run out of goodies, at which point Murli Chowkidar would try placating extended hands with textbooks no one wanted. When all done and the crowd still clamouring for more, Murli Chowkidar would use his bamboo lathi to cane the herd fearlessly, while the Texan retreated with phoren awkwardness into the mysterious, dark cool of the Golf Club. Sindhi Camp gutters would choke up with textbooks in their wake, and late evenings saw *David Copperfield* and the *Baburnama* being used as fuel in the jhopadpatti. Come next morning, and America's glutton for punishment would be out there again.

Hanson sat wearing a Scally cap today, instead of his twelve-gallon, holding his wife's hand in a bear paw. Her blonde hair was stiff with spray—like they prefer in their southern states. Capri slacks and high heels completed the picture. Doris she was, Doris Hanson. A nice, quiet woman with a troubled inner core. Ernst was good by now at reading the bad stuff. He felt he should go up and thank Hanson for rushing the dead Arjun to hospital. Also, for making a dent in Salim Ali's worldview, although impossible to say for sure.

On the other hand, he felt tired and so hell with it. The Hansons made it easier by signing their chits and getting ready to leave. Bearers stood to attention out of respect at the American-size tips left behind.

~

The verandah's decibel levels were up and Ernst felt unwell. It should concern him, how normal this back and forth had become—well, unwell, not ill, but not well. Someone touched his elbow. He found Sassoon by his side balancing a whiskey with superior, British, upper class and he started feeling better. It was good to be in the great man's inner circle once again. Brothers-in-arms. Shit happened between friends all the time. So what if he'd fired Ernst. He was at least trying to make up twenty-six years later by pushing business his way. It's really large, the order, Major Punjabi had warned on the phone. Three truckloads of stainless steel pipes. When you want to make up, do it like a Sassoon.

'All good?'

'Yes, Adam. You?'

'The Muslim bugger,' Sassoon said, 'He needs to step up. Return what his friend stole. Enough is enough. Seriously. It's impacting you.'

Funnily enough, Gomes had felt the same. We want it back, he had said, reaching into the one-eyed Fiat.

'Why?' Ernst asked, and a voice clambered up on his shoulder to whisper, careful now.

'Why? He works for you, that's why. What's he got you hang on to him like that? Tell me. Maybe, I can learn something.'

'Integrity,' Ernst replied. 'He has integrity. It can't be learnt.'

Only thing left now was to watch the train careen out of control. Sassoon's smile was reassuring though. 'I didn't hear that, old chap,' he said, allowing Ernst to breathe again. 'And anyway, why complicate matters now that both Iyer and Punjabi are on board with helping you? Talk to you later.'

Walking back to his entourage, Sassoon turned around to say, 'Need you on board too. So let's get the darkie to behave. Return whatever's been taken. Punjabi's waiting to sign off on your advance. God knows you can use the money.'

True, but how to get that darkie to behave? He felt a sudden heat pricking through his trousers, reminding him of the other matter. It was the cheque drawn in favour of the Seth, burning a hole in his pocket. He was here to give it to the Seth; the Seth's Lala would then give one back to him as promised, with a little extra for Salary Day, and his world would continue to revolve. Catching him look their way, the Seth waved from across the Great Divide, friend to friend, to assure Ernst venal commerce was the last thing on his mind; and the first thing he expected Ernst to bring up. The Seth was smiling, and over here Sassoon was smiling too. They didn't know each other and either one could swat him like a fly and no one would care. And just like that, Ernst's stomach started to cramp up and the cork up his arse clamped down, causing the cheque in his pocket to heat up further. Strange, because it should have remained stone cold, given there was no money in the bank.

Ernst allowed himself to be distracted by a flutter some sofas away in a bouquet of floral prints. There was a time Bombay Ingrid would sit in there, skirt swirling around her; a long stemmed rose coexisting with the bouquet, yet not part of it. Today, Daisy Lansdowne was present instead, articulating past the alcohol while chatting away with Cathy Sassoon. Cathy saw him and waved excitedly. He waved back. If Cathy Sassoon had any real passion beneath all the giggly, put-on charm, Ernst hadn't seen it in all these years. Rumour was, neither had Sassoon. Edging down the colour-scale and to Cathy Sassoon's left, Beatrice Taylor sat behind her horn-rimmed glasses. Pinker than Cathy she was, but so what. She was half-baked, an Anglo-Indian, which meant that in a gathering of white people she was tolerated at best. They made sure to be seen being kind to her.

'You saw *Gone With the Wind*?' Beatrice asked Ernst once. 'Can you make out Vivien Leigh's half-Indian? No? See? We Anglo-Indians don't look like bloody darkies one bit, so why treat us like them? Bloody racists, all of you.'

She had gone on and on. Her stunning breasts went well with the inferiority complex. They looked spectacular today, even from a distance. Right next to them and at the bottom of the colour-scale, sat Bhairavi. Ernst couldn't remember the last time he saw an Indian woman at the Golf Club. She was in that white sari of hers—the one with the maroon border—and her mouth was clamped tight. It caused her upper lip to bulge. Memsahibs everywhere, she kept close to Beatrice Taylor while hugging a red bound ledger for protection.

An alcoholic mist hung over the bouquet and Beatrice was getting loud. 'She won't disappoint,' Ernst heard her say, Cathy Sassoon nodding. 'Make sure Mr. Sassoon doesn't hand her any money. She'll simply spend it. You know how these people are. Best I keep it for her.'

20

Sethji's Gift

Thine to me is the swastika.
—*Vedic chant*

He tried catching the girl's eye and once again she ignored him, the cork up his arse clamping tight in protest. Beatrice Taylor threw a smoky smile his way as a consolation prize.

When Adam Sassoon walked over to the ladies, it was with that charm dialled up. He appeared to smile directly at the girl though, as if at Goddess Bhairavi instead of a buck-toothed darkie from Sindhi Camp. As if she was the most beautiful woman in the world and not an emaciated refugee girl. Given the Goddess legend (if she looks ugly, you live, if beautiful, you die), were Sassoon Indian and the way Bhairavi smiled back at him, it could mean ta-ta, bye-bye. Ernst tried picturing Sassoon an Indian and failed. The great man bent down to speak and Bhairavi canted to listen to him and so did Beatrice, her face reflecting a golden glow from the scotch someone else was paying for. Cathy Sassoon smiled relentlessly from the far end of the colour scale. Ernst felt he should go say hello. Daisy Lansdowne, however, peered like a riled bird-horse and with Bhairavi pretending he didn't exist while Sassoon established hegemony, today's bouquet appeared toxic. Ernst mulled doing a bishop and scurry diagonally across the chessboard without attracting any further attention, but it would still be touch and go. Then Mohan Driver signalled from the entrance and Ernst weaved toward him like the knight he knew he wasn't.

It was a phone call. Parvatibai had called the reception. Dr. Waller had called home. Ernst felt sick. His pulse rate went up; he felt feverish and broke into a sweat. He was a textbook hypochondriac learning the doctor just called, and to hell with Sindhi Camp Bhairavi and whatever she was doing here. Going into a tizzy, he tried to calm himself. I'm a hypochondriac, he said. That's all there is to it. Acknowledging his condition initiated a bout of relief and the cork loosened, pulse steadied, clamminess eased, and she could still go to hell. He became almost euphoric seeing how he had reacted to Waller's phone call. There was no cancer. How could a hypochondriac be ill? That would be a contradiction in terms.

Looking out at Sindhi Camp from the Golf Club reception area, he came down the club steps for some air, and stretched. It felt good. He was surprised seeing Tsering Tufan walk past the gate towards the police chowki. It wasn't often his two worlds collided. The man did not look professorial today, more like a sickly Chinese babu holding tight to a yellow file. He appeared to be deteriorating on a daily basis with a real illness, not from bullshit head games hypochondriacs play. It was surreal seeing him, though not half as much as seeing the little black man with the fuck-you look. Lip curled, Salim Ali ventured into the club courtyard without a qualm.

'You knew it was that ape, Gomes! Why didn't you tell us?' A dozing Murli Chowkidar jumped sky high, and Ernst reached to tease at his mole, feeling the plaster instead. When it came to Salim Ali though, he felt up to it.

'Why didn't you tell me you were accessory to a crime? Bad enough stealing something. No telling what else you'd do if you knew about Gomes. Yes, I was worried about you.'

Salim Ali was categorical. 'Bullshit. You were worried about your business. So, who approached you? Sassoon or the Yank? Or both? What was the deal? You keep shut and they give you the pipes and tubes order? All the orders you want? Was that the deal? Don't lie!'

'How can I lie when I don't know the fuck you're talking about? All they want is you return what Arjun took. They asked me to ask you, and I did.'

'They killed Arjun for it. So who's next? Me?'

'You just said Gomes killed Arjun. What have Sassoon and that American got to do with Gomes? Make up your bloody mind.'

'At least try and sound convincing.' Then, to Tufan. 'See how white people come together? That's why I don't tell him anything. Fuckers! All of them!'

'Look at you,' Ernst said. 'This is why I didn't tell you.'

Hands clasped behind, Salim Ali assumed the posture he had taken addressing the working class at Fertilisers. Lenin was back. 'I resign,' he proclaimed. 'I cannot work for a lackey'. It was all very grand.

Ernst looked towards Tufan in appeal. Tufan was apologetic. He had to get to the police chowki. Have them do something about Arjun. He looked regretful about Salim Ali. There was nothing one could do about him.

Salim Ali snatched the file from Tufan and waved it at the chowki. 'Dr. Waller's autopsy report. Let's see what they say now.'

Ernst watched them walk over to the chowki. Rubbished by both the Sassoon and Salim Ali blocs the same afternoon. A record, even for him. He felt cold in the afternoon heat. It was the facial mole, he concluded, rubbing the plaster again. It was sapping his judgement. The Seth waved at him from the desi half of the verandah. Walking over, Ernst put a hand in his pocket and took out the folded cheque. He held on to it because if it dropped, the cheque would bounce.

~

Bearers threw down everything at a snap of the Seth's fingers. They rushed to lower the bamboo chattais and shade their Sethji from the afternoon sun coming in sideways. Bania seths of the trader caste ruled Socialist India. And Seth Jamunadas Kejriwal, industrialist, gold smuggler, loan shark, patron of politicians, publisher of the nation's textbooks, as well as builder of temples across the land, ruled the seths.

The Seth's Lala placed his cloth-bound, single-entry ledger on the table but didn't reach out to squeeze Ernst's hand this time. He didn't pout either, or make googly eyes. Hindu swastikas danced all over the ledger's red-cloth binding, radiating good luck. They smiled at Ernst along with the Seth in one big welcome. The Lala did not. In the background, the club's Grundig was crying over the dead Prime Minister.

'Namaste, Sethji,' Ernst said, 'Very sad, about the PM.'

'Why sad, Mr. Ernestji?' the Seth asked. 'Not to worry. Nehru's back already.'

Ernst leaned forward. If there was one thing he had fine-tuned over the years, it was this posture. Indians opened up like faucets when he did that.

'Yes ji, the Prime Minister is back,' the Seth repeated. 'Reincarnated as a dog in Sweden within a few seconds of his death.'

Ernst was glad he'd stopped by.

'All very scientific,' the Seth assured. 'I was informed by His Divine Grace, Swami Prabhupada himself.' Those around the Seth nodded, and while his Divine Grace could well be full of shit, how hardcore Hindus felt about Nehru was no secret. The Seth was humming to himself when Ernst slid his dud cheque across the table towards the bania.

'Sethji, the loan amount due I discussed with Lalaji.'

The Seth recoiled, throwing his swinging foot out of kilter. The Lala hefted the offending item away and into his pocket. The leg fired up again, increasing its swing until oscillating optimally. Though getting a cheque in return would breathe life into this one, Ernst was tempted to let the matter go than fuck with the clockwork again.

'Sethji, Lalaji and I discussed another loan. Same interest, of course.'

The Seth sighed and looked at the Lala, who looked relieved seeing the pendulum swinging away.

'Difficult times, Mr. Ernestji,' the Seth said. 'Credit crunch.' Time for the Lala to wink at Ernst and remind him this was just chitchat, nothing more than a lead-up to the cheque with Sethji's signature. Lala Prem, however, was busy adjusting his turban and missed his cue. The Seth looked pensive as he spoke.

'These are tough times, Mr. Ernestji. But I would like for all of us to be happy.'

Ernst and the Lala took turns looking happy. The Seth reached into his pocket and brought out a circular, dark blue box made of the cheapest plastic money could buy.

'By the way,' he said, opening it with his fat fingers. Resting inside on red pincushion cloth was an electro-plated, gold swastika coin, the size of a rupee. 'For good luck.' He placed it on the table in front of Ernst. Pointing at the swastika on the medallion, he then said, 'I know Hitler.' One hell of a way, Ernst admitted, to get a Jew's undivided attention.

'He took our swastika and made it his. Did you know in one speech, he said nothing for the full first minute? Just stood there, hypnotising you people. I learned that trick from him. Fair exchange, one can say. After all, our swastika. Like you Germans, we Indians are also Aryavartas.'

True. Like Germans, North Indian Hindus claimed an Aryan heritage. Unlike Germans, they still believed the horseshit. Ernst didn't have the heart to break up the party and inform Sethji he was talking to a Yehudi, not an Aryavarta. The rest, all true. Sethji was spot-on about Nazis co-opting the Vedic swastika.

If he knew all that in the beginning, Bombay Ingrid had demanded toward the end, why did he bring her here in the first place? Should have warned her in Berlin itself, India was no place to avoid the swastika. Add to that, the weather, the people, the smells, and everywhere you looked, the shit. All in all, too much for Berlin's Jewish princess. She would take those white, German Aryans any day over these brown ones, thank you very much.

Their perfect sex was the first casualty after such showdowns, then the perfect love and finally, perfect Ingrid. When she walked up the roped gangplank towards the ship's smiling, First Officer in white—he might as well have worn a Gestapo uniform—Ernst had done nothing to stop her. He let her walk the plank.

'I love you,' he had called out, and recalled the idiot in white uniform grinning down at him. She had pretended not to hear, taking the Officer's practised hand as he gently heaved her over. The pregnancy had barely showed.

~

Sethji's imitation gold coin eyeballed him from its red pincushion. Unlike the swastikas on the Lala's ledger, this one didn't smile.

A cheap gold-plated swastika, gifted to a Jew. He wondered if that constituted insult to injury and thanked the Seth profusely. He hoped a cheque would follow.

'The swastika will for sure change your fortune,' Sethji said. 'Have faith in it, Mr. Ernestji. After all, you are one of us.'

'Sethji, about that cheque from you for the new loan.'

The Seth's demeanour was encouraging and he looked toward his Lala.

'We should discuss collateral first,' the Lala suggested. 'The cold rolling mill wasn't yours to sell, Mr. Ernestji. But you did. Now we have a problem.'

'I thought we sorted that out.'

'Did we? You had some requests. I had some suggestions. At the end of day, we are not here for charity. We must have collateral.'

The Seth clearly disagreed, the way he glared.

Ernst tried to visualise ten thousand dollars of collateral. Her father's Packard Clipper came to mind. The one left behind in Mauripur. Her father lost his ten thousand dollar-Packard Clipper to a mob that day and the mother lost something to them too, but at least the two of them escaped and Bhairavi was born. Escape was a wonderful thing.

'I need the money, Sethji. Or my cheque will bounce.'

The Seth understood, and turned once more to his accountant. 'Lalaji,' he appealed.

'No.'

'Please.'

'It's not possible.'

'I beg you, man to man.'

'Our hands are tied.'

'Why? Why is it absolutely impossible to help our brother?'

Ernst sat and watched it play out, the Seth acting miserable at his inability to help a fellow sentient being.

'Lalaji, you waived the collateral that day, and asked me to come for the cheque. I'm here because you asked.'

'Things change. The Seth was happy then.'

The Seth rushed to intervene. 'I'm still happy, Mr. Ernestji. Just not with Muslims.'

'And communists,' the Lala reminded.

'And communists.'

'And thieves.'

'Yes. Muslims and communist thieves.'

Ernst didn't know where all this was coming from, did not wish to know, and wished he did not know Salim Ali.

'The cheque I just gave you. What about it?'

The Lala appeared to be confused. 'What about it? You gave us cheque, so we deposit it. Do note there is no collateral anymore. So cheque absolutely must not bounce. Too much exposure already, Mr. Ernestji.'

The afternoon rays wriggled through the bamboo chattais to create a chequered tablecloth pattern on the Seth's face. Resting eyes on Ernst, he wagged a stubby, bejewelled finger. A sapphire flashed and light slanted towards it on cue, filtering past the chattais to highlight the cut. The Seth was emphatic.

'Remember Mr. Ernestji, I'm always there for you.'

Ernst's Tantaji, the gardener's wife at Purandhar Fort, used to say the whole purpose of any ritual was to meet expectations. No point otherwise, just like there was no point to the cheque ritual anymore. So Ernst did his namastes and got up to leave. It had taken the Seth twenty minutes of meandering to tell him, no money for you. Something Sassoon managed earlier in just five. Ernst couldn't say he preferred one to the other.

Preparing to leave, he had to watch his steps to avoid another ambush because Beatrice Taylor was eyeing him from across The Great Divide. She looked like a tigress—a fat one with tits. Ernst looked around for Beatrice Taylor's one-girl body shop, and found her on the sofa in a huddle with Sassoon over that ledger. The great man was locked in on her like she was Goddess Bhairavi and nothing less. Ernst glanced at his watch.

'Don't forget your good luck swastika, Mr. Ernestji,' the Seth reminded him. Ernst's dud cheque had reappeared in the Lala's hand; the man too busy studying it to say goodbye to a good friend.

Across The Great Divide, Beatrice the tigress was positioning herself to intercept him. He gave her full marks for trying. Sassoon walked over to the reception to take a phone call and the girl was left alone. A bearer walked by and Ernst heard her order chai. The bearer ignored her.

Meanwhile, Beatrice couldn't hold it any longer. 'Ernst,' she said, and he pretended he hadn't heard. Over there, the girl asked once more in her Sindhi accent. The bearer probably knew her from Sindhi Camp and wasn't amused. He may be a waiter, but she was a fucking refugee. There are limits. When he snapped, asking her to go to hell, the verandah stopped in its tracks.

Beatrice turned around to the girl, and then focused back on him. 'Ernst,' she called out again but fuck that, because Sassoon had come up from behind and tapped the outraged bearer's shoulder. 'Memsahib asked you for chai,' he said, and struck the man on the mouth.

No one moved except Beatrice, who did a slow, half-circle. The girl just sat there, and Ernst pictured a Lady Justice with buck teeth, wearing a blindfold. There was a confused silence on both sides of The Great Divide. This wasn't happening. Stepping up for one darkie by punching another in public, made no sense at all. Clearly, the great man wasn't himself, and Ernst felt Goddess Bhairavi was to blame. After all, he thought, look what she's done to me. But to Sassoon? Sassoon wasn't Ernst. Sassoon was Sassoon—letting Ernst know with a smile and a pat on the shoulder that Salim Ali needed to ante up, else no advance, no order; no more brothers-in-arms. That's how it's done, with scotch in hand. Yet there he was, the great man making a fool of himself over a refugee girl. It's that Goddess Bhairavi legend come true, but Ernst didn't find that funny anymore. He thought of distracting Sassoon with the news Salim Ali had just resigned. Save the great man any further embarrassment. Yes, the Darkie's gone and what got stolen may well be in my apartment. You're welcome to it. So, for fuck's sake, leave this poor bastard of a bearer alone and let's get on with it. I need the advance. Twenty-eighth is Salary Day.

However, Ernst was wearing his Indian hat and therefore, superstitious about saying out loud that Salim Ali had resigned. Because it would then come true.

21

Schwester Ingrid

Old acquaintances return to help you cross the river.
—*Yama, King of Hades*

Mohan Driver would do the ten miles from Chembur to Colaba in around forty-five minutes, throwing his timing back to what it was during Bombay Ingrid's short reign. He preferred to do it under thirty. 'Like with the whores on Foras Road.' Ernst overheard him say that once to Kirti, the shy caddie-boy loved by all, and also by Lala Prem—a bit more than necessary. Turns out, he's the girl's brother.

A shrill Bombay Ingrid was the brake those days, staying Mohan Driver from pressing on the accelerator. Now, it was burgeoning traffic around Chembur Naka. There at the Naka crossing, the Trombay and Chembur suburbs mated in a haze of diesel fumes while vehicular traffic stopped to watch. Chembur Naka jams were grand affairs. The bottleneck funnelled vehicles on to the Sion-Trombay Highway in a choked sea of yellow-black Fiat taxis, and private Ambassador dowagers with their superannuated backsides from the early Fifties. Both in turn dwarfed by overloaded Tata-Mercedes trucks of every vintage, swaying on the road to violate statutes by the dozen and help feed a police force. They were supposed to enter the city limits only at night, after ten, but they paid up, so who cared. Diesel fumes gave the air a mirage-like quality. Horns tore at eardrums. The obstruction ahead appeared to be pre-monsoon roadwork.

Taxis began cutting through the corner petrol pump with the smiling ESSO Oil Drop to get past the roadwork. An outraged Gujarati attendant hollered protests in the face of cheerful Sikh disdain. Still, Bombay was nothing compared to the disasters brewing in Calcutta and New Delhi. Ernst noticed the coy Esso Oil Drop tempt Mohan Driver. Taking the Sethji's round, little box with the gold-plated swastika from his pocket, he reached out to stay the man.

'For you. Just don't hang it in the car.'

There was another Krishna Temple coming up ahead at the Chembur Naka corner and resting behind it, the amber-walled, Sassoon Protection Home for Women & Children with its red roof tiles. That's where they dumped Foras Road whores after police raids. Facing the Krishna Temple was a Siva Temple—the compound already a beehive, work underway on the clay Ganesh statues for the immersion festivities in September. Temples populated every nook and every corner of every city, but Chembur Naka was special. Cars slowed to a crawl outside the temples, making the jam worse. One could only hope they slowed down to peek at Krishna and Siva and at the fat little Ganeshes being crafted. However, heart of hearts, everyone knew it was to crane and stare at the Sassoon Protection Home, hoping to catch a glimpse of whores nestled amidst the gods.

~

Ernst's mind drifted away from thoughts of money, and back to it. To what would happen were the Lala to try cash the dud cheque and whether there was room left to get fucked further. Given his history, there was always room. He looked out at the roadwork instead, and was distracted by formations of big, Lambadi breasts behind their mirror work. The women were sifting gravel, the line-up of mammoth titties moved along the roadside as if choreographed—to and fro between heaped gravel and an inclined, wood-framed wire mesh. They could just as well be working the sulphur pits at the Fertilisers, or for that matter, digging into radioactive dirt at Atomic Energy. Their bodies glistened in sweat from the enervating heat, and remembering Salim Ali telling him about the radioactive shower, he could see how they must have run to the fountain gushing out from the manicured grounds around the CIRUS nuclear reactor. First, made to work on radioactive lawns, then allowed a radioactive shower to cool off.

Were any of those irradiated, out there working in the heat? Were those facial blisters from the sun, or the radioactive shower? Reasonable enquiry. They were, after all, the itinerant engines behind Industrial India, moving from site to site until they dropped dead from exhaustion, malnutrition or radiation exposure. How did one feel being exposed to just enough caesium to not exfoliate you right away; only blisters for now? Like him? Not yet ill, but not well?

He caught a svelte, non-existent frame with platinum hair and in a starched, white uniform observe the women labouring away. She had calves to die for. Passers-by seemed unfazed by a foreign nurse at Chembur Naka—like she didn't exist. She did to Ernst, who saw her looking at the labourers as if she understood a country she disliked so much. Hindu philosophy and especially the Sahajiya's Tantric school had several explanations for why an eidolon would appear like this—none that augured well. All his euphoria at being a healthy hypochondriac vanished in a rush seeing Ingrid in her nurse avatar. Schwester Ingrid is what they called her, over at the Jüdische Krankenhaus in Berlin. Ernst saw her stare at the working women and sniff.

Feeling short of breath, he lowered his window for air, trying to deal with his wife showing up in a nurse's uniform and all that it implied to a Tantric Sahajiya. He didn't need a Goddess Bhairavi smiling at him to know his time was up. A dead wife appearing out of thin air was enough.

'Sa'ab, are you okay?' Mohan Driver could read the rear-view mirror like a book, while tearing down Sion-Trombay at snail's pace during rush hour.

No, he wasn't okay. Because to now have Schwester Ingrid appear out of nowhere and deliver a diagnosis in full uniform, where was the need to call Waller? He already knew the results.

'Stop the car.'

Muttering away, Mohan Driver swerved left on the grass shoulder flanking the highway's seaward side and braked. Salt pans rose from the marsh—white crystalline heaps filling up perfect squares in neat triangles. Ernst got out, staggered towards them and threw up. People craned out of crawling car windows to stare, see a white man retch. Mohan Driver tried willing the whole thing away by gazing into space instead. From the looks of it, there was a fire alarm ringing in his head, at seeing his gora sahib behave like this. 'Make this go away,' his eyes screamed. 'Make this go away.'

On his part, Ernst tried to think his way past what was happening— beat back a hypochondriac's terror with some suitable argument on hand. This time though, calm refused to take hold. Blistered Lambadi titties lined up in his head, Schwester Ingrid inspecting the guard of honour. The message was clear. Prepare. Tantra tells us that preparing to die is an important element of keeping it simple. As a Tantric Sahajiya of sorts and given his age, he should have started to prepare some time ago. He didn't, forcing Schwester Ingrid to now come remind him. That she would do anything for him was a bigger miracle than her appearing out of thin air.

Walking back to the car, Mohan Driver held the rear door open for him. When he fell to his knees instead, Mohan Driver watched in horror. Ernst realised his own state was not from fear, as much as sadness at how things turned out. Not just for him, but also for Ingrid. Not just because he knew he was dying, but also because he now knew for certain she was dead. Not just because he would never know how she died, but also because he knew that's how she would want it. Times like these, kneeling in dirt, and so what if constipated, a man takes stock of his life. Finds he never served any purpose. He was a complete waste of time. When the tears came, he let them run.

All the way home, Mohan Driver and he refused to look at each other. On arriving, he got out and bolted up past Parvatibai straight into the bathroom. Splashing water on his face, Ernst yanked the plaster off and tried muting the sliced mole with some Max Factor pancake—left behind by Daisy Lansdowne after their forgettable tryst. He saw Parvatibai filling up the bedroom doorway to watch him apply it, his hand shaking in fear at all this change hitting at him from all sides. He turned to her in his terror because she was the one, safe place left.

'Phone,' she said, calming him with her presence.

~

Dicky Waller was Salim Ali's reason for deigning to even speak with Ernst again; not resign immediately; not tell him go fuck himself.

'Dr. Waller asked you to see him tomorrow for the results?'

'Yes.'

'After what you did, you deserve to go alone.'

'Yes.'

'It wasn't just Gomes, was it?'

'There could be others.'

'Chhote?'

'Possible. I saw him hit Arjun with his hockey ball. Then Gomes goes and kills Arjun, and on that same day meets Chhote in the Golf Club compound. I was there. Chhote saw me and walked off.' So did the girl, and how, but that's for another day.

'Who else?'

'I know you suspect every white man on the subcontinent, but really? More to the point, where's the gunny bag? Parvatibai won't tell me what she's done with it.'

'Of course she won't. It doesn't concern you.'

'It's lying at my flat and doesn't concern me? Or is it you won't tell because white people can't be trusted?'

Silence prevailed, and Ernst let it go. It was best to treat Salim Ali like an adult. And set an example by being one.

'Like your father?' Schwester Ingrid whispered and he dropped the phone with a start, but of course she wasn't there.

22

Das Jüdische Krankenhaus

Nichts Juden. Juden kaputt.
—*Russian soldiers, surprised finding Jews in Berlin*

Those days when Germany's Jews craved escape so much they would even pay to get out, the platinum blonde Bombay Ingrid became the only Jew to return. Once in Berlin, she donned a nurse's uniform and became Schwester Ingrid. She didn't just survive the German fly swatter, but safe to say, she thrived; something Schwester Ingrid never tired telling Ernst. There were several letters, long letters, pages and pages trumpeting a triumphant survival, written on onion paper and real ink that even real Aryans couldn't get their lily-white hands on.

Ernst's father on the other hand did not display the requisite skill set to survive, let alone anything close to her level. Also, unlike Schwester Ingrid, he never bothered with letters. Actually, not entirely true. There was that envelope Ernst received several years after it was handed to whomever, to hand to someone, to give the Red Cross for safekeeping with the reminder, not to forget to deliver to this Jew in India. Oops, the Red Cross said, when he finally received it five years later. On opening the envelope, a photograph fell out. It was his father's last message—that picture of Schwester Ingrid in uniform behind barbed wire, with the children on her lap and calves to die for. There was nothing else inside. Still, Siegfried couldn't have sent his son a more eloquent suicide note. His visits began soon thereafter.

When Siegfried Steiger wasn't sneaking into his son's dreams to demonstrate how he slit his wrists, he would whisper about the goings-on at the Jüdische Krankenhaus. He looked nervous popping up without warning, aware his acerbic daughter-in-law could do the same. He complained to Ernst that despite his best efforts, it was getting intolerable.

'I'm not talking about the detailed records on Jews they make her keep. And as for keeping a tally in the Sammellager, someone had to do it.'

The Gestapo set up a temporary holding camp—their Sammellager—in the Pathology Department pavilion at the Jüdische Krankenhaus and cordoned it off with barbed wire. When Schwester Ingrid's tally hit one thousand, trucks would come pick up the parcel of Jews for shipment and she would begin a new tally, as the Sammellager began filling up again. The rule was applied, German-style. Ship a parcel only when it totals one thousand—not one less, not one more—and that's what she did. Jews have done worse things to survive. Besides, his father understood if she didn't do it, someone else would. When she tallied off friends and relatives, once again, he understood. What choice did she have?

Her boss was this Herr Doktor Doktor Walter Lustig. He held a doctorate in Philosophy and was also a doctor of Medicine. Hence the two Doktors he insisted upon at all times. Even after July 1938, when they stripped Jewish physicians of their medical licenses. Legally, he was now just one Doktor. No worries, because Lustig was a powerful Jew. Unlike Siegfried, they needed him. Like Siegfried he was also married to an Aryan. Unlike Siegfried, his wife was still alive. Like Siegfried, he was associated with the Jüdische Krankenhaus. Unlike Siegfried, he headed it. As a cherry on the top, he authored several books including a nurse's textbook, as well as the popular, *Little Lustig*—an indispensable handbook for Germany's medical administrators. In a rare exception to the rule, the Aryans let this Jew and his two Doktors be.

No surprise therefore, that Herr Doktor Doktor Lustig cultivated some serious Aryan friends because of all of the above. One being the commandant of the SS contingent at the Sammellager, with whom Herr Doktor Doktor Lustig shared his nurses. As one nurse put it, 'It was not good to be pretty.'

Schwester Ingrid was not pretty. She was sensational.

A platinum blonde, Marlene Dietrich. Siegfried would see his daughter-in-law walk to the Sammellager after work, in the evenings. There, she would spend some time consoling those waiting to be shipped. Something so out of character that Ernst refused to believe it. That picture of her in uniform, seated on a bench in the Sammellager with two children on her lap was relegated to the back of the picture corner in his living room; as if he didn't want to deal with the subject.

Coming to complain after Ernst was fast asleep, Siegfried said he would see her sitting on a bench in the Pathology Gardens behind the barbed wire, holding some woman's hand and whispering, or comforting a child, speaking to a group of worried-looking men. Once it got dark and those interned taken indoors, she would walk to the area sequestered for housing the SS. Her father-in-law would watch as the sentries let her past the guardhouse and see her disappear into the Commandant's living quarters.

Siegfried would stand and watch all night from his window. He would walk up to the Sammellager early morning to allow everyone see him witness his daughter-in-law emerge; freshened up and showered in hot water, smelling of real soap and wearing a laundered uniform. 'Look!' he'd say, smiling at the Nazi guards and the impassive Jews. 'My daughter-in-law!'

She wouldn't react and would continue with the morning routine—spending time with the Jews parcelled in there before exiting to the hospital section to begin her day. She would walk past Siegfried without a word but in a silent fury that Ernst knew all about; the kind that makes a man's knees buckle. Even so, Siegfried would be there the next morning, and the next.

'What was I supposed to do?' he asked.

'Slit your wrists?' she suggested, popping into the dream out of nowhere, all of a sudden, all in white, platinum-blonde hair like a halo around her face carved in white marble, and the blood-red lipstick she wore to hit men between the eyes with the contrast.

~

When Doktor Doktor Lustig finally had enough of Siegfried, he had Schwester Ingrid reason with her Göring-fat, Jew father-in-law. It wasn't difficult enumerating why he should behave, including for example, staying alive. The difficulty was in getting anything through, past all that fat. When Lustig saw Siegfried outside the Sammellager risking it again one morning, he took matters in his own hands.

'And by that,' Schwester Ingrid wrote to Ernst, 'All I mean is he tried to personally talk him out of it. Herr Doktor Doktor Lustig is that sort of a man, a negotiator and humanitarian. He saved thousands of lives, including mine. He is the reason your father was not in a cattle car already, a yellow star on his chest, en route to Auschwitz or someplace similar.' Let's not forget, she reminded Ernst, Herr Doktor Doktor Lustig never had to wear a Star of David; more importantly, he made sure nor did his Jewish doctors, nurses or patients.

Herr Doktor Doktor Lustig's gentle persuasion did not work its magic this time. Siegfried continued making a nuisance of himself over his daughter-in-law. Finally, the SS Commandant had a word with the good Doktor Doktor. Now the matter couldn't be ignored without taking their little Jewish world apart. 'You piss off Nazis, you end up with pissed-off Nazis,' the Doktor Doktor said, explaining why he did, what he did.

Refusing to endanger the whole Jewish community in the hospital because of one fat, fool of a Jew, Herr Doktor Doktor Lustig washed his hands off Ernst's father by declaring him fit to travel. Those days, there was just one direction a Jew could legally take. East. Also, remember how Siegfried would go about driving people crazy saying, they should've let that homo teacher run the entire verdammte school system, and saved themselves a Second World War? Well, for the coup de grace, Herr Doktor Doktor Lustig went registered him a homosexual. A twist to the thrust, just to show who was boss and what happened to those who forgot.

One may want to sit back and let this sink in. Think what it meant being a Jew in Nazi Germany. Then, read up on what happened to homosexuals. Simply adding the two together doesn't do justice. For Jewish homosexuals, the persecution needs to be compounded—like the Seth's interest—to get at what lay in store. Reasonably good at math, Siegfried Steiger knew he was in for the compounded fucking of his life.

23

Doctor Waller

Neither Indian or English, but both.
—*Frank Anthony, MP, on the Anglo-Indian community*

'No question,' Salim Ali claimed, epistemologically speaking, 'the patient knows more than his doctor. Don't forget that.'

'I don't know what that word even means. Your accent isn't helping.'

'Oh, and yours is perfect? What's wrong with you? Coming to Sion Hospital instead of going to Breach Candy like other Europeans.'

Waller's Mallu nurse showed up and there was this silent, ethnic moment with Salim Ali. She was perky, this one, and openly checking him out. It didn't take long to establish though that when one looks like Salim Ali, he being a fellow Mallu wasn't good enough. She tuned off and beckoned Ernst to follow.

Walking behind the nurse, Ernst decided to remain upbeat. After all, he wasn't in pain, still alive, and leading a life of sorts. He couldn't help wondering though if this was the turning point. When his body took a look at the rest of his life and decided to follow suit. The nurse left him at the door, refusing to go a step further. Entering Waller's surgery, Ernst made straight for the operating table, clambering up to get his feet off the floor. He tried not taking in the pungent urine smell and musky odour. Seeing the snakes on display, Ernst understood why the staff left Waller alone. And even though he was sure the Russell's Viper scare was nonsense, people swore they had seen snakes slithering around.

Waiting up there gave him time to study the nearest glass vitrine on the stainless steel shelf, a few feet from his face. It looked like a plumpish, brown eel coiled in there with a distinct snake's head: triangular with a blunt, raised snout. This one had big nostrils—you would think they were eyes. Ernst could count each scale on the snake's fragmented crown. He had never been close to one before—not even near a harmless rat snake from the hospital compound, which is what this probably was. The Mallu nurse peeked in, shuddered and stepped aside for Dr. Waller. He pointed at the snake staring at Ernst through unblinking horizontal slits.

'That's a Russell's Viper. Poisonous bugger, what?'

Ernst scooted up the operating table to the far end. He cursed, calmed himself and got ready for Waller to begin with a dissertation on Russell's Vipers before coming around to the medical report. Knowing Waller, he would read it aloud then say to him, there's nothing to worry about, you bugger.

'It's skin cancer,' Waller said.

He turned grave, stern almost. 'The cancer from the melanoma may have spread. Possibly the colon, given your related issues with constipation and all.' The man delivering that blow to the head was all British. Where did the half-baked dingo go? 'To confirm the diagnosis though,' he went on to say, 'X-ray's a must.'

This was an outrage. Ernst wanted to tell the idiot he was a confirmed hypochondriac and therefore he couldn't possibly be ill.

'The other day you said it was all in my head.'

'Relax, you bugger. You have in the neighbourhood of several years with proper treatment.' The meandering Anglo-Indian was back to blunt the blow. He then went, 'Possibly more,' before his British Army alter ego qualified that going, 'with a catheter and other aids.' Over these past years, certain aspects of Dr. Waller's personality weren't obvious. Like his having two of them.

'Let's go get you an appointment at the Tata Memorial,' the British Army version said. 'Sooner, the better. They have the latest Canadian teletherapy machine. But first, an X-ray's required to identify the spread.' He spoke as if the spread was certain. 'However,' the drug addict intervened to add, 'whatever the diagnosis, I still ask you, bugger, lead your life normally. Remember, every man has to die one day.'

Ernst knew he would die one day. Just, not one day soon. Which is where maya comes in. Why it's such a necessary illusion. But the curtain before his eyes was rent now. He felt trapped by a growing terror and became short of breath.

'Don't quote me,' Waller said, 'but late cases sometimes outlive the early ones, simply because they escape invasive procedures.'

'Did exposure to sun cause this?'

The British Army Waller was back again, and categorical. Nothing just appeared out of nowhere. Cause-effect principle. Excessive exposure to the sun, smoking and now, they say, even the human sperm when it enters the female cervix.

'We can eliminate that last one though in your case, what?' the half-baked dingo said with his crazed smile.

'Anyway, no time to lose.' The British Army surgeon was back. Chop-chop. 'Off to Tata Memorial with you. Let's not delay the appointment.'

'How worried should I be?'

'Relax, bugger. They have this Canadian Theratron Junior over there. It can cure anything.'

'Even cancer?'

'Ha ha. That's the spirit. Humour's key. But faith too, you bugger. Times like this, keeping faith is what matters.'

Ernst wanted to reach across and strangle the man who, seconds ago, advocated against invasive procedures and now wanted to blitz him with radiation, based on faith. What he needed, was a second opinion. Sassoon would find him the right doctor at Breach Candy once he got past Salim Ali. The Seth would get him into Bombay Hospital, once again if only Salim Ali weren't blocking the way.

Alternatively, he could surprise himself by taking charge. Stop looking for handouts; go get admitted to the Jüdische Krankenhaus. Like him, Berlin's Jewish hospital had survived. Unlike him, it had flourished. He should make a trunk call. He was still German. Still a Jew. See how the Jüdische Krankenhaus protected Bombay Ingrid after she returned. Maybe it would hold back cancer the same way it kept the Nazis at bay. Then there was the matter of an air ticket. That admittedly, would need one more handout.

He felt a shortness of breath, and sat on the bench outside Waller's office. Behind her desk, the Mallu nurse was a tight, little package and he didn't care. That Waller though, was something else. So was one's life—going, going, gone, and nothing to show for it. This feeling of emptiness stemmed more from time wasted, than over what little remained. He had done nothing with his life, and now there was nothing left to do. Someone touched his shoulder—Salim Ali, with his best, disinterested expression.

'Do you need me to assist you?'

'Why?'

'You should look at yourself. Does he actually have snakes on the floor?'

'What?'

'Nothing. What was the diagnosis? Nothing to worry about?'

'He confirmed it's cancer.'

Salim Ali curled his lip. He looked disappointed.

'We'll fight this. If not here, then Moscow. I can arrange it. Socialist medicine is the answer.'

They walked out to the one-eyed Fiat.

'Fuck Moscow,' Salim Ali said. 'Don't listen to me. You have to get to West Germany.'

An impressive a volte-face as any. It struck Ernst that the panicking Salim Ali was too young to have people dying around him. Arjun gone, Tufan going, and now this—the last straw.

During the ride home, Ernst paused to ponder the diagnosis. First you fail, then you die. For once, he empathised with Salim Ali and found himself in agreement. This was the last straw.

24

The Last Straw

Black as night,
Her tongue is red,
Demon blood is what's been shed.
When she's a frightful sight,
Means all right,
When she's smiling though,
It means you're dead.
—*On Goddess Bhairavi*

'Goddess Bhairavi, Shiva's daughter, is the sixth Mahavidhya or great teacher,' says Andhi Ma.

'But you already know that,' she says, 'unless you're a bigger fool than I thought. More importantly, seen her recently? No longer ugly as sin, is she? Even those teeth look good. Well, please don't shit your pants, but your time's up.'

First and foremost: even while speaking to no one in particular, the crazy, blind woman outside the Krishna Temple has an Assamese, Convent-School accent. She sounds like the dead Arjun's mother, Tobi Basar. Other than that, there's nothing in common with the Oriental Butterfly.

Second: Who is she going on about? Which Goddess Bhairavi? Shiva's daughter, or the one from Sindhi Camp?

'What difference does it make?' she asks in that Assamese Convent English. 'When time's up, it's up.'

Third: if this was a dream, how does he know to call her Blind Mother, or, Andhi Ma?

Maybe, because it is a dream.

His panic comes in waves cresting above chest level while Andhi Ma sits it out beyond the surf. He takes deep breaths, does his 'Oms', tries to focus and tell himself he is there for a purpose. When one has Waller as his doctor, going to a blind mendicant for a second opinion actually makes sense. Besides, it's no one's business what he does in his dreams. Her legs are crossed and feet sticking out from her unwashed, saffron, kaftan-type sackcloth she has on, day and night. He cherishes his foot fetish like nothing else, and would never place himself near ones as dirty as these. Let alone hold them with both hands to press against his head in supplication, Hindu-style.

She looks pleased to death when he does that.

'I'm scared, Maaji.'

'Think I can't see that?'

But you can't. He feels an idiot. In a way, good she's blind. Her crusted braids are alive with lice and it's impossible to maintain eye contact. She appears philosophical. He tries not to stare at her caked feet but it's either that, or the lice.

'Stop staring. What's this nonsense about last straws? Tell me how you feel.'

'Relieved because I'm with you.'

'You're relieved because the uncertainty's over.'

'How do I fight this cancer?'

'Why? What's it ever done to you?'

That deserves a pause.

'You're a tantric acolyte. A Sahajiya.'

Pause.

Then, 'Really? You think I wouldn't know? Being Sahajiya, shouldn't you be displaying more sense? I mean, what's the big deal? Whatever's happening inside you is helping you prepare, getting you ready for when time's right. But your type either wants to fight it, or surrender. Looks like it's only bookish knowledge, your tantric studies.'

It's supposed to be, he wants to tell her. This is India. No need to practise what's preached.

'Or maybe, you are Sahajiya just for the tantric fun and games? You know...' Andhi Ma winks. What he feels seeing her nictitate, Ernst wouldn't wish on anyone.

'When's the time right, Maaji?'

She doesn't bite his head off. Instead, 'How should I know? Your body will tell you,' she says, looking up, distracted. 'That glare, can you see it?'

He tries not to look stumped, not to follow her finger tracing past Sindhi Camp with its frightened Nissen huts and towards Trombay Hill hiding India's nuclear reactors from view—a permanent backdrop looming large. He struggles dealing with her not just being blind, but stoned.

'Treat it like a friend, your illness,' she advises, now back on track. 'You may see it as evil; I see it being considerate. Spreading painlessly, until it is time.'

Painlessly?

'Yes, painlessly. Do you know how long it's been inside you without causing any problems? What has it done that you want to tear at it? A mole appearing? Some weight loss? Irregular bowels? We call that ageing.'

'They say I have to begin radiation.'

'Why? Not getting enough already?' She points at the air at absolutely nothing. 'Look at all that light. What do you think that is? Eat almonds instead,' she says. 'Bitter almonds are better than X-rays. And recite your *Bija Mantra* every morning. Not just for time-pass, the way you recite it now. Outrageous. A total waste of time, just so you know. Who taught you?'

He touches her feet once more, and offers his namastes. Time to get away from this, and that, and all the other clutter in his life.

'Maybe you're taking death too personally,' she suggests.

He pretends he didn't hear that gem.

'Your local is rushing towards VT,' she explains, meaning Victoria Terminus, the big, paan-stained and urine-smelling but otherwise exquisite Indo-Saracen, Victorian, Neo-Gothic railway terminal the British built where Mumbai ends and Bombay begins. He has taken a local from Chembur Station to VT a couple of times on the Harbour Line.

'What do you remember from your rides? Tell me about the sights and smells. I've never been on one.'

You don't want to. Passengers overflow from each compartment, and from the roof of every moving train at all times, every day. Overhead you have power lines, killing those on the roof when they stretch up. The compartments have no doors, killing those inside when they lean out. Of course, no air-conditioning either. With a wide-open entrance on either side, the cross-ventilation brings in smells from people squatting alongside the tracks, trousers down, saris up, faces averted, taking a dump. There you have it—sights and smells.

'Your train's heading to the terminus,' she says. 'Soon, your time will be up, and all you want to take away are sights and smells of people shitting?'

There's a riposte waiting at the tip of his tongue but he can't find it. She plays along, not saying anything either. He looks at her. She looks in the air.

He remembers his first ride on the Harbour Line local. He had purchased a First-Class ticket that should have come with a printed warning: Oye Bhenchod, First Class means shit.

That ride established what every commuter knew—there was nothing about abject poverty a train ride through Bombay couldn't trump with something worse. Cutting through the world's largest slum, it was as if seeing India for the first time. All of Bombay wasn't one, big, festering slum just because that's all you saw from a local. But most of it was. He had covered his nose with a handkerchief, and hell with whoever got offended.

Then they rolled into Masjid, one stop before VT.

Masjid is Bombay's wholesale spice market. No more smells of shit and urine. Instead, cloves, cardamom, nutmeg and black pepper filled the air. Hitting Masjid, he was transported to his classroom in Berlin where his homosexual class teacher would read him the names of these spices out aloud. After coming to India, the sight or smell of any of them would whisk him back to the Berlin classroom; he alone with the teacher behind closed doors, but that was another story.

'Stick with the analogy,' Andhi Ma says. 'You're at Masjid now and the shitty, smelly portion of your life is over. Enjoy the smell of spices because the next stop is final. You are lucky to be where you are. It's like approaching the Place of the Hidden Moon. I envy you.'

She means that place in your head, inaccessible even to you. Where the perfect union takes place every second of every day, with Lord Krishna loving a Radha who's married to another and therefore unattainable. That way, the Lord teaches us to reach for the impossible. There is purity in an asymptotic trajectory—getting closer to, but never touching the curve of the Hidden Moon. One is unable to cross the horizon to get to where they aspire to be, but so what? Getting as close as possible is what matters—the journey is everything. It takes three minutes from Masjid to VT. Sticking with her analogy means he has three minutes' equivalent of life left. That was meant to be comforting? She senses his panic at being caught between a rock and a crazy place. It irritates her.

'We are talking about three whole Technicolour minutes. Who asked you to perform tantric rituals if you want to live in black-and-white and die in bed?'

He tries protesting once more. This is India. All theory.

'Now that the end's near, enjoy the ride. Enjoy the food, the smells, the air. Everything is now in Technicolour, like the smell of those spices. Your cancer has done half the work for you. You go, do the rest. Do things you thought impossible. No one can stop you, except yourself. Or maybe, her.'

From the corner of his eye, he sees Sindhi Camp Bhairavi hurrying past ration queues. She is headed toward the jhopadpatti slums that garland Sindhi Camp. He catches the sway to her backside as she weaves past one slapdash tenement on top of someone else's.

'See? You're already becoming adventurous.'

Andhi Ma looks at the girl as if she can see her. He on the other hand can, and notices the ankles and feet are Sindhi-white in this dream.

'Is that what you want?'

No. He just wants to be free of cancer.

'That, my friend,' Andhi Ma says, 'is not going to happen.'

25

The Men's Room

Eat at an Udipi, shit at the Taj
—*The College Mantra*

Turns out, Andhi Ma was an amateur when it came to Jewish anxiety. He did ponder her advice though, sitting in an Irani restaurant with cancer for company. His mole asked to be caressed and he gave in, wondering if the restaurant had those bitter almonds she'd recommended in lieu of radiation. Who knows, bitter almonds could work, just like being blitzed by the Theratron Junior at Tata Memorial could work. Doing nothing could work, or nothing could work. He would keep an open mind.

Waiters surrounded the gora backpackers on the next table and were giving them the professional treatment. One gora wiped a plate of pork vindaloo clean with a folded piece of bread, then joined his travel companions to stare at the bill because clearly, it was adding up to nothing. So why were the waiters fawning? The foreigners looked confused about what it meant being white in India, and appeared unsure of their power. Seeing Ernst, a waiter peeled off from the encirclement to bring out the fruit plate and espresso for him as usual. Sliced chikoos and bananas, a vati with a liberal dollop of honey, a frosted glass of yoghurt set last night and left in the groaning fridge. Three rupees for fruit plate, honey, yoghurt and the espresso. He wanted to tell those broke kids on the next table they could live here forever on next to nothing, as long as they used their whiteness judiciously. Don't fuck around too much, don't be arseholes, and step out of the way from both oncoming traffic and creeping cancer.

He sipped at his coffee. Outside, vestiges of British India peeked from behind billboards, garbage and betel nut paan stains applied in broad swipes to Colaba walls. Colaba was meant for an era without Indians cluttering the place, and with never more than fifty thousand Englishmen spread across the subcontinent. These days, there were ten times as many people clambering all over the Causeway alone. The architecture was beginning to buckle under and it was only a matter of when. Being early morning, there was still space to breathe. The crowds would be here after ten, spilling on the roads amidst cars, BEST buses and taxis. Then growing by the hour, to inch past Arabs, goras, and pickpockets with their children tugging at tourist arms, while slender men with kohl in their eyes led blonde, Scandinavian types to unknown fates like determined little tow-tractors pulling 707s through the crowd.

He took a spoonful of yoghurt to mix into the fruit and honey. The ritual being, to keep pouring until some of the yoghurt spills over, at which point he'd stop, taste a spoonful, and follow up with a sip of coffee. Once in a while the chikoo would melt in his mouth, the chilled yoghurt would be creamy perfect, the honey sweet as imported American Tupelo, and the espresso kicking back like a horse. It all came together today, in Technicolour. He chewed and poured the remaining honey into the glass, stirred it around until the yoghurt turned gold, then drank it. The sheer taste of it sent his head spinning. Three rupees later, he stepped out on the Causeway to buy a straight razor.

~

The Taj Hotel ran for four blocks parallel to Colaba Causeway. Its length obstructed the sea view, so you couldn't see the tour boats bobbing like corks around the Gateway of India. Same as Victoria Terminus, the Taj too was Indo-Gothic, neo-Victorian or Indo-Saracen, and one hell of a structure—a Tata owned, phoren-looking, Indian design. Unlike VT however, not a single paan stain anywhere. Its exclusiveness, more than any architectural beauty, made pedestrians pause but not spit. Cars too would slow down, bumping into each other. It loomed ahead, the Taj dome, crowning the grey-and-white stone structure, but with doormen missing from the big, wooden block of a door that faced Colaba.

That's because two Sikhs manned the door facing the harbour on the opposite side instead—the entrance to what technically, was the hotel's arse-end but deemed the main entrance because it faced the sea. The debate on what was, or was not, the Taj Hotel's front door trailed across a century of agonising over the architect's motives in positioning the main entrance away from the harbour. The man allegedly committed suicide at the shame from such an obvious fuck-up. The architect was Indian, so people knew that story wasn't true. Not about the fuck-up. The fact he would commit suicide out of shame. Rumours being what they are and therefore, true or not, the Taj became associated with suicides. So much so, they said the Tatas had a budget allocated to keep any such talk out of the newspapers.

A Tata Mercedes truck inched up from his right. It crept past the traffic sign warning in English and Marathi, TRUCKS NOT ALLOWED. If all Tata Mercedes trucks didn't look so alike, Ernst would say this one looked familiar. So did a gorilla squeezed in the cabin along with more than a full load. The driver's handlebar moustache cramped the confines further. The Tata Mercedes stopped as if to check out the Taj. Ernst got the feeling it was also checking him out. It struck him how since the cancer shock, he had so easily put aside the dead Arjun and his dying uncle, as well as the headless Sardar and the gorilla at the centre of it all—now staring past the Tata's windshield with those beady, little eyes.

He walked in through the back door that was the front door, and headed for the Men's Room. In the whole vast expanse of the hotel, he was most comfortable in the toilet. There was no place in Bombay that compelled a better shit. This was his first time inside the premises since he turned invisible twenty-six years ago, even though a ten-minute walk from his flat. The lobby had carried on without him.

'As if I never happened,' Ernst said out aloud to no one. Walking towards the toilets he felt dizzy, and slumped on a sofa with a suddenness that brought the Guest Relations Manager running.

'No worries,' he said to her. 'Pretend I don't exist. It's easy.' The Guest Relations lady didn't know what to say, and waited while he sat out his emotions.

Cowering in the Irani restaurant that morning, trying to look cool and remain calm, he had reviewed Andhi Ma's advice and concluded that he was right, she was wrong; this was the last straw, not some final journey in Technicolour. Buoyed by all that sugar and coffee, he had decided on the Taj. Now sitting in the foyer, the sugar buzz was gone. He was no different from all the other white patrons, scattered around the lobby like foreign exchange. The Guest Relations Manager would probably beg to differ. Her expression suggested he was different. Unlike them, he was a problem. Her hotel would only get back to normal if he would kindly leave quietly. She offered to have the doorman escort him out.

Ernst pulled himself up from the soft, downy sofa much to the Manager's relief, and walked down the vestibule leading to the Men's Room. He tried to find amusement in the episode and flashed a parting smile. She stared in response. It made him feel superior and he started to feel better. He was on a different plane. He had a sense of purpose and a more important thing to do than most people, including this woman. He held on to the feeling, and it shored him up.

26

The Toilet Stall

Yield not to unmanliness,
Follow your Dharma wherever it goes,
Cast off fear—become more not less,
O Parantapa, Scorcher of Foes.
—*The Bhagavad Gita*

The toilet attendant was missing. He showed up on afternoons and evenings when tippers came in to piss and preen. No one else there either, and the wide, luxurious, teak and marble toilet stalls were empty. A jhopadpatti slum family could live in one. Given there was a functional toilet inside, they would never leave.

Ernst removed his wallet after locking the stall door. The only identification he had on him was a few visiting cards and a driving licence. Indian drivers' licences did not need photographs. He sat on the shut commode with his trousers on and as he tore up the licence and cards, it felt strange the way his sense of purpose was carrying him through this. He could have used it with Ingrid. He stood up to flush and it took three rounds with intervals of waiting before the itsy-bitsy pieces of a man gurgled away. Ernst then sat back and took out the straight razor he just purchased. It was Soviet, an OKA: four-inch stainless steel blade, plastic handle with a splatter of Cyrillic and no box or case.

His heart began to pound, knocking at his chest with loud thumps. Soon the whole cubicle was vibrating to the thump-thump-thumping.

He felt a vein throb on the side of his forehead and marvelled at how easily all this thumping and throbbing could be stopped. Also, if he didn't put a stop to it, there was something inside him growing with every thump that easily would. His options came down to this, or that; fucked, or screwed; now, or later; on the commode, or in bed; be like his mother and die of cancer, or go his father's route and kill himself. I'm spoilt for choice, he thought and started to tremble.

Growing up in Berlin and around the time jackboots became fashionable, he would be unable to sleep, screaming with terror inside his head while waiting for his father to get home safe. Later in Bombay, he would scream while asleep, watching his father slit his wrists again and again until Parvatibai showed up with her poultice.

Sitting on the commode with its lid down, there wouldn't be any screaming today. That would be ridiculous. He had no argument handy, however, against the quiet panic that took over, and he watched his hand shake trying to wield the straight razor. Even that drug-addict of a Waller exercised better control. He was going to botch it and hurt himself if he didn't get a hold. Leave quietly without a fuss, please, and without Parvatibai having to clean up the mess. He thought of Parvatibai, and all that bulk barely left space to squeeze in Salim Ali; but he managed to do it, acknowledged his presence, and thanked him. When the only two people who cared a fuck wondered why he did it, they would place cancer first on the list, followed by, in no particular order, everything else. In reality though, it was the other way around. Everything else came first with cancer being the last straw.

The camel started to buckle under, way back when Bombay Ingrid walked up the gangplank to leave him for reasons he couldn't fully fathom because by the time she left, they had mostly sorted things out. One day announces she's pregnant, and next day says she's leaving. He would still wake up on mornings surprised she would leave just like that. On other mornings he would marvel at how everything unravelled so quickly after she left or because she left. Who knew?

'I want you to know however,' he said, sitting on the commode, 'that I have loved you like no other. I think of you, and think of you more and more every day, and after all these years, still you alone matter.' He went on to say to the empty stall that she should know this, and if she didn't, then she should just look into his eyes to know who was the thief of his heart.

He took a deep breath and though his hand still shook, he felt it was time to calm the mind.

> Sai, Your presence grants me the comfort I seek.
> I do as You ask,
> Act as I must,
> It's not difficult this task,
> My transformation to dust.

He stopped chanting because it wasn't working. He felt like praying to Ingrid, instead. A strange and disturbing thing for a Hindu-Jew, but she was still the only thing close to Christmas in his life. If she showed up now, nothing else would matter.

Who wouldn't show up after that? She appeared in aseptic German white, in the uniform he had never seen outside of the photograph; didn't matter because all he cared about was her face. Bombay Ingrid's petal-like beauty had hardened, become more muscular and attractive on Schwester Ingrid. There were crowfeet around those ocean-blue eyes. A line etched down her left side of the face alongside the nose and she had never looked more stunning. Age had worked wonders and it was like Christmas in the toilet stall. He decided if she tried to stop him, he would let her. She looked at the straight razor hovering over his wrist and her eyes widened. She reached forward, as if to stay his hand.

Slice firmly along the track to slit it properly, she advised, not across the vein—apparently, a common mistake.

~

She did look unhappy however, at his trying to slit his wrists with a cheap Soviet razor and that too on the commode.

Sordid. Any idea what a mess he would make? And to top it all, you're doing this at the Taj? The one place that made Bombay

somewhat tolerable? Had he really thought this through? She had
loved passing time at the Sea Lounge on the Taj mezzanine—sipping
tea, nibbling pastries. He once managed to hold her hand across the
table over there for a little longer than usual. Later, they'd walked
home and she'd spread herself on the bed to allow him a go. She
had laughed, seeing him slobber over his Christmas present in July.
Now here he was, ruining yet another memory. Why not in a nice,
warm, bathtub instead? He should know—she never failed to remind
him in letter after letter and now once again—his father did just that
before the Nazis came a-knocking.

They had kicked open the bathroom door at the Jüdische
Krankenhaus, to find Siegfried in the tub bleeding from both wrists.
Schwester Ingrid wrote it was quite the sight, what with Emmy
Destinn soaring from his turntable like an eagle to crap all over the
soldiers. The Nazis couldn't be bothered and froze into a rock-solid
cohort sealing the doorway better than any Parvatibai; mesmerised
by Siegfried's penis sticking out through the soapy water like a
fist. His father's erection had kept them at bay allowing him to die
undisturbed; avenging the embarrassing, pink homo-star they had
forced him to wear. Whereas towards the end, all he wanted was the
solitary, yellow, Jew one.

Why? Schwester Ingrid had asked in one of her letters, just before
they stopped altogether. Why did it come to this? No one wanted
ripples at the Jüdische Krankenhaus. Not the Jewish staff, not the
patients living in constant terror, and definitely not the Nazis. It
was their staging post for boxed and parcelled Jews shipping East.
They wanted everything to look normal for those being shipped
to die. To the extent of sparing the Jew staff and Jew patients for
appearances sake. His father had to go fuck with that. Then slit his
wrists to escape the consequences.

That reminded Ernst. Lala Prem would have deposited that
cheque today. He felt a surge of adrenalin at the thought of it bouncing
like Chhote Bhai's hockey ball. There was something to be said for
escaping the consequences. It shored him up into pressing down with
the razor and take charge. He wanted to pray to Lord Vishnu while
doing it, to Gurudeva, Maheshvara; ask them for strength. Once
again, Schwester Ingrid was the one who came through. Firmly, she

advised, while he prayed. Steady that hand and be firm. For once in your life, be firm.

'Jai Gurudeva, Jai Guru Vishnu, Maheshvara. You will prevail. Jai Mahadeva. Jai, jai.'

Caught up in his chant, when Ernst first heard sounds from outside the toilet stall, they didn't register. Marathi isn't spoken in the Taj. When the shouting persisted, it threw him. As if a Maratha army had stormed the Indo-Saracen structure and into the Men's Room. Impossible really, until Ernst heard a familiar voice growling instructions.

The Men's Room door opened again with a clickity-click-click. The same male voice was now articulating in English, and a female going, 'Yes, Sir, I understand Sir, but I simply cannot be searching among foreign guests and international VIPs. I told you, he was not feeling well and left.' She sounded a lot like the Guest Relations lady.

'Maybe he did, maybe not,' the familiar voice said. 'What's the harm in making sure? You say he was not well and we are his friends. We are worried. You need to do as I ask, before we do something to your bleddy establishment. You know whom you are talking to?'

There was the fading clickity-click-click of stilettos on marble, as the lady scooted off to save the Taj. The male voice then reverted to Marathi and a war council came to order. Ernst would recognise the gorilla's rumble anywhere. Henry Gomes.

Gomes spoke and no one interrupted him. The others listened. No arguments. Ernst looked around and Schwester Ingrid was gone. Too many Indians.

Outside the toilet stall, Gomes continued with who searches where, and does what. Ernst scrambled behind the Marathi syntax to try and understand. Gomes was now laying out whom they had to find. It was a disparaging description of the shitty, old, European fuck they saw entering the hotel. Ernst grudgingly conceded the description fitted him. Then he heard the Guest Relations Manager rush back in a race against her own clickity-click-click.

'We have searched all public areas, Sir,' she said, breathless in the service of her hotel. 'I can assure you, unless he has a room with us under a different name, he has left the premises.'

There was silence around the urinals. Then Gomes muttered in Marathi, 'That motherfucking chutiya couldn't afford a room.'

'Go, look around once more,' he ordered. 'Let me think.' Ernst could picture the man—more gorilla really—with those shoulders and red beads for eyes.

He heard the flowing Maratha river debouche through the door. The Men's Room was now empty except for him, and the gorilla gone silent. He probably was deep in thought, because he was an intelligent gorilla. Not intelligent enough though—Ernst was thankful—to consider checking the toilet stalls. Then, he too was gone, leaving a hollow feel to the place.

Peeking out into the vestibule to make sure the coast was clear, Ernst realised he had forgotten to kill himself.

27

The Marxist Passion Play

*The permit room is a peculiarly Mumbai institution: drinks are generally
served in six-ounce bottles, the lighting tends toward dingy and the
clientele is almost exclusively male.*
—*The New York Times*

The Golf Club's permit-room was a tight fit for a working day and
Japanese everywhere.

Ernst tried to engage D'Souza past the large Japanese presence
at the bar. Japanese or no Japanese, today cried for a Bloody Mary
because next week was Tata Memorial. Waller had managed to get
an appointment for him with their Radiology department. Best
then, to let them decide what to do with the rest of his life. Left
to his own devices he couldn't even kill himself. It was a growing
list—the things he couldn't do. Dr. Waller would be there at Tata
Memorial to hold his hand while they X-rayed his insides. The
good doctor would then help decide what to fry further with more
X-rays. The only other alternative was Andhi Ma's bitter almonds,
even though the Jewish Hospital in West Berlin had come back with
a resounding, Yes!

A German Jew wanting to go back to Germany? The West German
Consulate on Peddar Road was ecstatic. Frau Schmidt—the terror of
Indians seeking visas—couldn't do enough. Ernst became her personal
project and she single-handedly proceeded to wipe out Germany's
past. As long as Frau Schmidt manned the tele-type machine, there

was no question of him spending a pfennig on healthcare. The telex had chattered over Ernst while matters of state waited it out. He should have his doctor send over his files, the telex suggested. A September check-up and even admission were possible, it declared. Of course no charge, it stuttered, and Frau Schmidt had given a tight smile. He would of course need an aeroplane ticket. That could pose a problem, he felt. On the other hand, bitter almonds wouldn't.

~

Trick to a perfect Bloody Mary, he heard D'Souza explain to the Japanese men nodding away at the bar, was to make it fresh, from 'highly fresh ingredients.' Because, 'It's a highly unstable concoction.' The Goan bartender couldn't stress that enough.

'Has to be fresh. Must be highly fresh.'

This accent on high freshness hit a chord with the sushi eaters and they went, 'Aaah so!'

'Also ice. Lots of ice. It neutralises acids in tomato juice and other ingredients that ruin taste.'

D'Souza wasn't your typical, Western-style bartender. On any given day, he required a gun to the head before eking out monosyllables. How come then, this non-stop monologue? Could be from addressing people more deadpan than he. Each Japanese held a glass and sipping in unison, they went, 'Aaah so!'

As for these sons of Nippon being here, turns out there was a perfectly logical explanation. If one was Willie Lansdowne. While still under his stewardship some years ago, the Bombay Presidency Golf Club found itself at a tipping point from a steady decline in Westerners. Compounded, one could say, by Willie's reluctance to enrol Indians. It seemed silly to cede more ground just to balance the books. Made no sense. Then one fine morning, a flock of Japanese flew into the permit-room. Then more. Then a few more. They would fly in to golf over holidays and long weekends; people said cheaper to fly here than pay the green fees back home. In the process, they saved the club from more Indians. Willie reckoned there must be a God and as his last official act, gave away memberships to any and all Flying Japanese. They thought the club was holding a fire sale.

The incoming club secretary was Brigadier Bunkim Kumar Chatterjee (retired), who had done a stint in South East Asia. Mainly as a Japanese prisoner of war. He smiled in disbelief when his predecessor hollered during his last board meeting as secretary, 'Better Nips than wogs!'

Seeing the Japanese at the bar, the Brigadier went up to his beloved Victrola parked by the bar (polished it himself) and had it crank out 'Sukiyaki', in honour of his tormenters from those balmy days in Singapore he had enjoyed as their house-guest at Changi Prison. It was now the Japanese's turn to smile in disbelief as their global number-one hit ricocheted off the walls. 'Aaah so!' they went, clapped, bowed and then got all confused when the Brigadier responded with the correct bow.

'Sukiyaki means beef-broth,' the Brigadier said to Ernst, while smiling at the Japanese. 'It's a love song.' He waved. 'They'd do it all over again, you know. In a heartbeat.' The WWII veteran then gave Ernst the once over. 'Looking buggered, what?'

Over at the bar, D'Souza broke away from his mesmerised audience to answer the intercom. Placing a black handset on the bar-top, he came up to where Ernst and the Brigadier sat. Someone Indian at the reception was asking for Ernst, who wilted further. The reception area was like a border crossing for Indian guests. Brigadier Chatterjee nodded to D'Souza who went conveyed the nod over the phone.

Turned out to be Salim Ali, mustering superhuman strength to creak the heavy teak door open. An aura of class warfare preceded him by yards, making it difficult for people to remain on even keel. The Europeans stared, and Salim Ali right away sensed where the gentry were coming from. It's that remarkable Indian antenna seeking out any sliver of hidden hostility in a look. Not harbouring the remarkable Indian eagerness to please however, the little Marxist transmitted back a big, fat, fuck-you-too at the permit-room. The Brigadier appraised Salim Ali and appeared fascinated by the company Ernst kept. Willie too was staring their way, so Ernst excused himself and edged Salim Ali to the far end of the bar. Best to keep a safe distance from Willie, who looked more like Colonel Blimp every passing day. There at the bar, Ernst appeared exaggerated next to a Salim Ali struggling up his bar stool. It was as if he had violated a slew of by-laws to bring his illegitimate, black child into the permit-room. Salim Ali stabilised. Once his stool's rotation was under control, Ernst ordered him his lime juice, vegetarian samosas and a plate of little, green chillies that would take down a rhino.

Playing with the glass of nimbu-pani, Salim Ali said, 'You wanted to see me.'

'Come, sit, relax. See how the other half lives.'

'Who plays these silly-bugger games on a working day?'

'What working day? Thanks to you, all they do at the workshop is discuss PL 480 food aid.'

'Sure,' Salim Ali said. 'Blame the workers.'

Ernst did not take the bait. Andhi Ma had granted him three Technicolour minutes. That sort of a deadline made you want to smell the roses and hell with everything else. He looked down, and cringed. Salim Ali was in rubber slippers. The reception had no choice but to let him in following the Brigadier's intervention. His toes were wet and shrivelled, making the uncut nails much bolder to the eye. Clueless what that did to the people around him, Salim Ali got down to business.

'How's the bookkeeping coming along?'

'Why the interest in accounts?'

'Parvatibai thinks there's more than just double-entry going on.'

'Parvatibai's being Parvatibai.'

'Bhairavi could be your daughter.'

Five minutes with Salim Ali, and now he wanted to kill himself again.

'Yes.'

'Indian. Hindu. Sindhi. There've been riots for less,' Salim Ali said.

'Just a thought. Could you be jealous?'

'Why am I not surprised at that? However, unlike you, I have other things on my mind.'

'Like that gunny bag Parvatibai's holding on to for you?'

Salim Ali's lip curled on its own volition. 'Good try.'

'Where's Tufan?'

'At the bleddy police chowki, where else? Asking them to act on the autopsy report. Bleddy thugs in uniform.'

The room parted, and Adam Sassoon was seen approach the bar. The way people reacted, as if they wanted to applaud. Except for Salim Ali. Already tottering on a bar stool, the last thing Ernst needed was for him to stand up on his soapbox. Didn't matter. The great man pretended Salim Ali wasn't there and it appeared, neither was Ernst. While Major Punjabi was also not there today, a young, sharply creased minor Punjabi carried the great man's briefcase for him.

~

Adam Sassoon's presence reminded Ernst of Salary Day; also that no advance was forthcoming; no pipes, nothing. The only cheque doing the rounds was his dud; the one the Lala would have deposited today. Thoughts of it bouncing didn't bring about the usual shortness of breath, or tighten the cork up his arse. Surviving a suicide attempt seemed to have advanced the mind. Sassoon wasn't authorising Major Punjabi to pay up? Fine. Fuck it. No money for salaries? Fuck that too. His cheque was going to bounce? Great.

We'll see what happens. 'Bloody dekha jayega!'

Salim Ali dropped his samosa and looked at Ernst. Eyebrows rose across the permit-room. Sassoon had this interested look to his face. No longer invisible, Ernst raised his glass to the bar. The minor Punjabi recovered, and touched Sassoon's elbow. Jehangir Merchant had walked in, suited-booted—dark patches under armpits and a babu in tow holding a long, rolled blueprint. The same Indian gentleman with the pince-nez, Ernst had seen scurry alongside Jehangir that other day at Fertilisers. Now holding the same rolled blueprint Jehangir had dropped all over the floor. Paranjpe. That babu with the pince-nez. His name was Paranjpe. Ernst patted himself.

'Bugger. There goes my drink,' Sassoon said. 'Can't take it over there now, can I?'

'Why not? They all drink anyway, the sods.' Willie knew Indians. There could be no argument. They were all secret alcoholics. He was a social drinker.

Leaving his scotch behind, Sassoon walked the short distance towards a table Jehangir had sequestered. Willie reached out a paw for some bland peanuts from one of the bowls decorating the bar. They were without masala to placate Western palates, or intentionally bland to keep Indians out.

Across the cramped room, Sassoon's group settled in and Jehangir let loose that oversized blueprint with a flourish, knocking a cheap tin ashtray off the table. Meanwhile Paranjpe had turned invisible, folding himself into a corner chair. He re-emerged under Ernst's squint. The man had a general sense of apology at being there. With his suit drying off to deliver the proper effect, Jehangir Merchant was back to being his patronising best with the bespectacled babu. It was Sassoon though, who blew Ernst out of the water by asking D'Souza, 'Bring some orange juice over for Paranjpeji.'

'First he sacrifices his scotch for an Indian babu,' Salim Ali noted. 'Now he is playing host. I smell something.' He craned his neck to check out the blueprint's generous expanse.

'Pipes,' Ernst said, before the idiot became any more obvious. 'It's a schematic on a building full of pipes.'

'Same pipes the bugger Punjabi wants us to draw?'

'You tell me. What's a reprocessing plant?'

'You mean a refining plant.'

'I mean a fuel reprocessing plant. That's what that blueprint says.'

Salim Ali blinked. 'Fuck,' he said.

'What?'

'The Atomic Energy facility at Trombay. You bleddy sure it reads reprocessing plant?'

'Yes, I'm bleddy sure. Why? And stop staring.'

They are building a nuclear reprocessing plant at AEET, that's why. Bleddy Sassoon's sneaked in there too? Nothing's sacrosanct in this country. He blinked a couple of times. 'Those pipes are specialised. You telling me that capitalist rascal plans to have us draw them? Reprocessing nuclear fuel requires concentrated nitric acid to dissolve plutonium and uranium from the spent fuel,' he said, and Ernst sincerely wanted to know if there was anything—anything at all—the little fucker didn't know.

'You need zirconium or austenitic stainless steel to hold the radioactive acid. Even then, it's dangerous. Very. Even the Americans announced a full stop to their nuclear reprocessing. They plan to dig a hole in some mountain, dump their spent fuel and forget about it. I tell you this is too big. Not something we can do.'

Would be nice if we could, Ernst felt. 'We could end up becoming accredited suppliers to AEET.'

'Listen,' Salim Ali said, stepping out of character to grip Ernst's forearm. His black claw dug in. 'I know you're joking. But what if the pipes Punjabi's sending us are really for AEET? Is this how these cheap bastards plan to supply a nuclear facility? By having someone like you draw the pipes?'

Ernst decided not to take offence.

'Relax,' he advised. 'There is no order any more. No one's sending us anything. Didn't you see how Sassoon ignored us?' Salim Ali's look suggested he saw nothing unusual in that. People ignored him all the time. The heavy door creaked open once more, and Venky Iyer walked in. The scene now had all the elements of a Marxist passion play, with the proletariat playing Jesus.

'Someone's getting fucked,' Salim Ali concluded.

Iyer saw him. His look said, yes, and that someone is you. Then he too went and joined the cabal: industrialist, bagman, babu and now, senior civil servant. Running a socialist country together in a business-like manner.

'I'll wait for you in the car.'

With that, Salim Ali climbed down to walk by Willie and he must have brushed past or something, because Willie spilled his drink. Salim Ali ambled along—no apology. Surprise broke out over Willie's face like a red rash, but the teak door creaked again, distracting everyone from what an Indian had just visited upon the club's former secretary and current cuckold.

A woman in a sari stood at the door. Ernst had never seen the permit-room getting shoulder-to-shoulder like this. He had also never seen an Indian woman enter in here. Nor had the gentry, especially one like this. Sindhi Camp Bhairavi's buck teeth shone like pearls.

'What?' Willie gaped.

Adam Sassoon on the other hand was behaving as if Goddess Bhairavi—the beautiful version, the one to die for—had lit up the dingy permit-room. He leaped to attention at her toothy smile; her sari fluffed around an arse custom-made for a tight fit. With a red-cloth ledger in hand, she smiled only for the great man and the rest could go to hell.

28

Ground Fighting

Ground on which we can only be saved from destruction by fighting
without delay, is desperate ground.

—*Sun Tzu's Art of War*

It was around four-thirty and in blinding heat, when Mohan Driver
held the rear door open for Ernst. The man had probably stopped
by a temple because there was a smudge of saffron on his forehead.

Salim Ali was inside the Fiat and compressed into the far corner
by some overbearing weight. Could be Sassoon's stainless steel pipes
that never showed up at the workshop, or maybe the ones showing
up on that blueprint. Or, could be the sight of his Bhairavi walking
into the permit-room as Sassoon's guest.

Ernst got in the rear seat with Salim Ali and settled back into
the body odour. Outside, Sindhi Camp played dead in the afternoon
heat with Jhama Sweetmeats deserted, shops shut, no traffic, no
roadside cricket game, no water queue, and crows ruling the skies.
Nothing, except for the ration queue winding alongside Trombay
Road as proof of some life. The Seth's driver was there in line and
Sassoon's chauffeur was present as well, both to collect ration rice
for the household servants while waiting for their masters. With
their fingers intertwined, they held hands the way Indian men do,
and chatted. Ernst tried picturing Sassoon and the Seth being friends
Indian-style, and failed. Looking around, the only other activity was
in the police chowki compound.

Henry Gomes sat there amidst Bombay's Finest, peeling a banana. One couldn't escape him anymore—gorilla to albatross in one month. Ernst wasn't surprised. He had already seen him as a murderous worker in blue, then a conscientious hospital orderly in khaki, and this morning, as the leader of a pack hunting him down in a five-star hotel. So why not now, relaxing at a police station? That he was not in police uniform was the only surprise. Instead, he had on a tight sort of white T-shirt and was admiring each slab of his abdominal muscle on display, while eating his banana; therefore, he didn't see them drive by. Someone must have, because turning right onto Vashigaon Road, Mohan Driver slammed on the brakes a few yards from where Chhote Bhai's Mian Building stared down at the Krishna Temple.

Frozen at the steering wheel, he took in the Marathas blocking his vehicle going forward. One of them came around, bent over the driver's open window and Mohan Driver shifted his stare down to the foot pedals. Reaching in, the Maratha pulled at Mohan Driver's cheek. Then he tapped on Ernst's window. Ernst wound it down with ten rupees in hand and leaned out, all set to play the genial European. The man took the money and hit the flat of his palm against the Fiat's side.

'Get out. Take the driver and walk away. Leave the Madrasi thief in the car,' he said, staring at Salim Ali. 'He has something we want.'

Ernst put on his European face while Mohan Driver looked shaky, but stayed put.

'Kerala,' Ernst said. 'He comes from Kerala. He's not Madrasi.'

'Don't be a hero. Get out.'

Salim Ali sat back as Ernst leaned across him to lock down his side. Instantly, there was hammering against the glass. Salim Ali watched them bang away for a bit, then went and unlocked the door before Ernst could stop him.

'Both of you, wait inside,' the little man instructed. An astonished mob made way as their Madrasi thief stepped out.

~

There was a friendly tug to Ernst's sleeve and he saw a white T-shirt forming a perfect V-shape outside his window. Gomes peered in, showing off equally perfect teeth. He nodded towards Salim Ali. Some five men surrounded him doing nothing. Any one of them could have taken the little engineer apart.

'Look at them,' Gomes said to Ernst. 'My Portuguese grandfather used to say, "Individually, Indians are intellectual giants. Collectively, their IQ won't fill half a tea cup."' Reaching in, he yanked at the locked door handle and invited Ernst to step out. Putting an arm around Ernst's shoulders, he walked him toward where Salim Ali stood within the sweaty semi-circle, nary a flutter in the still air. Seeing Gomes, Ernst suspected where there was one, there has to be the other, and so he looked back at the Mian Building. Sure enough, Chhote Bhai stood on his second floor balcony carved out of granite, sipping tea. The Grand Mufti overseeing the proceedings, ensuring a fellow Muslim and his Jew boss were brought to book.

'Why are you looking there?' Gomes shook off his irritation. 'Talk to me. Where did you go this morning? We were searching all over the hotel for you! I wanted to say hello.'

'Just the Men's Room.'

Gomes's eyes glazed as his gorilla brain began processing. One waited for the coin to drop. The little red eyes widened, and he must have pictured Ernst cowering in the toilet stall because his mouth spread into a smile. His teeth sparkled.

'Sorry about that,' Gomes said. 'We just wanted your mian. He needs to return what he's got. You know, all this really has nothing to do with you. But you go embarrass me, bribing that drug addict Waller to perform an unauthorised autopsy. You realise how much trouble you people have caused? The fucking Chinaman now comes daily to try and file a police report over his dead nephew. He is in there now. Every time he goes to the police, I have to be present. Chutiya is driving us crazy. He may not have any work, but we do.'

'I'm sorry,' Ernst said, with utmost sincerity in his voice. 'But there was no bribe. And you did kill his nephew.'

Once again, Gomes demonstrated maturity by not reacting. Instead, he gave Ernst's neck a friendly squeeze. 'We shouldn't be fighting,' he said. 'I am here to help. The Chinaman should do the right thing and come to me. Have him give me the autopsy report.

I know everyone in the police. I can be of assistance.' Asking the murderer's help to investigate the murder. It had India written all over.

'Sure,' Ernst said. 'I'll let him know. But for now, why not let my friend go?'

'You mean the Madrasi thief? Tell you what. Ask him to return what they took and I may even let you go.' He gave Ernst's neck a gentle squeeze and shouted something in Konkani—lingua franca down the upper Malabar Coast. Salim Ali's assailants jumped back to life. One of the five men reached out and slapped Salim Ali tentatively, just to see what would happen. Ernst tried to pull away, but Gomes's arm was still across his shoulder like a yoke. And as any buffalo will tell you, a yoke is a yoke.

Gomes put out a sterner Konkani, and more realistic blows slammed Salim Ali against the Fiat. A fist smashed against his face followed by another blow to the head. Ernst struggled again to break free, but that didn't seem to bother Gomes. Salim Ali lay sprawled, and one could see the gash under his eye. There was more blood running down the side of his head. Before you knew it, he was back up again on his moral high ground, eyeballing the assailants. Although in a chokehold, Ernst couldn't help but feel a pride of sorts.

A passing vehicle slowed down. It was a silver Mercedes with D'Souza's Japanese flock staring through hermetically sealed windows. They looked out with identical mouths wide open. Gomes waved with his other arm like a friendly native and sent them on their way. Slowly, Ernst's yoke turned into a vice while over there, the five Marathas continued playing ping-pong with Salim Ali's head.

Way back when Ernst was interned, he would practise holds every day with Purandhar's few Japanese POWs. Ground fighting, the Japanese prisoners would yell in exasperation. Ground fighting! All very well, except that he was now running on empty. The morning's rush was gone. He could have used some of it now. Besides, it had been a while since he had gone limp the way he now did, becoming a dead weight to throw a confused Gomes into letting go. Ernst fell to the ground and waited.

Seeing him in the missionary position apparently stirred Henry Gomes. Enough to kneel and grasp at his collar for purchase, allowing Ernst to wrap his legs around the Goan's waist. This put a jiujutsu cramp to Gomes' style, literally, because he needed his hips to swing his arms. Probably why those punches raining down on Ernst didn't kill him.

They did hurt. Feeling his lower lip tear, Ernst tried to mentally assess the damage as his face kept getting slammed by Gomes. There was something ringing in his ear. Seeing a massive fist bear down once more, he shut his eyes. When he tried to watch out for the next blow, his right eyelid remained glued. It felt mushy and his nose flopped as he moved his head. There was this strong taste of blood and his mouth began filling up. He swallowed, and it filled up again. Gomes didn't seem too worried about Ernst choking on his own blood. He did look irritated at the legs wrapped around his waist, stumped how they cut the locomotive power to his pistons. Then shrugging off the situation as ridiculous, he worked past Ernst's weakening guard and freed himself from one leg, then the other. Within a few seconds, he was at ninety degrees, chest to chest, freed and back in charge.

By the time Ernst reached into his pocket, Gomes had mounted him again and was sitting on his chest. He placed his hands around Ernst's neck and in a gradual squeeze brought his face down close. His breath was cinnamon fresh.

'All this,' he said, 'could have been avoided, no?'

'Not really,' Ernst replied, 'not after what you did.' Pressing the straight razor into Gomes neck, he then said, 'I may be dying anyway. Why don't you join me?'

~

Cold steel to his skin and beady eyes gone wide, Gomes let go Ernst's throat and froze, displaying no interest in shifting even an inch. Ernst was beginning to feel they were finally getting somewhere, when Gomes went and jerked as if kicked. Blood painted the straight razor and Ernst's hand turned red. A form carved in granite hovered above them casting a black shadow. The bloodied razor fell to the ground.

Chhote Bhai lifted a groggy Ernst before kicking out once more, this time at Gomes' six-pack showing off through his tight T-shirt.

Gomes howled and doubled up, hands going from neck to stomach, and back again, leaving bloody palm prints walking all over that muscle encased in white.

'Aaiee ghuh,' the gorilla grunted, calling out in Marathi for his mother.

Ernst was starting to see things, because it appeared Chhote Bhai was protecting him from his own pet gorilla. Confusing, but all for the best. He was certain Dr. Waller's two personalities would come together with Chhote Bhai to agree that cancer patients shouldn't get into a fight. He felt feverish and wasn't sure whether that actually was Mohan Driver, over there with smudged Hindu caste-mark still on forehead, bending over Salim Ali to take the beating meant for a Muslim. Ernst found it impossible to function on his own steam and Chhote Bhai had to hold him in both arms. Something round pressed against his armpit and unless he was imagining things again, the man was holding on to that bloody hockey ball of his while cradling him. Delirious he may well be, but this was worth noting. Talk about a fetish.

At least he wasn't imagining her standing across the street in the same khadi sari she had worn to the club. She would've been shimmying home and stopped to watch the tamasha. A dark waif she was, standing over there, watching along with her brother, Kirti, who made for a milky white replica, minus those teeth. This wasn't the time to think about how her teeth had grown on him. What Ernst could not pinpoint earlier, was now clear in his befuddled state. Standing next to each other, their kinship—she and Kirti the caddie-boy—couldn't be more obvious. She, on the other hand, remained confusing as ever, her eyes ablaze with either anger or some strange excitement. Who knows? Let Chhote Bhai figure it out. Or Sassoon. He couldn't be bothered. But he couldn't take his eyes away either, and she stared back as if on fire. Held like a child, he remained pressed against Chhote Bhai's torso. Feverish from all that dark flesh here and there, everywhere, his mind wandered. He tried pulling away.

Chhote Bhai let him struggle, settling him down in the rear seat of the one-eyed Fiat. Curled up at the back, Ernst found he had an erection. How could he not be in perfect health? He studied his blackened fingernails. They looked just like they would in the schoolyard in Berlin, after turning black and blue in the cold and dangerously close to frostbite. His teacher would cup those freezing hands in his own and blow to warm them before kissing the cold away.

Salim Ali was still out there with Mohan Driver, so Ernst raised himself up to squint in that direction. The pummelling had stopped; Chhote Bhai's presence saw to that. The Marathas stood away from Salim Ali with injured, 'who me?' looks. While Gomes remained in a pool of blood, there was no arterial spray, so Ernst guessed he would live. It wasn't the cut on his neck that had kept him curled up, nor the kick to a stomach designed for road rollers. There was something else. A gorilla assumes that position only when facing an angry alpha-male.

'The Madrasi has the gunny bag,' Gomes whimpered. 'So I thought…'

Chhote Bhai bent low on his haunches and took a swing with his right hand—how badminton players sometimes sweep the shuttlecock just before it touches the court. There was a crack when Gomes' skull made contact with the hockey ball.

'Don't ever say Madrasi again,' Chhote Bhai said. 'And next time, don't think. Ask.'

Gomes lay there, motionless.

Chhote Bhai turned to where Salim Ali stood, face bloodied from the head wound. Mohan Driver stood by Salim Ali's side, as formidable as any henchman. Looking Chhote Bhai in the eye, Salim Ali said, 'I won't thank you,' his voice so different, it penetrated Ernst's haze. 'I know what you and Gomes did to Arjun. Why? What did he ever do to you?'

This would be where Chhote Bhai demanded the gunny bag with all those wires sticking out. 'We know it was you,' Ernst remembered Chhote Bhai asking Arjun in his Tamil English. 'Bleddy bastard. Come on, just return the gunny bag.'

Instead, he stared at his feet and it was Salim Ali who spoke.

'You wanted something, I know, so you go kill him? How does that work?'

And then, 'Namaaz five times a day. For what?'

The incorruptible are unlike the rest of us. Salim Ali made that clear from as far back as his job interview five years ago, and Ernst had hired him on the spot. Surely, Chhote Bhai saw something similar in Salim Ali today, because he couldn't look him in the eye. Salim Ali had advised Ernst: 'These past so many years I've greeted him, looked down and walked away. Next time, you do the same.'

This time though, it was the slumlord who looked down and walked away.

'I hope you don't suffer too much,' Salim Ali called after him, and once again, the voice wasn't his.

If this was Salim Ali going Buddhist, Ernst preferred not to be around. Slipping into darkness, he slumped unconscious in the back seat.

29

Rusalka, Song to the Moon

It's a simple fact of Indian life: there are too many Indians.
—*Paul Theroux*

The crowds were gone once past Haji Ali, and the buildings along
the gentle upward climb at Peddar Road could be any European city.
They entered Bombay, and Ernst was glad to leave Mumbai behind.
He also wanted to leave his illness behind; whiz past the cancer that
was now his shadow. He just needed some naphtha in his tank, get
back his energy, then run like a bhenchod. He had proved incapable
of killing himself. On the other hand, surviving a gorilla attack—no
problem. Why not cancer? In a pivot from earlier that day, he now
felt there were at least some things he could do properly. Saving his
arse appeared to be one.

Marine Drive opened up as soon as Mohan Driver turned the
corner at Walkeshwar to take the Queen's Necklace. It was past the
magic hour, when golden sunrays angle to light the three-kilometres of
whitewashed art deco arched around the Arabian Sea. Street lighting
took over instead, setting ablaze the four-lane road that cupped the
waterfront giving it its name. The light struck at welts on Mohan
Driver's neck, making their dark blue stand out. Blood caked around
his left ear. Ernst wondered how his own face looked with the nose
flapping every time he moved. He dozed off again, until Mohan
Driver screeching around the Regal Cinema roundabout had him sit
up, cursing.

Mohan Driver was an illegal sub-tenant in the police quarters behind Colaba's British-era police chowki that ruled Colaba Causeway. The police quarters rose behind the chowki—socialist cubes cocking their snook at the Gothic artwork in front of them. Le Corbusier's Chandigarh-style cubes were sprouting all over urban Indian landscapes; each copy diminished from the Chandigarh originals, until left with the kind of despondent block where Mohan Driver resided, paying under-the-table rent to a police sub-inspector for the use of one room, no toilet. He would come to Karim Court every morning for a shit, turning Parvatibai into the harridan she became for the rest of the day. They hated each other like a married couple. Ernst asked him to park by the curb.

'I'll drive from here. You go home. Clean up and get some rest. Just look at you.'

Mohan Driver shook his head the way one does at an idiot. His eyes darted back and forth in the rear-view. Unbelievable, they seemed to say and he gunned forward instead, throwing Ernst back. Mohan Driver knew something was wrong. Not the damaged nose from the scuffle. Something else. Something deeper. Ernst's hands started to shake again. He wanted to pull away and regress to some earlier date. Any date. The worst moment from the past would do, as long as pre-cancer. He wondered how his hand had remained rock steady while holding the straight razor to Gomes's neck. But then unlike the cancer, Gomes, one could see.

Jai Gurudeva, Jai Mahadeva, Jai, Jai...

3rd Pastor Lane was still another few minutes up the Causeway. Turn right on to Pastor Lane, then up the third lane to the left, and you get a row of mildewed buildings lining either side. The whorehouse ruled the lane from above Ernst's apartment, lit up as if every evening was Diwali.

Once home, his head rang like an alarm clock to remind him what a chutiya he was—trying to kill himself today to avoid dying tomorrow. The telephone too, started to ring. He attempted shrugging off a semi-hysterical Parvatibai, failed, threw Mohan Driver at her and dove down the corridor. Could be Salim Ali on the phone, maybe Major Punjabi, possibly, Bhairavi. Why not? She saw what happened. She would be concerned about his well-being. She had his number. It was Adam Sassoon.

~

'They're beating up white men now? Hell's going on? You defended yourself with a straight razor?'

Yes. After trying to kill myself with it.

'Told you to get rid of the darkie. You never listen. They were after him. He has stolen property. Don't you get it? They won't let that go and I won't have you killed in the process, you hear? For God's sake. At this point in our lives?'

True, they were after Salim Ali. Gomes had said as much. But then, who wasn't? Still, Ernst had to ask how the great man knew. And by the way, who were they? Iyer? Hanson? The police? Chhote Bhai and Gomes? The one thing they all had in common was, nothing.

Hell with all that. The only thing Sassoon wanted was Ernst's safety. 'You win. I'll have Punjabi deliver those bloody pipes along with the damn advance. Satisfied? Just be safe.'

Ernst assured him he was satisfied and safe. Sassoon was unconvinced.

'That darkie of yours. Get him to return what he's got, or he goes. No argument.' Ernst didn't argue and placed the handset back. As he walked to the bedroom, Parvatibai followed right behind, breathing down his neck like his very own, three hundred pound grim reaper.

Inside, he found Schwester Ingrid afloat on the bed. It was the Western Classical Hour and AIR no longer mourning the PM. Delibes' *Lakmé* poured from the Grundig Radiogram. Not the 'Flower Duet' that got that teacher of his killed along with his dachshund, but the 'Bell Song' with Lakshmi standing in the town square, forced by her Brahmin father to sing and lure her English lover out in the open. Schwester Ingrid had her eyes closed, caught up in the deceit.

'You should clean up first,' Parvatibai said. Ernst ignored her. Sensing the mood, Parvatibai shut the door behind him.

It had been a long day and yes, he needed to clean up first. The plan was to then dwell on Bhairavi. How and why she walked into a gora watering hole like a Goddess and straight to Sassoon's table. Then later, stood alongside her brother, watched Chhote Bhai cradling Ernst like a child, placing him in the one-eyed Fiat, kicking the shit out of Gomes.

Schwester Ingrid, however, was spread before him, bringing on Christmas early and so nothing else mattered. Not the torn lip, nor the flopping nose or the taste of blood. Not Arjun, or how Salim Ali or Tufan was doing. Not Chhote Bhai, not the Seth or the Lala or the cheque, nor the sister or the brother—the black-and-white duo. Not even the fact he was back in business with the great man, who was worried about him.

To set the mood, Ernst went to his ragged row of seventy-eights lining one side of the shelf above the bed. He switched off the radio, picked out and placed an Emmy Destinn on the turntable. Not one in her native Czech, but from the time she sang 'Rusalka's Song To The Moon' in German to a hysterical Berlin audience.

The Aryans loved her across generations and listened to her encore performances ad nauseum over their subsidised, little Volksempfängers. That is, until Mein Führer decided on Czechoslovakia for dinner. After that, the next time any Berliner would hear her sing 'Rusulka's Song To The Moon', was when his father had played it from his window ledge at the Jüdische Krankenhaus overlooking Iranische Strasse—the Victrola dangerously resting on the ledge to allow the Czech opera singer continue soaring over the city she once owned.

The sight of a big, fat, Jewish Göring playing a Victrola on the window ledge drew passers-by. The gathering crowd in turn drew soldiers and a couple of SS men from the Sammellager who couldn't believe their eyes. When his father started to dance a jig, it was too much, and the SS officers commandeered the gawking soldiers to charge the hospital. Seeing them rush the compound, Siegfried had gone inside and stripped, to famously wait for them in the bathtub.

A young Ernst had once asked his father what 'Rusulka's Song To The Moon' was about? 'It's about sacrifice,' his father had explained. 'Not the Wagnerian bullshit. But how it's always fucking futile. Remember that.'

Reclining on the bed with the record wobbling to Emmy Destinn from the radiogram, Schwester Ingrid was not amused. Is this how he planned to seduce her? It was impossible to hear that song, and not think of his father playing it in his bathroom while the Nazis were at the door.

After the incident, Schwester Ingrid had helped move Siegfried's body to the morgue in the basement of the Jüdische Krankenhaus, under the Pathology section. Below the garden that they cordoned off with barbed wire for their Sammellager holding area, from where they packed and shipped Jews. The Sammellager is where his father should have been in the first place, waiting to be shipped East like the other Jews, she wrote, the familiar vitriol rising from the priceless onion paper like fumes.

When the Nazis managed to edge past Siegfried's penis, they smashed his Victrola to prevent Emmy Destinn flying around and embarrassing them further, but it was too late. The suicide spread amongst nurses like wildfire—his father's cock growing a full inch with each narration.

Why embarrass her like that, Schwester Ingrid had asked Ernst. 'If he wanted to die,' she asked, 'why come to the Jüdische Krankenhaus? The Nazis would have obliged him outside.' She would never forgive Ernst for so many things, and his father was one more. Be that as it may, here she was, laid out on the bed. It was all he wanted earlier that day in the toilet stall. It was all he wanted now. Schwester Ingrid waited and waited and here he was, unable to open his mouth. Not even to ask why she left him. Why didn't she come back? Who was back there in Germany? What was so wrong with me?

'Why change the music?' she asked. 'Just because it reminds you of your homo class teacher? Guess what? This Czech bitch reminds me of your father. I can be a bitch too and bring up that homo, but do I? How he made you feel special? What went on behind closed doors?' She then mimicked their dead teacher by singing the 'Flower Duet' in an exaggerated falsetto and he thought, how can I possibly love this person the way I do?

They remained on the bed wedded in silence, and in complete agreement nothing had changed. All this while, Emmy Destinn flew around the bedroom after the arpeggiated chords did their overture. The two of them listened to her until Ernst fell asleep, just after that bit at the end, when she lulls you before the build-up.

Fast asleep, he knew Schwester Ingrid had left. He looked around and saw Bhairavi sway toward the jhopadpatti. She had Chhote Bhai in tow with his head down. Quite the role reversal. Once again though, she was Sindhi-white in his dream. White like that, she could be Kirti, but for the sari.

30

So Many Zeroes

A cancer cell is, what it is,
For it does, what it does,
And it does, what it does,
For it is, what it is.
—*The Other Face of Cancer*

The world doesn't stop because you have cancer.

The locals kept running and people continued falling from open carriages. They died on impact and those squatting along the railway lines continued shitting. Politicians continued printing money and famine continued looming over the rain-shadow side of the Western Ghats. People continued starving than consume American PL 480 wheat they couldn't hold down. The brave ones, though, went ahead and risked the shits tomorrow, just so they could fill their bellies today.

Sethji continued smuggling gold so Hindus could marry off their daughters. Hanson continued distributing biscuits, anna coins and school textbooks to pavement dwellers, who ate the biscuits, pocketed the money and burned the books for fuel. Chhote Bhai continued with his Matka gambling business and fixing cricket matches, even though they said his heart wasn't in either. Didn't matter because people continued to bet on matches, or play the Matka numbers, or do both. Most of India continued without healthcare, running water or electricity while the father of Atomic India, Dr. Bhabha, Mastermind, continued repeating the same message to the nation over AIR: a nuclear program didn't mean The Bomb; it meant medical breakthroughs and cheap electricity for all. Sure, said the nation as one, and winked. They were positive a bomb was about to be reprocessed by the Mastermind out of thin air. Anytime now. Phoenix became the new buzzword.

Over at Sion Medical College, the de facto Dean continued to fuck with his student body. Perched safely on the far end of the operating table, Ernst watched as several unhappy interns shuffled their feet at the unsafe end near the glass vitrines. Waller looked happy as a pig in shit holding a syringe. He placed the syringe on the operating table adjacent to a half-glass full of what could be red wine, though Ernst had his doubts. Another glass tumbler, next to it, had a thin rubber sheet stretched tight across its mouth and held in place with rubber bands. There was a small quantity of yellowish liquid in it. The students experienced a harrowing moment when, reaching into a vitrine with a metal rod, Waller snared a snake with the hooked end. It was the same plump, brown Russell's Viper that had eyeballed Ernst the last time he was here. Ernst was back today to have his damaged nose checked, find out what the damned X-rays had to reveal on the cancer spread, and be gone. Looking at the snake being freed from its confines, he swore never to return.

Before the snake knew what was happening to it, Waller had its head pressed on the operating table with the metal rod while he held on to the tail. He let go after taking a comfortable grip just behind the Russell's Viper's triangular head. With the tail hanging free, four feet of snake coiled itself around Waller's forearm and the girls screamed. His arm now had a triangular head at one end, its pink tongue flickering. When he took it to the glass tumbler with the rubber sheet, the girls screamed again, alarming the head into becoming bigger. The entire class cowered as one, stumbling back against each other in retreat. Ernst couldn't recall Waller this happy. When the arm's triangular head neared the tumbler, it struck and was a sight to behold—walking across the tightly stretched rubber sheet on its two-inch fangs seeking purchase. The fangs finally buried themselves into the rubber sheet and a drop of urine-yellow venom welled from each tip inside the tumbler. After the screaming had quietened down and the snake—poor bastard—returned to its glass container, Waller began.

'Okay, you buggers,' he said, and never mind there were three female students in the group, pale as death. 'Today we do Disseminated Intravascular Coagulation, or as I like to call it, DIC,' and he cackled. 'Under normal conditions, your body is in finely tuned balance between coagulation and the fibrinolysis that prevents unnecessary blood clotting. Fuck with the balance, and you have DIC.'

Most of the students were Marathi vernacular, so that one flew right past; they just stared, not sure who was scarier, the snakes staring back from their glass confines, or the cackling dingo. That his pun failed, seemed to simply embolden the crazy old coot.

Waller syringed venom from the tumbler and pressed out a single drop into the wine glass. The blood in the glass went from liquid to frothing semi-solid in seconds. When Waller tipped the wine glass, a foaming, red disc fell into the petri dish. He looked at the two female students.

'Here, have some DIC,' he said.

The students stared, wide-eyed. Done showing off, he threw them out.

'Short shrift,' he said. 'Short bloody shrift. That's how you treat them.'

Why not treat my flapping nose instead, Ernst suggested, and he would be glad to get the fuck out of here too.

'What do you mean nose is flapping? It cannot. You just think it is. Keep it iced and it will be fine in a few weeks. There's nothing else to do. It will remain a bit crooked, but what do you care?'

The drug-addict bastard was right. Ernst didn't care. They moved on to the X-rays. Ernst tried to focus on Waller's finger, pointing at something in his abdominal area that meant bugger all. Why couldn't an X-ray be like any other photograph?

'A mild spread, around stomach. Intestines clear.'

Ernst was impressed, but then the good doctor continued. 'Cancer rarely hits the small intestines, I've noticed,' he said. 'Maybe shit's antiseptic.'

~

'Why not?' was Waller's response, when Ernst suggested the Jüdische Krankenhaus as an alternative to Tata Memorial. 'Europe, after all.'

Spoken like a true Anglo-Indian.

'At least they take you buggers back into Germany. The British don't want us. We're just dingos to them.'

After all these years, Ernst finally went and asked. 'Why dingo?'

'Because when the Brits left,' Waller replied mournfully, 'we could've buggered off with them too, but we dingo.'

He stared into the X-ray, looking resentful at the unfairness of it all before elaborating on the advantages of Europe. If Ernst went into surgery, he would need catheters after that. Urinary or renal—probably both. If so, infection was guaranteed in Indian hospitals. Ernst found it hard to remain calm in the face of tubes sticking out from his lower anatomy. He drifted off to the safety of the Jüdische Krankenhaus.

When it came to harbouring Jews, no place was safer. Right through the war, even as they plucked them like low hanging fruit in Occupied Europe, the Jüdische Krankenhaus stared Nazis in the face from a Berlin suburb. It remained a sanctuary the Nazis refused to violate, except that one time to retrieve his father and who could blame them. They could have also plucked Bombay Ingrid without any qualms when she returned to Germany, packaged her off in a cattle cart to be processed at Ravensbruck if lucky, otherwise Treblinka, Auschwitz, Kulmhof, or Janowska—pick one. Being pregnant though, she got admitted at the Jüdische Krankenhaus as early as her second trimester. That must have required some doing.

Bombay Ingrid went in, Schwester Ingrid didn't come out. On their part, the Nazis did not encroach beyond the cordoned off Sammellager holding area, allowing the small Jewish community of doctors, nurses and patients inside the hospital campus to exist, even flourish, given the circumstances. Schwester Ingrid was proof.

'What are you waiting for?' Dr. Waller asked, irritated why anyone would want to remain in India. 'Send your medical file to that Jew Hospital along with these X-rays. Bloody get on with it.'

Ernst thought of all the reasons why he couldn't.

~

Salim Ali pointed a dirty fingernail at why he could. 'We have money.'

The great man's cheque lay on the table, his whorled signature declaring emancipation. Salim Ali's bandaged head gave him the undeserved appearance of a Somalian Haji. With his crooked nose on the other hand, Ernst knew he looked ridiculous. He studied the cheque. All those zeroes could make a man dizzy.

'Punjabi had it delivered last night.'

Ernst counted the zeroes.

'Now, why would he do that?' Salim Ali asked.

Ernst could still hear Sassoon dealing with the horror of white men assaulted on Bombay streets. At this point in our lives? Just be safe, the great man had asked of him on the phone. He would send the pipes and the advance. Just be safe. Still, all these zeroes? Salim Ali had a point. Why would Sassoon do that?

'Because you European people stick together.'

'Technically, he isn't one. Sassoons are Baghdadi Jews. But why don't you just simply return whatever Arjun took? Then see how many more orders come.'

'I see. Bribery and blackmail. I try not to sell my soul for twelve pieces of silver. And why do you keep saying we took something? What proof?'

'You're joking, right? I saw the damn gunny bag. It's probably still at my flat because you're too scared to keep it.'

'Conjecture. Conjecture and lies. Typical. Go search your flat. Ask Parvatibai.'

'Sure. She's just waiting to hand it over. The two of you should get married. Listen, you and I both know something was taken. Knowing you idiots, can't be for money. It's some idealistic nonsense that got Arjun killed. And you're right. You could be next. I am worried. Why won't you tell me? You really think I'll go squeal? How paranoid are you?'

'Did I tell you about the French and Americans in Vietnam?'

'You did. I'm not French or American.'

'Germans, French, American, same thing.'

'You still think of me as German? Know what? Forget it. Just tell me, now that we have the advance, how do we draw the pipes?'

'You should've thought of that when you took the order. Lying about the Cold Pilger like that.'

'There are other cold rolling mills in Bombay. We'll find one.'

'No need. Just tell that Punjabi he'll get his pipes back in two weeks,' Salim Ali said. 'Drawn to spec, cut, and bent, along with the flanges.'

'Whoever's the supplier, you'd better involve me. Bargaining isn't exactly your forte.'

Salim Ali curled his lip.

'Prepare to be surprised,' he said.

~

They took their tea over to the balcony.

'How is Chhote Bhai?' Ernst asked. 'I want to thank him.'

'Why for? You had Gomes under control that day. There was no need for him to intervene.'

He had a straight razor to the gorilla's neck, if that's what Salim Ali meant. A lot like holding a tiger by the tail. Flat on his back and in a clutch with Gomes, Ernst had no idea what to do next until Chhote Bhai did it for him.

'Maybe you should give yourself more credit,' the Somali Haji advised. They gazed out from the balcony in silence, but Chhote Bhai refused to go away.

'You said he wanted to break your legs at one time and didn't.'

'I grew up in that jhopadpatti around Sindhi Camp,' Salim Ali said, as if nothing to it. A boy from the jhopadpatti and Muslim to boot. Stray dogs in a mad city—that's what Bhairavi called Arjun and Tufan. This stray dog goes on to graduate from one of the best engineering schools in India, if not the world.

'Chhote Bhai is seven years older than me. His family's hut was at the other end of the slum, but he was all over the place. Even as a boy if there was money to be had, he was there before anyone else. He killed a man by the time I was ten. In a couple of years, he was the person you went to. We kids had a cricket team and approached him for a donation. He bought us equipment and bulldozed an empty couple of acres to make us a playground with a proper cricket pitch. Just behind Sindhi Camp.' Salim Ali paused. 'He bought us white cricket clothes, so we could compete with the kids from AEET and other colonies, like normal people.' Salim Ali went silent again, still mulling the white uniforms after all these years; that someone would do that for jhopadpatti kids.

'That's how I met Arjun. He was an AEET man. They beat the shit out of us every game because of his batting. One day, he showed up alone at our playground. He started playing with us, became part of our team and the next time, we beat AEET. He would walk the two miles to come over play with us every evening after school. We became friends.'

'And Chhote Bhai?'

'Chhote Bhai never liked Arjun. Of late, it's been almost like he hated him.' Ernst saw Chhote Bhai smash the hockey ball against Arjun's porcelain head.

'Our matches became a big deal what with all the betting. I left for IIT, but he would make me come back every month to play the match. He'd begun to make too much money. He had Arjun play too, because he was an ace batsman. Also because otherwise, I wouldn't.

'Anyway, I also used to fool around with Matka gambling those days. Played the numbers to pay for my tuition. I had a system. It's all probability anyway, a number game. Easy as shit.'

For him, sure. Then there was her father, losing four pouches full of diamonds trying to do a Salim Ali.

'I bought my Vespa with the winnings. Paid for college and boarding. One evening Chhote Bhai came by the IIT dorms in Powai. Said he'd been asked to break my legs for cheating at Matka. However, he was proud to see a fellow Muslim in IIT. So instead, he'd break my legs if I ever bet again. He said I could pay him back by throwing a few cricket matches. I refused. He blew a gasket. No one refuses Chhote Bhai. He asked me how come I had no problem cheating at Matka but wouldn't throw a match? He didn't understand. To win at Matka, I had to do something. To throw a match meant doing nothing. How demeaning is that?'

Maybe Chhote Bhai did understand, because Salim Ali said he had a strange look on his face when he left. When Salim Ali graduated,

Chhote Bhai invited him to move into the Mian Building for a ridiculous rent. Because of that, Salim Ali could move his mother out from the slums. Yet, they had barely spoken since.

'You would look down, walk away.'

'Yes.'

'Now he looks down and walks away? Chhote Bhai should break your legs for that gunny bag you're hiding at my place. Instead, he walks away?'

Salim Ali shrugged. 'When he sees me, he thinks of Arjun. That's why. The dead take over your life. It's the price you pay for killing someone. Why do you think he intervened with Gomes and his men that day?'

They stared out from aqua armchairs at the skies over a darkening harbour invisible from here. One could feel the seafront. Then with a little effort, sense Dubai across the Arabian Sea, and the Seth's dhows bringing back gold from there to feed Hindu marriages.

'So Arjun steals something from the Americans. And Chhote gets his pet gorilla to kill him. Why, because the Americans wanted him dead?'

'Something like that.'

'Granted Chhote didn't like Arjun. But you don't just go kill someone you've known all your life, just because someone asks you to. As for the Americans wanting Arjun dead, did you see Hanson's state? He was more distraught than you were.'

'And yet.'

'Yet what?'

'Arjun's dead.'

'Killed by your landlord's goon. So, let's blame the Americans? You may want to re-think your thesis.'

There was nothing to re-think. He was a good Marxist and therefore American complicity was mandatory. All that was left was how Chhote Bhai fitted into Salim Ali's conspiracy theory—elegantly simple, yet total without basis.

'Who knows why? But he has to live with it now. I feel sorry for him.'

'What's in that fucking gunny bag?'

'It's eating you up, isn't it?'

~

They could hear kids on the neighbouring terrace yelling taunts at the monsoon clouds brooding over the Arabian Sea. The clouds rose in dark tiers above the invisible harbour, holding on to their waters for now. Parvatibai lumbered over, yelled at the children to shut the fuck up and squatted on the floor with a grunt. Doing so, she completed the circle that made India so liveable. As long as this equation added up the way it did, Ernst felt he would manage whatever was lodged in that stomach X-ray.

He shut his eyes to enjoy the sea breeze squeezing its way past buildings to the balcony. It helped him squeeze all of the peace he could, from all he had. Those zeroes on the cheque helped of course, while the whorehouse parrot hopping about its cage upstairs, cursed away in Marathi. It reminded him the way she had abused the E.M. Foster Brahmin, the one they caught shitting outside her home at Sindhi Camp. He found himself missing her, somewhat like how he would miss Bombay Ingrid.

The three of them sat and stared at the invisible harbour. Just the thought of ocean could make one feel better. If you looked past the rows of flaking, art deco style buildings struggling in the same repair the British left them, then peered to the top, right hand corner of the panorama—there it was, a glint of water—a sliver of hope that refused to go away even when the rest of everything was hopeless beyond redemption.

'You have cancer,' Salim Ali said, 'and look at you. Calm as the ocean.'

Parvatibai snorted. At times, she understood English perfectly.

Salim Ali pointed to Sassoon's cheque again. 'So, we're going ahead with the aeroplane ticket?'

'Is that so? Where's the money to draw those pipes for Sassoon? What about Salary Day? Who clears the Seth's cheque?'

'There are enough zeroes there for salaries, and your aeroplane ticket. Let me worry about the pipes.'

'What about the Seth? He can pluck aeroplanes off the sky if his cheque bounces.'

'I have a solution for that too,' Salim Ali said.

'What?'

'Tell him go fuck himself.'

He looked at Parvatibai, whose eyes showered praise. They fed off each other—overweight cat and little black mouse.

'You're going to Germany for treatment. Why worry about paying back the Seth? You probably won't even see him again.'

'Thanks. You don't appear confident about my chances.'

'You know what I mean.'

Ernst did. For most Indians, leaving for the West was a one-way ticket. Salim Ali then spoke to Parvatibai in Marathi. 'Other owners fire workers left and right, or simply don't pay them. He goes sells his imported machine to pay us. Now he wants to pay that crooked Seth.'

Then in English to Ernst, 'Why can't you think like a bania for a change?'

'He's right,' Parvatibai advised. Then we can move away from this whorehouse. Even I've been approached. The shame of it.' There was a stunned silence. Salim Ali coughed.

'By the way,' Ernst said, 'how come you're suddenly fine with supplying those pipes to Sassoon? What if they're for that plutonium reprocessing plant?'

'Can't be. Punjabi's pipes are pharma grade. I checked,' Salim Ali said.

'So?'

'So, they can't be for plutonium reprocessing. I told you already. To reprocess spent fuel, the stainless steel has to be nitric acid grade, otherwise it corrodes. Punjabi's pipes are for something else. Just relax.'

'I'm relaxed. You're the one who went into a tizzy over Sassoon supplying our pipes to AEET.'

'Why do you think I checked?'

The question remained. Then what was Sassoon doing with blueprints for a plutonium reprocessing plant?

'Supplying something or the other. Needn't be pipes. These people will sell anything for a profit.' Salim Ali's Marxist credo declared all businessmen guilty of making a profit and therefore untrustworthy—Ernst being the singular exception. When once asked why he trusted Ernst, Salim Ali had looked surprised one would even ask. 'Because he's so unsuccessful,' he said.

Later, and in a decent enough ending to a good day, Parvatibai went off to the ration shop for rice against Ernst's ration card. Then to Colaba Market for vegetables, and mutton on credit.

Salim Ali left for the 6-Limited bus ride back to Chembur. Well before Bhairavi came over for an hour of translating the Munshi's books into double entry. Beatrice could well be keeping her money, but this Bhairavi was Sindhi and would be on time. Walking Salim Ali to the door, Ernst gave it another shot. 'I know the gunny bag's still here, somewhere. Just tell me what's in it. She won't let me even enter the servant quarters. Locks the door. You people seem to forget this is my flat.'

'You have no proof of anything,' Salim Ali said. 'All you need to know is we would never do anything illegal.'

'Maybe. But your definition of what's legal is somewhat elastic.'

'I repeat. Arjun didn't do anything illegal.'

Maybe. But something was stolen and Arjun was dead.

31

Rubbing Knees

The Kamasutra defines four types of women. It fails to say the vast
majority belong to a fifth type that cannot be defined.
—*Sir Victor Sassoon*

Like Salim Ali, she too was categorical. Arjun was incapable of any
wrongdoing. 'He was my moral compass.' As for Chhote Bhai—guilty,
not guilty—Bhairavi couldn't care less and remained deadpan. Ernst
wanted to protest on behalf of the slumlord. You're fucking him for
Chrissake. Then there was the other thing.

'What were you doing with Adam Sassoon at the club?'

'Madam Beatrice wants me to help Sassoonji with filing and
accounts.'

Sassoonji needs help with filing and accounts? He let that go.
Adam Sassoon had grinned like an idiot seeing the moonlighting,
part-time accountant from Sindhi Camp shimmy up. As if Goddess
Bhairavi herself strode into the permit-room. He had beaten a waiter
to pulp for slighting the refugee woman who smiled at him like a
Goddess. Ernst felt, maybe, someone should advise the great man
what a smile from Goddess Bhairavi implied.

Bhairavi then went got lost in Ernst's ledgers until Parvatibai
rang the doorbell. She put down the pencil to go answer the door
before Ernst could react. Later, when Parvatibai brought in Bombay
Ingrid's Wedgewood teapot to the living room with two matching
teacups, she got up to help.

When Parvatibai stumbled and spilt chai putting the tray down, she gripped her forearm to support all that weight with ease. Not just that, she then took the tray and things back to the kitchen with Parvatibai wrapped around her little finger.

~

'What made you leave your own country?'

That was an easy one for most German Jews. Not all that easy for one from Berlin. Berlin was a Jewish city. They built it. No Jew was going to pack up and just leave because of some effete, Austrian arsehole. Moreover, almost half of Berlin's Jews were married into gentile families. In fact, Aryan women preferred them to their own men; Jewish men worked hard and didn't drink or beat their wives. So even after the rumblings, the Jews stayed put. Everything would be fine, they said to each other. This is our home. Let the Arschloch go back to Austria if he wants.

That was then. A few years down the road, Jews were marrying Jews they didn't even know, just to have someone by their side while herded to the camps. People marrying people they never met in their lives. Everyone marrying anyone, to avoid dying alone.

'At least, I left Germany safely with the woman I loved. Look what happened to the others.'

'Then why did she go back?'

Yes, Ernst, why did she?

'Ingrid never liked India. She was out of here and back home even before the war started.'

Be that as it may, Bombay Ingrid broke all sorts of records the way she flung herself back into Nazi arms. When was the last time a Jew did that? It would take all evening to try explain why, because one would need to first understand the different Ingrids—the one from his Berlin school days, who became the one in Bombay, who went back to Berlin and became a nurse. Besides, Bhairavi was wearing a green-and-white salwaar kameez today, and her hair in pigtails.

'When did you last see her?'

Ernst hesitated. His knee accidently touched her's and she didn't retract.

He pointed at Bombay Ingrid posing deadpan from the Kashmiri salver in front of the "Zaankert" at Sassoon Docks. One could see the First Officer in white and out of focus up the roped gangplank. She was polite that day, but couldn't wait to turn around and leave. Ernst remembered her stiffen when he hugged. Better not to have hugged at all.

'Where was the other picture taken? That one. With your wife in that white uniform and those children on her lap.'

Oh. You mean my father's suicide note. The uniform went with the platinum blonde hair. Schwester Ingrid's face had aged somewhat from that day when Bombay Ingrid couldn't wait to leave, get on that boat. The figure though, suggested nothing of that sort.

'At the Jewish Hospital.'

'She liked children?'

Ernst pondered the possibility and gave up.

'She never came back to India?'

'No.'

'Where is she now?'

'In a better place.'

'Who took that picture?'

'My father.'

'Something about him,' she said in her Sindhi Hindi, looking at Siegfried standing next to Ernst's mother. 'Where is he now?'

'Definitely in a better place.'

She impressed him by changing subjects.

'Your nose. It's going to be that way forever, you know. Whatever happened that day with Gomes?'

~

The ceiling fan spun thick air around, leaving a pre-monsoon sheen on her skin. Back to work and inspecting the Munshi's ledgers, she leaned over to drop a bead of sweat on his wriggles. Her breasts made tiny dents in the kameez.

'I can't believe that Munshi of yours…who taught him accounts?' She snatched at an eraser to correct something pencilled in a column, pressing her knee hard against his and continued annotating. She remained irritated as hell, and not the slightest acknowledgement of any trespass beneath the table.

He wanted to ask, what's going on? What is it—rubbing against my leg or rolling on grass with Chhote Bhai? Or bloody both? Besides, you really think you can take on the Ingrids? Her knee kept applying pressure, moving away, then pressing again. At which point he decided, fuck it, and reaching below with his left hand, rested it first on his own thigh, then placed it on hers. No response. He squeezed. Nothing. He stroked her salwaar across the length of her thigh. Nothing, but her eyes were those of a kitten held by the cuff of its neck. He stroked some more, squeezing the thigh, feeling hard muscle through her salwaar. She looked vacant, swollen lips agape as she stared at the ledger while holding the pencil so tight, her fingertips went white. Jews, however, know good fortune comes in discrete packets. So enough was enough, and he brought his hand out from under the table, placing it on hers.

She pulled away violently. 'What do you mean?' she barked, leaving him with nothing to say about his indecent, above-the-table overture. She stared down at the page as if furious with it, her eyes raging. He had never seen a female face contorted like this and it sent a chill down his spine.

But the years had rendered him a practical man, and he didn't question the rules when her thigh brushed up again. The face however, continued to rage at the Munshi's single-entry ledger with its red-cloth binding.

32

Atomic India

I remembered the line from the Hindu scripture, the Bhagavad Gita;
Vishnu is trying to persuade the Prince that he should do his duty
and, to impress him, takes on his multi-armed form and says,
"Now I am become Death, the destroyer of worlds."
I suppose we all thought that, one way or another.
—*J. Robert Oppenheimer, on the world's first nuclear explosion*

Tsering Tufan could barely stand, but stood waiting for them at Atomic Energy in Trombay.

Ernst wanted to know why. Why were they going there, and by the way, what about the pipes? 'Have we found a cold rolling mill yet? We may want to start earning all those zeroes on Sassoon's cheque.'

'Leave it to me,' Salim Ali said. More and more, Ernst seemed to have no problem with that.

Getting to India's beloved nuclear facilities meant Mohan Driver doing a sharp right from Trombay Road, just before one fell into Thana Creek. Then, a smooth and unbelievable four-laned, metalled strip cutting a corridor through a thick crop of mango, betel nut and stately banyans came to view. Mast trees lined the sides like folded green beach umbrellas and a sixty-foot divider of green grass ran through the middle; two lanes on either side. The road sign read, CENTRAL AVENUE. It was surreal enough to imagine the four lanes cutting through AEET and continue all the way to become the world famous Central Avenue in Hollywood, where every Indian moviegoer dreamt of speeding in a Chevrolet Impala.

'Welcome to Atomic India.' Tsering Tufan said as they went past the main gates left wide open. The security guards yawned as they drove past.

The Atomic Energy Township glowed grey under New Delhi's love and care. The grey buildings reached out fifteen storeys into the sky from the grey pavements. It was the surrounding greenery, however, that overwhelmed Ernst as grey buses moved grey, be-spectacled, Brahmin engineers around. All this hidden behind Trombay Hill, just a few miles from Sindhi Refugee Camp. Who would've thought? Ernst made sure to look impressed for Tufan's sake, and so what if the residential township was spooning Bhabha's nuclear reactors? If you think about it, so was the rest of Bombay. Besides, he liked Tufan.

They left the burgeoning township behind as the four lanes cut past dense forest on the right and a cricket field to the left. A young boy was running in from the far side, angled to deliver a tight spin at the batsman. The field was dressed in spotless white. This wasn't India. It was however, where Tufan's dead nephew would have been playing. If he didn't opt to play in a slum instead. Ernst could guess why a Chinese-looking, tribal kid from the Northeast preferred playing at the jhopadpatti with other outcasts. These here at AEET were all upper caste, Brahmin boys. A low caste tribal in their midst was chum for sharks. A stray dog in a mad city.

Another gate came up, looking meaner than the previous one with its lolling guards they'd left behind. There was an arch over the gate and the sign said, North Gate. The army sergeant on duty heard Tufan out, hand resting on the canvas webbing holding his holstered sidearm.

'Nahien,' he said. No.

'Why for no?' Salim Ali asked. 'We were cleared by security back there.'

'Oh them, were they asleep when you drove past?' the sergeant enquired. 'After all, it's afternoon. We, on the other hand, we don't sleep. We are army. Not rentals.'

'Really?' Salim Ali asked. 'You were awake when the Chinese came?'

Tufan stepped out to better make his case. Also, to take the conversation away from Salim Ali.

'Who said guests allowed inside?' The sergeant's belligerence was up a notch. Could be for any number of reasons, or could be Salim Ali.

'I pre-registered them, Subedarji. Please check.'

'Check what? There should have been a phone call. There was no phone call.'

A white Ambassador with dark, tinted glass windows approached the gate from inside and honked. The gates swung open in style and the sergeant stiffened, stamping one foot hard to the cement while the Ambassador gave him the once over before coming up to the Fiat. The missing headlight made Ernst's Fiat look like a boxer with a black eye, facing off the new champion parked alongside. The Ambassador's dark, rear window rolled down and a chin stuck out. It had a cleft you could lose a coin in. A famous face followed—deep, dark eyes nesting below a forehead the nation watched inch back every year. The jet-black hair was slick with Brylcream. In a more equitable universe, men this good-looking would be brainless gigolos, not nuclear scientists. A monogrammed Louis Vuitton valise lay in the front seat alongside the driver, taking the full brunt of the brutal air-conditioning.

'Bhabhaji!' Tufan said aloud with folded hands held up high in salutation, as if evoking Govinda, another name for Krishna—most beloved of all gods.

'My Smiling Buddha.' The good-looking Parsi looked deep into Tufan's eyes with a love that anoints. He turned serious and wagged a finger. 'They tell me you're not looking after yourself.'

'Where to, Sirji?'

'The PM, my friend. Where else?'

'The PM,' Tufan said after the receding Ambassador, waving at it. 'It's always the PM.'

~

North Gate onwards driving south, the four lanes converged to two, and the sixty-foot green divider disappeared. They cut through a good mile and half of dense forest before seeing cement again in the shape of an upright North American penis. The CIRUS nuclear reactor just stood there, befouling Salim Ali's mood.

'The Russians were giving us one. But no, it has to be American.'

'It's Canadian actually,' Tufan offered. 'America just provided the heavy water.'

'There's a difference?'

Fountains flowered from cooling ponds arrayed around the CIRUS reactor and its peripherals—concrete hexagons showing off their Islamic-style geometry. If this was where a fountain of radioactive water had gushed out for Lambadi women to shower, there was no sign.

There was however work still going on, as Atomic India flexed its pectorals using another expendable Lambadi formation. The gypsy women formed lines from portable cement mixers on wobbly wheels, to masons laying bricks. Using their trowels, the masons slapped, spread and smoothed the gritty, grey mush that the women relayed in dented, shallow tin vessels. The rotating cement mixers, moving trucks, and trudging feet raised clouds of dust and at one point the Fiat's occupants had to wind up the windows. The Lambadi had their faces veiled against the grey powder, settling layer upon grey layer on blistered skin. Choli mirror work on their blouses reflected light from breasts arrayed in their usual tight formation.

'Look at them,' Salim Ali said. 'The proletariat at work. One day, they'll fuck you all.'

'One can only hope,' Ernst said.

'Over there.' Tufan pointed at the new construction to change the subject. 'The plutonium reprocessing plant. Bhabhaji's Phoenix.' Bhabha may not be around, but he was everywhere.

'He designed it to use the American Purex process.'

'Something the Americans themselves abandoned as too dangerous,' Salim Ali said to his friend, who should've known better than to lob so feebly. 'When do we stop taking hand-me-downs from the West?' Salim Ali asked.

The answer of course was, never. But who was Ernst to further disillusion heroes marching to a new tomorrow?

Mohan Driver slowed down and parked on the left to wait out the Lambadi-style Ho Chi Minh trail cutting across Central Avenue. The women emptied long, shiny, stainless steel pipes from a curbed Tempo with brutal speed, to have them disappear in the maw of the Phoenix building. It was an elongated structure, adjacent to a smoke stack as tall as the building was long. The chimney reached out into the sky. Men wielding clipboards supervised the work detail with non-verbal hand gestures at the Lambadi—speaking to lower caste types, verboten. Leering though, was permitted. Tufan waved at one of the clipboards Ernst recognised. 'Mr. Paranjpe,' he said, waving away like a school boy. 'Our Purchase Manager.'

It was the same man scurrying behind Jehangir Merchant that day at Fertilisers when Jehangir the bagman had dropped the blueprint on the floor—blueprints for a building full of pipes. The same man in the permit-room, sitting next to Jehangir and trying to go invisible. The same man now moving pipes into a building with a chimney the length of Dara Singh's dick—turns out it's a plutonium reprocessing plant. Paranjpe saw Tufan and waved, then saw Ernst and froze. Hand stilled mid-wave, it was impossible to turn invisible the way he had managed in the permit-room that day.

Invisible maybe not, but miserable, absolutely. His assistant looked puzzled at a Paranjpe suddenly so out of sorts. By now, Ernst was used to his general unpopularity in certain quarters. This though, was embarrassing, the way Paranjpe dove into his clipboard and buried himself.

'What's wrong with him today? Such a friendly fellow otherwise.' Tufan asked.

Past CIRUS, the forest closed around them again. The Central Avenue remained its silky smooth self—like her skin—and not a pothole in sight.

'Strange.' Tufan shook his head and looked confused. 'Those pipes Paranjpe was unloading. I don't recall issuing them.' Then, back to normal. 'Seedha Barkhurdar!' he said to Mohan Driver, slapping his shoulders. 'Straight ahead, young man!'

Ernst studied him. This serene tribal from India's Northeast border with China. 'My Smiling Buddha!' is what Dr. Homi Bhabha had called out, knowing full well his Smiling Buddha was burning up behind that smile. Tsering Tufan's illness sidled over to settle next to his. What was there to nitpick between the two? One was frying his innards to eventually show up outside. The other, burning Tufan from outside to burrow in. In either case, the end was the same. He felt grey, like the buildings they had left behind.

'We left everything behind,' Mohan Driver pointed out. 'Where to now?'

Tufan displayed his shy, Smiling Buddha side and Ernst gave the lush greenery a closer look. Low-slung, pillbox-like structures nestled here and there. Bhabhaji's subtle handiwork. One had to wonder whether there would be any forest cover left to hide India's nuclear program, if the Parsi scientist wasn't around. It was difficult for Indians to keep their hands off timber. The straight road began curving right as they neared the tip of Bombay's northwest land mass. The forested turf to their left turned mangrove. Up ahead would be the stretch of water tapering into Thana Creek to the North, opening into the Arabian Sea to the South. Tsering Tufan thumped a resigned Mohan Driver again and pointed where to park.

They were in deep forest and could make out a well-maintained concrete structure behind a shiny, chainlink fence. Such impeccable upkeep with rust-free fencing was like a pair of Wranglers, a colour TV, or Toblerone chocolates for that matter—taken for granted only in the West.

'Come,' Tufan said, in spite of all the tiredness. 'Come, come, come!' Cicerone for the day, Tufan was taking the tour very seriously.

~

Past the fence, a brick path led them to an elongated whitewashed pillbox, complete with sealed turrets. The humidity was overpowering. Ernst felt his feet heat up in their plimsoles. His legs went into a slow bake inside the trousers. He would have worn shorts, but there are rules in India: no long-pants for boys, no short-pants for men, unless Bombay Police. The police wore dark blue shorts that ballooned from the waist like skirts, just in case someone were to take them seriously.

A three-wheeler Tempo was aligned with the pillbox when they drew up. Shiny stainless steel pipes laid flat along its open payload section and stuck out from the back; the tailgate was down to accommodate their length. They looked like the pipes they just saw Paranjpe unloading over at the reprocessing plant. Five workers in blue overalls and one Sikh stood by, next to the Tempo. The workers in blue were Mallus and had Salim Ali written all over, while the Sikh, he would be the Tempo driver. The blues were barking at each other in Malayalam, making the Sikh grimace. To a North Indian Sikh, these were an unfamiliar and alien race.

Not so to Ernst, because these were his employees from the Goregaon workshop. He watched Tsering Tufan work the brass Nav-Tal lock on the door and reeled from a blast of cold air when it opened. All his years in India, Ernst had never known an air-conditioned shop floor. 'I'd left it on for you,' Tsering Tufan said shyly. Ernst thought of the ceiling fans back at Goregaon circulating sweaty body odour.

'West German,' Salim Ali crooned, once inside and caressing a Siemens lathe. Air-conditioned workshops, imported machine tools and now communists salivating over Western products. Meanwhile, Tsering Tufan was pouring over the In/Out logbook kept by the door—black ink scrawling what came in, went out.

'Strange,' he registered again, as he had in the one-eyed Fiat at seeing Paranjpe unloading pipes for the Phoenix plutonium reprocessing plant. The same confusion seeped from his tired face as he studied the In/Out log. 'Those pipes Paranjpe was unloading. I was right. They are not registered here. Why not?' Ernst empathised. After all, he too had no idea why his workers were here in AEET.

'Paranjpe could be procuring the pipes elsewhere?' Ernst suggested. Anything to get the Buddha smiling again.

'Cannot,' the Buddha said, deigning him a smile. 'It's critical we quality control what goes into Phoenix. That's why Bhabhaji gave us this workshop. See?'

~

At Ernst's workshop in Goregaon, Salim Ali's Marxist labour had the walls decorated with every deity known to man. From Rama to Krishna to Jesus with his big, Sacred Heart on full display, to Karl

Marx and the unseen presence at Mecca's black, draped Ka'bah. Plus 2 x Buddha-heads thrown in for back-up.

Tufan's theme over here was more monotheistic; his gallery of framed black-and-whites celebrating a single God. There was Homi J. Bhabha striking a pensive pose to outclass any Bombay film hero with that face, the chin, those large, liquid eyes. Homi J. Bhabha speaking at the Atoms for Peace conference in Hiroshima. Homi J. Bhabha with Prime Minister Nehru, watching his nuclear reactor take wing. One more of Homi J. Bhabha with the PM, this time with two Americans; the looming one resplendent in a 12-gallon Texan hat, that looked a lot like Jack Hanson's. Which would make sense, because the man was Hanson. Homi J. Bhabha strolling with Albert Einstein. Homi J. Bhabha with UN Secretary-General Dag Hammarskjöld. Homi J. Bhabha with J. Robert Oppenheimer and the shorter American from the picture with Nehru and Hanson. There was something about Oppenheimer, while the American alongside him looked like anybody. Oppenheimer had fathered the world's first atom bomb, but Bhabha was the centre of this universe.

Homi J. Bhabha, out there in the air-conditioned Ambassador, rushing off with his Louis Vuitton luggage to meet India's new Prime Minister and save the world in style, rather than save his Smiling Buddha. Ernst felt like questioning Tufan on his blind devotion but knew he shouldn't. Bhabha like any God had better things to do and a world to save. Instead, Ernst lingered over the expensive machinery lining up at their deity's shrine, there to control what went into Phoenix. Whereas, Salim Ali was already at the far end of the room behind the stamping machines. Tufan shut the In/Out logbook and hurried over to lead them through a narrow passage. Looking at Tufan muster the energy, Ernst was tempted to take the man home, make him lie down, rest, and do the same himself. The two of them lying side by side, then letting go together at the count of three.

The other end of the passage held more drawing equipment, and a Cold Pilger. Everything one needed to draw stainless steel with precision, make flanges, deliver a building full of pipes. Like the one they had seen Paranjpe fitting out over the human conveyer belt. Ernst looked at the cold rolling machine. He remained polite. 'Those pipes we saw Paranjpe moving into the Phoenix building. You're very sure they were drawn on this Cold Pilger? Not somewhere else?'

'Where else?' Tufan said. 'However, I don't recall that batch coming in, or going out. Nothing entered in the In/Out log either. We can be lazy at times, Mr. Ernest. And forgetful.'

'What about the Tempo load outside with my workers?' Ernst asked. 'Have those pipes been entered in your In/Out logbook? Better check, because I think you may have forgotten to enter them too. Actually, no need to check. I think you know very well they are not entered. What you may not know, is that they are the same pipes Paranjpe is unloading. You are a damn fool, but that's okay because so am I.'

'There is no need to be rude to Comrade Tufan,' Salim Ali said. 'Try being grateful, instead.'

Ernst wanted to do something bad to him.

'Those are Sassoon's pipes in the Tempo outside?'

'Yes. You can tell Sassoon that delivery has already begun.' Salim Ali's chest swelled. An inch more, and he could take on Gomes.

'You illegally processed his pipes here at AEET?' Ernst asked. 'What, for free? In a highly restricted, Government facility? Just because you know the Head Machinist? Are you out of your bhenchod mind?'

'Depends on what you mean by illegal. The facility belongs to the people.'

'You were the one not wanting anything to do with AEET.'

'I don't want us drawing bleddy pipes for their reprocessing plant. We don't have the expertise. I have no problem with them drawing pipes for us.'

'Not for us. For Sassoon. These pipes go back to Punjabi, yes? No? Yes. And no record coming in or leaving this place. After all, Tufan's letting you use this facility illegally. So obviously he can't show them in his In/Out log, can he? Funny thing is, Tufan just found that lot Paranjpe was offloading at Phoenix, that's also not in the In/Out log. How come? Maybe because they're one and the same. You got these pipes drawn by Tufan at AEET to supply Punjabi, who then supplied them via Paranjpe, back to AEET. Punjabi's pharma-grade pipes are ending up in the plutonium reprocessing facility, after all. Exactly what you feared. And it's because of you. If you feel like a chutiya, I'll understand.'

Salim Ali curled his lip. Tufan looked bemused. Ernst so badly wanted to kill one and kick some sense into the other.

Ernst's Mallus were carrying out more of Punjabi's pharma-grade pipes to the three-wheeler. They looked like they knew their way around. No one bothered with the In/Out log. There was no record of the pipes leaving the facility. Tufan could put hand to heart and say AEET's Cold Pilger was never used to draw these pipes for Ernst's Salim Ali to sell to Sassoon's Punjabi to sell back to AEET's Paranjpe. On the other hand, you knew it was. It made Ernst India's most unique middleman.

'Why?' Ernst asked, once in the one-eyed Fiat on Trombay Road heading back. 'Why, now that we have money? You couldn't find another cold rolling mill in all of Bombay? Why make Tufan do this? Put the poor bastard at risk? Just like you did with the girl, making her play that communist anthem.'

'I didn't make anyone do anything.' Salim Ali asked. 'Besides, I'm telling you, those pipes simply cannot be for Paranjpe. Why would Sassoon supply substandard material to a nuclear plant? Fuck with something this big? You're wrong as usual.'

'What's costlier? These pharma-grade pipes or ones that are nitric acid grade?'

'What do you think? Of course, the austenitic stainless steel for nitric acid.'

'There you have it. I've known Adam Sassoon since before you were born. He is that same capitalist who features in your Marxist nightmares. The one who does anything for money.'

'No one in his right mind would do such a thing.'

'This is India.'

Silence.

'Quite the role reversal, you'll agree. My pointing out a capitalist's culpability and you defending him.'

'Conjecture. You're very good at that.'

'I'm good at that? Anyway, tell me, would you have processed these fucked-grade pipes if you knew they were for the plutonium reprocessing plant?'

Salim Ali considered the matter carefully before deciding to ignore Ernst.

'Why?' Ernst asked. 'Why did you do this?' Ernst persisted. 'I'm not letting this go, you know.'

'Your aeroplane ticket, that's why. I told you, tell the Seth to go fuck himself. But, do you listen? No. You had to go honour his bleddy cheque. Now after salaries, you'll have just enough left for your ticket. Or the pipes. One, or the other. Not both. But thanks to Tufan, I've gone got the pipes done for free. We can now go buy your ticket with the money left. Get you to a proper hospital in West Germany.'

'You shouldn't have.'

'Why not? Someone has to think of you, because you don't.'

Ernst leaned out into the humid, tropical night to hide his face. It had turned red and his ears burned. Salim Ali, though, was busy looking out from his side and that, therefore, was that. All for the best, because Ernst didn't know what to say, what to do. Unlike him however, everyone else clearly did; Salim Ali over at Tufan's workshop, taking care of business and Paranjpe at the reprocessing plant, doing the same. Installing Sassoon's pipes. Probably, bribed silly to do it. By Adam Sassoon. Ernst was there in the permit-room when the great man was seen taking care of business. With someone he wouldn't normally touch with a barge pole. Paranjpe was the kind of person normally left for Jehangir to sequester.

Yet, 'Bring some orange juice over for Paranjpeji,' the great man had ordered D'Souza, the barkeep, that day in the crowded permit-room. The great man knew exactly what he was doing, playing host to this Indian. It was unprecedented, stepping down from Olympus to get a wog aligned. Could be because in this case, the wog would need to bypass Bhabha's quality control and install substandard pipes in a nuclear reprocessing plant. Too big to be left to a Jehangir. Given the price difference between austenitic stainless steel and pharma grade, what did that translate into, Ernst wondered. Double the usual profits for Sassoon Industries? He settled on triple. Still, what a risk to take.

Then there was Bhabha—this other great man who knew what to do. Not just a great man, but God. Goes builds a national atomic program from scratch. Installs the finest machine tools money can buy. Ensures key components are machined in-house. Total quality control over what goes into his nuclear reprocessing plant. But then goes appoints a Paranjpe as Purchase Manager.

Nothing from the pictures arrayed in Tufan's workshop would suggest that gods fucked up too. They looked infallible in the line-up. Well, at least Bhabha did. After China, one couldn't look at Nehru anymore and ignore the clay feet. As for Oppenheimer, when was that picture taken? From the look in his eyes, definitely after his atom bomb, but before or after he resigned from America's nuclear program in remorse? They took away his security clearance in retaliation and he was no longer God. One thing America couldn't deal with was rejection. Ernst on the other hand, was good with it. To be rejected was his natural state. Anything else was disconcerting.

33

Dress Code

Englishness remains the primary qualification for
membership into an Indian club.
—*Daily Mail*

Sassoon stared at the greens. He could be searching for the meaning
of life. He leaned back into his rattan sofa and smiled at good
friend, Ernst—rehabilitated for a second time. Sassoon's cheque
would have cleared today, raining zeroes all over Ernst's overdraft.
In turn, Ernst's cheques to the Seth would have cleared—circle
of life.

Ernst was at the club just to make sure. Cover all bases. Look
Adam Sassoon in the eye to find out if his cheque would pass. Better
than to learn the next day that the great man had reclaimed the zeroes
on a whim. Or, because of Salim Ali. Jewish by birth and Hindu by
choice, it was okay to be insecure.

'The pipes,' Ernst said. 'Punjabi never mentioned what they're for.'

'Did he provide the specs? Thirty-one millimetre, I believe?'

'Yes, of course.'

'Well, that's that, then. What more do you need?'

'Those blueprints with Jehangir, the other day in the permit-room.
Couldn't help but notice. They're for Atomic Energy's reprocessing
plant. That means nitric acid grade pipes. These ones we're drawing
for you, they're not. Just saying.'

'You're wide awake these days, old chap. Good to know. But if you're saying they are not Atomic Energy grade, then they're not for Atomic Energy, what?'

'The man with Jehangir. That same day in the permit-room. He's Purchase Manager over at AEET. So, thought I'd ask.'

'Eclectic sort of a bloke, our Jehangir. Can't be bothered whom he drags along.'

With that the great man went got lost in the greens again. After a bit, he emerged to ask, 'By the way, what if they are?'

Ernst went, 'Eh?'

'The pipes. I mean, what if they are for the reprocessing plant you're all worried about. What then? You wouldn't do the job? Not accept the money?'

Ernst wondered how many lifetimes would it take and how many good deeds over each of those lives, to be granted by Lord Vishnu, by Krishna, by Maheshvara, the strength to say, 'No, in that case I won't accept the money.' Just like how Arjun had shook his head and said "No!" to Chhote Bhai.

And died for it, he reminded himself.

'Thought so,' the great man said. 'No worries, old chap. Punjabi tells me the money's in your account.'

Instead of relief, Ernst felt the cork tighten up his arse. Sassoon shifted his on the rattan sofa and nodded towards the Hansons, seated on an identical sofa with red cushions. In all fairness, it wasn't just darkies and Salim Ali; the great man didn't care for Americans and Hanson either. The rest of the Golf Club followed suit and kept away, leaving the Texan with more or less his wife for company. For some strange reason he appeared content with that, and it baffled the Anglos.

'Always wondered if she carries them too.'

'Carries what?'

'Those damn biscuits.'

Hanson looked subdued. Holding his wife's hand, he stared out, seeking the same solace Sassoon sought within all that grass. A bearer lowered his tray to serve them. Over at the next table, Willie Lansdowne downed his fifth gin tonic. The empty glasses around Daisy Lansdowne suggested she must have long, lost count. Encouraged, Ernst ordered another Bloody Mary to celebrate all the zeroes and walked over to the Hansons. To go say hello. Shake hands, meet the missus, shoot the breeze. Find out what Hanson was doing towering over everyone in that photograph on Tufan's altar at his AEET workshop. The one with Nehru, Bhabha and that other American.

'You mean, Nichols,' Hanson said, after his wife strolled off towards Daisy Lansdowne, assessed the damage, and did a quick right turn towards the greens.

'Kenneth Nichols. We met the prime minsiter and Bhabha together. Nichols was once with Oppenheimer on the Manhattan Project.'

He was also with Oppenheimer in the other picture with Bhabha. Bhabha looking at Oppenheimer. Oppenheimer looking at Bhabha. Nichols looking sanguine.

'You know,' Hanson said, 'they asked Nichols to vouch for Oppenheimer after he resigned from the nuclear project. Was he a communist, they wanted to know. Why else would he resign? They asked him whether Oppenheimer be allowed to retain his security clearance. Nichols went threw him under the bus instead. It became claim to fame. Said Oppenheimer was a communist in every way, except that he didn't carry a party card.'

So what was this Nichols doing in that picture with Prime Minister Nehru and Bhabha?

'Selling them a nuclear power plant. He had retired from the army and was working at Westinghouse by then.'

What was Hanson doing in there?

'Chemerica was the sub-contractor,' Hanson said.

'You guys are everywhere.'

'I like that. We should use it in our brochures. Chemerica is everywhere!'

Then he went got pensive again. 'You know, we were there to sell them a nuclear power plant for the fucking electricity they need, and all Nehru would talk about was the bomb. He asked Bhabha in front of us how long would it take to build one. A year, Bhabha said. Just one year to build the bomb. You should've been there. It was as if they had found the answer to famine, starvation, power blackouts, Pakistan and China in one go.'

Nearby, Willie was getting louder by the minute and Daisy ready to pass out. Ernst tried taking past him but then Willie was up and gesticulating towards the entrance and there was no point.

~

When Brigadier Bankim Kumar Chatterjee, Club Secretary, walked down the carpet pretty much master of his domain, a buzzed Willie eyed him with more ferocity than he otherwise reserved for wogs. It was a lovely evening and standing there on the verandah, Brigadier Chatterjee struck a pose—legs apart, an imaginary swagger tucked under an arm, and a satisfied demeanour.

'Bloody good, what?'

'Tell us, Chatterjee,' Willie asked, dispensing with unnecessary titles. 'Do we still have a dress code in this club?'

Now, the Brigadier wasn't particularly in awe of the white man. Stationed in Singapore, he had witnessed Brits and Australians panic, leaving Indian sepoys to deal with the Japanese pouring in from Malaya on bicycles. Willie, however, was a paying member and civility was in order. Besides, Brigadier Chatterjee wasn't the kind to hold a grudge against all Englishmen just because most were arseholes.

'Independent India, old chap. As long as you're in a pair of pants and shoes, it's fine by us, what!'

'Over there. Do those look like bloody pants and shoes to you?'

Willie's rudeness was beginning to rankle, and it showed on the Brigadier's face. Nevertheless, the reigning secretary followed the ex-secretary's sausage of a finger—pointing at Seth Jamunadas Kejriwal.

'Don't even go there,' the Brigadier advised.

'Is that man complying with the club's dress code or not? A simple yes or no should suffice.'

Both men studied the bania foot innocently swing back and forth, while hangers-on and bearers fawned. Sticking out through his dhoti, the leg stopped each time someone bent low to whisper something. Then start on its own volition, waiting for the next minion to step up.

'What would you like us do?'

'Go talk to him,' Willie said.

Ernst didn't want to know where this was going, and waved down a bearer for another hit. His third Bloody Mary for the evening. One above his limit, but at this point, what would that do? Kill him? He watched Willie cross The Great Divide, with the Brigadier dragging from behind. Resplendent in his dhoti and waistcoat, the Seth brightened on seeing them.

'Brigadier Bahadur! Come, please! Sit! Now! Here!' and he patted the cushion by his side.

Lowering the treble a bit, his voice took on an inclusive tone to co-opt the two and Ernst could no longer hear what was being said, until Willie spoke up. 'Chatterjee, explain to the man. This is not a bloody, Indian hangout. There's a dress code.'

Instead, the Brigadier stood aside to allow the Irresistible Force direct access to the Immovable Object. No matter. The Seth had sized up Willie. In such situations, a bania from the trader caste will freeze momentarily. He will withdraw to mentally regroup. His outer personality becomes even more pliant, if that's at all possible. He becomes his accommodating best, bending backwards while a hard knot forms inside. He explains in broken English how being a simple man, this is how he dresses. Surprisingly, no one had raised this matter before. He'll then go on to say, not to worry about anything. He'll take care of everything. No rules should ever be broken, he agrees. After all, where would that leave us? All will be resolved, he assures them, and looks at Willie with a big smile. What? Never again enter the club in a dhoti? Really? Okay. If you say so.

Then after he has Willie withdraw in the face of his performance, and after done with all the acting for the white man, the bania turns and stares at his minions. The eyes have gone cold and the demeanour more in line with the hard knot in his stomach. He snaps his fingers to send people scurrying and Ernst, who has seen this go down before, knows Willie is fucked. If not today, then tomorrow. But he is fucked.

~

The evening ripened with an overpowering smell of jasmine—incomplete without her sweat. With a fourth Bloody Mary in hand, he wondered what Sassoon had to say about Goddess Bhairavi's body odour. Did he wrinkle his nose, or breathe it in? A wail went up in the air. A cuckoo, this late? Could mean just one thing: the monsoons were here. Peering up to see if he could spot the harbinger, Ernst stepped out on the lawns. Trying not to dwell on Willie's upcoming travails, he swayed toward the club fence. Everything seemed amplified. He could handle his alcohol, so this heightening had to be Andhi Ma ratcheting up the remaining three minutes of his life. He didn't feel ill at all, as if he had outrun his cancer. There was a hole in the fence beckoning him and he floated over. He placed an eye to it and backed away.

There was someone peeking back from the other side. When he peeked again, the huge Indian eye was still there and the waft of sweaty jasmine was unmistakable. It sent him lurching for the rusted side gate—the one used by caddies to go in and out. He opened it and saw a woman walking away with that familiar shimmy. A blast of neon from Jhama Sweetmeats caught her neck, painting it white.

34

The Haunted Whorehouse

In abandonment of the scriptures, is the birth of love.
—*Tantric Sahajiya belief*

From where he stood in the jhopadpatti, Sindhi Refugee Camp appeared an advanced civilisation.

Warrens of jute bags came alive around him, breathing in their sleep. Crazy shanties made from flattened Castrol tin cans and cardboard, jute string and stolen plastic sheets crept up like his cancer. And everywhere, above, below, sideways: the heat, humidity and most of all, the hunger.

The place was asleep, and maybe that helped somewhat. Even so, the jhopadpatti made it clear: it was hungry. Not starving like the villages on the other side of the Ghats, but hungry nevertheless across its length and breadth. And it was endless, this jhopadpatti, spreading like a virus in the whole open area behind Sindhi Camp; extending, and extending, and growing, looping where necessary to squirm past housing societies and factories and roads and anything blocking its progress, until it reluctantly stopped from where the marshland mangroves walked out into the sea. These jhopadpatti would swallow a person whole unless one stuck out like a white thumb. It pressed Ernst from both sides, allowing him three feet of mud and faecal matter to walk on. There was no electricity. No public taps. No running water. No drainage like the Sindhi Camp's sophisticated, open sewage where one could squat and shit. Ernst remembered the

E.M. Forster Brahmin with a lota of water in hand, sneaking into Sindhi Camp under the cover of darkness to crap in style.

Distracted, he almost stepped on a little boy asleep on the three-feet of a footpath, curled snug against a tin shack. The kid could be Salim Ali before his Great Escape. The tiny lady sleeping inside that shack with her tired, cracked feet sticking out could be his blind mother. The man lying drunk further up, a wayward father. No Sindhi would be seen dead around here but there she was, Sindhi Camp Bhairavi, afloat over the mud and heading deeper into the slum as if she knew where to go and blind to her surroundings. He wondered if it was a case of the blind leading the drunk. The back of her neck wasn't dark brown anymore and instead, looked a pale white under the moon. Like the flutter of her sari, it guided him forward. He shouldn't even be in Sindhi Camp at night, and look where he was.

The moon disappeared but her neck remained white. He saw her float past a stall. The stall-owner was packing away his bhelpuri ingredients: peanuts, puffed rice, tamarind chutney. He placed them underneath the display area in a box with a disproportionate, Nav-Tal lock. The stall was in front of what looked like a school. It was a school. Chhote Bhai stood on display above the entrance in black and white—the school's patron—framed and garlanded with his aura intact. Nothing like how he looked the other day after Salim Ali was done with him.

Behind the school, there was a wide-open, empty space—two acres of it in a demarcated rectangle. It was staggering that the jhopadpatti wouldn't think it appropriate to encroach. Equally improbable, an expensive length of canvas pegged smack in the middle of the playground. It was sixty feet by ten feet—cover for a regulation-size grass cricket pitch to protect it from moisture. Keep it dry for a cricket match with people betting money. Going by the loving care on display, lots of money. A heavy, manual roller rested at the far end of the playground, used to even the pitch and compact the expensive clay bulli that Chhote Bhai must have paid for. Ernst could see Chhote Bhai bouncing his hockey ball on the ground to inspect the grass pitch—more the bounce, faster the pitch. At other times, he used it to smash in people's heads.

The playground filled up with ghosts in white after Chhote Bhai was done bouncing his hockey ball. Ernst stopped to watch Salim

Ali deliver his spin—the ball taking an innocent trajectory away from the wicket before heading back to demolish some batsman. Arjun was behind the wicket; Chhote Bhai busy taking bets from the sidelines. Ernst saw the girl Bhairavi looking on from the edge of the playground, with her teeth sticking out and eyes on fire.

Whereas, she had actually gone on ahead, so Ernst followed. It wasn't for him to unravel the threads within this group of childhood friends—their love, and hate, and all their history clouding his judgement. More so now, with one of them dead, another the accused, Salim Ali the accuser, and the girl up ahead crossing a rope bridge swaying over a stretch of darkness. He approached after a mental coin-toss, and looked down into fetid waters you could probably walk on without sinking. The jhopadpatti had taken root on both sides of the ooze with a section down there to shit, and a little further up, to wash clothes.

The other side of the bridge was an incline with clustered huts clinging on for dear life. Tin and thatch playhouses strung next to each other, and there was that smoky air from burning cow dung that hangs over a jhopadpatti. A large, pukka structure stuck out from top of the incline, lit up like someone's mother-in-law had died.

The first sign of electricity. If not blazing so recklessly, it could be a textbook haunted house: a bhoot bangla. He remembered the suburban myth about a churail blowing evening gusts towards Sindhi Camp from just such a place. The girl walked up its porch and into the incandescence like an angel without wings, opening the front door as if she owned the place. A voice sprang from the door and Ernst groaned. It was the fucking churail, and only his hard-on kept him from making a getaway.

Stepping on to the wooden porch, he was careful to walk around the powder mandala design radiating from dead centre, the triangle's apex pointing where the sun would rise a few hours from now. She had left the door ajar, and he walked into a Tantric, Bhairavi Chakra ceremony just about to begin. Seated inside, feasting on him with sightless eyes, Andhi Ma cleared her throat, imitating the practice that singers of her calibre do with the scales, before tearing you apart with their voice.

~

Here's how a Sahajiya fairy tale goes. There were two young people, very much in love, who each day laid together in the flower grove behind the palace. The girl's father was the king, and one day he discovered their tryst, and forced them to get married. Their bed of flowers turned to thorns and their love, to ashes.

Taking the fairy tale to heart, the Tantric Sahajiya decided early on that love within marriage was profane. Love had to be with the unattainable for it to be sublime. Just like Lord Krishna's dalliance with his consort Radha—the Perfect Woman, because she was married to another.

~

The evening's Tantric ritual celebrating the Perfect Woman would have started the night before. The decision on time and day would be arrived at through astronomical calculations—as complicated and scientific as her father's desperate Matka math to play the numbers. And just about as accurate. No matter, as with Matka gambling, it's faith that counts.

Ernst could see he was in a mujra-style dance hall inside the haunted house. There was another Tantric powder mandala on the floor of the dance hall. This one was king-size and made of sand, built with great care by the Tantaji—the ceremony's Tantric guide. Really big—over ten feet in diameter—the powder mandala allowed the Tantaji to enter through its doors and move around the streets. Men and women sat around it in a circle and no one could enter the powder mandala except the guide. Ernst knew the Tantaji would destroy this king-size work of art after the ceremony. Erase it to demonstrate maya and the nebulous nature of all material things. The Romans had slaves whisper, 'Memento Mori!' in the victor's ear. 'Remember! You too will die.' The much more sophisticated Indians have maya to tell them something similar, or the exact opposite; depending on what one wants to hear.

~

A Tantric guide would be typically female, like the gardener's wife at Purandhar Fort. Or Arjun's feminine half—the one Bhairavi claimed had a full fifty per cent of Arjun in its thrall. The bhoot bangla's Tantaji was all male, but working under Andhi Ma's instruction. He looked to the blind woman for permission every now and then, as if she could see. Andhi Ma sat cross-legged in one corner with her musical instruments, and nodded back as if she could.

'The way of truth is different from the way of society,' the Tantaji said in a standard Tantric preamble, and a caution of sorts. 'The two may overlap, or they may not.'

Quoting Chaitanya, the patron saint of the Sahajiyas and Lord Krishna's last reincarnation, he then intoned, 'At one time my mind was calm, but in the name of Radha-Krishna, my rationality disappeared.'

First caution, now licence.

An equal number of Krishnas and Radhas sat in the circle, man, woman, man, woman. As Ernst watched, they were asked to hold hands, which they did. In thirty years, he hadn't seen an Indian couple hold hands in public; now this. The participants were instructed to consider each man in the circle an embodiment of the divine consciousness, each woman as the embodiment of divine energy. Typically, as he knew from the Tantric texts, husband and wife would not be next to each other. In this way, adepts and acolytes together build an approximation of the Place of the Hidden Moon—one can never get there but there was no harm in trying.

As the ceremony heated up one had to ask, who led him here? Sindhi Camp Bhairavi, or was it the blind Andhi Ma—trying to liven up what was left of his life? This did beat having to die from whatever it was Waller had pointed out in the X-ray. No matter. Seeing the living, breathing chakra move in front of him, his illness wasn't important, nor was this orgy. He just wanted to locate the girl because his heart was in a free fall. The women in the room, though, all looked married—a line of red sindoor parting their hair, or a mangalsutra around the neck, or both. Sindhi Camp Bhairavi wasn't in the room and he buckled in relief.

The Tantaji then said, existing interpersonal relationships stood dissolved for as long as the powder mandala remained on the floor. He sat at the centre of the circle and asked the congregation to do their asanas, just as he had taught them. When they began, it was almost like a dance; the Tantaji reciting his mantras while the participants concentrated on their respective chakras, and on each other's wives. By the time Ernst ventured further into the room, the group was entangled and intertwined into a single, labouring organism.

Tantaji intoned from deep background, confident he was still being heard. The room was told the aim of the practice was not sexual, but to be able to see the divine in all beings. He chanted simple autosuggestions so each unit of the writhing circle looked at the rite from a spiritually elevated perspective. Dissolution of temporal relationships, he said, assist people in redefining their own in a spiritual way, and blah, blah, blah.

Ernst couldn't be bothered. He sensed Andhi Ma trying to engage him, but with all due respect, not today because there she was, Sindhi Camp's Bhairavi. In the chakra, caught red-handed in repose with some lout of a man—full-paunched, moustached and gasping under her ministrations. The man's Krishna-style, peacock feather headgear was askew. Ernst's heart sank like a stone. Just when the pain had become physical and he clutched at his stomach, he realised it wasn't her after all. The woman though had the same dark skin that was the bane of his life, and huge Tamil eyes plumbing pelagic depths.

It wasn't Bhairavi, but the girl's Tamil eyes almost made up for that. The most beautiful face in a circle of beautiful faces. Skin like ebony, she too had those broad forehead and cheekbones to make fashion photographers squeal with delight. He watched Tamil Eyes whisper into the lout's ear, readying to pull the trigger. Given how tiny it was, one almost didn't see her Adam's apple bob.

~

The most sexually repressed nation on earth, and one just walks into a room full of compliant Perfect Women? The Sahajiya wife swapping was supposed to make a theoretical point. Like most Indian thought though, impossible to put in practice. Having said that, India is as much the land of make-do, as of make-believe. So if women aren't playing along, dress up the men.

Acknowledging the room for what it was—transvestite Radhas with their Krishna clients—he was impressed no end. It was like the nation's import substitution programme. Caught up with the faux Krishna splatter himself all over Tamil Eyes' hand, he almost didn't see the other Tamilian in the room. Luckily, Chhote Bhai was hard to miss: all black and all in white, with his back to the proceedings, he was staring into an open door.

The Sahajiyas believed caste is not a matter of birth but of attitude. He, of any caste or religion, becomes a Brahmin on worshipping Krishna. That included Muslims, though clearly not this one with his back to the ceremony. You would think the man would have at least some interest in the goings-on behind him. Even the dead would die again just to watch Tamil Eyes giving a hand-job. If the five-times-a-day-namaaz-type Muslim wasn't here to get off in the Bhairavi Chakra, then why? That Chhote Bhai was here for Sindhi Camp Bhairavi, was unacceptable.

Seeing Ernst storm up to do the white man thing, Chhote Bhai registered no surprise at what should have been a big one. From behind all his bluster, Ernst couldn't help but feel somewhat offended at the way the big, black man ignored him to return his attention to whatever was inside that open door. Ernst didn't seem to matter and were he to die tomorrow—a real possibility—Chhote Bhai would not miss him.

Doors lined the corridor feeding into the creaking bungalow from the mujra-dance hall; their symmetry marred by one that remained wide open. Looking in past Chhote Bhai, there was no mistaking her backside. She had changed into a heavy, red, brocade sari in keeping with the evening's faux-bride theme, and she wore the same white ankles from his dream. Seeing her alabaster-white neck, he panicked. He had to run away from here and do it right away, because there was nothing left of his erection to afford him that earlier courage.

She sat at an elaborate dressing table, probably not unusual in a whorehouse for transvestites. Being spoilt silly, it appeared, by two men, both of whom Ernst recognised from the flock that flew in from Japan to play golf.

A Flying Japanese brushed her hair in long strokes, making it cascade down to the floor in a black waterfall. The other man massaged a porcelain-white foot resting on his lap. That is, until she pushed him away with a languid stretch of her leg, pressing her foot into his crotch to make him moan. And they said the Japanese flew here from Tokyo to save on green fees.

After the cross-dressed Bhairavi Chakra, Ernst wasn't up for more surprises, but Lord Krishna—or Govinda if you prefer—didn't care, because it wasn't Johnson's Baby Powder on that foot, or caking that neck and covering those bare arms. She had magically gone creamy-white and when she swivelled to face him, her bunny rabbit teeth were missing.

The woman in the red sari ignored Chhote Bhai and stared at Ernst instead, startled at first, just like that evening, emerging from the Golf Club greens with Chhote Bhai. Just like then, she turned away, but there was no trace of panic, nor was there a need to hide the face this time. Granted, Kirti the caddie-boy was a good-looking kid, but as a woman he was stunning.

~

'I would get bullied,' Kirti said, leaning back to talk to no one in particular, his sari pallu falling to the floor. 'So I learnt to deal with male-dogs. I learnt how to calm their fury, tame them with a look. Now instead of me, they kneel with their mouths open. I think I'll stick to wearing saris from now on.'

Kirti then deigned Chhote Bhai a glance and turned away, bored. Ernst could see what the boy meant. The sari was empowering. Chhote Bhai had ruined Kirti's father; taken four pouches full of diamonds over Matka. Going by Chhote Bhai's face, the son was doing a pretty good job getting even. All this while Flying Nippon#1 hadn't missed a stroke—counting to a million—and continued to work at unknotting Kirti's hair. Flying Nippon#2 was kissing the caddie-boy's foot. An irritated Kirti would shrug his shoulders every time #1 caressed an ear. Ernst couldn't decide what was more disconcerting: the cross-dressing or the arrogance that came with it.

'Sorry Princess,' said #1, not looking sorry at all. Down at the caddie-boy's foot, #2 was in a world of his own. No idea how long Ernst stood there with the humiliated Chhote Bhai, watching the Japanese worship their caddie-boy princess. When Chhote Bhai decided enough was enough, he didn't just leave; he slunk away. No goodbye, no protest, no threats, and no hurry to get back to anything resembling a slumlord. Ernst almost stopped him.

I understand, he wanted to say, because the man was clearly hurting. I now know it was the brother with you that day on the greens, not the sister. Wearing a sari, like right now. You like boys in saris. It's your thing. Fine. Whatever gets you off. But, why kill Arjun? And don't tell me it's because he stole something from the Americans. You wouldn't care if he stole America itself, as long as he wore a sari for you like Kirti here.

Salim Ali almost had it right when he said Chhote Bhai hated Arjun. It looked like hate because there's such a fine line. The two were lovers. Then something happened and Arjun stopped wearing saris for his slumlord. Safe to say, he was in love with someone else. There was after all that look to Arjun's face when they carried away the Headless Sardar. The way he reached out with his arm. Arjun's grief seeing his new lover's headless torso was enough for Chhote Bhai to smash the boy's head in with a hockey ball. Arjun may very well have stolen something, but doesn't matter whether he did, or what he stole. That's not why he was killed. Because by then, love had become hate and any excuse would do. Homicidal slumlords don't make for forgiving ex-lovers.

What was it with boys wearing saris? First, the dead Arjun, now this kid here; her brother, now sister.

Ernst remembered her saying the two boys would play with her, make rangolis. Like boys playing with dolls. Beautiful boys, who then began wearing saris to drive grown men insane. Insane enough to kill one of them.

He wanted to ask this one here, how close were you to Arjun? As close as your sister? Can you help cut through this damn thicket? I mean, look at you, so empowered and all.

A stench of condensed semen flowered from the Bhairavi Chakra; a double dose if you will, given there were no women in the room other than Andhi Ma.

'Still here?' Princess Kirti asked, looking at Ernst as she would at any male-dog. 'Something you need?'

If nothing else, it was the perfect cue for him to follow Chhote Bhai's example and slink off.

~

A wide nullah ran down the incline and emptied into the canal near the rope bridge. It was clogged—the sludge alive and bubbling with oil skeins floating on top. At least here, shit didn't necessarily flow downhill. Lengths of black coaxial cable tracked the nullah, running illegally up the incline to the Haunted Whorehouse. Some of the huts had wires drawn to them from the thick, winding cables. It explained why electrocution cases piling up at Sion Hospital's morgue were second only to bodies falling off trains.

When Andhi Ma ambushed him from behind as he stumbled down the incline, something happened to the jhopadpatti. It appeared to calm down further, if that was possible. Cow dung smoke rose to join Andhi Ma's rising octaves, as she sang about what the Tantric Sahajiyas claim, is the Place of the Hidden Moon.

'Morey Mann ke Kanhaiya,' she sang to the Krishna inside her head, and also inside each one of us. She sang to Him like a petulant child demanding attention, asking to be allowed into the Place of the Hidden Moon. That Perfect Place barricaded from us, even though it's in our heads; where He resides, fucking a married woman—Radha—every day, every hour, every second, creating the Perfect Union through Perfect Sex with a Perfect Woman. All the goings-on in all our heads collectively powers up the universe and keeps it from dissipating back into nothing.

'Bhairavi's tongue sticks out,' Andhi Ma complained in her song to Krishna, 'she's still ugly as sin.'

'Make her beautiful for me,' she pleaded to Govinda, 'have her carry me in.'

Ernst felt something crucial being said and it was important that he listened. Maya helped out by whispering in his ear. 'If you were following Kirti all that while, where's his sister?'

35

When Wishes Become Horses

Women typically defy math by giving two hundred per cent.
—*Sir Victor Sassoon*

Karim Court's cage of a lift wasn't working and he dragged himself up four floors. The building wasn't designed for cancer patients. Ernst's nostrils flared even before he stepped on the landing. She was there with Parvatibai, both squatting over a rangoli at the doorstep, huddled together like schoolgirls preparing the ground for hop, skip and jump. Schoolgirls in silk saris, giggling like hookers from the penthouse upstairs. The rangoli had their undivided attention.

Her bottom hovered above the floor as she worked with the coloured powder. Staring at her behind, he tracked their story from when he first saw it stare back at him through a maroon sari. Then her brother's—the one he saw that night at the Golf Club, taunting him from alongside Chhote Bhai. Chhote Bhai was fucking that one, not this. The brother, not the sister. Except of course, in Ernst's head. His head, by the way, turned out more prescient than he; painting her Sindhi-white in his dreams. Although if one wanted to sit back and get uncomfortable, one could say the cross-dressing brother was the one in his dreams. Schwester Ingrid would smile at that. She remembered things he preferred to forget, because of what they had done to his schoolteacher left hanging in the school courtyard alongside his dog. Or, because of what the schoolteacher had done to him behind closed doors. Pick one. Or both. It didn't matter all that much anymore. Whatever happened between him and the homo teacher wasn't why Bombay Ingrid left, or why Schwester Ingrid never returned. It wasn't why he got fired, or why he got cancer.

He stayed in the corridor behind the girl's glow and she ignored him for a bit, working side-by-side her new best friend. Then, she turned around to smile and the world lit up, like the first time she had smiled at him past her teeth, from her porch. It was he all along, not Chhote Bhai. Wishes were horses, after all.

Silly man, her smile said, and he felt good things happen to those who wait.

Then there are those who wait, Schwester Ingrid whispered, until it's too late.

~

Afterwards, they sat on the balcony while Parvatibai fussed around the living room.

'So, it was me all along?'

She didn't reply and instead offered her hand openly in what, for an Indian woman, could only be total surrender. He could check her pulse for the truth but there was no need because her pupils flared. She was on fire.

'Why me?'

'You do have a confidence problem,' she said.

'If it's because Salim Ali's been jabbering on about my fighting for workers, let me assure you he's far better at it than I am.'

'That's true. You're only good at saving friends from under trucks. He is right about one thing though. You may be a hero to some of us but you're zero to yourself. Is that a curse or blessing? To not see what others see in you?'

'Salim Ali says he doesn't know what I see in you.'

That made her giggle.

'I know. He likes women soft and white, like rasgullas. I don't mind.'

He kept his grip on her feminine hand with its raw, masculine strength, hoping he could draw on it like Sassoon's cheque. All of Colaba now smelled of her jasmine blend—laced with sweat and loaded with youth. Parvatibai brought them tea in Bombay Ingrid's Wedgwood set with two cups. She served her before Ernst and then lingered on, reluctant to leave, as if he couldn't be trusted with that hand. He agreed. Parvatibai should remain so he may try explain what a cancer patient his age was doing with someone young enough to be his daughter. Not easy because he couldn't even explain it to himself.

Sindhi Camp Bhairavi had smiled at him, not at Chhote Bhai. Why would she smile at Chhote Bhai? Chhote Bhai ached for creamy-skinned boys—the Kirtis and Arjuns—not her. Even when the creamy-skinned boys stopped reciprocating, the slumlord continued to ache. He ached for Arjun who refused to wear a sari for him. Whether the Not-Chinese boy stole something or didn't steal anything, or stole everything, nothing mattered to the spurned Chhote Bhai, except that he'd been spurned. Salim Ali had said only Chhote Bhai knew why he got involved in the boy's murder. Now Ernst knew too.

Sitting next to him on the balcony she was done acting the coquette. Forget all that, her eyes said, I ache for you. That's all you need to know. She looked at him and laughed, teasing him with all the marriage proposals being imposed on her these days. Tauba! From all sides! Who would think, she said. Someone as dark as me!

But you want nothing to do with those marriage proposals, right? You want to be with me. I know. I'll talk to your father. It should be easy. He and I are the same age.

There was this one family. Sindhi, of course. Amil, her caste. They were being very persistent. Dada couldn't be happier. Wants it over with quickly. Have her out of his hair. He forced her to stop with those embarrassing powder mandalas she did every morning; the ones Arjun had taught her.

No worries. Forget the Amil family. It's you and me now. I'll keep you on a pedestal. At least, when you're not changing bedpans.

This time she did not demand what he was going to do about Arjun. What are we going to do about us, her eyes asked instead; in an adult conspiracy. They were partners in crime. Frankly, she couldn't have made it any easier for him.

'Is there anything you want to ask me?' she prodded.

Yes. Do you know what a catheter is?

'Is there anything you want from me?' she asked.

He thought of the age difference. He considered the gora thing and Salim Ali's heads-up. There have been riots for less. He visualised sex with a catheter sticking out. How would that work? Oh, yes of course. It wouldn't.

As a woman she must have known how men get tongue-tied when propositioned, because she gave him time, lots of it, while she sat and smiled. A happy smile, relaxed, now that it was all out in the open and above the table.

Then as time passed and he still didn't say a thing, she must have felt more and more naked because when she understood what was happening here, she pulled her sari over the head to cover herself somewhat better. When he finally tried saying something, she stood up and moved away, pulling the sari even tighter to protect what remained of her modesty.

'Don't you dare,' she said, shiny streaks tracing down her face. 'You think I am that type of a girl? That was a proper proposal. I wasn't being challu. You understand? Good-for-nothing fellow.'

He tried telling her he understood. Her tears however, declaimed faster than he could. When she walked off, it was with such dignity, that Krishna in his avatar as Jagannath, Master of the Universe, rumbled awake to insist Ernst erase all record of past, under-the-table dealings. To show he meant business, Jagannath opened the city gates and the monsoons—laying siege for over a month now—arrived in one big, hissy fit, sending Parvatibai scrambling for the windows.

Between a bout of severe stomach cramps, Ernst watched the household batten the hatches. He hoped Andhi Ma was getting soaked nice and bloody proper out there, for giving him more Technicolour than he would ever want. He would tell her what she could do with the Place of the Hidden Moon. With his stomach cramping up like that, it was small comfort that he too may have grown along with the cancer.

After all, he had let Bombay Ingrid go because he couldn't take a decision. He let Bhairavi go today, because now he could. Not that it made him feel any better. He was relieved when Willie Lansdowne called to cancel the morning's golf game.

~

The boss wanted Willie in early tomorrow for something, was why. 'Head office apparently called about that Golf Club wog of yours.'

'Who?' Ernst asked with innocence piled high, so he could deny owning any and all wogs, while praying it not be that one wog he knew it was.

'Your bloody Seth, who else?'

Ernst felt a cold wind blow. He forgot his own travails and he put aside Sindhi Camp Bhairavi. His heart went out to the Englishman and he wished Willie could remain his innocent, harmlessly racist self forever; not face what was coming his way. But Willie had gone insulted the Seth and so he too needed to batten the hatches. Maybe not today, but definitely tomorrow.

'Wants a favour, I bet,' Willie said. 'That's what wogs are all about. Favours. Well, we'll see.'

However hard Ernst tried, it was impossible to dislike the fool. 'I'll give you the Seth's number,' he offered. 'Just call him and apologise for that other day. Do that, and I'll talk him down.'

Willie though, wasn't listening to anyone but Willie. 'How does he get the nerve, I ask you,' he demanded.

Hearing that tone, Ernst knew he wouldn't be able to get a word in edge-ways, or get the Englishman to apologise to an Indian. To a wog. At least, not in time to save himself. The white man's ego helped him rule this country for two-and-a-half centuries. The same ego would now destroy him. The Hindu in Ernst accepted it as par for the course. The rest of him wanted to shake Willie like a rag doll.

36

The Golog

One, two! One, two! And through and through
The vorpal blade went snicker-snack!
He left it dead, and with its head
He went galumphing back.
—*Through the Looking-Glass*

Ernst peered around Jhama Sweetmeats and up the side gully leading to her Nissen hut, trying to catch a glimpse of the girl without making a fool of himself. A short while ago, he had asked Mohan Driver to drop him outside the club gates instead of going in like any normal, white human being; so he was a fool already. And not just to Mohan Driver. Salim Ali stood by his side with a sword in hand. Ernst had yet to ask why. Together, they looked even more ridiculous. People gawked at the gora being harangued by a little black man flourishing a weapon.

'Know where Comrade Tufan is right now, this very, bleddy minute?'

Ernst declined the bait.

'He can barely stand, but he's in there,' Salim Ali answered. He brandished the straight blade, nodding towards the police chowki with his bandaged head—courtesy Gomes' goons from the other day. Gomes stood at the chowki gates with his own bandaged head—courtesy Chhote Bhai from the same day. He was eating a banana, his Enfield recklessly blocking the police chowki entrance to make a point. He stared with beady eyes at Arjun's mother, waiting across the road for Tufan to come out from the police chowki. Tobi Basar had her back to Gomes. It didn't matter because when it came to those breasts, Gomes had x-ray vision.

'Just look at that murdering ape. Staring at Aunty like that.'

Gomes turned to Salim Ali as if he heard that. So? he seemed to ask. What do you plan to do about it? And by the way, yes, I killed her son.

'Comrade Tufan's showing Dr. Waller's autopsy report to the bleddy bastards in there for the nth time,' Salim Ali said. 'Thanks to that ape, they still won't act. Good-for-nothing buggers. I tell you, I've just about had enough.'

Now Gomes was waving. He shouted out, 'All well, Mr. Ernestji?'

Ernst felt he should demonstrate some outrage. Show more interest in Tufan's plight as the man and his sister pursued justice for her son. It was getting difficult to be interested in anything, including himself.

'Stop twirling the damn thing,' Ernst said to Salim Ali.

'It's a Golog I practise with. Belonged to Arjun's father. I've to return it to Aunty. It calms me, their sword dance.'

He walked off towards Arjun's mother. In rubber chappals and armed with a dangerous weapon, it was impossible to take him seriously.

A banner fluttered astride two bamboo poles driven on either side of the Golf Club entrance. 'WE WELCOME THE HONOURABLE DR. HOMI J. BHABHA, CHAIRMAN, AEET.' A crudely painted Indian tricolour remained frozen above the lettering, mid-flutter.

Turning around as he made past the banner, Ernst saw Salim Ali in a huddle with Tobi Basar, and Henry Gomes' beady, gorilla eyes still not ceding an inch. There was this look to Tobi Basar's face as she put her mouth to Salim Ali's ear and started to whisper. Ernst could see Salim Ali stiffen with each whisper, her forehead touching the side of his bandaged head. Somehow, he didn't look comical anymore. Over by the police chowki gate, Henry Gomes touched the bandage on his skull where Chhote Bhai's hockey ball had struck. Whatever Tobi Basar kept whispering in his ear, it was doing wonders to Salim Ali's posture. Ramrod erect, he stood there

eyeballing Gomes. He could be demanding a re-match with Gomes'
Marathas, the way he stared.

~

Ernst picked up the evening's programme from the reception;
the engraved, white marble card also placed on every table
across the verandah. The club typewriter's Courier font announced
Brigadier Chatterjee had pulled out all the stops. The evening's guest
of honour, India's Oppenheimer, Dr. Homi J. Bhabha, Chairman of
Atomic Energy, father of Atomic India and sexiest man alive, was
giving a violin recital.

It was too much. 'Is there anything he cannot do?' Jack Hanson
asked. He looked up from the programme, his wife squeeze-fitted
into the sofa by his side.

Folding chairs radiated out in semi-circles from the repaired club
piano standing on its little podium and looking a lot less resigned.
Like waves, the chairs went past the red carpet at the entrance on
one side and crunched-up against the Seth's divan on the other. This
left Seth Jamunadas Kejriwal's leg just enough room for minimal
oscillation. The permit-room appeared blockaded for the first time
in living memory. The white gentry looked confused. They checked
the programme card on their tables and appeared more perplexed.
A wog playing Schubert?

There was a buzz and people turned towards the entrance.
The doorway framed Sassoon, Dr. Homi J. Bhabha, and Cathy
Sassoon. Together, they looked like tomorrow's *Times of India*
front page. As bulbs popped, Bhabha stood still with black hair
slicked back, as if ensuring they capture his good side. Adam
Sassoon appeared somewhat diminished next to India's shining
star, while Cathy's smile conveyed if this was the new normal, she
wanted out. Men in bush shirts shuffled behind the three VIPs as
the line-up advanced. They were the crème de la crème of India's
Brahmins, and Bhabha's immediate cohorts. Ernst recognised
Dr. Raja Ramanna, Dr. Bhabha's right hand, the left hand busy
with the PM at all times. And apparently, Dr Ramanna recognised
Jack Hanson.

'I know you!' he called out.

Hanson waved. 'It's going to be their India,' he said, 'or that fella's,' and nodded toward the Seth, resplendent today on his velveteen, divan sofa. The smiling bania waved, looking every inch the safer bet. Ernst checked the crowd trickling in. One expected Tufan to be here to cheer for his deity. Maybe, once he was done getting fucked over at the police chowki.

Earlier outside, Salim Ali had told Ernst, 'They screw with Comrade Tufan daily, making him wait so they may stare and snigger at the smiling Chinaman. They crack Chinaman jokes to his face. Yet he's there every day after work, smiling patiently and waiting forever to petition on behalf of Arjun.'

A dying man petitioning on behalf of the dead—a strange circumstance. Ernst would be glad to see Tufan again. There was something about the Smiling Buddha.

~

The Brigadier had been at it for a good five minutes and was beginning to ramble.

Brigadier Chatterjee declared his debt to Western classical music and how it helped him survive Changi Jail in wartime Singapore. Locked in a cell, he'd played arias inside his head while the Japanese tattooed a beat on top of it. When the Brigadier finally came around to introducing Bhabha, he left nothing to chance. He laid it out, reading aloud from a typewritten list on white foolscap. Not only an accomplished violinist, but also world-class painter. Not only world-class painter, but also the Father of India's nuclear program. Not only the Father of Atomic India, but also the builder of India's first ever radio telescope. Not only all that, but who do you think gave the meson particle its name?

Finally, 'Quite the Renaissance man, what?' So without further ado, the Brigadier invited Dr. Bhabha to commence with the recital, accompanied by, 'His very own Dr. Raja Ramanna on the piano.'

Dr. Homi J. Bhabha leaped on the stage, violin in one hand, bow in the other. Pointing into the audience with the bow, he said, 'I see my Aunty Coover. The nation owes her a debt of gratitude.

Dr. Ramanna and I refined India's first gram of uranium in her kitchen on Peddar Road.'

The beaming Aunty shone like the sun from a wheelchair in the first row; could be all that radiation absorbed from her kitchen. The VIP rows grinned, India roared in applause, Sethji clapped in childish glee, and the gora sahibs came to grips with the meaning of Dr. Homi J. Bhabha.

Someone yelled, 'Homi! That a Stradivarius?' It was a lanky, well-dressed twenty-something, sprawled on his chair and showing early signs of another Jehangir Merchant.

Dr. Homi J. Bhabha laughed. Ernst could see his eyes sparkle from where he stood. 'You forget I'm a Government servant,' Bhabha replied, and Louis Vuitton luggage notwithstanding, well fielded, Ernst thought.

'It's a 1923, Canadian Auguste Delivet,' the Government servant offered. 'A gift from W.B. Lewis, father of Canada's nuclear program.' He ran the bow across it with a flourish. 'Just so you know,' Bhabha continued while rubbing the curlicued end of the instrument against his shirt, 'it's the property of the nation and on display at AEET.' Then with a big, fat, innocent grin, 'Just borrowed it for the evening.' Party to his conspiracy, the crowd grinned back.

Young Jehangir yelled out again. 'What else you got on display behind that hill, Homi? Tell us!'

Bhabha flung back his killer smile. 'Read the third Five Year Plan, Dikkra. Remember, no secrets in our country. We're just making salad oil, that's all.'

'Is that what they call reprocessing spent fuel these days?'

Jack Hanson. Asking he be accepted as one of them, be party to all these inside jokes. The crowd parted to take him in—impossible to refuse a white man. Young Jehangir invited him over, pointing to a vacant chair and together with the other Parsi bawas, the rest of the Indians, and alongside Jack Hanson, began badgering an indulgent Bhabha.

'Tell us! Tell us!' the verandah demanded. Ernst hadn't seen Indians so unanimous on a subject since Gandhi asked they go fuck with the British.

Bhabha caved, moving on to provide an exegesis on India's state religion. The verandah went still. As with a reading of the Holy Ramayana, such nuclear talk left Indians raptured.

'Like I said, it's simple as Italian salad dressing,' Bhabha explained to the Atomic India Fan Club, his violin resting in one hand, the bow waiting in the other to make a point. 'The plutonium and uranium we dissolve in nitric acid at the reprocessing facility, is like the vinegar-water mixture at the bottom of your bottle of salad dressing. The tri-butyl-phosphate and kerosene mixture we use is like the salad oil you see on the top. Now just shake the bottle, and the plutonium and uranium are extracted into the kerosene. Next, pour off the plutonium and uranium rich kerosene, then mix it with concentrated nitric acid. Voilà, the plutonium is extracted into the nitric acid, leaving the uranium in the kerosene.'

Young Jehangir was relentless. 'What will you do with the plutonium, Homi?'

'Tell us! Tell us!' the Indians asked as one. That the salad-oil analogy would register en masse was astounding. An Indian will absorb concepts like a sponge. It's only when he puts it to practice that the fuck-ups begin. In theory, Indians are the most intelligent people in the world.

'Tell us!' they roared with a patriotic fervour that had doubled after the bruising from China.

'To produce electricity of course,' Bhabha said, and the big, wide, innocent grin across his handsome face left the Indians squirming with pleasure at the duplicity of it all.

'Hell with that, Homi,' Young Jehangir yelled out, and Ernst was impressed at how closely he resembled the original. 'Just give us the bomb!'

'I know how you must feel.' Bhabha started playing his crowd instead of his fiddle. 'After all, why should America decide who goes nuclear?' Somewhat like the Deputy Commissioner's complaint—why are only Americans allowed to be cowboys?

The demagoguery got the crowd roaring. They were savouring their moment, when Jack Hanson boomed across the packed verandah. 'You're shaking the salad bottle in a radiation field two miles from here. Hopefully, you're not doing it in anything like your Aunty's kitchen!' He laughed to establish it was a joke. Portions of the fan club laughed with him while others digested the comment; those who had seen Hanson amongst slum dwellers, maybe, glimpsed where he was coming from. Others weren't that charitable.

'Pulling a Nichols on my boss, Mr. Hanson?' Raja Ramanna asked, deadpan, fingers poised over the piano keys. Dealing with white men, clearly not a problem.

Dr. Homi J. Bhabha smiled. Leaning over, he whispered to Ramanna—steadfast by the piano, owning it. Ramanna nodded back to his boss who tucked the violin under his chin and hit it, leaving Ramanna to come casually from behind on the keyboard. All across the room, Parsi bawas scrambled for Brigadier Chatterjee's programmes on white cards, as Schubert's 'Ave Maria' floated out from the Delivet. A wog playing Schubert, accompanied by another on the piano.

The 555VMOT microphone on the stand in front of Bhabha came with a poor, high frequency response. It didn't matter though, when Bhabha took off low and deep on the violin. Two minutes later, when he stopped to make way for a bit of keyboard play by Ramanna, and then returned sweeter and quite a few octaves higher, the microphone's thin metal diaphragm struggled. That didn't seem to matter either. Ernst saw D'Souza at the permit-room door, listening to 'Ave Maria' with tears in his eyes.

Five minutes later, Bhabha lowered the violin and the Indians rose as one around the scattering of grim-faced goras, who remained seated. Not Jack Hanson, he cheered alongside the people he loved. His big-boy grin notwithstanding, Ernst couldn't help but notice the troubled look to his eyes. It reminded him of the confusion that had crawled up the Texan's face that day at Fertilisers, holding onto a dying Arjun in a pool of Indians while trying not to drown. And yet, Salim Ali blamed him for Arjun's death. The man didn't seem to catch a break. Now it was Ramanna pointing a finger. Pulling a Nichols on my boss, Mr. Hanson?

Kenneth Nichols had thrown his boss Oppenheimer under the truck, after Oppenheimer refused to participate any further in the American nuclear program. Fingered him. Declared him a communist. In America that would be the kiss of death. It was still vivid though, how Hanson had broken down, cried, with Arjun in his arms. He wasn't capable of throwing anyone under a truck. So what made Ramanna think he would do that to Bhabha? And anyway, who could do anything to Bhabha? He looked invincible standing there with the Delivet in his hand, taking a bow.

'Show 'em, Bhabhaji!' the Indians yelled, and while you could say they were rooting for his music, one knew they were asking for a bomb.

~

Bhabha was charging his batteries with a glass of orange juice when Ernst stepped out for some air. He looked around. Thankfully, no Salim Ali in sight. Surprisingly, no Willie either—otherwise a permanent verandah fixture this time of the day.

In lieu of both, Henry Gomes sat astride his Bullet Enfield in the golf club compound. A brooding Chhote Bhai stood next to him. Today for some reason, Gomes looked the man in charge despite his bandaged cranium. He dismounted, leaving the new, subdued Chhote to go fuck himself. Ernst noted the role reversal and whispered Krishna's name, acknowledging maya and the transient nature of things. At the far end of the compound, a group of men was busy with Marathi chitchat. Their thickset potbellies and standard moustaches said they were plainclothesmen and part of Bhabha's security detail.

Seeing Ernst, Chhote Bhai looked like he wanted to step up and say something. Then his helium started to leak and it left him just standing there, a vacant expression on the face. Ernst was deliberating over what Chhote Bhai had gone done to himself, when Salim Ali and Tsering Tufan went appeared at the gates. The bond between the South Indian Malayalee and the dying tribal from India's Northeast was palpable even from a distance. Tufan was in a white, hand spun, khadi kurta, white trousers, leather chappals, and the gentlest of smiles. In his left hand was that worn, yellow file—a permanent appendage he now slept with; every little detail on his nephew's death next to him at all times and ready to present at a moment's notice.

'The autopsy report says it was a stab wound to the femoral artery. Please take down an FIR complaint, Mr. Policeman. I can also identify the culprit who killed my nephew. He is standing outside.'

'Oye, Chinaman! Look at you. Don't get too close. What bleddy autopsy report? Who issued it? Only the Coroner's Office is authorised. Not some medical college. Who is this Dr. Waller fellow? We don't recognise him. Kindly get the autopsy report from proper authority first. Until then, the only culprit is you, for wasting our time.'

Standing at the club gates, the Smiling Buddha looked a lot like a man back to square one. When Ernst returned to Gomes, the gorilla appeared petulant at the lack of respect. One minute they were eyeballing each other—the proper thing to do—and then without any warning, Ernst was waving at Chinamen. Tufan had waved back, of course. Not Salim Ali, who also held a yellow file in his left hand like Tufan. Whatever Tobi Basar whispered in his ear had worked like a tonic. When Salim Ali strolled into the club, it was like he owned the place; behaving as if he were Adam Sassoon.

Walking up behind the glowering Gomes and a muted Chhote Bhai, Ernst could have sworn his engineer's right hand was empty. That's because the short, straight, tribal sword, the Golog, was in Salim Ali's palm and flat against the back of his wrist, pressed along the forearm.

Meaning, he had to first walk past the two men, drop the file, and only then slash backwards. Bhabha was at it with his violin again, and this time it was Beethoven. His 'Seventh in A Major'. Salim Ali's skinny right arm floated back and toward the more muscular men with such grace, Ernst thought for a moment he had decided to dance to Bhabha's music. Gomes was nothing if not a sharp fuck, and saw it coming. He sidestepped the sword like a ballet dancer, but it didn't matter. Salim Ali ignored Arjun's killer and homed in on Chhote Bhai instead. One could argue Chhote Bhai too may have reacted like Gomes if he was fully there, or for that matter, if he cared. Could have parried Salim Ali's arc, if not so caught up in the web a relentless Arjun kept spinning from the dead.

Salim Ali's sword cut deep across Chhote Bhai's stomach and with an ease that didn't do justice to the muscle it shred like gauze. It looked easy, probably because Chhote Bhai didn't make a peep. Salim Ali slowly brought the blade back to Chhote Bhai's navel and stood erect. One would think he did this every day. A surprised Chhote Bhai looked down at the sword sticking into his black, dead centre, then at Salim Ali, standing in front of him just shy of five feet tall. The security, caught up in their chitchat, failed to notice the artistry underway. Chhote Bhai, though, watched mesmerised as the sword then cut upwards through his diaphragm; something like what a Japanese committing seppuku would do to himself. Only Chhote Bhai was having it all done for him by his tenant with a bandaged head. Several long and silent seconds after organs and messy bits and pieces started falling out from his stomach, Chhote Bhai decided to follow suit without protest. Salim Ali pulled the sword back, allowing the huge body enough space to land with a thud. Bhabha continued with the Allegretto in the clubhouse and it was Gomes who began yelling as if he was stabbed.

He must have felt a lot like Salim Ali; like a man who had had enough. This was it. No more. First, Ernst with his straight razor, now this. Gomes appeared to have had it with arseholes welding sharp objects. He jumped to avoid Chhote Bhai's entrails slithering toward him. Then with a cry, almost plaintive and no other way to describe it, Gomes the gorilla headed for the gates. Turning left, he took off down Trombay Road and kept going. The last thing Ernst saw before returning to Tsering Tufan was an also-screaming Murli Chowkidar following in hot pursuit. Their two banshee wails came together to wax before dying off into the distance.

By now the police registered something may have happened and they froze, fixated on a bloodied Salim Ali looking back at them. Salim Ali surveyed the battlefield and his eyes seemed to gravitate towards the old banyan behind Murli Chowkidar's abandoned guard post. Its base was at an elevation; a neat circle of bricks packing mud around the thick bole with its dreadlock of vines that became trunks on touching ground. It was a massive banyan, competing with the one over at the Krishna Temple. Salim Ali walked over to the tree as if not a care in the world; probably true. The little Marxist then hopped up and ritually circled the trunk three times. No one else budged. The police remained frozen, rock-solid. Salim Ali had their undivided attention.

He could be performing some tribal ceremony. Salim Ali walked back to Ernst with the dripping sword in hand and came to a standstill, a foot from his face. Then he raised the drawn weapon and reached up to tug at Ernst's hair with his other hand, running his fingers through it. From behind eyes shut tight, Ernst was surprised how a fistful of his blonde hair parted company with a single swipe; Salim Ali holding the hair with barber-like aplomb. Something wet trickled down Ernst's face. Opening his eyes, he saw Salim Ali now holding the sword to his own head. There was a red smear on the little man's forehead, like a caste mark. The black tuft he took from his head stood out against Ernst's gold.

By now, Tufan had stumbled inside the compound and had the same look of calm panic from when Arjun died. He pulled himself together as Salim Ali approached and the two men folded hands in namastes as part of whatever was unfolding. Salim Ali whispered something into his comrade's ear. The Smiling Buddha's body heaved with silent sobs. This was the same man who observed his nephew's post-mortem with the equanimity of a Buddha.

'On behalf of Arjun's dead father,' Salim Ali said to Ernst, as if explaining some arcane ritual. 'I had to use his sword for this. It's a Golog, tribal thing. One has to do it.' Whatever it was Tobi Basar had whispered in his ear earlier by the police chowki, it must have been a complete education.

What did she tell you, Ernst asked, and Salim Ali looked to make sure Tufan was out of earshot. 'Bad things,' he said. 'That Chhote Bhai did bad things to our Arjun.'

Holding the sword under an armpit, Salim Ali then proceeded to braid his black strands of hair flocked with Ernst's gold. Moving around the gore at his feet, Salim Ali walked towards the tree again. The policemen backed off in a hurry, competing with each other to get behind the sturdy rear fin of the Seth's Impala. Selecting a slim vine from the banyan—one not yet touching soil—Salim Ali knotted the braided hair around the strand, in whatever conclusion this was to his ritual sword performance. To do that, he had to grip the sword under an armpit once again. That still wasn't reason enough for Bombay's Finest to act, and they remained protected behind the Seth's American armour.

'Hands up!' one of them did say however, peering up from the Impala's fin. He sounded tentative.

Salim Ali ignored the order and smiled at his friends as Gautama Buddha would. It had taken a murder for the man to become serene like never before. You could say the same for his disembowelled landlord. Ernst noticed the dead man's face lit up with pure relief. He had never before seen the bored, brooding Chhote Bhai this positive and upbeat.

'I'll be at the police station next door,' Salim Ali said.

37

Girl on Fire

We tribals had no idea we were low caste, until the Hindu informed us.
—*A.Z. Phizo, Naga nationalist leader*

The constipation welled up again soon after Salim Ali's sword dance and the cork back up his arse, along with a slight fever that came and went like the cork. He felt feverish even when the thermometer confirmed there was nothing of that sort. A phantom fever. Like the phantom cork. To him, both as real as Schwester Ingrid—also popping in and out at will whenever he was alone. He led a full life these days.

The cork loosened in surprise when Bhairavi opened the door to Tufan's flat at Atomic Energy.

'Do come in,' she said.

Frankly, he was a bit taken aback. As if that other day at his place never happened, as if he didn't make a fool of himself, as if she did not walk away bereft. Seeing her made him pucker up, down there. He tried to relax and pushed downwards. Relax the sphincter, then try again. The cork didn't feel figurative at all. If he reached into his pants from behind, it would be there.

Tsering Tufan was reclined in a chair amidst a floor full of Ernst's Goregaon workers. They had taken over the room. They straggled up to wish him and collapsed back into a squat one by one. Ernst settled amongst them and was soon squirming on the tiles. Compared to the constipation, his recent on-off fever was nothing.

Tufan leaned back against the chair like an enervated Buddha resting up. If Salim Ali's personality had done a volte-face after Chhote Bhai, so had Tufan's—his equanimity was now a thing of the past. Along with the luminosity from his eyes. Looked like he was dying some more every day and too lost to care. The trade union man by his side looked equally lost. His soda glasses displayed big earnest eyes and his spindly legs folded up like a grasshopper.

The balcony doors were open, allowing the sea breeze to enter with a whoosh and the curtains bellowed like sails. They were on the fourteenth floor of Alaknanda, one of Atomic India's many high-rises and named after a Himalayan river. The flat was spacious, modern, and with the living room wall straight from Salim Ali's flat. The same charcoal portraits of Lenin and Fidel Castro hung at eye level. Vietnam's General Ngyuen Von Giap too, resplendent in green uniform and red stars. Here though, there was also a black & white Bhabha, who would never have looked this satisfied with things over on Salim Ali's wall. Castro too, appeared more comfortable pondering a ceremonial sword instead of holy, Arabic calligraphy. The Golog sword was in its hewn, leather scabbard, inclined on two thick-padded nails in the wall. Coloured threads trailed down from the nails.

The grip was familiar. Ernst had seen it on the weapon Salim Ali used to fillet Chhote Bhai the other day. Salim Ali had borrowed that sword—one just like this—from Tufan's sister and it was now in police custody as Exhibit A. Ernst could visualise Tobi Basar teach Bhairavi all the right moves; have her dance the way Salim Ali had with the sword in hand. He went hard instantly and was ashamed.

'You think Salim is okay in the police chowki?' Tufan had the look of a little boy seeking solace.

From what people said about that place, who could say? And after what Salim Ali had done, who could tell?

'He'll be fine.'

'I hope he's getting some sleep.'

Henry Gomes had stabbed young Arjun in May. It was almost August and Salim Ali had only just carved up Chhote Bhai. He was behind bars, surprisingly serene, and arguably, Gomes the one not getting any sleep. Ernst wondered if Henry Gomes had at least stopped running.

Not bothered about Gomes or much else, Tufan looked done with this, and that, and everything else. The grasshopper next to him hiccupped and turned his head to the wall. Tobi Basar stood behind Sindhi Camp Bhairavi in her Thai-style, shiny silk sarong and a green blouse.

'Did you make him do it?' Ernst asked her.

'Are you asking about Salim Ali?'

He wanted to say, yes, but chickened out. He was sorry he asked. It didn't matter. You whispered in his ear, he went tribal and whatever happened, happened.

Standing there by the corridor, she looked like the Statue of Liberty in a sarong with a Jacqueline Kennedy haircut.

'You're blaming me? No, no, it's okay. I can see that you are.' She paused to crank up the voltage. 'Being European, maybe you don't know about this country. What these Indians do to us. That man Salim Ali killed, do you know what he was doing to my boy?' She looked at her dying brother. 'We should all have run amok like Salim Ali long ago.'

The room was not expecting this. Putting aside his Marxism, the grasshopper unfolded his legs. 'Aunty, this is your country too. You're Indian, just like us.'

'I am? They say we are Indo-Mongoloid. What is Indo-Mongoloid? Do you know even a single case of an Indian Hindu marrying a tribal? I mean proper marriage, not rape. There is no such thing. Hindus are too racist for that. They actually enjoy it, being openly racist. It allows them to look down on others, be like the British. Our people came to the region from China and East Asia. India colonialised us, like the British before them. There is no Indo. We are not Indian.'

When Tufan hawked, collecting his phlegm and folding the handkerchief neatly back into his trouser pocket, she went somewhat bitter. 'Don't try telling him though. He couldn't understand why Arjun refused to play cricket with Hindu boys in Atomic Energy. Why he preferred playing in the slums with Salim Ali instead. They were kindred souls, Salim Ali and Arjun. Both victims of India. How many times I pleaded with my brother, "Let's go. Let's get out from here." He refused. Said he was Indian. He preferred to stay in Bombay with his Bhabha instead and get irradiated, see his own nephew murdered. Now he can die with my dead boy on his mind.'

With that, she went back to deadpan calm. Tufan looked confused at the attack, and the grasshopper's face had contorted. Some people should never cry.

Still speaking to Ernst, she nodded toward Tufan. 'You know, I woke up at night a few weeks ago, and came to the kitchen. He was sitting there, pen in hand and staring at the waiver papers they wanted him to sign before allowing him medical treatment. I watched him, God knows for how long. He kept looking at the papers, unable to sign them and save himself.' She paused once more, and Ernst understood that her dislike for India wasn't like the one Bombay Ingrid held so dear. Or like Willie's, for that matter. With Tobi Basar, the hatred had developed one wound at a time.

'It's best you die,' she said to her brother. 'You may love this country, but it has no use for you. They're waiting for you to go. Everyone knows it.'

'These same people also know the soil around the CIRUS reactor is contaminated. If radiation were visible to the naked eye, the glow would light up the skies. They employ Lambadi gypsies as daily wage-workers and not one dosimeter badge between them. The Lambadi children play on the contaminated lawns where their mothers work without protective gear. If that's the value the Indian Government places on Indian lives, what can those like us expect?'

She was done. The Smiling Buddha and the grasshopper looked ready to slit their wrists. She turned to Sindhi Camp Bhairavi and said, 'We have dance practice.'

~

'I am sorry about the other day,' he said.

They were alone for a bit, standing by the corridor; Tobi Basar back in her bedroom, the grasshopper gone with the rest of the trade union gang, and Tufan staring out into middle space from his chair.

'Why sorry?' Sindhi Camp Bhairavi's eyes weren't ablaze anymore. 'You were right not encouraging me.'

No, he wasn't. He knew women enough to know what had happened. They gave themselves with the same absoluteness with which they tuned off. She was past him now, and it showed. He was an idiot. He waited for her to ask about Salim Ali. What are you going to do about him? By now, she would know he could do nothing.

'Parvati says you are going to Germany.'

'Yes.'

'Anyone still there?'

He thought of Schwester Ingrid, and he remembered Siegfried, and he remembered his mother. 'No.'

~

It took the German in him to understand his father's genius: going straight to the nearest police station after he buried Ernst's mother— Betty, the Aryan.

With her gone, the Gestapo would have sooner or later come for Siegfried anyway. Betty, the Aryan, had held them back all those years. Hitler didn't know how to deal with mixed marriages and there were a lot of them in Berlin. Jewish men were, after all, a catch—didn't get drunk, didn't beat their wives, had jobs. So, the Gestapo would wait until the Aryan spouse died before boxing and shipping off the Jewish catch. Siegfried pre-empted them by surrendering as soon as his Aryan wife was buried. Not to the Gestapo, mind you, he went to the police instead. His crime? Being a Jew, he explained. While they mulled over him walking in like that, he informed them that besides being Jew, he was ill and needed medical attention. He coughed a couple of times and the police station went, Aaah Ha! At least now they knew where he was coming from. Unlike the Gestapo Manual, the Police Handbook pre-dated Hitler and was crystal clear: sick detainees to be hospitalised before any legal proceedings and / or incarceration. They knew what he was up to, but they were Germans, and law was law. The boxcar would have to wait until the Jew recovered.

The Jüdische Krankenhaus was the one hospital still accepting Jews. He was admitted into the Polizeistation police ward and remained there for four years. Schwester Ingrid wrote that Herr Doktor Doktor Lustig would have covered him for four more. After all, he was doing it for others. The Jews behind the hospital walls included genuine patients and doctors and nurses of course, but also those pretending to be patients and doctors and nurses. Schwester Ingrid was an outstanding example. If only Siegfried hadn't been such an arsehole.

After saving his life by declaring him too sick to be killed, four years later the Jüdische Krankenhaus would declare Siegfried Steiger fit enough to die. By doing so, Herr Doktor Doktor Lustig gave up on him and Siegfried gave up on everything to go dance to Emmy Destinn from his open window.

'Do you think of your father a lot?'

'Every night.'

'Do you think of your wife?'

'They come arguing in the same package.'

'You never told me what happened to her.'

'I don't know. I never saw her again after she returned to Berlin.' A lie. She was all over him last night, going on and on about his father. Sindhi Camp Bhairavi cocked her head and squinted as if peering through to the other end of the galaxy, at Berlin.

'You said she didn't like India.'

'Yes. The heat, the dust, everything was wrong.' He pointed at the Hindu swastika hanging from her neck. 'Even that upset her.'

She rubbed the pendant. 'Does it upset you?' she asked.

'No.'

'Do I upset you?'

'No. Of course not.'

'Why not?'

He felt himself shrivel. No guts in the face of a bunny rabbit half his age.

'No reason.'

'That's not a good reason. It means, no feelings at all. Not even dislike. Who wants that?'

There was finality in the way she said it. Who wants that? He wanted to ask her not to give up on him. He didn't mean what he just said. He hadn't meant it that last time either. Of late, when he thought of what's missing from his life, he saw her face with the buck teeth, not Ingrid's perfect beauty. He wanted to tell her that.

Fall back in love with me.

That, like escaping cancer, was not going to happen. There was something almost triumphant about the way her eyes glittered while she stood there, reading his heart. She was back on fire. The word he was looking for would be: victorious. She was done with him. It was over. This was closure. They were through. She was victorious.

'How's Kirti?' he asked, acknowledging a lost cause. Did she know about her brother? The cross-dresser?

'She's fine. Why?'

She knew.

'And your father?'

'Kismet. All he wanted was a son...now he has two daughters. One isn't his, and the other isn't one.'

Tobi Basar was signalling from the bedroom. 'Coming!' Bhairavi said, and reaching around her neck she took off her pendant with that swastika.

'Please...' she pointed to the dining table, handing it to him. 'If you don't mind. It gets in the way when I practise.'

'Of course.'

She then went to the wall and drew the Golog from its scabbard.

'The sword dance,' she explained. 'Teaching me keeps Aunty occupied, otherwise...you just now saw.'

They knew he was watching when Tobi Basar took the Golog from her and Bhairavi tied her dupatta like a sash so it didn't come in the way. She crouched with legs spread like Tobi Basar demonstrated; how the Japanese POWs at Purandhar would take a stance doing karate katas. When Tobi Basar's sword arm floated in a wide arc and then back to the centre, it was how Salim Ali had shredded through Chhote Bhai's abdomen—just because Tobi Basar whispered something into his ear. And now he was in jail.

'Why did you have to tell Salim Ali about Arjun and Chhote Bhai?' Ernst asked, and the two women stopped what they were doing. He couldn't see Tobi Basar's face, but the girl was frowning.

'Why? Where was the need?'

Tobi Basar remained in the shadows and he knew it wasn't fair on her, but what had happened wasn't fair on anyone.

'What am I supposed to do with him gone? Did you think of that? What do I do now?'

He stood there watching Bhairavi twirl the sword listlessly, when instead of just asking him to leave, she turned around to say, 'Look after yourself.' There was something final in those words and maybe regret too, but by now his judgement was anyway suspect.

Mohan Driver was waiting downstairs, so Ernst lugged himself to the lift. Heading towards the one-eyed Fiat, he wanted to know why was he now wearing her gold pendant. She'd asked he leave it on the dining table; instead it was now around his neck. How, no idea. Except that on top of everything else she had on him, he was also a thief.

~

The rains were back to fucking with the city after showing up that other day, so the car windows remained rolled down to allow air. The breeze brought in a strong, wet whiff of clean jasmine; not the same without her sweat. Ernst looked back towards Atomic Energy—leaking away from behind Trombay Hill and making Bombay glow. Now he could see the light the blind Andhi Ma had been complaining about; yelling, as she did, like the mad woman she was, pointing at the skies and calling everyone idiots.

And being an idiot, Ernst found himself still wearing her gold pendant. Parvatibai could return it to Bhairavi, for all he cared. That girl was gone as far as he was concerned. And it didn't matter. After all, could anything with anyone come even close to how Bombay Ingrid would spread out once a month to allow him his Christmas in July? No? Then why bother? Besides, there were other things to worry about.

Saving his arse for one. Not depend on Waller being the other. Man was a placebo, not a doctor. First and foremost, then, was to find sufficient courage and call the Jüdische Krankenhaus. In spite of all evidence to the contrary, he remained terrified Schwester Ingrid would answer the phone. Almost as terrifying as the thought of Salim Ali alone in some cell at the police chowki.

38

Bhairavi's Engaged

Draco Dormiens Nunquam Titillandus.
(Never tickle a sleeping dragon)

With Salim Ali's Buddha avatar locked inside, the police chowki developed an aura.

At least one knew where Salim Ali was. Where was Willie?

When Ernst called, Daisy Lansdowne answered.

'Hello Daisy. Willie around?'

'Hello Ernst. Actually, no.'

'Haven't seen him in weeks.'

'Funnily enough, neither have I,' she said cheerfully, before disconnecting.

Back at the chowki, the moustached havaldars were quite surprised at Ernst's audacity, showing up with the half-dead Chinaman.

'We have a full confession from the Muslim communist. This is now a national issue. Death sentence guaranteed.'

Tsering Tufan leaned against the police chowki wall, rich with moss, yellow paint peeking out from here and there. He slid against the green slime and fell. Rushing to him, Ernst was riveted by the defeat and fear in the man's eyes. He heaved him up and held him tight.

'I said don't come.'

'Salim Ali's in there.'

'I know.'

Farther down Trombay Road, Jack Hanson was dispensing charity by the club gates. He appeared done with doling out loose change and biscuits to mobs clamouring for more. Murli Chowkidar too had finished handing out textbooks to those who didn't want them. The road was littered with discarded school textbooks. As the pavement dwellers drifted off, the jhopadpatti folk moved in to collect the textbooks for fuel.

Seeing them approaching the club, Hanson came up with a smile the size of Texas. Tsering Tufan politely shrugged Ernst off and waved back.

'Why this daily early morning tamasha?' Tufan asked with the gentlest of smiles, reverting to his half-dead normal. 'Why not assist in a more structured manner?'

'Structured assistance?' Hanson asked. 'Oh, you mean like the American PL 480 food aid you don't want?'

Tufan did not see that coming, but continued smiling. Ernst could have kissed the American's arse for resuscitating the Smiling Buddha.

'You are a good man, and I'm indebted to you for Arjun,' the Smiling Buddha said. 'But doesn't it bother you why American aid always comes with a catch?'

Hanson didn't look bothered. Instead, he looked in the direction of India's nuclear facility nesting behind Trombay Hill in the distance.

'You know first-hand that people are getting irradiated over there,' he said, sweeping a paw, large enough to scoop up Trombay Hill. There was an American-style pause, the way they do on Madison Avenue. Next, he turned ninety degrees to point eastwards at Bombay's hinterland behind the Western Ghat mountains. 'And there's a famine brewing over there.' Another flourish. 'PL 480 food aid is the least of your worries.' He paused again before a classic First Amendment close. 'Having said that, I respect your right to hold a contrary view.'

Ernst was bent over the reception desk signing-in Tufan, and missed the detente failing to get underway.

'People getting irradiated?' Tufan was still, all smiles. 'What are you basing that on? A single incident?'

Hanson looked at the Smiling Buddha and his eyes widened. 'You can say that after what they did to you?' he asked.

'They didn't do anything, Mr. Hanson. We all have to go, one way or the other. It's no big deal.'

'I'll tell you what's a big deal,' Hanson said. 'You know about criticality excursions? Of course, you do. They happen around reactors, they happen in the PUREX reprocessing plants, and they happen during experiments like the one your great Bhabha conducted in his Aunty's kitchen. By the way, fucking around with radioactive material like that, we call it Tickling the Dragon. People die when they tickle the dragon. Except in India. Here, it's as safe as Italian salad dressing. In the rest of the world, criticality excursions are accidents waiting to happen. Even with all the fail-safe shit we put in, we still have accidents. The Soviets have them all the time. As do the F   Brits. All of us are guilty of somehow, at some point, doing something wrong and inducing radioactivity in open surroundings. All of us, that is, except the Indians. Not a single recorded incident! Experiments in kitchen sinks, labourers taking radioactive showers, workers manually handling fissionable material and yet, a hundred per cent safety record. What a country!'

'Maybe because we have people like Dr. Bhabha.'

'Then what happened with you? How come your Dr. Bhabha lets you burn up from the inside? How many roentgens did you take in his radioactive shower? Hopefully no more than a hundred, because then you may survive a while. But that's not what I hear. I heard you were in there far too long, pushing those labourers away, taking samples. Looks like you have a death wish. Let's say you absorbed a conservative two to three hundred roentgens. In which case, you have barely a couple of months unless you received immediate medical care. What's the great Bhabha doing about that?'

Hanson had maintained a sarcastic tone through the monologue. The kind you adopt in friendly debates. Now, he was angry.

'But you didn't get medical attention, did you? How could you, when the accident never happened? India, after all, has a hundred per cent safety record. Prepare to shit blood in about a month, and be dead in two.'

Even a Salim Ali would have backed off in the face of this Texan blowout. Tufan and Ernst were mere mortals.

'America no longer risks reprocessing spent fuel,' Hanson said. 'But, it's fine to play around with it here in your largest city? The damned reprocessing hasn't even started, and look at what's already happening.'

Tufan remained silent, Hanson continued to smoulder and Ernst felt it incumbent to contribute at least a line or two.

'India needs nuclear energy. Don't forget, old chap, the country has a power shortage.'

'Old chap? What are you, fucking British? If there's a power shortage, old chap, build more commercial power plants. Reprocessing nuclear fuel has just one outcome,' and Hanson mimicked an explosion with his big hands. He then looked the Smiling Buddha in the eye. 'So, Mr. Tufan, why waste time protesting food aid you need, instead of a reprocessing plant that you don't?'

Jack Hanson raised his hands in cowboy-style surrender and walked away to seek sanctuary in the permit-room. He opened the heavy teak door like it was plywood and was gobbled up by the air-conditioning. And over there hanging from his divan, the Seth's leg was a pendulum keeping time while he watched the exchange. He nodded towards the permit-room door. 'A den of inequity, I tell you, Mr. Ernestji,' he said loudly, 'brother to brother.'

Ernst did his namaste and led Tufan away, out of the club and down the steps to the compound.

'How does Hanson know so much of your medical history?'

'It's this American desire to be loved,' was Tufan's take, shuffling along with Ernst help. 'So they show an interest in everything and everyone.'

~

The skies above the Mian Building went dark, as if someone had switched off the lights. Ernst remembered lazier sunsets. Way past nine over July evenings and the sun would still linger behind the Quadriga atop Berlin's Brandenburg Gate, making the golden horses glow. Berlin Ingrid and he would watch it trying to set while they strolled by the Unter den Linden—minus the lindens. The Nazis had cut down the trees so they could put up their flags. A swastika every ten yards. He had made a grab for her hand. Those being different days, he remained undefeated by her lack of cooperation and had tried again. Cheerful Nazi flags fluttered in the evening breeze nudging him on. To embellish the evening further, Mein Führer's strutting line-up of Aryans had erected these tall, ugly, black posts blazing Klieg lights from either side at the Brandenburg Gate. Still, Kristallnacht was nowhere on the horizon, allowing Jews a few more years. Almost happy days.

Across the road from Salim Ali's balcony, the ringing Krishna Temple went about its business of trying to drown out the namaaz time prayer at the local mosque. A cow tackled the traffic with the equanimity of a Buddha. Jhama Sweetmeats lit up like a Roman candle and lined up behind it, the Nissen huts were glow-worms trying to follow suit. Compared to 1935 Berlin, 1964 Bombay was a garbage dump. Looking down over it from the balcony, Ernst never felt more at home.

Inside, Tufan was seated on a sofa across Salim Ali's mother, holding her hands and explaining meaningless shit. Fact remained, her only son was in police custody with no way out. The blind old woman was in the same black sari and the same black mood from the last time Ernst was here. Whether what Tufan was blabbering registered or not, was an open question. Ernst hoped Tufan's bullshit on Salim Ali being fine was getting through, because, how would it matter? Best she remained blind.

She turned to glower at him and he thought, so now she can read my mind.

~

Outside, Bhairavi's father stepped into view from inside Jhama Sweetmeats' pink radiance. Chabildas presented an impressive silhouette. His barrel of a chest made matchstick figures out of the others who were out and about in Sindhi Camp. He balanced a pile of rectangular Jhama cartons in his hands. Gulab jamuns and samosas would be a good guess. Rather than taking the gully and risk slipping on Jhama grease, he walked up Trombay Road to track back to his home.

This evening, her family's half of the elongated Nissen hut shone almost as bright as Jhama Sweetmeats. Just for me, Ernst decided, looking down at it from the balcony. Just for my eyes. Rented florescent lamps made two crude 'V's on either side of the door, and little bulbs thrown across the front wall, blinked happily.

Clearly, a celebration was underway. Although come to think of it, why? Why were fresh strings of thick marigold lining the top of their doorway? Why was the father shopping for sweetmeats when his only son had taken to wearing saris? Why were people coming in and out of her home? They weaved around the traditional rangoli design chalked on the threshold—an orthodox Hindu blessing this time, and nothing Tantric.

The father reappeared in the inner room behind the window grill, struggling with his jute, charpoy cot. He placed it down, facing the steel Godrej cupboard. She appeared in the window frame to sit on the charpoy. Looking down at them, Ernst felt it was a movie being played out just for him. Tufan came up to watch the movie and placed his elbows on the balcony parapet.

'She'll be fine, under the circumstances,' he said. Looking at the girl, Ernst wondered how Tufan knew she would be fine or not; then realised he meant Salim Ali's mother still sitting back there in the living room, tearing a hole through his back with eyes that couldn't see.

They let the old woman be, and both surveyed the girl together. That red zari sari she was wearing, with all those sequins. A bit much, he thought. Even for a Sindhi. She looked like her brother, from that day in the Haunted Whorehouse—just a lot darker. He needed to reach down two storeys across Vashigaon road, all the way past that grill, and touch that face. A gaggle of women converged into the inner room around her. She stiffened before disappearing from view. When the women eventually dispersed, she continued sitting there—ramrod straight and face caked with everything the women could throw at it. Her mouth was shut tight the way she did when self-conscious and her upper lip bulged. They had exhausted every trick to try whitening her up. His heart lurched even with her looking like that. For a moment there he thought he could smell her jasmine sweat, and took a deep breath that amounted to nothing.

There was a commotion outside her half of the Nissen hut, as if the entire Sindhi Camp had converged at the doorstep. Chabildas came out in a spotless white churidar to greet a man who stepped up on the porch with a namaste. A plump fellow, this one. He too was in white churidar, and around the same age. Chabildas got boisterous, spraying bonhomie like an air freshener. A hearty handshake followed the namastes and then came an embrace, with this other man's head nearly making it to her father's chest. The crowd released two more actors on to the stage: a purse-lipped shrew, followed by a young man in a drooping brown suit with tie. The young man came with a standard moustache. The celebrations moved indoors to the living room-cum-kitchen.

And all this while she remained seated on the charpoy, alone in the inner room and magnified by how he felt. The grilled window was transparent to her stiff hostility as she stared into the mirror on the Godrej. Staring into it, she could get a good view of the goings-on in the other room. He knew she was looking at the suited-up boy and he waited for her face to contort, like it had when he tried holding her hand the first time. This time though, he would understand where she was coming from. He felt for her, being forced into an arrangement like this. It wasn't right and he felt his outrage build. Probably, that is why it didn't make sense at first when her mouth relaxed open, and her face softened staring into the mirror. A short while later, she broke through the ridiculous make-up and reached out with a smile on her face to wrap that boy around her little finger.

Tufan put an arm on Ernst's shoulders.

'Let's go in. Salim's mother insists we eat something.'

'She's fucking crazy,' Ernst said. 'Like you. Climbing those stairs in your condition. Leave me alone.'

'It's an engagement ceremony,' Tufan said, squeezing his shoulders. 'Not for us to attend. Come on, let's go in.'

Ernst knew what it was. He wasn't blind and besides, his heart was in free fall like that evening at the Haunted Whorehouse. There were no big surprises here. Between him and a cross-dressing brother, it was impossible for her to have remained single any longer. The only surprise was how brutally the change in her demeanour affected him. Still seated on the bed and surrounded once again by women, she appeared less edgy, more gracious. She glowed as they huddled for a bout of giggles and whispers. Seeing her join in and giggle helplessly, his heart sank as if it had expected another outcome. And just when he wondered where they had hidden the cross-dressing brother, a growing murmur brought him back. There seemed to be another tamasha underway, this one outside the police chowki. Salim Ali was in there, so again, no surprise. You could depend on him to stir the pot from even inside a jail cell.

The intermittent drizzle started up once more. Then, it became a torrential waterfall, monsoon-style.

39

The Marxist Buddha

Better than waiting for court date.
—*Final word on suicides in police lockup*

His yells brought Parvatibai running into the bedroom. This dream was a complete break from standard Nazi fare and slit wrists. From Cold Pilger being carted off. Or the ones where Bombay Ingrid leaves a hole in him the size of Gateway of India. Instead, Ernst finds himself soaking wet in Sindhi Camp with Tsering Tufan swaying by his side, blisters glowing red in the dark. He remembered asking him to go home for fuck's sake, and he remembered the dying man smile. They are on Trombay Road, separated from the police chowki by a vertical sheet of water. Even in his dream, a Bombaywallah knows when an umbrella means fuck-all.

He is drenched, but the cold stems from something clutching at his insides. Could be the cancer, or could be because in the police chowki compound, a cross-dressed Kirti in sari—imperious as ever—is doing sit-ups in the pouring rain. At least now we know where the cross-dressing brother's been sequestered, to allow his sister to get engaged without shit hitting that ceiling fan in the living room-cum-bedroom-cum-kitchen with the Bushane cylinder on full display for the future in-laws.

Kirti is in full transvestite regalia, though far from picture perfect today—crumpled red sari, mascara trailing down that creamy-white face, red sindoor smudging the hair and forehead. Looking at the kid, Ernst decides there and then if the boy wants to be a girl, who is he to quibble? Hands crossed across her flat chest, Kirti does her sit-ups—up and down and up and down and holding her ears in penance. If she has her sister's thighs, this can go on forever.

At the doorstep and safe from the rain, the sub-inspector version of Johnny Walker, India's famous film comedian, keeps count. The resemblance is uncanny. Also noteworthy that his sidearm is in place today—the polished, buttoned-down, brown holster with its Indian Ordinance, .38/200 Webley. Somewhat peculiarly, it had gone missing from his side just that one day. The day Ernst pointed out the bullet-hole in the Sikh's severed head. 'What bullet hole?' the sub-inspector had asked, and his posse had shrugged. No one would see the perfectly bored aperture staring them in the face.

Ernst sees Salim Ali standing behind Johnny Walker looking atypically at ease. Even though, knowing Bombay Police, he is on next, once Princess Kirti is done. The thought of Salim Ali doing sit-ups in the rain to amuse the local constabulary gets Ernst's heart pumping. He wants this drama to end. The little bugger's had a huge personality makeover; he still won't accommodate the police. Over that, there can be no argument. Not because Salim Ali can't do sit-ups like Princess Kirti (he can't), but because he won't. In all fairness, neither would Lenin. Nor would the Buddha. So now what? Panic starts to build. He worries for Salim Ali. He also worries about himself. He knows he cannot be without the surly, little fuck.

Over there on centre stage, the way she's going at it, Princess Kirti should meet her quota of sit-ups anytime now. The Bombay Police will then reasonably expect Salim Ali on next—to limber up and begin. They like to be kept amused. They don't like being kept waiting.

When Ernst pushes past the crowd to break into the police chowki compound as if all robust and cancer-free, no on stops him. When he grabs the Princess and drags her from the rain back inside the chowki, no one stops him either. Instead, Johnny Walker makes way. Once inside, Princess Kirti shrugs him off, ignores Salim Ali, and walks on ahead into the police chowki. She does look at Tufan with respect but other than the police, who doesn't?

The whole sit-up tamasha-in-the-rain for police pleasure fizzles off in the face of Ernst's bluster. It leaves the lot looking at each other. In the face of nothing else to do, Salim Ali invites Tufan and Ernst back to his cell like he owns the place. And while Johnny Walker asks the gentle Tufan to go fuck off, when it comes to Ernst, he simpers. 'Actually not allowed, but please do come in,' he says. 'Go,' Tufan says, 'go.'

Making way for Ernst, Johnny Walker offers, 'Chai, Sirji?'

Inside the police chowki, box files, yellow files, and bundles of files bound in red cloth pile up like supporting pillars. They buttress weakened load-bearing walls, support wobbly Government-issue tables from beneath, and overflow into hallways. There wouldn't be a police force without them.

Salim Ali's twenty square metres of a cell however wears a barren look, furniture wise. Not just no supporting files, but no mattresses, bedding, or charpoys either—not even a stool. It makes up though, with more than a roomful of squatting and standing detainees pressed against each other on the stone floor. And while there's also no light bulb, no ceiling fan and no running water, there is a tap. Unmindful of all that, the two dozen or so pre-trial detainees squeezed together all nice and tight, are busy feeling up nine transvestites drowning in their midst. The room also has an overflowing Indian-style toilet. The smell is overwhelming. One cannot imagine Princess Kirti squatting in public with sari raised, should nature call. At some point however, nature may insist.

'A bit cramped, so we sleep in shifts,' Salim Ali says, smiling at how crime and punishment come together in the lockup. He demonstrates the equanimity of a Buddha. This avatar isn't anyone Ernst knows. Salim Ali takes off his bush shirt and manages to look that much more elegant.

'Much better,' he says, 'It's too hot, even for me.'

It's too hot for anyone. There's no window. No ventilation. However, up by the roof, there are two rectangular vents for some iterant whiff of the outside world. Also, the cell's rusted grill-door is kept wide open for cross-ventilation, as if the detainees can leave should they so wish. They don't. The Princess is still soaking wet from the rain and the object of incarcerated, male eyes. She rakes the male-dogs with her disdain.

Cross-legged on the dirty stone floor, Salim Ali invites Ernst to join him. The other male-dogs squeeze up some more against the shemales to allow the European his space. All these years, and Ernst still cannot hold the lotus position for more than a few minutes without squirming.

'I know what she whispered in your ear,' he tells Salim Ali. 'But to go kill Chhote Bhai for that?'

'That's my burden to bear. Even Comrade Tufan doesn't fully understand why I did it. Let's keep it that way.'

'Man's not a fool. Besides, Arjun's mother knows. After all, she made you do it.'

'A mother always knows. And please don't blame her. She has suffered enough.'

Ernst can't recall Salim Ali ever saying, please. Definitely, a first. This personality makeover thing begins to worry him.

'You have to get away from here.'

'Where would I go?'

'Anywhere. Cross over to Tibet. To China. From there, to Russia if you want. I know how much you love that place. Just get away from here.' He doesn't want it to sound like he is pleading, but he is.

'I am Indian,' Salim Ali says. 'What will I do over there?'

'Are you serious?' Ernst asks. Fear grows inside him for Salim Ali, for Tufan, for himself. A fear of all this shit that keeps piling. 'Ask anyone whether you're Indian. You're a low-caste, Muslim convert. A communist mian, a China lover, and a murderer. I'd get the fuck out of here.'

He pulls money from Sassoon's zeroes like a rabbit out of a hat and for a moment there, the detainees forget all that shemale flesh they've been feeling up. It's true then. About white people and money.

'I will get you out. But you must do as I say.'

'That's your ticket money,' says Salim Ali. 'Stick to the plan.'

'Besides, I prefer my own country,' says the man who only recently broadcast the Soviet National Anthem over a public address system. Bare, upper torso erect while seated in the lotus position, he asks about Tsering Tufan. Ernst stares at the emaciated, little Marxist with his legs crossed in a Perfect Lotus. This is how the Buddha must have looked towards the end, under the Bodhi tree.

'He is suffering,' Salim Ali said. 'Please take care of Comrade Tufan.'

'Your mother is suffering too. Think of her.'

'She'll be looked after,' the Marxist Buddha says, eschewing family ties in favour of Universal Compassion. Probably, Ernst admits, given Comrade Salim Ali's standing in the Party. Besides, Chhote Bhai isn't going to come knocking for rent any time soon. Salim Ali surprises Ernst further by asking him to take care of the girl, Bhairavi. 'Her brother too,' he asks, looking towards Princess Kirti like the Buddha would. 'Some people need more help than others.'

There's a rumble down the corridor, as if Johnny Walker and sundry police are rushing over for an audience with this Buddha in lockup.

However, it's only Willie Lansdowne storming the barricades.

~

Figuratively, because while Willie does rush in like a big, fat, steam engine with mayhem on its mind, the policemen are careful to not step in harm's way, or to try stop him by any means possible. They remain safely in his wake and congregate around the wide-open grill. From there, the police watch in awe as the gora turns red like Hanuman, the Monkey God, looking this way and that, searching for Sita. Ernst can see something's wrong—the drawn face, week-old stubble, or maybe it's the way Willie looks at Kirti the Princess, as if nothing else matters.

Willie is clearly surprised seeing Ernst in there, but he has other things on his mind.

'I'm in love, you bugger,' he says.

Ernst remains cautious. 'Why not start at the beginning?'

Willie doesn't reply. He is busy looking at the Princess and you should see how she looks back at him. The Ramayana analogy gets tossed for a six.

'Kirti the caddie-boy? You're fucking with me. Say you're fucking with me.'

Willie remains stubborn. One of his strengths.

'She loves me too.'

'Kirti, the male prostitute, loves you too? Anyway, where have you been?'

'Ask your Seth. He got me thrown out of the club. Next, I get fired. Then, I lose my bungalow. Have to vacate in a month. Now the income tax buggers are after me.' Willie looks flummoxed. 'A wog can do all that to a white man?' Looking at Kirti, he admits only she kept him sane.

'Have you lost your mind?'

'Yes,' he says, apparently unable to tear away from the Princess. 'And it isn't because of what you're thinking. Wish it was that simple.'

Willie proceeds to explain his way past the indestructible edifice of his racism to reach across to Princess Kirti. Indian men may be useless, bloody wogs, but the women are different. 'And she's a woman,' he says out loud, to establish the fact once and for all. 'Get that straight.' If there's a Princess left in this godforsaken country, it's Kirti. He wants to spend the rest of his life with her.

'What about Daisy?'

'What about her? Think I don't know what you've been up to?'

Ernst freezes. He can try telling Willie that fucking his wife was the most miserable thing he ever did; see if that works.

'Don't take this personally, but Daisy doesn't feel the same towards you,' Willie said, smiling with wisdom beyond his IQ level. 'Told me so herself. Simply not interested, old chap.'

Ernst may be awash in relief, but it's impossible not to feel protective towards the fool.

Willie doesn't feel he needs protection, or anyone's permission to scoop his Princess up. She is weightless in his thick, hairy arms. Carried out of the lockup like that, this can only be straight out of a movie. The police remain in a trance and part to give way. They press themselves against the walls to allow the couple down the corridor, and out the entrance. There is huge all around disappointment because of no mouth-to-mouth kissing.

All that enormous love in Willie's eyes; for once, he leaves everyone else looking the fool. Ernst feels that if simple, racist Englishmen are also allowed a go by Lord Krishna, then William Lansdowne is well on his way to the Place of the Hidden Moon, with his Perfect Woman. Perfect, because she isn't one.

~

It dawns on the Indians that the British just invaded them again. It brings back painful memories and even the detainees look patriotically unhappy. Johnny Walker looms over the open cell door. He appears energised now that the invader has departed.

'Deputy Commissioner Sa'ab will see you,' he says.

Ernst doesn't want to leave Salim Ali behind with two-dozen or so men, nine transvestites, no running water and a running toilet, but try telling that to Johnny Walker.

Supplicants are lined up outside the Deputy Commissioner's office, and even though Johnny Walker is being an arsehole after this second British invasion, Ernst is still white, and therefore first in line to meet the Deputy Commissioner. He totals five plainclothesmen lounging around. They sit, stand, chew paan, spit it out on the stone floor, and gossip. Bolstered by the company he keeps, Johnny Walker spits a red stream while staring at Ernst. Ernst decides to take that personally, and reminds himself to decline the chai Johnny Walker offered earlier.

The door reads, "Vijay Jahagirdar, Deputy Commissioner of Police." The same Jahagirdar from outside Sion Hospital. The one persuading Tufan to accept his nephew's body; accept the death as accidental. Tufan hadn't, for all the good that did. He should have done as asked—taken the body, cremated it, moved on. If people would only learn to move on. To those who don't because right is on their side, listen up: it means bugger-all. And those taking a stand against injustice should remember: you will lose.

The Deputy Commissioner's room has a leaky roof, and yellow Government files buttress the walls against gale-strength monsoon winds howling outside. The desk is cocooned in an outcrop of box files encroaching from both sides. The window behind it remains shut tight to ensure Deputy Commissioner Jahagirdar remains dry. The sealed window can't keep out the damp chill, and Ernst remembers feeling his nipples perk up in his dream.

'That boy Kirti,' the Deputy Commissioner begins. 'Today was his sister's engagement. An auspicious day, and the idiot decides to go wear a sari. The family couldn't afford that kind of embarrassment and the father approached us to do something. So we brought the boy in. The poor father was beside himself—son dressed up in a sari like that. Just not right.'

Having said that, it also wasn't right, the Deputy Commissioner openly admits, making the chhakka do sit-ups in the rain. He pauses before going Western with his upmarket, St. Stephen's accent. 'This job can make animals out of us. By and large though, the Bombay Police are known for their restraint.'

The way Jahagirdar talks, reminds Ernst of someone he knows—someone who says one thing and does something else. He can't put his finger to it though. It's tantalising, trying to guess. Like her jasmine-laced sweat. Sitting in his igloo, the Deputy Commissioner is in plainclothes this wet evening—white linen shirt and khakis. A David Niven in mufti. His imported watch, shining sterling silver, must be the ballpark, combined yearly salary of all the havaldars and plainclothesmen lounging outside his office, and way above anything a Deputy Commissioner can technically afford.

'More than the Indian Constitution, or any specific law, it's our self-restraint that allows India to function.'

The Deputy Commissioner settles back to allow Ernst time to digest that preamble.

'Far easier to be cowboys, you know,' he says, 'and take out undesirables expeditiously. Be done with them.' He became wistful at the thought of going cowboy, and while his forefinger is raised and ready, the Deputy Commissioner exercises restraint. Ernst remembers him going bang, bang, bang outside Sion Hospital. He feels he isn't up to clutching at his heart and doing the whole dying thing all over again.

The Deputy Commissioner comes out of his reverie. 'Anyway, what may I do for you?'

He appears confident Ernst doesn't have the balls to reopen the past, do a Tufan, ask why Arjun's murder wasn't investigated even after Dr. Waller's autopsy, or dare suggest should the police have done their job, Salim Ali wouldn't be here today. Not misplaced at all, the Deputy Commissioner's confidence, because all that matters to Ernst is Salim Ali, and how to whisk him away. Thankfully, there's enough money in his pocket to do just that; the one-eyed Fiat waiting outside, with Mohan Driver inside gunning the engine.

'Just between you and me, your English friend made fools of us with his angry white-man act. Coming into my police station and walking away with the chhakka like that. Any idea how I look? What do I tell the boy's father?'

Having got that off his chest, the Deputy Commissioner appears ready to let bygones be bygones. 'By the way,' he asks, 'the communist mian in lockup, he's your friend too?'

'Yes. I wanted to talk to you about him.'

The Deputy Commissioner reaches under his desk. The door opens to present Johnny Walker. His brown belt gleams with its shiny, buttoned down holster.

Deputy Commissioner Jahagirdar asks Johnny Walker in Marathi about Salim Ali. About his paperwork being in order, things like that. Ernst pulls out the money. It's a thick wad. And to think not too long ago, he couldn't meet payroll. Look at you now, bribing Deputy Commissioners.

'No,' Deputy Commissioner Jahagirdar says. 'No need. Please put the money away. He is after all, your friend.'

He then instructs a disappointed Johnny Walker to ensure Salim Ali is removed from the general riff-raff. That he has no complaints. 'In fact, let's make sure he never has any complaints going forward,' Jahagirdar instructs. Johnny Walker's face lights up.

The Deputy Commissioner leaves his chair to tell Ernst, 'Don't worry. We'll take good care of him. In fact, if you kindly wait here, I'll go attend to it personally.'

Jahagirdar's not a bania but he smiles like one, and Ernst realises whom he resembles. He recalls the Seth assuring Willie not to worry, that everything would be resolved. Look what happened to Willie. With Johnny Walker masticating paan like cud while leading the Deputy Commissioner out of his office, it became clear to Ernst that no amount of zeros can add up to a positive conclusion. A Bombay Police officer had declined money for the first time in living memory. That can only mean one thing for Salim Ali, and one thing alone. Because the British just humiliated India for a second time, nothing

can be done to save him. Money can't buy everything, even in a
police station. Johnny Walker's satisfied look moments ago, means
the die is cast. Barging in like that, Willie went kicked off Ernst's
Law of Unintended Consequences. And so, just because the Deputy
Commissioner is attending to Salim Ali personally, doesn't mean
nothing will happen.

~

Something did happen. Ernst realised that as soon as he woke up to
his own yells. Parvatibai was at his bedside in no time at all, clutching
a glass of milk and that wet cloth of hers for his forehead.

'You're begging for a heart attack,' she said, as he pushed her
away. 'Waking up like that at your age. What's wrong with you? It
was just a dream.'

But it wasn't. He clearly remembered going for the door, not
too long after the Deputy Commissioner left to personally attend to
Salim Ali, but it was locked from outside. And anyway it was too late.
Ernst remembered three loud gunshots reverberating off the chowki
walls. He remembered thinking the leaky roof would come down.
And just because all he wanted after that happened, was to crawl
into bed and pretend nothing had happened, doesn't mean it didn't.

40

Swastikas & Synagogues

The closer to a synagogue, the farther from God.
—*Some smart-assed rabbi*

He tried explaining to Parvatibai he wasn't dreaming, that he had seen the body. They had even let him curl up at Salim Ali's feet, with its overgrown, black nails extending from shrivelled toes. Seated against the wall at the other end with Salim Ali's head on his lap, Tsering Tufan showed no signs of life. Unlike the dead comrade's head on his lap with halo intact. That smile on Salim Ali's face—as if chasing Americans in his sleep.

Having said that, there was havoc all around the smile that didn't belong to any Salim Ali anyone knew. However beatific the smile, it was unable to distract from the tears to the chest and neck, and the small, neat hole between the eyes. Ernst had to wonder if once again, the bullet-hole was only meant for him, or whether others could see it too. As with the Headless Sikh and Arjun, so with Salim Ali. An autopsy would be an absolute waste of time.

The lockup had been emptied of detainees and shemales, although the rest of the police chowki was packed with mourners. Ernst's workers from Goregaon overflowed into the compound. Slowly, more began to show up. The police looked on nervously as the crowd started assuming proportions disproportionate to Salim Ali's size. It was as if Lenin had died.

Bhairavi was in a white sari of the kind worn by Partition widows all over Sindhi Camp. Seeing her, one couldn't tell that only just now she had been all in red, face plastered with whitening make-up and engaged to be married. Standing by the wide-open grill, she clutched at Salim Ali's blind mother to save herself from drowning. Holding up the old lady's other arm was Princess Kirti, as if keeping the three of them afloat. The other shemales were nowhere around but princesses don't disappear that easily. Any other day, and Ernst would've lingered over the black and white contrast between brother and sister, two sisters, whatever.

Salim Ali's mother was in black as always. She had her goggles on, and muttering away in Malayalam.

Ernst found himself mumbling a Sahajiya prayer in Bangla that the Purandhar gardener' s wife—his Tantaji—had taught him in another life.

'Please don't,' Tufan said from where he sat holding his comrade's head.

~

They brought a worn-out, white bed sheet and shoved it at Ernst. Johnny Walker had a bored look pasted across his face. He wasn't even trying.

'Detainee used this to hang himself.'

'Look over there. That's a bullet hole in his head. Two to his torso.'

'Who says? Are you an expert?'

'Where's the bed?' Ernst asked.

'What?'

'Where did he get that bed sheet to hang himself? There's no bed in the lockup. Let's ask the other detainees. They must have seen it happen.'

The Deputy Commissioner swooped in. Returning after a massage, that's how relaxed he looked. Tension released by doing whatever he had done, his eyes sparkled, but he remained solemn.

'This man's an idiot. No idea how he became a policeman. There was no bed in there and of course, no bed sheet. Mr. Ali hanged himself from a ventilator in the toilet, using his vest. Our fault. We take full responsibility. We allowed him use of the private latrine as a special consideration. I see now why we shouldn't have.'

Deputy Commissioner Jahagirdar then took some time to stand sombrely before Salim Ali's bullet-ridden body. He wasn't the type to leave loose ends, and would, 'personally make sure everything was in proper order and verifiable.'

He hoped they were completely satisfied.

'Salim Ali didn't wear a vest. I left him bare-chested after he took off his shirt.'

'Did I say vest? I meant his shirt.'

'You know his family and friends too can see the bullet holes on his body. This time, it isn't just me.'

'People see what they want to see, Mr. Steiger. It takes professionals to decide how death occurred.'

'Look at you,' Ernst said. 'So confident you will prevail.'

'The truth, Mr. Steiger. Ultimately truth prevails.' The Deputy Commissioner pointed to a black-and-white Gandhi smiling from the wall.

'I've seen it before, Commissioner. Confident people like you. So confident, they kept meticulous records on the Jews they killed. You should read up on what happened to them.'

'I hope they were dealt with the utmost severity,' the Deputy Commissioner said.

~

When Ernst tried getting Tufan to stand, he refused to budge. Looking into his eyes, it wasn't just Salim Ali who had died that evening. Giving up on Tufan to edge past Bhairavi, Ernst mumbled words of comfort to Salim Ali's mother who remained stone cold unlike her dead son with that smile of his. As for Bhairavi, she wasn't adamant or anything this time, or demanding Ernst does something about what was visited on her Salim Ali. She didn't even notice him wearing her gold, swastik pendant from the other day. Princess Kirti was another matter, and her eyes flashed to ask: What do you plan to do?

Crawl into bed and die.

The one-eyed Fiat was waiting outside with Mohan Driver gunning it to whisk the Mian away. Where to, no idea, but one look at Ernst's face and Mohan Driver could tell it didn't matter anymore.

'Man, ich will nach Hause,' Ernst muttered, stumbling in through the car's rear door; numb with shock, and tired from loss after loss, one after the other, tired from being sickly, and from this and that; from the fact that there was no respite at all. Listening to Ernst mumble, Mohan Driver shook his head at the rear-view and turned the ignition off. The engine choked and died. After all these years, and despite it being clear something must have happened, there was still a part of him that expected white men to be white men, and for Ernst to behave like one.

Wide awake after Parvatibai woke him to put an end to his screaming, Ernst remembered swearing at Mohan Driver for refusing to re-start the engine. He needed to go home, fall into bed and die.

'Sa'ab,' Mohan Driver had said. 'If you behave like this, how do we get even?'

~

The next day, Salim Ali's mother refused to listen until they all had chai.

She got busy in the kitchen over an open flame with tea leaves, sugar, milk, and no eyes. When she returned to the crowded living room muttering in Malayalam, she looked directly at Ernst. It didn't surprise him anymore.

'She wants you to cremate Salim Mian as quickly as possible,' a workshop fellow translated.

Mohan Driver corrected the man. 'Chutiya. You mean she wants Salim Mian buried. They're Muslims.'

'I know.' The worker was belligerent.

'You know what?' Mohan Driver asked. 'Idiot.'

There was a stream of Malayalam from the old woman, who kept facing Ernst through the rapid fire. Then it was the translator's turn.

'She says, I am Muslim. My son wasn't. He wanted to be cremated. So cremate him.'

~

The smallish doors to the Keneseth Eliyahoo Synagogue at Kala Ghoda in South Bombay looked west, past the Gateway of India and across the Arabian Sea toward Jerusalem. It was a hole of an entrance and not worthy of either the stylish pediment above it, or the building. Indians called it the Kala Ghoda Synagogue, after the statue of a black horse sporting King Edward (VII) erected nearby by the Sassoons. Others called it the Gora Temple, since only white people were welcome. Brown Jews—here since antiquity— worshipped more modestly at Jacob Circle near the city jail, in their own synagogue adorned with "good luck" swastikas. Ernst envied the untainted bastards.

There being no set blueprint for synagogues, the Keneseth Eliyahoo choose to look like a blue, birthday cake with white icing—a large, ornamental, neo-Baroque, Christopher Wren of a cake that Ernst found hard to swallow. In Berlin, synagogues would face into courtyards, ashamed of themselves and resisting the urge to show off. This building was an open declaration of Jewish wealth in British India—not so much these days, but still.

Inside the doorway was an old armoire—thin and narrow, minus doors—remodelled ages ago to hang outerwear no one wore anymore. The mirror inside remained unobstructed by coats or jackets. Mottled with large, red oxide spots where the spluttered aluminium had worn off, there was still enough mirror to confirm Ernst's decline from rock bottom. His face a shock— as much by its age and sickliness, as by disarray and defeat. It was a reminder he had thrown himself into bed after Salim Ali's cremation without taking a shower. He had woken up, brushed aside Parvatibai's chai, brushed his teeth, not bothered with much else and walked all the way to Kala Ghoda clutching the earthen pot with Salim Ali in it.

'You'll know what to do. Just make him happy,' Salim Ali's mother had said, refusing to keep the ashes.

It took him twenty minutes or so to get to Kala Ghoda past the stares and with passers-by giving him wide berth. Looking into the mirror in the armoire, he could see why. Hair stiff with dirt, his eyes were bloodshot from illness and everything else. He looked befuddled and not particularly sane holding an earthen pot to his chest. People had edged away from him on the pavement. India has no time for slovenly, white men. The least a gora can do is look like one.

~

The synagogue's cantor was winding up. Bobbing yarmulkes lifted the Torah to take it back to the Ark, placing it against the wall nearest to Jerusalem. It was a full minyan today, crowding wooden benches around the raised Tevah. Looking out for the divine presence that hovers over any gathering of ten Jews or more, Ernst found Adam Sassoon holding court.

'Quite a Shabbat,' Sassoon offered loudly, and waved. When Ernst walked over to him amidst the chattering yarmulkes, the great man said, 'Every bloody Jew in town's here.' He, of course, meant the white ones.

Ernst couldn't help but notice every one of them staring at him. He took in the interior, built by one Jacob Sassoon—1885, it said on the pediment—to commemorate his father, one David Sassoon, the original prophet from Baghdad who dressed like one—turban and all—preferring to speak in Farsi even after buying himself a baronetcy.

'By the way, Old Chap,' Adam Sassoon said, all pukka and plummy and with no signs of Baghdadi ancestry, 'you do realise you're wearing a swastika around your neck.'

~

She had removed and asked he place her swastika pendant on the dining table the other day at Tufan's flat, so she could practise with the sword. Instead, he didn't just keep it, but was now wearing it. Inside a synagogue. Still, why the fuss?

A yarmulke stepped up to tell him. 'You are, after all, inside a synagogue.'

The sun broke through the lights on one of the stained glass windows behind the Ark. It caught the gold in her pendant and set the swastika aflame. Lit, it took on a life of its own, spreading its presence amongst the Anglicised Sephardics like wildfire. When Ernst followed Sassoon's gaze, the women were lined up along their gallery—a clutch of pursed lips looking down at him. Cathy Sassoon stood out in stark relief.

'Please remove the swastika,' the yarmulke requested. 'It's causing offence.'

On the face of it, a reasonable request.

'It's a Hindu swastik. Got nothing to do with you.'

'Is that a German speaking, or a Jew?'

Not bad. The yarmulke couldn't help looking pleased with himself. The outrage he fanned was silent, but it was sucking up oxygen from the room and it scoured Ernst's skin. When Cathy Sassoon chirped in from above, her voice was like an angel from heaven—the disapproving kind.

'If you won't remove that thing, Ernst, please leave. Don't spoil Shabbat for us.'

When her husband stepped up, Ernst didn't know whether to be surprised or not.

'You heard the man,' His Divine Presence said to the congregation. 'It's bloody Hindu. Got nothing to do with us.'

'Moving on,' he continued, 'What's that you're clutching, Old Chap? Makes me nervous.'

'Salim Ali.'

There was a pause while Sassoon struggled.

'Know who's that?' Ernst asked.

Sassoon admitted he didn't.

'My communist darkie. He's dead. These are his ashes. I loved him like a son.'

'Forgot his name for a second there. I'm sorry.'

He did recall Arjun's name though—the boy killed at Fertilisers. The darkie's friend. Thick as thieves, they were. On the other hand, the great man had no idea they knew the Sindhi Camp girl, Bhairavi.

'The one doing accounts and filing for you.'

'I'll be damned.'

Great men however stay on point. 'Your man. What was it? Suicide?'

'Funny you should say that. Because there's this Deputy Commissioner who absolutely insists it is. Man named Jahagirdar. You may know him. Fond of aiming between the eyes, cowboy style. He shot that truck driver they scrapped off the burner, and he shot Salim Ali. There's a bullet hole through his forehead, but the Commissioner tells us he hanged himself.'

Ernst had forgotten about Cathy Sassoon, who hadn't forgotten about him.

'Adam! Are you going to have him put away that awful swastika or not?'

'Bloody had it with her,' the great man muttered and reaching into his breast pocket, took out a gold-plated coin, the size of a rupee hanging from a thin chain. Looking straight up at Cathy, he put it around his neck. The cheap, gold-plated swastika had a glint to it while smiling to demonstrate the meaning of friendship, or maybe tell the wife go fuck herself; Ernst couldn't be sure.

'Are you sure?' Sassoon asked. 'About this Jahagirdar bugger?'

'Pretty much. Man gets off on shooting people.'

'So what do you plan to do about it?'

'I wanted to ask you the same thing.'

'I'll have someone look into it,' the great man promised, the swastika pendant still around his neck.

Jews wearing swastikas, Ernst thought, and almost asked Sassoon where he got his. But it would ruin the moment, so he let it go.

41

Salim Ali's Happy

Death is a delightful hiding place for weary men.
—*Herodotus*

Ernst woke up coughing blood. He saw himself shrinking by the
day while this thing inside him grew bigger—sometimes corking his
arse, sometimes giving him stomach cramps, at times a fever, and
now there was blood in his spittle. Yet, given the circumstances, he
felt calm and generally fine. One day, he wouldn't. He didn't need
Andhi Ma to tell him no amount of radiation therapy could stop
that day coming.

Knowing the final outcome, to then say, 'No'; to say, 'I decline
this needless treatment'; to say, 'I'll be fine, I've lived with this for
so long it's now a part of me—just my own cells going a little nuts,
wandering off and continuing to just do what they do'; and then to
go on to say, 'I don't wish to fight my own body, so thanks, but no
thanks, I won't bombard myself with X-rays'; it was beyond his powers
to do that. Come September, he knew he would be on an aeroplane
to West Berlin and the Jüdische Krankenhaus, where they could go
ahead and irradiate the shit out of him as long as it bought time.
Having said that, he still hasn't sent them his file with those X-rays.

Outside, the monsoons pondered their next move and the sun
took charge back after two weeks in purdah. Roads surrendered their
moisture and looked like mirages in the kind of cowboy Westerns
Deputy Commissioner Jahagirdar loved. Humid and hot once more,

Sindhi Camp reeled after two weeks under a waterfall. Even the dead Chhote Bhai's all-pukka, concrete Mian Building had had enough, while the rows of leaky Nissen huts across from it looked buggered beyond repair.

Over at Sion Hospital, portions of the roof caved in, and it started to rain bronze-back snakes from the nests they had built between the tiles. Dr. Waller stalked the screaming wards collecting terrified reptiles. He used his stick to prod them out from hiding places, then to press the head down while the snake whipped and coiled and people ran. In an impossible feat for a drug addict, he would then snatch it, fist just behind the head while the snake licked at the air with its darting tongue like, what the fuck just happened?

Salim Ali's mother came out to the balcony when Tufan and he stepped out from the Mian Building. They had met her up there in Salim Ali's flat one last time before leaving to deal with his ashes.

'What's she saying now?' he asked Tufan.

'Spread his ashes properly, she says. Make him happy.'

Staring directly at him, the blind woman went to town. She wagged a finger while declaiming in her nasal Malayalee, so even the roadside cows looked up. Perched on the temple patio, Andhi Ma appeared totally impressed at how her role had been usurped; how someone else was ranting for a change.

'What's going on?'

'She says you'll know what to do.'

'Since when do I know anything? There, she's still at it. What's she saying now?'

'That's about the gist of it,' Tufan said. 'That you'll know what to do. Also, she thinks you know who did this to her son.'

'Sure, I do. So does everyone. It was the Deputy Commissioner of Police. She wants me to arrest him?'

'She's saying hell with the police. She says you know for real.'

'I know what, for real?'

'I don't know. My Malayalee's not that great.'

They left her behind, going all Mussolini on them from the balcony.

Up ahead, the police chowki reminded Ernst of a body with cancer and beyond complaint. A low nesting building in municipal yellow, it had sagged further after the rains, the exhausted, red stucco roof tiles now almost at eye level. The tiles had surrendered and had holes that were football-size jagged circles. The next sheet of water would come down on the Deputy Commissioner's head.

The slums lining Sindhi Camp were the only ones left smiling. There's an advantage to being rock bottom. If this last deluge was the monsoon's best shot, they had little to worry. The slum kids ran past taxis, screamed, sang out loud, and jumped puddles without a care in the world.

Johnny Walker must have felt the same, or at least until Ernst showed up with Tufan. Moments ago, he had been smiling to himself and at peace with the world, having his chai, seated on one of the benches lining the police compound. Seeing them, he was now triggered, and stood up to further increase the threat level.

'You look not so good, Sirji,' he said to get things going. Acknowledging the standoff, Sindhi Camp Radio came alive with the theme from *Come September*. The soaked air quivered and Ernst thought it best to bring things down a notch.

'We're just here to collect his possessions.'

Johnny Walker came out past the wide-open, police chowki gates to energise the situation. 'What's in that pot? Go to Sion Hospital for his possessions, no need to come here unless you want to hand the Chinaman over.'

Ernst felt his insides light up and his hands shook, struggling with the earthen pot as if there was a pit bull inside.

'Bhenchod,' the plainclothesman said, and Ernst was once again struck by the contrast between the man and his comic screen version. 'Had it not been for you and that Chinaman, Sirji, your mian would have still been alive. Next time, kindly be mindful.'

From Tufan's face, it was clear Johnny Walker had landed a direct kick. Ernst gently nudged Tufan down the road, past Murli and into the Golf Club compound.

In time to see Adam Sassoon standing ramrod straight, holding the rear door open to his shiny, white Mercedes parked right next to the Seth's shiny, black Impala—each with their opaque-tinted glasses impossible to see through. Perfect for owners who didn't acknowledge each other or the general riff-raff outside. Sassoon's uniformed driver looked confused at his owner standing to attention and holding the door open as if he was the chauffeur. However, playing the chauffeur or not, Sassoon had eyes on the back of his head and he stiffened a notch, before turning around. An uneven playing field is how Ernst felt about any face-off about to happen.

'You look like hell,' Sassoon said, eyes fixed on Salim Ali in the earthen pot. Ernst realised the great man didn't know about the cancer.

Sassoon continued looking at the pot. 'Hell you still holding onto that for?' he asked.

'Just doing what his mother wants. That's why I brought him over to the synagogue yesterday. But then you went and wore that swastika pendant and it threw me. Meant a lot, by the way, you doing that.'

'One values friendship too, old chap. A two-way thing, what?'

'Then, I realised where you got that swastika pendant. Not wearing it today?'

Ernst placed the earthen pot on the Mercedes bonnet and when the uniformed driver jumped in outrage, Tufan stepped in and blocked him with the gentlest of smiles. When Ernst pulled at the red cloth covering the pot, the rubber band holding it in place broke. When he trailed Salim Ali's ashes on the Mercedes, some flew to also spread on the Seth's jet black Impala. When he flung the rest of Salim Ali at the great man, the remains flew everywhere and back at Ernst, and into his mouth and nostrils. The ash stuck at the back of his throat, and he gagged. Hacking away, he knew there was blood in his spittle and not due to the bony bits from the ash in his mouth. Adam Sassoon was coughing too, his hair and face ash-white from Salim Ali—the little man spread all over him, his T-shirt, and around and inside the collar.

'What are you doing?'

'His mother kept saying, make him happy. There, he is happy.'

Sassoon spat out bits of bone. 'Bugger,' he said. 'You know what you've gone and done now, don't you, old chap?'

'I know, Adam. Problem is, you don't know what you have done, because you keep doing it. A great man would know when to stop. You never did.'

'I just asked one thing of you,' Adam Sassoon said.

'I know. But Salim Ali's all over you, now. So ask him yourself for the damn gunny bag with whatever was stolen.'

If Sassoon didn't find that funny, neither did Tufan. Salim Ali's gentle comrade had let the driver brush past and just stood there mouth agape, staring towards the club portico.

It was quite the backdrop, Ernst had to admit. Sindhi Camp Bhairavi descending the Golf Club steps as if she was Queen of Sheba.

'Goddess Bhairavi,' Ernst said. 'Have you seen anything like it?'

Of course he hadn't. But then who had? When was the last time anyone saw Goddess Bhairavi go from coal-black demon to a stunningly radiant, to-die-for harbinger of death? If that's just a fairy tale, no one told Ernst who sensibly concluded he was done for. And if this was an augury for real, no one had informed Sassoon who began dusting himself, eyes riveted on her with the eagerness of a schoolboy.

Covered though he was in ash and bones, with chalk white face, hair a mess and T-shirt ruined, Adam Sassoon pushed his chauffer aside and went back to holding the rear door open, his eyes still locked on Goddess Bhairavi. And when she came up, it was crystal clear Ernst was back to being invisible. Nor did her beloved Uncle Tufan exist. When she stopped by the Mercedes as if she owned it, Sassoon could've been covered in shit or gold dust, for the difference it seemed to make. However, when she lowered herself onto the rear seat, one leg was left resting on the ground, deigning the riff-raff a prolonged stare at a Goddess' sandalled foot and up her calf. Only for me, Ernst was convinced. She's doing that only for me. However, the way Sassoon was staring, reminded him of the gentleman from Nippon caressing her brother's foot at the Haunted Whorehouse.

'Fools,' he said to Sassoon. 'We men are fools, each and every one of us. You and I though, may soon be dead ones.'

'The hell you blabbering?' Sassoon asked. He brushed Salim Ali off his shoulders the best he could, got into the Mercedes, and leaned back against the rear seat headrest, Goddess Bhairavi smiling by his side. Seeing Ernst look their way, Sassoon shut his eyes. Only then, the uniformed driver went scrambled behind the wheel. As he reversed, Ernst saw the Goddess lean over to the great man. Holding a cloth, she cleaned his brow, carefully collecting ash and bone, then dusting the cloth with great care into a square plastic box she held in her other hand, as if it was the most precious thing in the world.

When the Mercedes went past, Murli Chowkidar held the gates wide open and turned his face to avoid looking inside. When gods and goddesses go by, his mother told him some centuries ago, we look away lest we go blind.

42

The Mule

She has many forms. Some, you don't want to see.
—*On Goddess Bhairavi*

Willie was officially missing since he raided the police chowki to rescue his transvestite. What makes it more of a scandal—that one's fucking a male cross-dresser, or that it's a darkie? The Golf Club wasn't sure. Where's Willie hiding out, they wanted to know. Ask someone who cares, Ernst wanted to say, and went locked himself in his bedroom.

He coughed before reaching for the handkerchief and now his blue pyjama top was speckled red. It did not bother him and neither did the fever that came and went. It also didn't bother him anymore that like the cork plugging and unplugging his arse at will, the cancer felt more at home every day. The past weeks he hadn't left the flat, barely moving from the bedroom—his inglenook.

Adam Sassoon had turned out superior to cancer, or a straight razor. Schwester Ingrid would approve how he had torpedoed Ernst amidships. The Ingrids and the Sassoons had always held each other in high regard, each side wondering what the other saw in him. How does one ever overcome the ignominy from having someone's ashes flung at your face? You do it, Ernst would have to agree, by being Adam Sassoon and driving away with the girl. He had aimed and fired Salim Ali at the great man. Turns out he fired a blank.

There was a knock on the bedroom door but he shut it out. His bathtub's claw-foot was visible inside the bathroom from where he lay. If he stretched forward a bit, the straight razor was tempting him from the low stool next to it. If he craned any further, his father would be in the soapy water with wrists slashed and the sneer on his face Schwester Ingrid wrote about. The one the Nazis never got to see, so focused were they on his erection.

Parvatibai started banging at the bedroom door because she could read minds. He kept his eyes shut as if that would work. Finally, it became too much and he stumbled for the door. He was at a loss what to say, but Parvatibai was a monument to calm itself, with just a cursory glance towards the swastik pendant he still wore, or maybe at the red specks on his pyjama top.

'Someone's here to see you.'

She didn't ask he change his pyjama top, but stared some more at the rusty, red specks of blood.

Fine, but he wasn't changing for anyone.

~

A newly-wed stands out like a red beacon. With blood-red sindoor parting her hair, dried red henna on hands and feet, blinding red sari, and a ruby studded mangalsutra to make it very clear. Since last ignoring him while reclining in Sassoon's Mercedes as if it belonged to her, she had found time to get married.

'I came to see Parvatibai.'

Her eyes sparkled as they danced around the room—the happy newlywed visiting her best friend; saying a quick hello to the best friend's employer; doing a quick tease. She sat at the edge of the bed, and now he wished he had changed the pyjama top. Looking at her, he was struck by the resemblance with Princess Kirti—like black and white twins. Almost, but not quite, because her teeth came in the way. Although, frankly, not that much anymore. Married, she was less gaunt. Her face had filled-out and the teeth less emphatic. He found himself missing the bunny rabbit look.

He took off the swastik pendant.

'I keep forgetting to return it.'

She touched the mangalsutra around her neck.

'I have this now. You hold on to that for me.'

'And this too,' she said. It was the square box. The one in which she had carefully collected Salim Ali from all over Sassoon.

Sitting on his bed, when she broached his illness, she did it like Dr. Ramanna's keyboard from the other day at the Golf Club, in no hurry to catch up with Dr. Homi J. Bhabha's violin. Also, there was the question of how she knew. Maybe, the bedsprings vibrated an SOS on his state of affairs. Maybe it was his heart, visible only to her, warning her to look past all that love in there and focus instead on the corroded insides. Maybe Parvatibai had already whispered pointed Marathi in her ear. Maybe it was the speckled front of the pyjama top that she pretended to not notice. No matter.

What did matter was how, and without any warning, she lay back in her red sari to stretch like a panther on the bed and once again become Goddess Bhairavi.

~

She sits on the chakra at the base of one's spine. Her role there, is as destroyer of the nine mental impediments to reunion with the Supreme Consciousness in the Place of the Hidden Moon.

Bhairavi: who multiplies herself into any number of beings and forms, depending on where you're at.

Bhairavi: evokes images powerful and graceful, as well as discordantly seductive when associated with aggression and violence. Like for example, taking on a Deputy Commissioner of Police.

Bhairavi: causes the Universe to come into being.

Bhairavi: praised and blamed for everything.

Bhairavi: here to remind you of your shelf life, dangerously dependent on how beautiful she comes across. It grips him that she hasn't ever looked more beautiful. Fact is however, she's been beautiful since he first saw her—buck teeth and all. He settles back to ponder the simple implication of being a dead man.

She peers into the bathroom and asks, 'Why's there an open razor by the tub?'

She looked at the bright red specks all over the front of his striped, blue pyjama top, three sizes too big these days, and says, 'It's okay. Don't make a big deal about this. We all have to die of something.'

'Look at me,' she asks. He can barely hear her past a heartbeat making him vibrate like Waller.

'Look at me.' She's on one elbow now and bears down with those lake-size Indian eyes. He obeys, breathing hard. He would like to think dipping in those lakes will cure him and remains torn—jump right in, or run like hell?

'You declined me,' she says, 'because of your illness. I know that now.'

Saying that, she sticks her tongue into his ear and feels around tickling his brain. He waits it out, only daring to move after she vacates his skull.

Glowing in the darkened room, she begins burning him up. He knows he is done for.

'What are you going to do with me?'

Ride you like a mule, Goddess Bhairavi informs him.

~

Crouching from above, she raises her sari to straddle his seventh chakra. Those corded thighs could only belong to a Goddess. And so what if he is hard as rock? He feels like the mule he is and all that hardness belongs to her. She raises herself and comes down, her thighs like well-oiled pistons. He is enveloped by a rainforest before being pulled away, and then thrown back again into a warm, damp, malarial swamp. He wants her to call out his name, but knows she won't. Indian women don't do that. Not even goddesses.

Her eyes are ablaze. She's on fire, and either greatly forgiving or mercifully easy to please. His confidence returns even though he hasn't been with a real woman since his last Christmas in July with Bombay Ingrid. Daisy Lansdowne doesn't qualify. Still, the other side of him—the one that ensures failure—wishes she would keep her eyes shut and those controlling hands to herself. No need to look down on his stained teeth or feel the bald spot when holding his head. The way she warms him with her gaze though, suggests he might be more than the sum of his shabby parts. After all, she did fall in love with him once.

Expelling a divine grunt, she informs him they didn't have much time and thrusts down. It leaves him gasping for breath. He wants to ask, what's the rush, and can barely keep pace with her supernatural thrusts, although, it's probably just youth. He is glad he didn't ask because it would be insensitive. She has a husband waiting at home. A boy of a husband wrapped around her little finger, but husband is husband.

Turns out she meant something else—asking him to hurry up— and was referring to what needed to be taught, what he needed to know before exhausting his three Technicolour minutes. Never easy, his baggage doesn't make it any easier. He wants to apologise but she thrusts down and once again impales herself, or him, not sure.

When he makes an effort to sit up while she is still atop, she allows him to suck on a nipple. They stare back at him, dark, thick, rubbery, one still wet from his saliva and he never wants to ever taste the pink variety again. That appears to please the Goddess. She holds the back of his head to bring his open mouth forward, and caresses his bald spot. He sucks like there's no tomorrow while she croons wisdom in his ear.

'Destruction begins from the moment of birth,' she tells him. 'Cancer is always within you. Death, or Bhairavi if you will, is present in everything. Don't think of me as a married woman; think of me as your constant companion.'

He disengages, but only to beg her not to stop. Please continue removing the clutter from my mind.

He reaches forward again, and she allows him a quick lick before pulling back. All this time she remains fixed, impaled on concrete—far removed from the dismal performance with Willie's wife. The only clutter, she assures him, comes from maya.

'We need to get you past her fog.'

'How?'

'Siksha.' She plans to teach the maya out of him.

'Right now?'

'What better time?' She comes down hard and he gasps.

'See? Carrot.'

Then raising herself, she hovers effortlessly, caressing his tip with her lower lips while denying entry.

'Stick.'

He thrusts upward, and she levitates still higher. 'What you just did,' she says from way up there, 'is because maya compelled you to. Maya nourishes your ego, makes you feel entitled. That in turn prevents you breaking free from your ways. Just as a man cannot see his own back, so also he cannot see his own mistakes. For that, he needs a guide. Let's get to work.'

She descends to give him a carrot. They both thrust at each other for a bit. Seeing how her pupils rolls back, Ernst suspects this may be a two-way thing going on, but what does he know?

'Tell me what happened to your wife.'

'What?' He waits for the concrete to leach away. It does not. 'She went into Berlin's Jewish Hospital during her pregnancy, and remained there until the war ended.'

'They left a Yehudi alone in their backyard for all that time?'

Instead of raising herself, she remains seated and rotating her hips, grinding against him in encouragement.

'They wanted everything looking normal to the Jews being shipped out to die. So they left the Hospital Jewish staff alone.'

'Still. All those years? How many others lasted that long?'

'Why are you bringing this up?'

'Because you are a little man, and you'll remain one if I don't.' She easily lifts herself into a half-squat, leaving a gaping hole in him. He stares at her thighs. All she needs now are two more arms to be the hottest Hindu Goddess in business.

She explains the ego-destroying principle of Prapatti. How true humility comes after a full admission of guilt.

'Okay, I admit. She was the SS Commandant's mistress. She did that to survive. What more do you want?'

'How is that your fault? By admitting to that, what are you not admitting? What are you not telling me?'

Seeing him starting to drown, she descends to make sure the concrete remains in situ; then grinds her pelvis to pour more concrete into his erection. Where did she learn to do that? Clinging to her while not letting go of maya, he finds it difficult to hang on to both.

'So your father killed himself because she became the enemy's mistress?'

'You could say that. He protested, and pissed them off. If you piss off Nazis, you're going to end up with pissed-off Nazis. He killed himself to avoid being shipped East.'

'But he was a sophisticated man. You said so. He would have understood she collaborated to survive. How could she be a traitor if forced at gunpoint? Your father would know that. What are you not admitting? What was so unacceptable he had to go protest in front of such dangerous men? Piss them off like that?'

He wants to defend Schwester Ingrid more than anything else. Ask, what does an Indian Goddess know about survival? Try being a Jew for one day in Nazi Germany.

Goddess Bhairavi hovers. 'What aren't you telling me?' she asks again. 'Why was your wife the only Yehudi to run back to the Nazis?' The Goddess then leans forward the way he does to get Indians to open up. When she does that to him, he becomes a faucet and pours his heart out.

~

Bombay Ingrid was waiting to be recruited all her life. A platinum blonde Jewess and more Aryan-looking than the most Aryan-looking Aryans, she resented not being one. Like Beatrice Taylor, she couldn't hide that longing. It must have shown on her perfect face, the huge relief at being back. So they got her admitted into the hospital, where she got rid of the baby and went to work.

The Goddess looks at him. That's a salty taste in his mouth. It's okay to cry, she says.

'She worked at the detention area keeping Jews calm. My father would watch his daughter-in-law—a beautiful, freshly showered Jewess smelling of soap—hold their hands to inspire trust, place their children on her lap so she could tell them not to worry. That the death camps rumours were nonsense. She would ask them to look across the barbed wire at all the Jews strolling the hospital grounds. See? Those are Jews, just like you. And you, well you're simply being sent to other nice, happy places just like the Jüdische Krankenhaus; to work, keep busy like them.'

The Goddess turns pensive. 'That picture of her in uniform with those children on her lap? The one your father sent you.'

'He sent it to explain why he killed himself. It was his suicide note. When their time came, she let those children skip happily to the boxcars.'

It had been a while since he thought of his father doing anything other than slicing his wrists in a bathtub. Things like teaching him to play the piano in their parlour. Teaching him to fly a kite. Ruffling his hair. Holding him in a bear hug. Doing whatever it takes to get his only son out of Nazi Germany. To get past the bathtub scene though, one had to first acknowledge what Ingrid did. Acknowledge that she enjoyed whispering lies to children. That she enjoyed being with Aryans, yearning to be one of them, as badly as Beatrice Taylor wishing she was a full, hundred-per cent European. Admit that Ingrid never did anything she didn't want to do in the first place.

'You acknowledging that would have let your father rest. Instead, he keeps slashing his wrists every night, trying to convince you there was nothing else he could have done. He didn't kill himself to escape the Nazis. He died to protest what she was doing.'

'You're asking me to blame her for his death? She is my wife. I loved her.'

'Did she love you?'

'She married me. Came with me to India. No one put a gun to her head.'

'You told me about your people marrying someone, anyone, those days, just so they weren't alone.'

When angry, Goddess Bhairavi is found on garish Hindu calendars, sitting on a faithful donkey with her mouth full of demon blood, her body covered with a tiger skin while holding a skeleton. Today, the Goddess rides a mule, and though there is anger at the size of his denial, she is here to open his eyes before they close forever.

'Look, what denial does. You won't even contact the Yehudi hospital for your own sake.'

He didn't want to deal with that now. He had all of his rest of three minutes left to do that.

'That's why you are not sending them your X-rays. Because then memories start to gush, demanding answers.'

'Yes.'

'Will you send them now?'

'Yes.'

'And what else?'

'Ask my father to forgive me. Allow him to rest.'

'And what else?'

'Ask for her forgiveness when she visits me again.'

'She may not. She's a woman.'

'I'll ask her anyway.'

'Oooh!' Goddess Bhairavi squeals. 'You're saying all the right things!' She leans forward while still riding him like a mule, and licks at his tears before kissing his open mouth to deliver a carrot he will never forget. Her pupils rolled back again as he surges inside her. If Parvatibai hears the Goddess screaming like this, she's going to come rushing in with that bloody glass of milk and a cold compress.

~

Her ankle scrapped his, the sari bunched around the swell of one calf. Light brown, wedding henna vines crawled across her dark brown feet. Each scarlet toe nested against the one next to it, with no need for pumps to align the formation.

Raag Bhairavi is morning music, and its strains filtered through the window grill from some neighbourhood radio. She sat up with a smudged dot on the forehead, like a red, third eye, her face crimson from the rising sun favouring her through the bedroom window. Seeing her glow, it dawned once again that she was too beautiful for his own good.

It was vivid, what he thought happened last night. But then, so were all his dreams. He had woken up a couple of times and watched her sleep, listened to her giving off little Goddess snores every once in a while. Sure, the face was smudged and hair spread on the pillow, not coiffured the way it had been with sindoor and all, but he wouldn't have had it any other way.

'Did something happen last night?'

'What do you mean,' she demanded, and he girded up for the face from the other day at the dining table, when he tried holding hands after feeling her up. She smiled instead. Urdu poets would line up to declare she looked like a piece of the moon. Gautama Buddha, the ninth avatar of Vishnu as Hindus have you believe, urges we go ahead and dig the pond without waiting for the moon. When the pond is finished, the Buddha says, the moon will appear in it. Just that, he's been digging away for so long now, when the moon's finally appeared, it's time to go.

~

When he brought up her brother, Goddess Bhairavi took leave and a frightened, over-dressed girl sat up.

'I don't know where Kirti is. She's simply gone and vanished.'

He wanted to tell her not to worry and that a big gora Englishman had her cross-dressing brother. That the English fool would die before letting any harm come to the boy. 'Kirti's fine,' he said, and they left it at that. Her look of relief had him worried she still thought he could do anything. Then there was this other thing.

'Sassoonji.' Smile, you idiot, smile when you say that. 'You in his Mercedes.'

'All the time you thought he was looking after you. Now someone has to look after him.'

She locked eyes, but then went wriggled her toes and he was distracted. Besides, just because she looked like a Goddess, didn't make her one. Rather than challenge her, he changed the subject. 'How's the accounting work getting along?'

'It's for your pipes,' she said. 'Sassoonji's Lala has me keep separate books.'

How could he let that one go? He asked about the pipes—what were they for? When she said for Atomic Energy, for the new, nuclear reprocessing plant, he explained, more to try convince himself, that stainless steel has to be nitric acid grade to reprocess spent fuel.

Salim Ali said so. 'Those pipes are not nitric acid grade. So, cannot be for AEET.' He didn't add—although, this was India and we're talking about Sassoon.

'You may make the pipes, but I do the books. So I should know.' She was emphatic. 'They have already been delivered to AEET,' she said, not telling him anything he didn't know.

He did want to know why though, as if asking himself. 'Why sub-par pipes for a nuclear facility? Why do something like that for money?'

She became a coquette again, wriggling her toes for him. 'Why don't you find Kirti and ask her?'

When Parvatibai came with chai for two, she didn't bat an eyelid at what looked like miscegenation and adultery rolled into one bed. Bhairavi used Parvatibai's thick forearm for support when sitting back up. They smiled at each other like best friends. Ernst felt under siege. He was relieved no end when Parvatibai left, and the two of them fell back to hold hands. One couldn't miss how married she looked.

'Like my wife, you went married someone you don't love. Do you hate him?'

'No,' she said. 'Of course not.'

'Why? Because you are a Goddess?'

She giggled like a schoolgirl. 'No,' she said, 'because I am Indian.'

Before turning to her side for a quick nap, she leaned over his ear again. He shivered waiting for the tongue to tickle his brain, but all she did was bend low and whisper. How exhilarating was it, she asked, to know that no one could harm him any more? To no longer be afraid of anyone? He should thank his cancer.

Later, when he spooned against her, she let him. When he thrust, the phone rang.

It was Dr. Waller. They had found Willie. He was no longer missing.

43

Directing Traffic

Without road accidents, India's population would double.
—*R.K. Karanjia, Editor, Blitz*

The Tata truck had adhered to the laws of angular conservation of momentum, twirled in a tight circle at high speed, and come to rest face-down. What would be incredible anywhere else in the world was nothing new at Chembur Naka. Nighttime, it becomes a racetrack.

The dead driver—half-in, half-out of the caboose—was a Marathi local. In this topsy-turvy world, Marathas were driving heavy vehicles now, not Sikhs. The dead man had the same handlebar moustache as the one in that truck at Sindhi Camp. The one who did a hit-and-run on a kid goat while aiming for Salim Ali. Sprawled like that, the driver looked almost bitter at how things had turned out. The cleaner was missing. Must have run like hell, leaving one shoe behind. It was a large, gorilla-size, and couldn't belong to your typical, little cleaner-boy—someone to spoon with over lonely nights. The gorilla-size cleaner had run away, probably just like how he did that day at the Golf Club after Salim Ali's sword dance. This time, Ernst was pretty sure he would keep running.

Another body lay more than fifty feet from the capsized Tata—almost too far to be part of the accident scene. A hand was stretched out towards the truck, trying to be part of the story or possibly commanding it to stop. The rest of Willie lay in a pool of blood.

Goras were milling around. It looked as if the whole Anglo-section of the Golf Club was at Chembur Naka this warm, sultry evening to mourn one of theirs.

Ignoring Ernst the way great men dismiss people from their lives, Sassoon wondered aloud. 'What the bloody hell was Willie doing here in the first place?'

When Daisy Lansdowne stepped out of his Mercedes, the great man rushed over to guide her away from the body, throwing a parting hiss at the hovering policemen. 'Someone cover him up, for fuckssake.'

The constables in their dark blue half-pants were alert lamp posts. There were too many white people around for business as usual. Between the police and their inertia, Willie remained as is—arm thrown out to direct Indian traffic from the afterlife—until Ernst gathered enough of the gunny bags floating around the Tata to go cover his friend. There was a nick at the side of Willie's skull, the kind that normally self-healed. All the blood around the body seemed to have drained from that single scratch. After the direct hit from a Tata, one guessed Willie forgot to clot. Ernst was surprised how removed he felt. Admittedly, not very different from the past so many days after Willie first went missing on getting fired, then went native, to finally go for broke. Ernst's mind had been on other things. Primarily Sindhi Camp Bhairavi—recently turned Goddess.

Deputy Commissioner Jahagirdar was also there and came up to commiserate. Salim Ali from just the other day, and now Willie. The way Ernst saw, he was all that remained between Jahagirdar and a hat trick. The way Jahagirdar looked him up and down, he seemed to agree.

They shook hands, old acquaintances meeting under unfortunate circumstances. Ernst remembered Willie raging through the Deputy Commissioner's police station, conducting a second British invasion. He had the distinct feeling the Deputy Commissioner was visualising the exact, same thing.

'Unfortunate.'

'Very.'

The Deputy Commissioner was suave as they came. 'At least we can both agree this time, there's no bullet-hole.'

'Commendable,' Ernst said. 'You must have exercised great restraint.'

Looking past Jahagirdar, Sassoon's Protection Home for Whores was visible from where he stood, peering at him from behind Chembur Naka's two temples. Its disarrayed red tiles demanded answers he didn't have. Logic after all, was in one's head. The outside world progressed with none at all.

'Ernst!'

It was Daisy Lansdowne brushing past a bemused Sassoon. Her face—red like the Sassoon Protection Home's roof tiles—also demanded answers. As if he would know why Willie was here past midnight, directing traffic. The Deputy Commissioner hightailed, than stay around to see how Ernst fared.

Ernst tried touchy-and-feely when she came up, but Daisy brooked no comforting from the likes of him. He understood, and flailing from want of an option, tried chitchat.

'I see you finally found some time for your friend,' she said.

Ernst protested; felt like telling her about the quality time spent with her husband in the police chowki.

'I called you the other day. You banged the phone down.'

'Yes, of course, thanks. One pathetic phone call. Adam calls daily. He worried about Willie, as a friend should. He located him some days ago and brought him back home. He sent his car again to pick him up last evening, and now for me. What have you done for us, lately?'

At times like this, a Hindu changes tack.

'What was he doing here at two bloody am?'

It was weak, but it was something.

Daisy had that look of eternal disdain cheated wives favour. She nodded toward the Sassoon Protection Home for Whores.

'What do you think?'

She then looked at Willie, his arm sticking out past a gunny bag. When the tears came, she said, 'Fuck him,' dabbing at her eyes. 'And fuck you too. Goodbye, Ernst.'

44

The Sassoon Protection Home
for Whores

In India, gods may cross-dress.
—*Krishna in drag vs Indian Penal Code*

Arrayed on the floor like that, Princess Kirti's life had taken a turn
for the worse. Or not, depending on where one stood.

Holed up in a room at the Sassoon Protection Home for Whores
and not permitted to leave, could be considered a turn for the worse—
result of defective karma. On the other hand, she had the room to
herself, no gang rapes by fellow prisoners scheduled on the calendar,
fed three times a day, and allowed to meet people.

Then again, Willie was dead.

For an audience with the Princess, one had to first sign the
register at the Protection Home reception. Then one had to wait
while the uniformed lady in khaki-sari at the desk called someone,
somewhere, for permission to allow the gora past warning signs in
Hindi, Marathi and English, exclaiming one after the other for good
reason: NO UNESCORTED MEN ALLOWED! The ceiling fan
was on and a pair of khaki trousers flailed helplessly from a hook
next to the multilingual warning signs.

'That chhakka can leave anytime, you know,' was Khaki-sari's
surly take on the subject. 'He just has to put on his trousers and I'll
personally throw him out. All this drama-bazi…such waste of time.'

'Don't call her chhakka.'

'Is it a hijra then? Really? A eunuch?'

'Just take me to her.'

'Chai, Sirji?'

Offering chai seemed the right decision, because the phone rang and someone, somewhere, gave Ernst a huge thumbs-up the way her eyes widened. Khaki-sari simpered and stood. Ernst thought she was going to pat herself on the back. He followed her past the warnings on the signboard and into a corridor cutting straight through rooms on either side. Recent repairs showed off through paan-stained, whitewashed walls.

Four carelessly thrown corridors made the Sassoon Protection Home for Whores an imperfect square with a compound in the centre. Khaki-sari led Ernst down the corridor, sort of parallel to the main road blaring outside. One couldn't look into the central compound from here but it sounded like an aviary.

One could look into the rooms though, the doors left open to prevent the bodies inside from stewing in their own sweat. As Ernst passed by each room, it would turn silent and eyes scour his white skin. Then he'd breathe easy again before the next door came up and once again the women would eat him up alive. Khaki-sari led on, unaware of the wrinkles to space-time in her wake. When they reached Marathi-numerical #47, Ernst was faint from too much of a good thing, and trying not to suffocate in female body odour.

~

Sick though he was, Ernst had come to see her, and bereft as she was, the Princess deigned him an audience. She even offered to strain him some chai bubbling on a primus stove. She sat in a corner just like at the police lockup, only this time not so bedraggled, and in dry clothes in an empty room.

Also, she had changed into widow-white. Khaki-sari rolled her eyes at the broken bangles on the floor and left him to deal with whatever was going on here. Hindu widows break their bangles on a husband's demise which, for all her genuine grief over Willie, even Ernst felt to be somewhat over the top. After all, she wasn't married to Willie, and though he didn't have the heart to bring it up, she was a he. Besides, there was a real widow in pain out there. He tried, but for the world of him, couldn't picture Daisy Lansdowne breaking her bangles on the floor at her company bungalow.

He declined the tea but concluded that for all the over-the-top drama, Princess Kirti's grief was genuine. When did this love develop? Over how many golf games? He asked instead, how she was doing. She asked about Willie.

'How did it happen?'

'Truck.'

'Did he suffer?'

'No.'

'You know, he was coming to see me when it happened.'

'Yes.' Either that, or he was directing traffic at 2 a.m.

'PL 480,' Princess Kirti said.

'What?'

'It's this PL 480 business. American food aid. That's why he was coming here. So we could teach the Seth a lesson he would never forget.'

'What's the Seth got to do with American food aid?'

Everything, she said, wriggling her toes, but it wasn't the same.

~

When Willie broke into the police chowki and stormed out with her, he went straight next door to the Bombay Presidency Golf Club.

'With you?'

'Of course. Why?'

'Nothing.'

'I know I am not allowed inside,' she said, sounding defensive. 'He asked me to wait at the reception.' Ernst stared at the boy's painted toenails sticking out from under the widow-sari. He corrected himself. Her toenails.

She reminisced about her hero. 'I saw him go straight up to Sassoonji. They spoke. You should have heard him yell. Just imagine. Yelling at Sassoonji. But it worked, because doors opened just like that and I was able to come here. Imagine what would have happened to me at the police chowki.'

He tried picturing Willie yell at Sassoon, and wasn't sure if imagining that was allowed. On the other hand, he had poured Salim Ali's remains over the great man and here he was, still alive.

He had to ask. 'You and Willie. Since when?'

'Two years now. You were there the first time we met. He hated me talking to anyone else. Even to you.' She smiled at that, reminiscing about her man. 'What people don't realise is we are women. We can't bear your babies, but we can love just as passionately. He was my life.'

A racist Englishman and an Indian cross-dresser. His head started to ring.

'What about Lala Prem? He's all over you too.'

'True. He will do anything I want. We share all our secrets with each other.'

'And Arjun? Did he tell you his secrets too?'

'Of course. We were childhood friends. He was an idealist. Silly boy. Where was the need to get involved? Look what happened.'

'You know what happened?'

'Of course. Arjun never hid anything from me.'

'Yes, yes. Neither did the Lala, I know. By the way, did Willie know about you and the Lala?'

'Of course. We promised to tell each other everything. No secrets.'

'But you just said the same about the Lala.'

'Yes. I would never hide anything from Lalaji. Nor would he from me.'

Ernst gave up and focused on the matter at hand.

He tried picturing Willie yell at Adam Sassoon and once again, he couldn't. Instead, he felt feverish.

'What did you two talk about?'

'What do lovers talk about?'

'And the Lala and you? What secrets did he share?'

'He would tell me about this American PL 480 food aid business. He complained it was taking up all his time.'

'And you told Willie.'

'He got excited when I did. Said it would solve all our problems. I believed him. Now, who cares?'

'I do. You told him what the Lala and Arjun told you. Now tell me.'

~

The Princess watched Ernst sip his tea. 'With him gone,' she said, 'I may not be here too long.'

She didn't have a bloody choice with Willie gone, but a Princess is a Princess and defines her own terms.

'Where will you go?'

'The hijras want to take me in.'

He felt a chill. He couldn't see the Princess a eunuch, doing the rounds at marriages and births, clapping her hands cross-wise and threatening to raise her sari if the baksheesh was insufficient. It was unbecoming. But before that, there would have to be a castration ceremony for the Princess to join the club. His stomach turned.

'I know,' the Princess said, reading his reaction. 'But I don't need it anymore.' She floated into a dream state.

'You know,' she said on coming back, 'he loved mine.'

'Yes.'

'Played with it for hours. He loved that I couldn't fake it. Called it my barometer. Hated anyone else touching it.'

Lala Prem came to mind and the flying Japanese, and God knows who else, but yes, I know what you mean, thought Ernst.

'What do I need it for, now that he's gone?'

~

Not only did she have a room to herself, but a room with a view.

Were the Princess to stand, she could have seen Ernst walking out toward the main road. Mohan Driver was parked by the Chagan Mitha petrol pump down at Chembur Naka. The Seth's Impala though, was parked on the opposite curb outside her window. Johnny Walker was in uniform, and along with his full-paunched posse could be seen clinging to the Seth's vehicle. The Impala's fin had protected the police against a Salim Ali doing his sword dance in the Golf Club compound, but why did they need protection today? Also, was the

Impala there just to serve and protect, or was there someone inside? That the Seth was inside wasn't improbable after hearing out Princess Kirti. Still, Ernst refused to consider the possibility. Sensible, because then he would have to consider the consequences.

'Are you the homo, Mr. Ernst?' Johnny Walker asked as he crossed the road and walked toward them.

Was he the homo? Almost, though, not quite. His schoolteacher notwithstanding and for all of Princess Kirti's obvious charms, only the Ingrids, and now the Bhairavis, did anything for him.

'Why for this homogiri?' Johnny Walker wanted to know, and then in a pensée that screamed of original thought, 'Why abominate, when you can conjugate?'

Sick and tired as he was, Ernst felt he should note that one down.

Preamble done with and bona fides established, Johnny Walker got down to business. 'You realise this cannot continue, Mr. Ernest.'

Given his deteriorating state, Ernst was willing to cease and desist, if he only knew what Johnny Walker wanted discontinued. The policeman kept going on with the threats, his broadsides becoming very general—rendering Ernst culpable for almost everything.

Ernst felt weak, tired and very ill. It showed, and he could see they sensed blood. One of them had a towel wrapped around something rod-like and wicked-looking. He wrung the towel. It could be Ernst's neck.

There was another way of looking at it. A thrashing correctly delivered could beat wasting away in bed from cancer. The policemen were beginning to resemble a viable alternative. If anyone were his friend right now, it was the leader of this pack. Ernst looked at Johnny Walker fondly. A good fellow, really. He found himself liking the man. To help speed up the process, he went up and slapped him across the face.

In retrospect, a mistake. While Ernst may have forgotten he was white, the policemen hadn't and they backed away. Uncertainty flickered over them like a desi florescent tube. They looked to Johnny Walker for direction. Johnny Walker looked at the Impala. The Impala looked empty behind its tinted windows. The Princess looked out from her room with a view.

'PL 480,' she said, talking down to the masses. She may well have been right, but Ernst wished she hadn't done that. Who knew, the Seth could be in the Impala. He could've heard her. On the other hand, it was true what Goddess Bhairavi had whispered in his ear. He had cancer. No one could harm him any more.

'Get out of here,' he told Johnny Walker, and took a step forward to within body odour distance. Johnny Walker took a step back.

'Go,' and pointing at the Impala, 'hide behind it. Hide wherever you want, but fuck off.'

All of this sent a rumble up his insides and he felt his arse corking up, then uncorking. No one spoke that way to the Bombay Police. Johnny Walker almost went pink, blood mottling his dark brown face, and in needless awe of a cancer-ridden white man who couldn't shit if he tried.

The police phalanx broke to let Ernst through to the Impala. As if aware what Ernst could do, the Impala rumbled into life. It crawled forward and stopped—in two minds—then tore off towards Chembur Naka.

Instead of walking on to where Mohan Driver was waiting, Ernst crossed the road again and ran back into the Protection Home, past the dire warnings to unescorted men with a startled Khaki-sari busy beneath it—her mouth forming a perfect O as she jerked up from a yellow file to see him go by.

He braked, and returned to the reception desk.

'Can you sign her out? I want her to come with me.'

'Cannot, Sirji.'

'It's okay. Make the call,' Ernst urged, pointing at the phone.

This time when Khaki-sari put the phone down, there was a sea change in her attitude and no more Sirjis.

'Cannot. The chhakka has to remain here until produced before Kurla Court.'

'Why?' Ernst asked. 'Prostitution is not a crime.' Technically correct, but weak.

Her disdain showed. 'Soliciting, vagrancy, cross-dressing and sodomy are.' All Indians are lawyers.

'What if he removes the sari and wears trousers?'

She looked impressed, despite herself.

'I'll have him thrown out in a second. No unescorted men allowed.' She pointed to the warning sign without looking at it. The khaki trousers hung next to it. She mulled over the huge technicality coming down to bear. 'The police may still file charges for sodomy. But that's their problem.'

The Princess was back in her corner in #47, squatting to drink tea from a glass. She sipped at it like royalty handling bone china.

'Put this on,' Ernst said, and held out the khaki trousers. 'I'll go find you a shirt. We're leaving. I am taking you to my place.' The thought of getting the Princess past Parvatibai had his penis go foetal in his scrotum.

The Princess looked at the khaki trousers with the contempt they deserved. Ignoring him totally, she got up to go stare out of the window. The police were still out there and they stared back. The Impala was gone.

'Put those fucking trousers on,' Ernst said. 'And do it now. Those men are waiting to get at you, not me.'

45

A Transvestite at Karim Court

Daddy's angry at my ways,
Be a man, he always says.
Daddy wants I learn to bowl,
Hit a six, score a goal.
Daddy said, it's for my good,
Then he beat me raw, but I understood.
—*Kirti the Poet*

A bristling block of hostility, Parvatibai barricaded the doorway. In comparison, Khaki-sari was a pussycat. Behind Ernst, Princess Kirti remained afloat inside gargantuan khaki trousers.

'Not a word,' Ernst said and pushed the Princess past.

Although taken aback by how easy that turned out, he doubted he could pull it off again. When Ernst wanted the Princess shown to the guest bedroom, Mundu the servant-boy sprang past a Parvatibai still coming to grips with what just happened. He snatched Princess Kirti's valise that looked like something Willie would own, and led her away, ignoring a frozen Parvatibai. Mundu's expression made it clear this was worth any martyrdom to follow.

Parvatibai regressed to a simpler Marathi for Ernst's benefit. 'All these years, he leads a nice, quiet life. Then he falls ill, and now look.'

Her comment brought his health back centre stage. He felt dizzy from too much for one day—a dead Willie directing midnight traffic through Chembur Naka and now Mundu directing Willie's Princess through the corridor. He instructed Parvatibai to make sure the Princess got something to eat. Hindi grammar allows the subject to be gender-free, in turn, allowing Ernst past any potential embarrassment of the he/she type. Or, so he thought.

'A snack perhaps, or does the chhakka want lunch?' she asked.

'Show some respect. That's your best friend's brother. Why? She didn't tell you about him?'

He slammed the bedroom door shut before Parvatibai could power back on. He would recall walking to the bed and the lights going out before he hit the pillow. He barely slept a few minutes before someone started banging away at the door. The clock declared otherwise. It was six in the morning and men were asking for him.

'Police,' Parvatibai said.

'Wrong floor. They probably want the whorehouse.'

'They asked for you by name.'

~

The Deputy Commissioner was not used to waiting by the door but he was a St. Stephen's man.

Kirti's father Chabildas, on the other hand, couldn't care less. His bulk was halfway through the corridor by the time Ernst emerged. Parvatibai surged forward seeing her citadel stormed again, and it looked like an imminent clash of the titans. As far as Princess Kirti's father was concerned, Parvatibai's three hundred pounds of dark matter didn't exist.

'You have my son.'

Ernst did not have the heart to correct the gender.

'Yes. There are people after him. So, I brought him here.'

'I know. People like you. I am his father. Let me handle his affairs.'

Behind him and still at the door, the Deputy Commissioner shrugged. Parvatibai turned in the narrow corridor—an oil tanker reversing down the Suez Canal. Ernst reversed in formation.

'She's gone,' Parvatibai said to Ernst.

'Talk to me,' Chabildas said, acknowledging the elephant in the room. 'What do you mean gone? Where's he gone?'

'She left,' Parvatibai said to Ernst. 'While you were asleep.'

'Where did he go?'

'She didn't tell me.' By now, the oil tanker had done the impossible and turned around on a rupee coin.

'I don't believe you. Show me where he is.'

From behind Chabildas, Deputy Commissioner Jahagirdar did that Indian thing with his head, suggesting Ernst acquiesce. Ernst nodded to Parvatibai, who walked backwards to allow Chabildas passage. This had Ernst reverse some more and trip over his golf bag leaning against the wall.

When Chabildas came through, Parvatibai said, 'The guestroom's over there, but she's not.'

Chabildas wasn't a Sindhi zamindar for nothing. He stared at Parvatibai but stopped short of making a fool of himself. Ernst pointed at the guestroom to help him along. He almost asked the Deputy Commissioner in but hearing Salim Ali voice a protest in his head, he demurred.

Chabildas was red-faced emerging from the guestroom, and giving off fumes. Ernst hoped the Mundu didn't have any lit beedies lying around.

'Where's my son?'

'I don't know. I was asleep.'

'Bhenchod. Where's my son?'

The temperature was going up and over at the far end, the Deputy Commissioner appeared torn between St. Stephen's College-style decorum, and being Bombay Police. The policeman won and came inside to take charge. Timing was good because Parvatibai reached for a nine iron sticking out of the golf bag. In that confined space, her swing could as easily take down Ernst instead of the father.

'The boy is an absconder. You cannot aid and abet,' the Deputy Commissioner advised.

The fumes were getting to Ernst. He turned to Parvatibai. 'What happened when I was asleep? And put that damned thing away.'

'Two hijras came and took her with them.'

Princess Kirti's father flinched but remained silent. Ernst ventured on his behalf.

'And you let them?'

'How do you stop hijras? All that noise they were making at the front door—the neighbours thought you had a baby boy. I had to get rid of them.'

Point taken. Indian eunuchs turn up out of nowhere at the front door to bless newborns; their noisy presence while auspicious, is fraught with embarrassment if not handled properly.

'Anyway, what's the problem? She left willingly.'

'Fucking whore,' Chabildas said. 'You are the type to go willingly, not my son. Your gora pimp and you have cast a spell on my child. I'll see you both in jail. That much I promise.'

Even the Deputy Commissioner looked impressed. He took Chabildas by the elbow to steady the man.

'We'll leave now,' DCP Jahagirdar said. But mind you, this is a serious matter. Chabildas-bhai has filed an FIR accusing you of kidnapping his son. At the Colaba Police Station, if you must know. There is only so much I can do for you.'

Walked to the door by the good policeman, Princess Kirti's father calmed down a bit and stopped to reflect on India's broad-spectrum antibiotic for homosexuality.

'He'll be fine once we get him married.' Hope radiated from the father and bounced off the corridor walls.

'By the way,' the Deputy Commissioner said, after instructing two dark blue constables to escort Chabildas downstairs. 'You know about Henry Gomes?'

'No. Why?'

'You don't know?'

Hindus and Jews will both tell you, the trick is not to engage.

'He was found dead yesterday, near Deonar. On Trombay Road. Outside the Tata Institute of Social Sciences.'

Where Arjun's mother worked.

'I see. I am sorry.'

'No, you're not!' The Deputy Commissioner laughed. 'But I am. I knew him well. A good, family man. God-fearing. Do you know how he died?'

'Bullet-hole between the eyes? Or maybe a truck accident?'

'You think it's funny?'

'We have both of those going around. I could make you a list of fatalities.'

'Yes, you are being funny. No, Henry was stabbed. Gutted. Some of that going around too.'

'I see.'

'Gutted professionally—abdominal area and right up to his thoracic cavity. There was pneumothorax and his lungs were collapsed.'

Ernst wondered if Jahagirdar expected him to comment.

'Similar modus operandi, don't you think?' the Deputy Commissioner asked. 'With what happened to Chhote Bhai? You think maybe Mr. Ali returned from the dead to extract revenge, or was it his comrade, the Chinaman? Or, maybe someone else? What do you think?'

To reiterate, there are times one may respond to a policeman. Most of the time though, just smile back.

'Don't worry,' the Deputy Commissioner said. 'We visited the Chinaman's flat at Atomic Energy. He was there with his sister, and half dead. Can't see him taking on Gomes. She showed us where the sword hung on the wall. The scabbard was empty. Maybe, because we have it in our custody since Chhote Bhai's murder.'

Ernst's relief must have been palpable, because Jahagirdar looked satisfied at the reaction.

'Still, somebody did kill Gomes with a sword.'

Ernst remembered the scabbard from the last time he saw it—not empty—the strong Golog-style grip sticking out of the hewn leather protecting the blade. Then Bhairavi had pulled it out for her dance practice. He wondered where that sword was now.

'I am sure you'll find out who is responsible. At least, you know where not to look.'

Deputy Commissioner Jahagirdar concurred. 'For sure. Like I said, there was no sword on the wall or anywhere in the flat. And of course, the one in our possession didn't kill Gomes.'

'Of course.'

'But something did.'

'Goodbye, Deputy Commissioner.'

After seeing the spry Deputy Commissioner take the stairs with a bounce belying his stature, Ernst returned to Parvatibai in the corridor—holding on to the nine iron and back in charge. A visual of her teeing off on the greens shook him up and he wanted to run, shut his bedroom door to recover. On the other hand, Salim Ali was now in a little square box on the mantelpiece, next to the Menorah.

'Parvatibai. Enough. Time to handover what Salim Ali gave you.'

'The hijras took it.'

'I see.'

But he didn't.

'They come for Kirti and you also give them that gunny bag you've been guarding with your damn life?'

'They asked for it, so I gave. You know how they are.'

~

When Parvatibai banged the bedroom door again, he wanted to shout out abuse for all the good that would do.

'The hijras. They're back,' she said through the shut door.

'What's it this time? They can take Mundu if they want.'

'They want you.'

46

The Sickle

Prince Arjun was the third brother to enter the king's palace.
His hair was long and braided and he walked with the gait of
a broad-hipped woman. His feminine attire attenuated his
masculine glory and at the same time, it did not.
—*The Mahabharata*

'Om Namashivai, Om Namashivai, Har Har Bole, Namashivai.'
Chants filled the air in praise of Lord Shiva. Krishna may well be
partial to cross-dressers but in the Hijra Township, Lord Shiva rules.

De facto though, Komal Guruji ruled the Hijra Township. She/
he/it pointed at a print framed on the wall next to their Goddess
Bahuchara Ma, standing on the aarti-shelf and decorated in a
green sari. It was a medieval, Pahari depiction of Krishna, the
most perfect, earthly manifestation of the divine in drag. Trumped
only by Shiva on Bahuchara Ma's other side, cast in silver with
a sway to his hips.

'Lord Krishna may have dressed like a woman, as did Prince
Arjun in the Mahabharata, but Shiva is half-woman. Half-half. Like
us,' Guruji said, leaving the ithyphallic Shiva's thick, black lingam
erect in protest inside temples across India. 'Anyway,' Guruji went
on, 'Thank you for coming. The boy Kirti wanted you here today.'

'Yes. But I've also come for what you took without permission.'

'I may be a eunuch, a hijra, but I am an honest person. It wasn't
yours in the first place. There was no need for permission.'

'I've seen you before, Guruji. There's this picture of the Communist Party Politburo on Salim Ali's living room wall. Very idyllic, that picture, with coconut trees in the background. You're in the line up.'

'We also saw each other at Fertilisers', Komal Guruji said, and Ernst remembered the older hijra ordering his troupe around. 'Why are you surprised about that picture? Hijras can't be politically conscious?'

'Politically conscious is one thing. You're a member of the Politburo.'

'Unlike the rest of India, my sexual orientation never concerned the comrades. It's why this basti is a Marxist commune.'

'A communist basti, complete with gods and goddesses.'

'Everything is fluid, ji. Doesn't have to be one or the other; India after all.'

'So it is. Anyway, Kirti must have told you what Arjun stole, and you people just came took it?'

'Not at all. We were the ones who learnt about it in the first place. Arjun volunteered to obtain it for us from the American compound at Fertilisers.'

'Who's us? The hijras or the communists?'

'What's the difference? The Communist Party is for the dispossessed, Sirji,' and Komal Guruji became all dreamy-eyed saying that. 'We look after all the stray dogs in this mad city.'

'And now you plan to look after Kirti?'

'Kirti always knew there was something different about him. I was the same. I would only play with girls, never boys. The girls would ask me what I was. I'd reply, I am a girl. But like I said, I'm honest. Even before my operation, I let clients know in advance what I really was. Because I was so beautiful, you would never know otherwise. The men came anyway. In fact, they came because I was pre-operation those days. Unlike a woman, you see, I couldn't fake it.'

'Fascinating. But about that gunny bag...'

'It belongs to the Party. Like I do.'

'I thought the Party belonged to the people.'

The room smiled. The puja-prayers continued in the background and Goddess Bahuchara Ma looked down from above at her Marxist hijras. The morning rays peeked in from dirty windows and through cracks in the bolted door.

'Maybe. I, however, belong to the Party. You know, at home, they were ashamed of my behaviour. They said I have to stop acting like a girl. But I couldn't change what I was. So I left home at fourteen. Wandered around a few years until the communists took me in. They kept me in their orphanage where I learnt about Marx and Lenin. About marginalised people, and workers' rights. And they learnt about me.'

'Funny thing,' Komal Guruji continued. 'No one questioned my gender preference. No admonition, no trying to convince me, and I was never ostracised or made to feel uncomfortable or different. Instead, one day they brought me here. I've been here ever since.'

'Guruji says today is auspicious,' Kirti whispered to Ernst, love in his eyes.

He was back to being the beautiful boy who broke hearts. Ernst felt like Willie by association. Around them, the tempo kept going up a notch every few minutes while out the grilled window, it was the start to a new day. Hijras played with a tennis ball in the courtyard, tossing it up high and catching it.

'When I first came here,' Guruji said, 'they called me Komal. It means tender, in Urdu. After all I was a tender young boy who aspired to become a girl. The elders gave me a home and work. I taught them their rights. This whole basti was communist before I turned eighteen and I was the Party's rising star. A year later, the hijra elders asked if I wanted to get operated.

'Of course, I agreed. It's why I had run away in the first place. I had no fear. The operation is the most important thing in our lives.'

Guruji kept talking as the opium took hold. Kirti reached out to take Ernst's hand.

'Remember the first time you saw me?' he whispered.

Ernst squeezed back. 'Yes.'

'You wanted me, didn't you?'

Ernst wasn't sure whether he meant the first time he saw Kirti the caddie-boy, or when he first saw Princess Kirti emerge from the greens, swaying an arse that drew men from as afar as Japan.

'Yes,' he whispered back.

'Tell me again, how I came in your dreams.'

~

Komal Guruji pointed towards Sion Hospital's Assistant Coroner with his sweeper standing alongside, wooden instrument box and all. 'Those days, a guru performed the operation with no medicines or injections.'

Guruji held up his right hand to display what they would have used those days. The sickle-shaped knife looked a shiny, miniature version of the garden implement used to cut grass; the curved little blade sharpened to a gleam. The blade was cranked—offset downwards from the grip—just as with the garden implement, making it easier to cut close to the stem.

'I was made to stand naked in the room while the elders talked to me. As we looked up at our deity, she seemed to smile down. They explained how the analgesic trance during the operation was but one strand of the dense relationship between our powerful Bahuchara Ma and us. Through her, we bring fertility during weddings when we dance. Without us, only girls would be born.'

The aarti ceremony's chanting began to heat up. The group surrounding the sari-clad brass statue on the shelf was going nuts. These were nirvan hijras: those in a state of bliss. The nirvan hijras prayed, did aarti, crossed hands across their chests to touch both ears in penance. After a while, the Goddess had had enough and stepped down from the shelf to enter Kirti lying on a wooden pallet on the floor.

Kirti's eyes rolled back though the smile didn't budge an inch. He held on to Ernst's hand, crushing it in a grip that wasn't his. Ernst blinked back the tears, and almost missed the sweep of the kneeling Guruji's right hand while holding Kirti in his left. He drew the sickle towards him in one, clean motion. The blood splattered on Komal Guruji's white kurta and Ernst's glasses went opaque with red mist. He took them off. He hadn't seen this much blood. Not when his father slashed his wrists every other night. Not when Gomes killed Arjun. Not even when Salim Ali gutted Chhote Bhai.

'Now,' the Brahmin Assistant Coroner said loudly from a safe distance.

Komal Guruji looked at the Brahmin doctor and turned back to Kirti.

'I know,' he said.

There was this cylindrical wooden plug that Komal Guruji picked up after a bit of searching around on the bloodied pallet. It was slim—a sliver—but machined cylindrical. He inserted it into the wound, in what would appear a fucked sort of way to stem blood gushing out by the gallon from a tear reaching across to the supra pubic area.

Having seen Arjun seep away, Ernst calculated Kirti should be dead in fifteen minutes from blood loss, with or without the damn twig. Kirti couldn't care less and continued smiling like an idiot with eyes rolled back while a Goddess galloped across his brain. Two nirvan hijras knelt besides the pallet, but there was no need to hold the boy down.

'We don't plug it to stem blood,' Komal Guruji said. 'We want the male blood to get out. The wood prevents full closure of the wound leaving a hole for urine. I have done this many times.' Komal Guruji brandished the bloodied sickle to make his point. Moments ago, Komal Guruji had also brandished the Princess Kirti's thick, long clitoris in his left hand—beloved of Willie and so many others. Now, it was gone.

'Fifty per cent mortality rate from such operations,' the Assistant Coroner offered up in English.

Komal Guruji wasn't impressed. 'Just do your thing,' he asked the Assistant Coroner, while the two nirvan hijras poured hot sesame oil on the gushing wound. They began rubbing herbs on it with a ferocity that belied their blissful state. Assistant Coroner Sahib approached the pallet with his sweeper and the nirvan hijras backed-off at Komal Guruji's silent signal. Wooden box open by his side and serrated scissors in one hand, curved needle and catgut in the other, the sweeper probed and sutured while Assistant Coroner Sahib peered and instructed.

'To avoid chronic urinary retention,' the Assistant Coroner explained in an aside, like an attending surgeon would while operating. 'Caused by incorrect amputation of the penis and urethra. Even though management of problem is simple, these people end up dying because of reluctance to go to doctors.'

Ernst wondered what would happen if the hijras did go to doctors regularly. Were there enough trained sweepers to go around?

~

'Kirti would worry about a beard showing up,' Komal Guruji said. 'He worried his lover (lovers, Guruji, lovers; in the plural) would notice the slight fuzz on his upper lip. If you shave it, it only grows faster. The hair around his nipples left him distraught. Now, no more.'

'Yes,' Ernst agreed, 'he just needs to stay alive first.'

Komal Guruji remained cordial.

'We would have tied a thin nylon cord tight around his scrotum and tightened in at regular intervals, while we kept him high on opium. In around a week, the penis would slough off. Kirti however preferred this; have the male blood gush off in one go. He wanted it out of him.'

The male blood had congealed around the boy, now dead asleep. Or dead. Fifty-fifty.

'Well, he should be all-woman by now.'

Today was auspicious and the hijras bulletproof. The sarcasm simply bounced off.

'Not yet!' a nirvana hijra squealed, clapping her palms together in anticipation of things to come. 'We still have to rub her anus against a grinding stone until it bleeds. Those first drops of female blood will signify menstruation.'

Ernst would've wished them well and staggered out, but there was this one thing.

'What's in the gunny bag?'

So Komal Guruji went told him.

Ernst wanted to know the hell they planned to do with it.

'My job is to hand it over to the Party.'

'Or, you could return it to me.'

'Why would I do that?'

Ernst leaned over to the member of the Communist Party Politburo, who also happened to be a eunuch in high standing, and told him.

'It's the Law of Unintended Consequences being played out, Mr. Ernestji,' the comrade eunuch in high standing said, after hearing him out.

~

The morning sun reflected off the bungalow's windowpanes like so much glitter. It formed pools of light on patches of rainwater lying around the courtyard. Well-dressed gentry carelessly squelched fancy footwear in the water while crowding the enclosure. It was impossible to visualise India's bourgeoisie pouring into a hijra colony, if not right there, right before his eyes. One isn't allowed into a hijra colony. One doesn't go to a hijra colony. The taboo is real in Indian society. Sorrow however is compelling, as is desire—no saying what one will do.

Ernst reeled at the sheer size of Kirti's clientele.

'Fuck.'

He surveyed the packed courtyard. Earlier, there had been a couple of hijras out there playing with a tennis ball. Now it was a sea of white kurtas, shirts, and even jackets; as much real pain in the air as witnessed the other day in the Friends & Family line-up at Sion Hospital.

All this sorrow? Somewhat nonplussed, he could still hazard a guess why so many men were hurting so much. Probably because now the Princess could fake it.

~

Mohan Driver had deserted the one-eyed Fiat, parked way back where the pukka road ended. Ernst found him squatting in a corner of the courtyard with his back to the world, as if being punished. Ernst added him to the growing list of Kirti clit-lovers. It included those he would never suspect. Seeing a stunned D'Souza holding on to a weeping bearer from the Golf Club, there were no surprises left, other than say, if one were to find a Waller in this motley crowd.

Seeing him, Ernst's jaw dropped. He first thought the junkie of a doctor was here to catch snakes in the hijra compound. But no stick quivered in his hand today.

'What?' Waller challenged. He didn't look particularly gora this morning. The Indian DNA was on the ascent and he could well have passed for a Komal Guruji in linen suit. 'What for that condescending look? You're here too, you bugger.'

Other than Ernst, Dr. Waller appeared to be the sole syndic from the European side of The Great Divide. 'Don't you worry!' he said, righteous anger banishing any embarrassment. 'Bloody buggers are too ashamed to show up, that's all. I can give you names, if you want! I have names! They were all after the poor boy. Damn hypocrites.'

It gave one pause that the packed courtyard was just a partial client list. Understandably and even though in mourning, many Kirti-lovers would be too embarrassed to be seen here. Not Nippon#1 of Flying Japanese fame however, standing there recklessly exposed with tears coursing down his proud, Japanese face. Nippon#2 was also present in silent solidarity. It must have been quite a walk from wherever they parked the silver Mercedes and straight into another universe.

Then, there was the Lala.

That he was in this line-up of pederasts was the least of the day's surprises. The Lala looked starved. Standing in the shadows, he could no longer be mistaken for a proud Pathan because no Pathan would care to look like a doped up fakir on a bad day. Tears flowing down hollow cheeks, his wrinkled salwaar kameez was awash in body odour and with his turban unwinding all over the place in an unseemly manner, he appeared consumed by his loss. Ernst realised this was about as vulnerable as the Lala would get. If he had to move in, the time was now.

The Lala's face became a flickering picture book on seeing him. He was in need of solace and his old friend Mr. Ernestji was here. He clasped Ernst to his bosom like a brother and wouldn't let go. Ernst struggled for air and gave up. The Lala smelled slept-in. He began to cry. Holding Ernst's hand like a lover, he cried like a baby. He cried for Kirti and that jumper cable of a clitoris Ernst had seen in Guruji's hand. It was Kirti the Lala wanted—the Princess was mere cosmetics. He was crying because Kirti was his first and only priority in life. That wouldn't go down too well with the Seth, but Ernst understood.

'Oye Lala,' he said. 'Shut the fuck up.'

The Lala's eyes widened as he disengaged to stare at Ernst, but retained his clasp-hold on Ernst's hand. Ernst shook it free.

'You people left Kirti no choice. Why cry now?'

But the Lala wouldn't let up. How he cried.

'Your Sethji was at the Protection Home along with his police dogs,' Ernst said. 'Kirti would be dead by now if I hadn't reached on time and got him out of there.'

'They wouldn't have hurt him. I know. They just wanted to ask questions. They wouldn't have hurt him.'

'They could kill a gora. What's a chhakka?'

'Please don't call him that.'

'You're right. Now he's a hijra, because you lot had Willie killed.'

'No, please.'

'Is it true? What Kirti told Willie about Sethji and American food aid?'

'What will happen now? They will kill the poor boy.'

'He's not a boy anymore.'

Seeing the Lala's state, Ernst silently thanked Goddess Bhairavi for giving him cancer instead of putting him through anything like this.

'I know about your PL 480 money laundering,' Ernst said, and saw newfound respect in the Lala's eyes. The Lala reached out to clasp hands, but Ernst declined.

'Smuggling gold wasn't enough, you people had to go sell your country?' Ernst asked the Lala.

The Lala refused to confuse issues. He buried his head in his hands like Mohan Driver, and mourned the loss of what was the mightiest clitoris in Bombay.

'I have to take Kirti away,' he said. 'Someplace safe. The Seth will have him killed.'

Ernst recalled how Komal Guruji had wielded that sickle.

'I wouldn't worry,' he said.

~

'Drive,' Ernst said. So Mohan Driver drove Ernst to Atomic Energy, grinding gears in-between sobs, openly protesting the injustice Kirti had visited upon him.

Tsering Tufan was asleep in his flat up in AEET's Alaknanda apartment building. He remained in bed after his sister woke him. He didn't look good but then, who did? He appeared confused why

Ernst would want to see Dr. Homi J. Bhabha as soon as possible, preferably right away.

'Why?' he asked. 'Besides, it may not be easy to arrange.'

'Those were our pipes being installed in the reprocessing plant,' Ernst said.

The Smiling Buddha continued looking confused. Ernst gave it another shot.

'That lot we saw Paranjpe unload at the Phoenix Building. They are the same ones you let Salim Ali draw illegally in your workshop. Salim Ali shipped them out from Atomic Energy to Sassoon's Punjabi, and Punjabi shipped them back to Paranjpe.'

'You said that before, but cannot be.' Tufan was emphatic. 'Your pipes are the wrong grade for a reprocessing plant. There can be a serious accident.'

'Precisely.'

Ernst laid out what Sindhi Camp's Bhairavi had said to him, without mentioning what Goddess Bhairavi did to him.

'Sassoon is supplying our fucked-grade, stainless steel pipes to your reprocessing plant. Phoenix is a nuclear disaster waiting to happen.'

'Are you sure?'

'Yes.'

'Why? Why intentionally supply pipes with the wrong specs?'

Ernst then told Tufan what he had learned from Princess Kirti. About Phoenix. About the Seth. About the murders, and how the Law of Unintended Consequences worked. About PL 480 food aid. And how India works.

After letting it all sink in, the Smiling Buddha stared past the bellowing white curtains and said, 'No one is born Marxist, Ernestji. But you can see why I became one.'

'Yes,' Ernst said.

47

Atomic Ganesh

They're already slain by me,
They have already died,
Just be my instrument,
The archer by my side.
—*Lord Krishna to Prince Arjun*

Major Punjabi had urged Ernst to deliver the pipes at his earliest convenience. He wanted them thin, not thick.

Thin! Making it easier for radioactive nitric acid to eat through. The dimensions were, therefore, crucial enough for even an Adam Sassoon to remember; 'Thirty-one millimetre, I believe?'

Intentionally thin, fucked-grade, stainless steel pipes to sabotage a nuclear reprocessing plant; making sure the pipes corrode at their earliest convenience. The nitric acid eats through and spills dissolved plutonium into the open, along with the rest of Bhabha's salad oil. On the bright side, Ernst would be long gone before Bombay lit up like Jhama Sweetmeats' neon—bright enough for all to see, not just the blind. He was going back to Berlin after thirty years. Maybe the Jüdische Krankenhaus would put him up in his father's room. It made him want to curl up on the back seat of the one-eyed Fiat.

~

Tufan of course failed to pull off a meeting with Bhabha. Even playing the illness card got nowhere. Gods have other things on their minds. Ernst would have picked up the phone, but knew with Bhabha the European thing wouldn't fly either. So he tore up that card too, and wrote a letter instead. Tufan promised to sneak it into Bhabha's In-tray. He would do that, he assured, and one thing more.

'The Phoenix Reprocessing Plant inauguration is this Sunday. You need to get invited as VIP. Bhabha will be there. See? Resolved. Why didn't I think of it earlier?' The old Tufan was back.

Be that as it may, Ernst didn't have the heart to tell him, it didn't matter. He was leaving for West Berlin that same Sunday. The ticket was in his pocket.

'Let's focus on the letter.'

The letter laid out what Sassoon did. Having spelt it out at length, in detail, Ernst had no more regrets about having turned a blind eye. Letting things slide. Regrets by and large were a waste of time anyway, and did nothing to save one from rebirth as a sow. Besides, any and all regrets over defective pipes and upcoming nuclear events were subservient to more immediate sorrows. That over the dying Tufan, his dead nephew, and over that dead fool, Willie. In turn, subservient to sorrow over Kirti. He should have rejoiced for Kirti, but because he was a man, he couldn't. Because he was a needy man, his sorrow over Kirti was subservient to that over Kirti's sister. Only Salim Ali could top that sorrow; he even managed to wriggle into nightmares past Ernst's father, Schwester Ingrid and the Cold Pilger.

And because Ernst was a little man, his sorrow over Salim Ali was subservient to that over cancer. It was a part of life, yes, but the kind of life he refused to accept—the fever, the blood he coughed up on his handkerchief, the plugged arsehole. So he planned to fight, and do it on his own turf.

Come Sunday, he would leave and take the fight to the Jüdische Krankenhaus in Wedding, West Berlin; it still felt strange. calling it West Berlin. The aeroplane ticket was in his pocket, paid for from Sassoon's zeroes and through Salim Ali's free and illegal use of Tufan's shop floor. What would happen if they found out? Nothing. He was gone one way or the other, and he couldn't wait to go. Salim Ali's crew was welcome to the Goregaon workshop. They could go ahead turn it into a worker's cooperative. He'd love to see that play out.

Mohan Driver did some hard math. If Ernst wanted to catch his 3 a.m. Air India out, he had to be at the Santa Cruz Airport around midnight. Meaning, leave Colaba no later than 8 p.m. Why? Well, because it was Bombay on a weekday. Furthermore, this was Ganesh Immersion Week. When Bombaywallahs took to the streets with their earthen Ganesh statues and cast them out to sea in a not-so-ancient ritual, less than a century old. This particular week, Lord Ganesh rode the city like his bitch. With Bhabha not yet having responded to his letter, a plane to catch that evening, and the Elephant God running amok in Bombay—best remain in bed, then straight to Santa Cruz Airport and the hell out of here.

So on Sunday morning when he instructed Mohan Driver to first drive all the way to AEET instead, a look of martyrdom crept into the driver's eyes. Seated at the back, the heat closed around Ernst. His jacket felt like one of the jute gunny bags they saw strewn by the roadside when they had passed Masjid Bandar's wholesale spice market.

~

Seeing him in a jacket, Mohan Driver had done a double take. Understandable. Yes, the man was going to Europe, but why couldn't he have worn the damn thing after boarding the bleddy plane? Struggling out from it, Ernst placed the jacket on his lap. It felt like climbing out from a heated pool. By now, the suburbs were in complete thrall to Lord Ganesh. Heavy-duty crowds billowed on either side of Trombay Road bringing the world to a standstill.

The crawl allowed Mohan Driver to fart at will and wax eloquent—the martyr gone and the Hindu back in charge. 'Only God knows how old this festival is,' he said, shifting his weight from left to right cheek. Ernst worked the crank to try lower his window in time, but it was stuck. 'Easily thousands of years, and celebrated globally. They say the Atomic Ganesh is the size of an atom bomb.'

'It's barely a hundred years old. And, celebrated globally? Since when?'

Mohan Driver tried to stare Ernst down through the rear-view mirror and Ernst was glad things were back to normal. He had been worried leaving behind the wreck Mohan Driver became after Princess Kirti surrendered her clitoris to Bahuchara Ma.

He owed Princess Kirti. There were too many variables around Arjun's death. The equation remained unsolved even after applying the Law of Unintended Consequences, until Princess Kirti provided the constant—PL 480. It helped solve the equation; just that Ernst didn't care so much anymore. The only thing that mattered was the fire burning him from the inside, and his getting to West Berlin in time to put it out. Going anywhere for anything else, would go nowhere.

Then there was the gunny bag at his feet. He reached into it to touch the box-like thingy with its jumble of wires Komal Guruji had surrendered. When holding it for the first time, the box-like thingy in the gunny bag had screamed, *Phoren*!

Salim Ali looked down from Ernst's shoulder at the technological marvel. 'For you,' he said. 'From Arjun.'

'Still think all Westerners are the same?'

'Yes, but you aren't one,' Salim Ali said before disappearing, not contrite at all.

~

They could see assorted festivities underway on the cricket field just before the North Gate—a Ferris wheel, food stalls, games and a stage for Atomic Ganesh. Mohan Driver looked distracted. 'Unnecessary delay, coming here. Salim Mian was supposed to organise entourage for your airport departure. Now I have to do it, but when? Aarti arrangements, garlands, sweets, whatnot. Where's the time?'

'Are you out of your mind? You will do none of that. Just drive me to the airport in the evening.'

'You have a problem with proper procedure, Sa'ab,' Mohan Driver said, 'take it up with Parvatibai.' Seeing someone off at the International airport and doing the aarti ceremony at the departure gate in full public view, was a prestigious ritual that gave a superior status to the one leaving for overseas, and those seeing him off. Only a white man would be selfish enough to deny that to friends, family, and employees.

Mohan Driver approached a formation of grey Atomic Energy buses lined along the cricket grounds' perimeter. The first two had a VIP placard stuck to the front, side window. He stopped and parked right in front of the VIP buses as if daring someone.

The cricket grounds were a raging carnival with festivities built around the covered pitch. Mohan Driver was right. The Atomic Ganesh statue was gigantic—an enormous, pink baby with an elephant head, taking up the entire stage, seated cross-legged in his cute, little dhoti. After the festivities, it would be taken to the sea for immersion. Looking at its size, one wondered how. While Atomic Ganesh waited for its devotees, the inaugurated nuclear reprocessing plant waited for a VIP tour the other side of North Gate.

Both events made possible, thanks to India's Oppenheimer, Dr. Homi J. Bhabha—father of Atomic India with the film star looks. The man could take on anything. Ernst glanced at the gunny bag at his feet. Almost anything.

~

Important people were coming out of Mercedes and Impalas to congregate around the VIP buses. Paranjpe, Atomic Energy's shy Purchase Manager, was attending to the august gathering. The absent Bhabha's presence though was everywhere, and it ignored Ernst completely. No question, the man hadn't looked at his In-Tray. If he had, he hadn't read Ernst's letter. If he did, he had dismissed it.

Ernst wriggled to put his jacket on and he was back in a sauna, fully clothed. He did not feel well. Mohan Driver was right that first time. They shouldn't have come here. He was melting. Seeing Ernst's sweat-sodden jacket, Sassoon raised an august eyebrow from amidst the circle of VIPs, Major Punjabi to his right. Maybe, it was the jacket or could be Ernst's face gone grey—allowing Sassoon an inside glimpse. Or maybe it was seeing Ernst on the right side of the VIP cordon with the wrong credentials.

The Seth too was present, and Ernst waved at him out of habit. Sethji returned a cold stare; far cry from the days they would sit thigh-to-thigh on the velveteen divan on the Golf Club verandah. It surprised Ernst to find he didn't shrivel. He felt buoyed instead. It was like he finally accomplished something.

Venky Iyer showed up, and stood to Sassoon's left. Deputy Commissioner Jahagirdar took his position next to Sethji. While Jahagirdar's role as the Seth's police dog was only natural, his presence amongst VIPs was the real reflection of his status. Moral of the story: get your hands dirty, keep your shoes clean, and important people will bring you along like a pet dog. Following his master's lead, the police dog locked eyes with Ernst.

How exhilarating was it, Goddess Bhairavi had asked, to know, now that he had cancer, no one could harm him anymore? To no longer be afraid of anyone. He wanted to tell her he didn't feel all that exhilarated. Just tired. It was overwhelming, this drop in energy and it made him buckle inside. The way Sethji and the Deputy Commissioner smiled, Ernst suspected they could see him crumble and they approved.

Like Sassoon, Mohan Driver too gave Ernst's jacket a long, lingering look. One couldn't get much past him. 'Sa'ab,' he said, 'do you remember the last time you wore that jacket? I was there to take you home.'

Yes. It was the day Sassoon had fired him. They both looked over to the great man, holding court by the VIP bus.

'You are wearing this jacket for the first time since then,' Mohan Driver said. 'Means, today you are unstoppable. Now, I understand.'

Mohan Driver came across to Ernst's side with the packet of red powder he had brought for his Atomic Ganesh darshan.

'They are already slain by me, they have already died,' he recited in Sanskrit from the *Bhagavad Gita*, dotting an auspicious red tilak on Ernst's forehead.

'Follow after me in the car,' Ernst said, escaping into the bus before the man pulled a full-blown Krishna on him.

'They won't let me through the gates, Sa'ab! Army, after all.'

'They let China in, didn't they? Find a way.'

48

The Pimp

As Shiva twisted and turned, leapt and whirled,
the age of Kalki came to its predicted end.
—*Gore Vidal's Kalki*

Ernst noticed the small tent outside the Phoenix Nuclear Reprocessing
Plant as the bus came in. More for show than any real protection
from the sun. It was stacked high with refreshments to give the VIP
tour a proper feel.

There was upturned soil around the tent pegs, but also around
the edges along the verge, piled into knee-high dirt pyramids. A
scatter of leaves lay collected at their base—swept there by some
cleaning crew. Tobi Basar had railed against the contamination
of soil around the CIRUS nuclear reactor. There was a lot of
digging evident in the circular gardens around the reactor, and
around the artificial ponds. Non-union, Lambadi tribals would
have done the digging—Bhabha's canaries. His Brahmin engineers
could use the women to assess pipe corrosion without damaging
themselves. The gypsies weren't around today, but their children
ran on the grass, playing barefoot. A slow burn baked through
Ernst's plimsoles. He reminded himself not to pack them for the
trip to West Berlin.

Instead of going into the reprocessing plant, the VIPs were first
ushered inside the insufficient tent. Marinating in the heat, they
sized up the enclosure. Paranjpe came by. He looked miserable in

the spotlight and had an announcement to make. 'While inside is not allowed, I am very glad to explain the completely indigenous reprocessing process to you, right here, in person. We have chalkboard for your benefit.'

'What do you mean, inside is not allowed?' someone asked. 'This is supposed to be a tour of the inside.'

'Minor repair work underway to replace some defective pipes, that's all. Nothing serious.'

'In that case, show us around.'

'Not necessary, Sir. Let's kindly begin.'

Damn. Bhabha had read his letter, after all. Ernst began breathing easier. He would have read it sometime over the past few hours; too late to cancel the VIP event. So they just cancelled the tour.

'What will you do with the defective pipes?' Ernst asked.

Paranjpe must have sensed danger. There were stories doing the rounds that discarded pipes from nuclear reactors were being sold in Bombay's second hand markets.

'Stored in deep underground concrete facilities in accordance with IAEA guidelines. We brook no deviation.'

As the world knew, they also didn't brook the IAEA.

'But this nuclear facility is not open to international inspection.'

Paranjpe, however, was in too much agony for Ernst to try persist. Besides, Ernst felt sickly from the torpid humidity; a taste of real illness making him giddy. He needed to sit down and only looking every now and then towards Adam Sassoon kept him going. He was sick from too many people around him, ill from what was within him and wanted out so badly it flashed like neon on his forehead; probably just fever.

There was also this strange sense of déjà vu and Ernst found himself sitting on Waller's operating table for a check-up. The emotion was strong enough to conjure up the oily, glandular, snake smells from Waller's surgery. Two Lambadi kids ran by, and one had a snakeskin wrapped around her tiny waist, the brown strip of sloughed scales trailing behind like a streamer while she chased another girl across the contaminated lawn, both shrieking with laughter.

~

Mohan Driver stood at the curb; allowed past a lax, Ganesh-struck North Gate. He looked at his watch. The one-eyed Fiat gave Ernst an accusing look. So did Johnny Walker, standing next to Mohan Driver and staring with a distinct lack of respect.

In the distance, a familiar, air-conditioned Ambassador drove away and up Central Avenue, towards North Gate. Dr. Bhabha departing, or distancing himself from a reprocessing plant destined to leak like a sieve; depending on how one looked at it. It tickled no end that Bhabha hadn't just driven away from the likes of Sethji and even Adam Sassoon. He didn't even bother to show up and say hello. There's a Vedic construct along the lines: however big your dick, someone else is bigger.

Sassoon did not appear pleased having the smaller dick. He walked into the open tent to take an empty folding chair and whatever shade he could grab. Going up to him, Ernst decided against being the bigger man.

'Those are your pipes in there, Adam, the ones being replaced,' Ernst said. 'The ones you had us draw. I warned you they were the wrong specs. You still went ahead.'

'Don't recall you refusing the money, old chap. You did cash the cheque, didn't you?'

'Bhabha knows what you've done. You're going to jail for this.'

'You mean like the Deputy Commissioner, for shooting your darkie?'

Ice in the veins. Ice in the veins is what differentiates the Chosen People from others. Being Jewish has nothing to do with it. Sassoon turned to Punjabi. 'When's the bloody car coming? I'm not taking that bus again.'

Meanwhile, Jack Hanson stood by the tent smiling at one and all, including the Seth—already seated and panting, one leg tucked under while the other oscillated. Sitting arm's length from each other, Sassoon and the Seth remained separated by a chasm. The dripping bania looked like a fish out of water. When Ernst caught him peering at Bhairavi's swastik pendant around his neck, he said, 'No Sethji, it's not one of yours. This one's real gold.'

The Seth's face clogged up, and Ernst was Indian enough by now to feel the need for background music. *Come September* would be perfect.

Sassoon too appeared tetchy, so Ernst asked, 'Bored? Why not the two of you chat? Pass time?'

The British upper classes can castrate you with just a look. Ernst continued as if there was no danger of that happening, as if there was no social divide at all. Somewhat like a court jester taking down the king.

'Go on,' he urged Sassoon, 'there must be something you can say to the Seth. After all, he owns you.'

Those in the insufficient tent looked around to see what just happened, because at that moment, Lord Shiva opened his third eye and reduced the world to ash.

In the new world that came about, a very pukka Adam Sassoon turned to an Indian bania for instruction.

~

The tent wore a puzzled look. So did Sassoon. Maybe, he realised what was happening here. Saw what Mohan Driver had seen in Ernst wearing a jacket for the first time in twenty-six years.

'At ten thousand dollars, I have to be the Seth's smallest debtor,' Ernst announced. 'At five crores, what's that, fifty million dollars, you've got to be his biggest. He owns you, Adam.'

Adam Sassoon glanced at his Rolex. Then donned his best, British, upper class expression and got up.

'Sit,' the Seth said.

The great man obeyed. He started to look spent—an isotope with not much of a half life. A couple of folding chairs away, Hanson flopped into one with a satisfied grunt. He too wasn't going anywhere.

The urbane Deputy Commissioner, still there on hand, must have decided, whatever was going on here, that civility be maintained. He barked in Marathi to Johnny Walker who hurried up to where the refreshments were laid out. He brought back marble-stop lemonade bottles to distribute and out of habit, white folk came first, including with some difficulty, Ernst. Handed two of them, Adam Sassoon looked confused and reached across the divide to pass one over to the Seth. Samosas came next, followed by napkins and a flurry of pops, as thumbs plunged down at marbles.

The lemonade did wonders and a spirit of improvisation took over. Sassoon's tan stopped glowing for a bit, Hanson went from red to pink, and the Seth burped like a baby with colic. Ernst felt the chill roar down his oesophagus in a racing car. The Deputy Commissioner glowered at him like weapon-grade plutonium. Iyer took a small sip. He was more like Paranjpe today than his usual, heaven-born ICS self—trying hard to blend into the background and disappear.

'All those zeroes in the cheque you gave me,' said Ernst, 'they belong to the Seth. Like you do. Sethji was bribing me through you for just one thing, and one thing alone. Get Salim Ali to return what that kid Arjun took from the American enclosure. It wasn't your money I received. Your money took off with the British. Everything you have here, belongs to the Seth.'

Sethji looked embarrassed. Do stop, he seemed to say; never did like discussing the one thing that mattered most to him. Ernst persisted.

'India is Indian-owned these days, Adam. Your time's up. So you decided to sell your nice Anglicised name to someone like the Seth, and become his pimp.'

~

'How did you learn?' Hanson asked. 'About these jokers?'

Americans. No respecting anyone. Ernst loved that.

'How? Because I found myself back in Adam's good books for no good reason, that's how. Not only that, we became friends again. Not just friends, we were back to being brothers-in-arms after twenty-six years. When I needed money, my workshop received an order to draw pipes. Lots and lots of pipes—the ones they are busy replacing in there right now. With the pipes came money. Lots of it. And when I was dumb enough to wear a swastik to a synagogue, Adam did the same in a spectacular show of support. Like brothers-in-arms. In return for all this, he asked for just one thing. For Salim Ali to return what they took from your compound.'

'Brothers-in-arms. That's bad?' Hanson asked.

'It's not. Just that the swastik he put around his neck was the same cheap, gold-plated coin the Seth hands out to his flunkies.

Adam Sassoon has no dealings with the Seth. How did he get it? More importantly, when was the last time a white man wearing a Rolex kept a cheap, Hindu trinket on his person? If you check his breast pocket right now, it's probably still there. Even I got rid of mine. The Seth and Adam don't even acknowledge each other in public, let alone talk. Why would he keep it?'

Adam Sassoon touched his breast pocket.

~

'Why for all this anger, Mr. Ernestji?' the Seth asked. 'You were one of us. What happened?'

Before replying, Ernst first thanked Jagannath, and Govinda, then Krishna—same difference—for his cancer. He then thanked Goddess Bhairavi for removing the fog of maya from before his eyes. It was like having one's cataract removed. Bhairavi was right. If he didn't feel like death already, he would feel exhilarated.

'Pillow talk, Sethji. That's what happened. But you know the story already. How a caddie-boy's been buggering your Lala, and how Willie was buggering the caddie-boy. The smitten Lala went whispered your PL 480 secrets to the caddie-boy, who whispered them to Willie. Willie insults you, you have him fired. When he blackmails you, you have him killed. Everything goes back to normal so you can sit here and ask me, why for all this anger?'

The Indian sun shone through the tent with a contempt reserved for white people. Sassoon usually tanned well, but went radioactive red. Indians weren't being spared either, and the Seth's fat melted in big glistening drops, straight off his face. Ernst was burning up and feeling impervious at the same time.

'Your pimp Sassoon over here, took care of Willie for you. Always considerate, ever the brother-in-arms, Adam sent his car to pick up Willie and take him to his caddie-boy at the Protection Home. Dropped him off in front of a moving truck instead.'

Adam Sassoon touched his breast pocket again.

'Kirti the caddie-boy told me what America does with its PL 480 rupees. The money India pays out, for what's definitely not food aid. The Americans can't take the money out of the country.

Rupees are useless outside India. So they use it to pay off the Seth for everything he does for them. Every month they buy up hundreds of thousands of overpriced textbooks they don't need. Besides being India's biggest gold smuggler, the Seth is also the country's largest textbook publisher. He's a textbook case of how many ways an Indian can screw his country. As for the Americans, it's a hat trick: feed, educate, and fuck India at the same time.'

Jack Hanson looked at the Seth. The Seth looked at Sassoon. Having nowhere to go, Sassoon stared at Iyer. To be ill is to be disorderly in your mind as well. Nevertheless, seeing the four of them, Ernst was reminded of an ancient symbol of the Eternal Cycle—an insect caught in a frog's mouth, the frog in a snake's fangs, the snake gathered by a pouncing eagle. All the archetypes in one motif and under one tent.

The American eagle looked impressed and bypassed the Indian snake to ask the Baghdadi frog, 'Man's dying of cancer and still refuses to let go. The hell did you do to him?'

Dying? Sassoon didn't appear concerned as much as curious. He still didn't know about the cancer. Hanson on the other hand, knew everything about everyone. 'It's this American desire to be loved,' Tufan had deduced.

The mere mention of his illness however, and Ernst found himself perched once again on Waller's operating table, reliving all the sights and smells from his surgery. The tang of snake urine was like smelling salts and that brought him back to the tent with a start.

'What's that smell?' Jack Hanson asked.

~

Ernst signalled Mohan Driver who pointed to his watch—a reproachful Krishna. He, however, hefted the gunny bag from the one-eyed Fiat to bring it over.

'Three-thirty already,' Mohan Driver muttered, lowering it to the ground. 'You decide, Sa'ab, if you want to catch that plane. Up to you.'

Ernst touched the gunny bag with his shoe. 'This is why,' he said to the archetypes, 'some poor truck driver was burnt to a crisp, his lover Arjun stabbed, Salim Ali shot, and Willie thrown before a truck.'

He dug into the jute bag to drag out the phoren thingy with wires sticking out from everywhere. It was an effort, and seeing what emerged, the zoo of ancient archetypes hiccupped as one.

'I'm told this is a Krypton-85 gas detector. The one stolen from the American compound. Very fancy, very expensive, very American. General Electric. Yours, I believe, Jack.'

Hanson remained seated and stared at the thingy—an estranged parent dying to reach out and not knowing how.

Ernst pointed at the tall smokestack extending into the sky from the reprocessing plant.

'The Indian reprocessing plant emits its secrets from that smokestack, and this American box smells them out.

'I learnt that with this thingy, the Americans sniff out the exact purity of plutonium being produced and can tell when it hits weapon-grade. No need for spy satellites if one of these is in play. Who can blame them for using it to sniff out what India's up to? They couldn't install it within India's nuclear facility, though I don't see why not. But America owns the Seth, who owns Sassoon, who owns Iyer, who runs Fertilisers, and there we have it. It is accurate up to five kilometres and the Fertilisers plant is within that radius. It had to be kept a secret, of course. Only Hanson's Chemerica was permitted into the enclosure where it was installed. No Indians allowed and that's fine with them. Even after Independence. Told to go fuck off, they go, yes Sirji.

'Then a Sikh truck driver in love, goes steals the damn thing. He'd probably do anything his petite, porcelain doll asked him to do. Must have climbed into the American enclosure with impunity. A Sikh would do that. He steals and passes the gas detector to Arjun—his porcelain doll. The kid who got stabbed. The one who dumped a slumlord for the truck driver. Why, who knows. There's this thing between Sikh truck drivers and young, Chinese-looking boys, so maybe I don't want to know. Anyway, they're both dead because of this. Your people had approached the slumlord, Chhote Bhai, to get back the stolen gas detector from his Arjun. Arjun was Chhote Bhai's lover. But once Chhote Bhai learnt about him and the Sikh, it was over for Arjun, and you were no closer to getting this back.'

Ernst let the heavy Krypton-45 gas detector drop with a thud. Hanson almost jumped off his seat.

The silence was total. One could hear the Atomic Ganesh festivities in the distance. He felt the phlegm tickle his throat and hawked into his handkerchief. He knew there would be blood—no need to check. More than ever, solitude was becoming his preferred state. He wanted to lock himself inside the Jüdische Krankenhaus like Schwester Ingrid. He had to get there first though, past this bunch, and past the Elephant God marauding the streets.

'With Arjun dead and the Krypton gas detector still missing, you people guessed right and came after Salim Ali. Came to me with money and friendship in return for just one thing. Have Salim Ali, the darkie, return the gas detector. You even tried running him over with a truck the same way you did with Willie. Why? Was it frustration, or to scare him? Or just for the fun of it? Salim Ali being a lower caste, Muslim convert made it more of a blood sport than a distasteful task. His colour allows Adam that extra disdain.'

Ernst hawked again, handkerchief to mouth.

'Then Arjun's mother goes whispers in Salim Ali's ear. Tells him about Chhote Bhai, and Arjun, and why Arjun died the way he did. Talk about unintended consequences. Salim Ali hears her out, then goes guts Chhote Bhai to end up in prison. My guy is done for, but there's an upside for you. At least now you can third degree the little fella to get at the gas detector. Except that, Willie stormed the police station and ended up humiliating your police dog, our trigger-happy Deputy Commissioner.'

DCP Jahagirdar smiled at Ernst—no offense taken. Ernst smiled back.

'Knowing Commissioner Jahagirdar, someone had to pay, and it ended up being my Salim Ali. Your darkie.'

He looked at Sassoon.

'Darkie this, and darkie that. What's it about a Salim Ali that gets your goat? He was top of his class at IIT, Bombay. He came out of the slums to become one of the finest engineers I know. And unlike you or me, he didn't owe anyone, anything. But he was a damn Muslim to the Indians, and a darkie to you. Not an engineer from IIT, but a stray dog in a mad city. Now, he's dead. What do I do with him gone? Tell me, you racist prick. What do I do?'

Jack Hanson shot up from his folding chair. His tone was emphatic. 'I wasn't involved in the crap these two pulled. I liked the little fella. You know that.'

'I know,' Ernst said. 'I also know your grief over Arjun was genuine. Americans never like to see the consequences of what they wreak. Upsets you being around when that happens. Yes, I saw how much it upset you.'

Ernst gave the Krypton-85 gas detector a friendly kick. Hanson flinched. Ernst offered him a smile to compensate. 'The ultimate puppeteer,' Ernst said. 'America may not win every time, but everyone else must lose. India cannot go ahead with its nuclear program. That's final, as far as America is concerned. So you pay your Indian lackeys to sabotage Phoenix. What was it Dr. Ramanna said? Yes, pulling a Nichols. He didn't trust you, did he? Knew you'd try do Bhabha in, the way your friend Kenneth Nichols screwed Oppenheimer. In your case, by getting fucked-grade pipes supplied to Bhabha's plutonium reprocessing plant. Guaranteeing a nuclear disaster. Imagine what happens to all those people you hand out biscuits and loose change to every day. But you won't have to see it because you won't be here when it happens. Besides, you're one of the good guys, so it's okay.'

49

Memento Mori

Approach me, stranger. Nothing in my story
should startle you. Your flesh has known it.
I just remind you. I'm Memento Mori.
                                    —*Rondeno*

The tent was useless against the sun and helpless against humidity. The eagle, snake and frog were getting listless by the second. The insect had escaped. An FCC station wagon had crawled up and Iyer crawled in.

Ernst noticed the Marathi labour standing by the curb. Next to them, Johnny Walker stood out in his uniform with sidearm. Close by, a Tata truck touching bumpers with the one-eyed Fiat. Mohan Driver continued being ominous—4 p.m. already.

The Seth's sodden kurta competed with Ernst's soaked jacket. Seth Jamunadas appeared as uncomfortable seeing him wear a jacket, as he would feel wearing one. To the Seth's right, the Deputy Commissioner was outgrowing his St. Stephen's College persona. He issued a guttural instruction in Marathi to Johnny Walker who walked up—somewhat unsure about approaching someone white, who had slapped him once already.

'We must move now?'

'You asking, or telling me?'

The Marathi labour was already on the move, leaving Johnny Walker to tentatively shove at Ernst under the Deputy Commissioner's watchful eye. The labourers formed a relay line from the waiting truck next to Mohan Driver, weaving into the Phoenix annexe through the front entrance. It looked like a guard of honour for a reluctant Ernst being goaded into the Phoenix building. The last thing he wanted was to get any closer to the invisible fires burning in there.

Then, shiny bits and pieces, stainless steel flanges and pipes—still dripping—started coming out over the human conveyer belt, now less a guard of honour and more like an irradiated, desi, Ho Chi Minh trail. The sabotage discovered, Bhabha's AEET was busy cleaning up. Finger pointing would come next. His Steiger Engineering logo stamped around the pipe threadings read, 'German-made', in case of any doubt whom to blame. The stainless steel pipes shone under the sun and probably glowed in the dark. He was tempted to have Mohan Driver move the one-eyed Fiat as far down the road as possible.

Johnny Walker started to get pushy, what with the Deputy Commissioner providing non-verbal encouragement—a bob of the head, the flick of an eyebrow. Sethji watched the shoving and pushing from the entrance.

'Where will they bury those pipes?' Ernst asked a Paranjpe trying to be invisible in plain view. The Seth must have heard, because he looked at Ernst as if at a complete moron. It dawned that yes, for all the enlightenment from Andhi Ma and the education imparted by Goddess Bhairavi, he was still a moron. Just as, for all his wealth, the Seth remained a cheap fuck.

'You are not burying them at all, are you?' Ernst asked.

Paranjpe squirmed and managed to go invisible, leaving the floor to his overlord.

'Do they look defective to you, Mr. Ernestji?' the Seth asked. 'They may not be for use here, but for elsewhere, they are first class. You should know. They are yours, after all. Besides, too many to just throw away. Such wastage would be unforgivable. This is not Europe or America where you use once, then recklessly discard.'

'They're radioactive. They have been carrying a plutonium-uranium solution. Does Atomic Energy know you plan to resell them?'

'The correct question, Mr. Ernestji, is do they care?'

'Do those men know what they're handling?'

'Once again, what do they care?'

He had a point. It was an established fact what you couldn't see, wouldn't hurt.

'You should go inside,' the Seth suggested.

Johnny Walker crowded Ernst, his sweaty body pressing the Seth's invitation. From behind them, Mohan Driver tapped at his watch. Searching around for Hanson, Ernst found the Texan staring at the desi Viet Minh carrying radioactive pipes. He waited for Hanson to say something. Do something.

Hanson stared for a bit more, just making sure what he thought he was witnessing, was what he was actually witnessing. Then his eyes glazed. He backed off from the radioactive pipes, from the Indians lugging them with bare hands, and from India. He did not stop until safe in an American frame of mind. Just then, Adam Sassoon's silver Mercedes rolled up and parked behind the truck. Sassoon's face lit up like a full moon.

~

If Adam Sassoon looked distracted all of a sudden, that's because the world stopped for him when Goddess Bhairavi stepped out from his Mercedes Benz. Ernst knew how that must feel.

Looking at her, Sassoon appeared stoked after what must have been a terrible day. She seemed to have an effect on Johnny Walker too, who froze, allowing Ernst to wriggle free. Ernst saw Hanson walk rapidly to where the Krypton-85 gas detector lay. He seemed to have recovered from the shock seeing actual human beings handle radioactive pipes with their bare hands.

Ernst beat him to it. Approaching the gas detector, he aimed and kicked. He kicked it again like a football, his eyes on the Texan, who flinched on cue.

'You need the readings, don't you?' Ernst asked him. 'As justification for sabotaging a nuclear facility? Or someone could pull a Nichols on you. Is that why you wanted it back so badly?'

Nothing Hanson said would have made any difference so Ernst kicked again, harder. He kept kicking and even in his enfeebled state those were serious kicks. He kept at it—kicking away at the Krypton-85 gas detector—and maybe he remembered Chhote Bhai slapping the young Arjun demanding: you bleddy well hand it over. Or, it could be the gorilla with those sharp scissors and orders to kill. Maybe, it was on behalf of Salim Ali that he kicked so hard, or could be for the country that had taken him in, no questions asked, but he kept kicking and wouldn't stop.

No one stepped up to end what could easily be stopped by shoving aside an ill, old Jew gone mad, whose loose shirt billowed in the non-existent breeze as he kicked away at an inanimate object. Johnny Walker grabbed at him only after he was done with the dead machinery. The exhausted Ernst saw Hanson beckon the policeman as if he was running the show. He pointed to Ernst and then at the Phoenix building.

'Are you very worried, Mr. Ernest,' asked Johnny Walker, reading his mind, 'that if you go inside, you may not come out?'

Very worried? He wouldn't go that far, but he did see himself all lit up and settling in a stainless steel vessel brimming with Bhabha's radioactive, Italian salad dressing. Cancer eating away his insides and he had problems with a quick ending? For the second time in a few days, Johnny Walker looked more saviour than villain. He should place his arms around the policeman's shoulders and stroll in to be reprocessed.

But there was that oily smell again, and this time he noticed it coming from the dirt pyramids, lining the verge as they came closer to the elongated building. It again triggered images from Waller's surgery. It was the same musky smell of snakes. Noon heat, earth piled into pyramids, and upturned mud everywhere. Leaves too, collected into piles and perfect for hiding from the sun. Ernst stepped to the edge of a pile like Waller would, and heard a rustle. Waller would have poked in there to bring out a garden-variety snake and pin it down with his stick. Instead, Ernst used his foot to scatter the leaves.

Johnny Walker didn't notice the danger, too busy shouting in Marathi. Ernst made out a demand for fucking instructions on what to do with this old coot once inside the Phoenix building. Did that fucking Paranjpe take him—Johnny Walker—to be a nuclear scientist? How to dispose off the bhenchod?

Paranjpe turned visible to address the issue, and it was with a look of deep regret. The look made it clear he would never have been party to any of this, if not for the money.

He signalled for Johnny Walker to follow him and the policeman shoved again at Ernst who stumbled against the leaves, scattering them some more. When Johnny Walker stepped on the leaves behind him, the snake that slithered out was just under four foot, enough to strike terror. Ernst recognised the beautifully ornamented, olive-brown back from Waller's glass vitrines. Ill and tired and weak and feverish, he took it to be a Bandied Racer, or that's what Waller called Sion Hospital's harmless rat snakes.

Resting peacefully moments ago, camouflaged within dead leaves, the snake looked pissed. And what with the desi Ho Chi Minh Trail confusing it further with shuffling feet, its triangular head swelled and one could easily mistake the large nostrils for eyes. Forming an S, it raised itself to almost half its length, hissing. Ernst didn't know a snake could hiss this loud, but did know rat snakes were harmless. So he remained calm even after it lifted itself and flew at Johnny Walker, who squealed like a pig seeing it go straight for his leg. Ernst remembered how Waller once pinned a startled rat snake in the hospital compound, pinched it from just behind its neck and held the whipping reptile with panache. Nothing to it, he had said, and people ran. For once, Ernst wished the old bastard were around.

The snake went for Johnny Walker's leg with jaws wide open to 180 degrees. Without thinking, Ernst grabbed its tail as it flew and yanked at it hard, but not before the two-inch fangs sank into Johnny Walker's calf. Tail in hand, Ernst twirled it for want of a better resolution, ripping the snake off the trouser leg. He could hear the terrified reptile hiss, its pinkish-green tongue smelling the air.

Everything came to a standstill and he saw the Seth freeze. Hanson too, and Sassoon seemed to forget he was keeping a Goddess waiting. As for the Deputy Commissioner, he could be watching a movie. And whether he meant to or not, whether accidental or after all those years, whether without thinking or to make a long overdue point like with the jacket, Ernst aimed for Adam Sassoon before letting go.

Sassoon's forearm rose to deflect the wriggly arrow, snagging it instead, the fangs burying deep into royal, Baghdadi skin. The four feet of plump, eel-like, brown muscle flailed as the triangular head chomped down. Like so many others that day, the snake too must have decided this was the last straw, because it didn't let go even with Sassoon tugging hard while keeping his royal head together, refusing to yell or behave in any way like that darkie screaming from behind Ernst.

Turns out, Johnny Walker decided he was going to die. Dr. Waller had once explained how people bitten by harmless snakes develop psychosomatic symptoms even when no venom had been injected. Johnny Walker being case in point—hyperventilating, with his hands and feet in spasms. By now, he had also developed the clammy hue one associated with a slowing heart rate. When the Deputy Commissioner ripped off Johnny Walker's trouser leg a vital few minutes later, the area around the snakebite was discoloured and swollen. There was blistering around the bite—like little flowers they were, those blisters, and already beginning to go up his leg in a straight line. The Deputy Commissioner was yelling—all Indian now, the strict discipline over 'V's and 'W's shot to hell, and being German, Ernst could empathise.

'Vere's the bhenchod jeep?'

Staring at the little red flowers creep up Johnny Walker's leg it dawned on Ernst that maybe, just maybe, this wasn't psychosomatic and that wasn't a rat snake. He may have chucked a Russell's Viper at Adam Sassoon.

~

Mohan Driver called out from behind the stalled human conveyor belt of radioactive pipes. He pointed at a Tempo pulling up next to the ticking Tata. It carried a full load of Mallus.

The Malayalee Ocean poured on the pavement. Ernst recognised his Goregaon workshop staff, and they appeared all prepared for a Santa Cruz send-off for their boss; ready with the garlands, the packet of red powder for dotting his forehead, the Rolleiflex camera. He wanted to tell them he wasn't even packed.

The Malayalee Ocean also served a more immediate purpose. It started roaring in testosterone-laden Malayalam, confusing the Deputy Commissioner who took cover behind the police jeep that showed up to rush Johnny Walker to the Haffkine Institute for polyvalent antivenom. It was the one thing that did the trick when it came to Russell's Vipers and there was only one place in Bombay you could get it. Haffkine was a good ten to fifteen minutes south from Sion without traffic.

All this time, Ernst's stumbling around, holding himself up like a wilted flower. He barely managed to walk up to Jack Hanson. Squinting at the giant American, and on behalf of Salim Ali and every other Indian, he said, 'You fucking bhenchod.' Then, he went slumped against Mohan Driver.

Sassoon on his part, was laid out on the lawn and dead still. The Russell's Viper had detached itself to make loud hissing noises and scare the shit out of everyone, before slithering away into the grass. The great man needed immediate medical attention and Goddess Bhairavi was seen hurrying towards the supine King of the Jews, even as the Deputy Commissioner's task force came up to remove him to the jeep leaving for Haffkine right away. Bitten on the arm, Sassoon had even less time than Johnny Walker if he were to make it.

Mohan Driver took the stumbling Ernst to the one-eyed Fiat and tried shoving him in. Not easy, because Ernst kept shoving back, waiting for Goddess Bhairavi to pass by. She did, ignoring him once again; those big, Indian eyes just for Sassoon. She did, however, put her arse up on display, swaying her hips the way women with that special something do. Understandable then, if Ernst did not at first notice the Golog sword held flat against the back of her wrist.

50

Krishna's Muslim Hordes

You say Allah, I say Krishna,
Only one can be right,
Although both may be wrong.
—*The sufi who lost his way*

It was a clear getaway past AEET's North Gate, and up the four-lane Central Avenue until they hit Atomic Ganesh heading out for his confirmed appointment with Thana Creek. Mohan Driver was certain about one other thing. 'Touch and go,' he said. 'Touch and go.' He had nothing else left to offer, except that, 'The traffic at Chembur Naka will fuck us like a Sikh.'

Mohan Driver tried a manoeuvre, the crowd snarled. The one-eyed Fiat buckled like a spooked bronco. Ernst didn't have the energy to protest. They inched on at Ganesh's pace. He anyway decided everything for you. With that thought, Ernst slumped back. Goddess Bhairavi had left him drained. Ahead, the float with Atomic Ganesh raised its huge arse to one side, like Mohan Driver about to fart, and the one-eyed Fiat lunged past. The crowd swore but held its peace, and they were on Trombay Road in no time, starting to inch forward once again behind another Ganesh statue. Following Ganesh into Thana Creek and to never surface again, appeared just the thing to do.

When Ernst rolled down his window for air, Mohan Driver said to the rear-view mirror, 'Don't worry, Sa'ab. Just sit back. We'll make it. I am there for you.'

When he coughed up blood, Mohan Driver said, 'Good, you're going to Europe. They will fix you up over there in no time. Not like here.'

When Mohan Driver averted his eyes, Ernst silently begged, 'Please don't cry. For my sake.' The famous RK Studios arose on the right, a mildewed block of grey concrete. To the left, a tract of forest stood cleared; another Government colony had decided to come up while he was busy dying of cancer.

'When did that happen?'

'Forget all that now. Focus on getting well. Pray to Bhairavi.'

That brought him back to Bhairavi standing above Adam Sassoon with that other Golog sword—the one DCP Jahagirdar wanted so badly after Gomes got killed. Sassoon's eyes were glazed going into shock from lack of blood flow. Ernst remembered Waller's lesson on Disseminated Intravascular Coagulation and the thrashing Russell's Viper he used to make the case. Left to Dr. Dicky Waller, Sassoon's death certificate would probably say, 'Buggered by DIC.' Sion Medical students should thank their de facto Dean for an unforgettable acronym.

Ernst had watched little red flowers blossom on Sassoon's arm around the bite, just like the ones that had taken over Johnny Walker's leg. The next time Ernst looked, the flowers had crept up the great man's arm.

Then the great man vomited.

Then his face had swelled.

Then blood trickled from his eyes, nose, then gums. His face was Middle Eastern now, Semitic features to the fore. As if all the British in him was being bled away.

Soon, the body would be one big sepsis if Goddess Bhairavi didn't let help approach; so she didn't. She had hovered over him with sword held up as a warning to any and all inclined to assist the dying man. Only when Sassoon was over and done with, did she stand down to go approach the Deputy Commissioner. He was alone now, his jeep having given up on Sassoon and rushed off with the uniformed Johnny Walker and his sidearm.

'Uncle!' she called out.

The Deputy Commissioner couldn't tear his eyes off the Golog he'd been trying to find ever since someone gutted Gomes. Seeing her approach, sword in hand, he must have regretted Deputy Commissioners don't come standard with a holstered Webley. Rather than panic, he wagged his finger at a naughty girl.

'I can have you arrested, you know.'

'Why Uncle?' Goddess Bhairavi asked. 'I haven't done anything yet.'

He didn't know what to do with that and whether she intended to keep it that way. One could see him doing Indian math, the way Ernst had calculated feverishly to try save Salim Ali that day in the DCP's office, and failed.

When DCP Jahagirdar's time came, there was no fuss or tamasha. Drawing up close, all she said was, 'For my Arjun,' and drove the Golog through his uniform and up to the hilt. No sword dance, no nothing and just pulling away after that, waiting for the Deputy Commissioner to sort out what had just happened. He had looked nonplussed in the face of someone other than the police committing a murder. Eventually, he sank to his knees with a whoosh of expelled air, and she removed this Deputy Commissioner's cap with its Ashoka Chakra and one star, chucking it to the ground.

'Salim Ali!' Goddess Bhairavi shouted while beheading DCP Jahagirdar with a single, practised stroke, making the name sounded like a Hindu war cry. Then she turned to the Seth. Seeing the Goddess approach, sword in one hand, and the Deputy Commissioner's head dripping from the other, Sethji took off. No fat man could run as fast as he did that day, but eventually she had caught up.

~

Ernst felt his spine jar as the one-eyed Fiat lurched forward and for a while there was nothing. Then, Sindhi Camp came in the way. Blocked and tackled by Ganesh's vanguard, for once Mohan Driver refrained from doing his 'I-told-you' routine in the rear-view mirror. Loudspeakers blared, neon blasted them with Technicolour, and jhopadpatti kids danced around one Ganesh statue after another, while Sindhi refugee kids just watched. They didn't have the moves, and wouldn't risk a display. He would miss this place—the colour, the kids, the heat, the people, the rampant radioactivity.

'We can still make it, Sa'ab. If I know Parvatibai, she must have had everything packed and ready by now.' That being the first time in thirty years Mohan Driver had anything positive to say about Parvatibai. Must be because I look like shit. He felt like shit. Going past Jhama Sweetmeats, Ernst saw a somewhat recovered Lala Prem buying sweetmeats, and he had his first glimpse of heaven in the Lala's eyes as they ate up dancing jhopadpatti boys.

The Golf Club crawled by to their right. He felt he should shout out to all the goras he was leaving behind; remind them not to inhale while teeing off—the ammonia guaranteed to make you slice. Then there was the leaking radiation only those blind could see—keep an eye out for it, but don't go overboard. This is India and one carries on. So what if your surroundings glow in the dark? Ignore it like Indians do, and all will be fine. Which left some other minor dos and don'ts like: don't glaze your eyes while passing a beggar, and do try to love this country you live in. He realised they weren't moving. Someone had aspirated all the oxygen and things were a blur.

The slow crawl was heating up the one-eyed Fiat. He would have to leave behind something extra for imminent repairs. The Mian Building was ahead and Mohan Driver primed to turn right. Salim Ali's blind mother was on the balcony looking down instead of looking vacant. Vashigaon Road though, looked clear all the way to Chembur Naka with no Ganesh, no singing and dancing, no crowds. Not even cars. Mohan Driver whooped, unaware he was up against blind fate.

The rat hole of a Krishna Temple came on their left, looking like never before and not just because a party was underway. A white sheet was laid across the porch for what, unbelievably, could only be a band of Muslim qawwali singers. The qawwali wafted into his ears.

Muslim mians singing at a Hindu temple? A manicured beard in white sherwani sat behind the tabla on the patio. A clone sat behind a peti—the venerable Indian harmonium. An older, untended greybeard in crumpled white kurta was belting it out, while Andhi Ma swayed. Making it that much more surreal, the local mosque's mullah sat in front and centre on the temple patio, looking sharp and impeccable. Behind him, the Mian Building's Muslim population congregated alongside Lord Krishna for the evening.

It would seem this time, the blind, Hindu nut-job of an Andhi Ma wasn't just fucking with Salim Ali's blind, Muslim mother, or with Sindhi Camp for that matter, but the world as we know it. This is how you kindle a riot. By trying to bring people together. Andhi Ma was a nuanced bitch though, and astute. The greybeard was singing paeans to Jhulelal, that neutral Sufi residing on a fish in the River Indus and revered by Hindu Sindhis, as much as by their mortal Muslim enemies. For now, therefore, no one took issue with Muslims singing at a Krishna Temple. The Hindu majority watched, swayed, even joined in singing praises to Jhulelal.

'Stop here a minute,' Ernst instructed, trying to stay Krishna the charioteer, all ready to charge down an empty Vashigaon Road.

'Why for?' Mohan Driver's calculations were implacable. 'Less than an hour for you to get to Colaba, and leave again for Santa Cruz Airport. Otherwise, don't even bother.'

~

Done with Jhulelal, the qawwali singer now went, 'Dhin, tanana, dhin, dhin, tananana...' in a classic dhrupad string, weaving Vedic chant with Persian melody. 'Dhin, tanana, dhin, dhin, tananana...' the greybeard sang. He took off, soared, and didn't let up. Ernst stepped out of the one-eyed Fiat to allow Mohan Driver tear at his hair in the privacy of the car. He found he couldn't walk, so Mohan Driver got out too, took his arm, and they stumbled forward together.

'Dhin, tanana, dhin, dhin, tananana...' It was relentless, the music. Descending from his high, the greybeard switched over to rustic Punjabi to better make his case to a lover, or maybe Allah. Just as with Tantric Sahajiyas, one could never tell with these Sufi types. Two Mian Building mians heaved Ernst to the concrete patio as if he weighed nothing. They were laying him down now and Andhi Ma slid on her arse to make space by her feet, mud-caked toes wriggling inches away from his face. From behind a prison-type window, the part-time, Brahmin priest watched Muslims defile his temple; allowed by the blind bitch. His hopes lay in their namaaz prayer time to approach. It would force the hordes to dissipate and the mullah go do his job at the mosque, allowing the priest to do his.

The qawwali simmered down, the mullah swaying to the dying strains of the greybeard's Punjabi lyrics, and in no hurry to leave. Andhi Ma cleared her throat. Apparently, her turn. Some more throat noises, and she erupted in a song to Krishna using words no Indian woman would dare whisper to a lover, let alone her husband. Some of the younger Muslims got up to leave, than participate in this sort of licentious idolatry. They were circumcised for a second time with a single look from the mullah and one-by-one sank back on their haunches.

Ernst inched forward to touch Andhi Ma's feet with his head. He clutched them and wouldn't let go.

'Maaji,' he said, 'I've seen the light.' Andhi Ma looked down at him and winked one blind eye without missing a beat.

It had to be close to namaaz time, but the Muslims weren't packing up. This was sacrilege on a grand scale. Ernst began to suffocate as if someone had cornered the oxygen again, and things got hazy. Andhi Ma took a deep puff from a chillum and offered it to him with another wink. He pulled at the ganja, coughed, and found he could breathe once more.

~

The crowd got bigger with every pull. The pain now throbbed from somewhere outside his body. They were all here, around him. Schwester Ingrid too, of course. He tried calling out to her—say, he is sorry. Will she forgive him? The way she looked, who could tell? And there was his father, hovering behind her. The huge fat, Göring of a Jew tapped at his slashed left wrist. It was time. Ernst forced himself to focus as Mohan Driver tried to say something. Probably, the same message his father was trying to convey: time to go.

'Here is good,' Mohan Driver said, instead. If only he would stop crying. He pressed Ernst back down to prevent him getting up. 'Don't go, Sa'ab. Here is good.'

Goddess Bhairavi had arrived too. When did she find time to change into a red sari after gutting the Seth and his police dog? He wasn't worried about her safety. The police couldn't stop a lone Englishman from storming their chowki, and they'd go fuck with a Goddess?

Her lips were swollen, the way newly-married women get, and she had red sindoor powder where the hair parts, like a Perfect Woman—married to another. He had never, ever, seen anything so beautiful in his life and knew his three minutes were up. He was also hard as a rock, and felt that's only fair.

She turned away to throw up. Something did happen that night, after all. The faceless little girl hiding in the folds of her sari had her jet-black hair, his skin. Not altogether a bad thing for a girl to be European-white in India. He tried to get Mohan Driver's attention. The Golf Club debentures were in his bedroom credenza. Could be worth something, some day. Split the proceeds with Parvatibai and the girl.

Namaaz time came and went. Greybeard started to sing to lyrics from the fifteenth-century mystic, Bulleh Shah. The mullah swayed alongside, eyes closed. Fucker was going to lose his tenure over at the mosque.

'Bulleh ki jana mai kaun'
Bulleh, I know not who I am,
I just know, what I'm not.
I'm not Hindu, or Christian,
Not Muslim, or Jew,
Not a liar, not a cheater,
Not a killer, nor a wife beater,
'Bulleh ki jana mai kaun'
Bulleh, I know not who I am.

He took another puff from Andhi Ma's chillum and began to cough. Goddess Bhairavi took on that disapproving look women reserve for their men.

'Ernest!' she berated, and lifted his head from the hard cement to her lap. People were somewhat startled, it being unimaginable for an Indian woman to take her man's name. Not even goddesses do that. The Tantric Sahajiya insisted however, the Perfect Woman can.

The Historical Context

Before the beginning and after the end.

ERNST STIEGER
Ernst Steiger is an amalgamation of German Jews who found
themselves in British India when World War II broke out. They
were interned in places like Purandhar Fort across the Subcontinent,
for being Germans. Their families and relatives were interned in
concentration camps across Germany and Eastern Europe, for being
Jews. Jewish humour draws on stuff like this.

THE JÜDISCHE KRANKENHAUS
While the Nazis were plucking Jews out of Occupied Europe, 'tis
strange but true they didn't touch the patients, doctors and nurses
in Berlin's Jüdische Krankenhaus. Why such un-Aryan behaviour?
For one thing, the SS had cordoned off an area within the Jewish
Hospital as staging post for those shipped to concentration camps.
Seeing fellow Jews walking about freely the other side of the barbed
wire, helped internees remain sedate and believe they were simply
being shipped to similar locations in the East. For example, like the
one in Auschwitz. Incidentally, the Jüdische Krankenhaus is still
around after surviving the Nazis. So are the Jews.

THE SASSOONS
By the time India became independent, the Jewish family that

single-handedly built Bombay was no longer around, with Sir Victor Sassoon moving on to go build Shanghai. Left behind, were minor relatives and pretenders like the fictitious Adam Sassoon from our story. Barely a decade later if asked about the Sassoons, Bombay-wallahs would go, 'Who?'

PUBLIC LAW 480

PL 480 made for big headlines in the Sixties, with America paid in rupees for 'food aid' shipped under this American law. While the money couldn't be repatriated, the Americans could use it for approved expenses or certain types of purchases—like textbooks printed in India. Consequently, America bought millions of dollars worth of Indian textbooks it didn't need. There's a theory this was essentially to launder money back to the CIA's Indian operatives. When the author brought this up with people at Langley, he was told we Indians suffer from feverish imaginations. Moreover, they took pains to inform him the CIA has an impeccable track record overseas.

DR. HOMI J. BHABHA

The father of India's Atomic Program was killed on 24th January 1966, when an Air India Boeing 707 carrying him ploughed into Mont Blanc. His body was never found. The crash was attributed to pilot error, or the CIA, depending on the point of view.

While his violin concert at the Bombay Presidency Golf Club never happened, he was a classical violinist, besides being a gifted painter along with the rest of everything else that makes him stuff of legend.

THE PHOENIX NUCLEAR REPROCESSING PLANT AT TROMBAY

After the Chinese nuclear explosion of November 1964, John Foster Dulles decided India shouldn't be allowed one. Krypton gas detectors were installed at the American Consulate at Bombay, to sniff the air for levels of Krypton gas that would suggest weapon-grade plutonium being manufactured at India's Atomic Energy Establishment in the Trombay suburbs. For our fiction, we smuggle an American Krypton gas detector closer to the Phoenix Plutonium Reprocessing Plant at Trombay.

For all of Bhabha's genius, the Phoenix Plutonium Reprocessing Plant never took off, producing mediocre quantities of weapon-grade plutonium. It remained shut for more than a decade. 'Poor choice of materials in early stage,' was the official reason, giving us an excuse to build our story around defective stainless steel pipes supplied by the CIA. Ironically, while America obsessed over Phoenix, it was the Canadian-aided CIRUS reactor with American heavy water, that provided India weapon-grade plutonium for its 1974 nuclear explosion, code named: Smiling Buddha.

In this novel, that's the nickname Dr. Homi J. Bhabha gives his serene Head Machinist Tsering Tufan, who is dying from radiation exposure.

India entered the 21st century still struggling to bring Bhabha's three-stage, nuclear-power based, electricity solution to term. As of 2010, nuclear energy provided less than three per cent of the total electricity produced. On the bright side, an inability to scale may have spared the country a Chernobyl, or Fukushima.

Given a nuclear program that continues to go nowhere, one may argue in favour of India applying that money to education instead. Then there's always health care, clean water and basic infrastructure like roads and commercial thermal, hydro and solar power plants. India's priorities remain different however, because of heroes like Dr. Bhabha and Pandit Nehru in the past and those that followed. An IAS officer once said to the author that maybe India doesn't need any more heroes, just fewer assholes.

THE SAHAJIYAS

Proponents of Tantra or the left-hand path in Hinduism, the Sahajiya have been targets of virulent attacks by the orthodox since their inception. Harassment prompted them to develop their own shadow language, resulting in further misunderstandings. Increasingly, they continue being exploited for purulent purposes, or by the sanctimonious making a moral point.

A prime reason for being misunderstood thus is their study around Lord Krishna's behaviour. The Tantric Sahajiyas have their own take on the Lord's dalliances with married women. Even his consort, Radha-devi, fundamental to the gigantic religious edifice built around the Radha-Krishna mythology, was married to another man.

This gave the Sahajiya pause, rather than to sensibly follow orthodox advice and, do as Krishna says, not as Krishna does. Instead, they decided early on, to take Lord Krishna literally and decreed that love within marriage was profane. Love had to be with the unattainable for it to be sublime. Just like Krishna's love for Radha—the Perfect Woman, because she was married to another.

This concept of reaching out for the unattainable is further perfected in their metaphors around the Place of the Hidden Moon. Edward Dimock, Jr. explains this best in his eponymous book. Citing examples, Dimock also shows that this concept of love outside marriage in not exclusively Tantric. Medieval Europe had its own Courts of Love where such matters were hashed out. Dimock tell us, 'One of the most famous of all (such) decisions is said to have been taken by the court of the Countess of Champagne in 1174 and is as follows:

'We declare and affirm, agreeably to the general opinion of those present, that love cannot exercise its powers on married people. The following reason is proof of the fact: lovers grant everything, mutually and gratuitously, without being constrained by any motive of necessity. Married people, on the contrary, are compelled as a duty to submit to another's wishes, and not to refuse anything to one another. For this reason, it is evident that love cannot exercise its powers on married people.'

The Tantric Sahajiya couldn't have said it better.

Bibliography

Albom, Mitch. *Tuesdays with Morrie, an Old Man, a Young Man, and Life's Great Lesson.* Broadway Books, 1997.

Andreas-Friedrich, Ruth. *Berlin Underground, 1938 – 1945.* Paragon House, 1989.

Arya, Pandit Usharbudh. *Meditation and the Art of Dying.* Himalayan Inst Pr, 1976.

Auboyer, Jeannine. *Daily Life in Ancient India from 200 BC to 700 AD.* Orion Publishing Group, 2007.

Baburnama. (Memoirs of Babur). Transl. by Annette Susannah Beveridge. Low Price Publications, 1989.

Baigent, Michael & Richard Leigh. *Secret Germany: Claus Von Stauffenberg and the Mystical Crusade Against Hitler.* Arrow, 2006.

Bhavnani, Nandita. *The Making of Exile: Sindhi Hindus and the Partition.* Westland Books, 2014.

Boo, Katherine. *Behind the Beautiful Forevers: Life, Death, and Hope in a Mumbai Undercity,* Random House Trade Paperbacks; Reprint edition, 2014.

Bose, Subhas Chandra. *The Indian Struggle, 1920 – 1942*; Edited by Sisir K. Bose & Sugata Bose. Oxford University Press, 1997.

Broyard, Anatole. *Intoxicated by My Illness and Other Writings on Life and Death.* Fawcett, 1993.

Chaudhuri, Nirad C. *The Autobiography of an Unknown Indian.* Jaico Publishing House, 1964.

Chowdhury, Indira & Anaya Dasgupta. *A Masterful Spirit: Homi J. Bhabha 1909-1966.* Penguin Books India, 2010.

Dalvi, J.P. Brig (Retired). *Himalayan Blunder: The Curtain-Raiser to the Sino-Indian War of 1962.* Natraj Publishers, 2010.

Dimock, Jr., Edward C. *The Place of the Hidden Moon, Erotic Mysticism in the Vaisnava-Sahajiya Cult of Bengal.* University of Chicago Press, 1989.

Egorova, Yulia. *Jews and India, Perceptions and Image.* Routledge; Reissue edition, 2009.

Forster, E.M. *A Passage to India.* Penguin Classic, 1989.

Forster, E.M. *The Hill of Devi.* Harvest Books; trade paper, later printing edition, 1971.

Gilmour, David. *The Ruling Caste, Imperial Lives in the Victorian Raj.* Farrar, Straus and Giroux, 2007.

Gupta, Chitrarekha. *The Kayasthas, a Study in the Formation and Early History of a Caste.* K.P. Bagchi & Co, 1996.

Hansard, Christopher. *The Tibetan Art of Positive Thinking.* Atria Books; 1st Atria Books Trade Pbk., 2005.

Haqqani, Husain. *Pakistan, Between Mosque and Military.* Carnegie Endowment for International Peace, 2005.

Jackson, Stanley. *Sassoons.* William Heinemann Ltd, 1989.

Jaffrey, Zia. *The Invisibles: A Tale of the Eunuchs of India.* Vintage, 1998.

James, Lawrence. *Raj: The Making and Unmaking of British India.* St. Martin's Griffin, 2000.

Kinsley, David R. *The Sword and the Flute: Kali & Krsna—Dark Visions of the Terrible & Sublime in Hindu Mythology (Hermeneutics: Studies in the History of Religions).* University of California Press, 2000.

Kothari, Manu & Lopa Mehta. *The Other Face of Cancer.* Bhalani Publishing House, 2009.

Kulkarni, Ramakant S. *The Diary of Balasaheb Shastri: Unusual Stories of an Unusual Cop.* Focus, Popular Prakashan, 1994.

Manto, Saadat Hasan. *Mottled Dawn: Fifty Sketches and Stories of Partition.* Penguin India, 2000.

Martin, Richard. *SuperFuel: Thorium, The Green Energy Fuel of the Future.* St. Martin's Griffin; Reprint edition, 2013.

Mason, Philip. *The Men Who Ruled India.* Rupa, 1992.

Menon, Dilip M. *The Blindness of Insight: Essays on Caste in Modern India.* Navayana Publishers, 2006.

Miller, Barbara Stoler. *The Gitagovinda of Jayadeva: Love Song of the Dark Lord.* Columbia University Press; 20 anniversary edition, 1997.

Naipaul, V.S. *An Area of Darkness: A Discovery of India. Vintage;* Reprint edition, 2002.

Nehru, Jawaharlal. *Glimpses of World History.* Penguin India; New edition, 2004.

Perkovich, George. *India's Nuclear Bomb: The Impact on Global Proliferation.* University of California Press, 2001.

Pradhan, R.D. *Debacle to Revival: Y.B. Chavan Defence Minister (1962 – 1966).* Atlantic, 2013.

Pradhan, R.D. *Dragon's Shadow over Arunachal, a Challenge to India's Polity.* Rupa & Co, 2009.

Shah, Idries. *The Sufis.* ISF Publishing; 7th edition, 2014.

Silver, Daniel B. *Refuge in Hell: How Berlin's Jewish Hospital Outlasted the Nazis.* Clarion Books, 2005.

Singh, Jaswant. *Jinnah: India–Partition–Independence.* OUP Pakistan, 2010.

Tendulkar, Vijay. *Ghashiram Kotwal, Essays & Annotations;* Edited by Neela Bhalla. Worldview Publications, 2002.

The Bhagavad-Gita: Krishna's Counsel in Time of War. Transl. by Barbara Stoler Miller. Bantam Classics, 1986.

V. Nero, Anthony. *A Guidebook to Nuclear Reactors.* University of California Press, 1979.

Venkataraman, G. *Bhabha and his Magnificent Obsessions.* Universities Press, 1994.

Wadhawan, Jaddish Chander. *Manto Naama: The Life of Saadat Hasan Manto.* Roli Books, 2005.

Wolpert, Stanley. *Jinnah of Pakistan.* Oxford University Press, 2005.

Websites

'India's Nuclear Estate: An Interview with Dhirendra Sharma—No Clear Reason—Nuclear Power Politics,' Radical Science 14, 1984, pp. 94-105.
<http://archive.org/stream/NuclearEnergyTechnologyFromHell/Nuclear_Energy-Technology_From_Hell_djvu.txt>
'Indian Program on Reprocessing'
<http://barc.gov.in/publications/eb/golden/nfc/toc/Chapter%20
6/6.pdf >
'Homi Bhabha Killed a Crow: The Nuclear Debate: Ironies and Immoralities'
<https://www.princeton.edu/sgs/faculty-staff/zia-mian/Homi-Bhabha-Killed-A-Crow.pdf>
'Tickling the Dragon: Nuclear Accidents in the USA and Russia'
<http://boingboing.net/2009/10/28/criticality-accident.html>
Country Report: INDIA, website
<http://members.tripod.com/~no_nukes_sa/overview.html>
'Plutonium & Uranium Recovery from Spent Fuel Reprocessing by Nuclear Fuel Services at West Valley New York'; (from 1966 to 1972)
<http://pbadupws.nrc.gov/docs/ML1219/ML12194A610.pdf>
'Nuclear Fuel Cycle Assessment of India: A Technical Study for U.S.: India Cooperation'
<http://repository.tamu.edu/bitstream/handle/1969.1/85860/Woddi.pdf?sequence=1>

'Nuclear Fuel Reprocessing Costs'
<http://web.ornl.gov/~webworks/cppr/y2001/pres/116757.
pdf?origin=publicationdetail>
'We Need to Reprocess Spent Nuclear Fuel and can do it Safely, at
Reasonable Cost'
<http://www.21stcenturysciencetech.com/Articles%202008/
Summer_2008/Reprocessing.pdf>
'Materials Used in a Nuclear Fuel Reprocessing Plant'
<http://www.azom.com/article.aspx?Articleid=627#_Austenitic_
Stainless_Steels>
'Criticality Accidents'
<http://www.cddc.vt.edu/host/atomic/accident/critical.html>
'Whether Ordinance on Self-Denial of Nuclear Power Harmful to India?'
<http://www.countercurrents.org/subbarao110612.htm>
'Nuclear Power: The Missing Safety Audits'
<http://www.dnaindia.com/mumbai/report-nuclear-power-the-
missing-safety-audits-1536223>
'Requirements of Near-Real-Time Accounting of Strategic Nuclear
Materials in Nuclear Fuel Repprocessing'
<http://www.fas.org/sgp/othergov/doe/lanl/lib-www/la-
pubs/00236897.pdf>
'India Won't Scale Back Nuclear Program, by Matthew Rosenberg'
<http://www.freerepublic.com/focus/f-news/1591642/posts>
'Ikonos Imagery of the Bhabha Atomic Research Centre, Trombay'
<http://www.globalsecurity.org/wmd/world/india/ikonos_
trombay_010-01.htm>
'The Long Jetty to CIRUS'
<http://www.globalsecurity.org/wmd/world/india/ikonos_
trombay_010-04.htm>
'Bhabha Atomic Research Centre, Trombay'
<http://www.globalsecurity.org/wmd/world/india/trombay.htm>
'Fast Breeder Test Reactor (FBTR)'
<http://www.igcar.gov.in/romg/fbtrintro.htm>
'Radiological Safety Experience in Nuclear Fuel Cycle Operations at
Bhabha Atomic Research Centre, Trombay, Mumbai'
<http://www.irpa.net/irpa10/cdrom/01175.pdf>

'Health Status of Indigenous People Around the Jadugoda Uranium Mines, Indian Doctors for Peace and Development and Dr. Shakeel ur Rahman'

<http://www.pragoti.in/node/2432?page=50>

'An Initial Analysis of Kr 85 Production and Dispersion from Reprocessing in India and Pakistan'

<http://www.princeton.edu/sgs/publications/sgs/pdf/10_3%20151%20179%20Mian.pdf>

'Measurements of Krypton-85 to Detect Clandestine Plutonium Production'

<http://znf.rrz.uni-hamburg.de/inesap_bulletin_27_Kali-Daerr-Kohler_krypton85-measurements.pdf>

'The Medical Aspects of Radiation Incidents'

<https://orise.orau.gov/files/reacts/medical-aspects-of-radiation-incidents.pdf>

'Nuclear Fuel Reprocessing: US Policy Development'

<https://www.fas.org/sgp/crs/nuke/RS22542.pdf>